Welcome to Marmot
Population 32

Published by 186 Publishing Limited 2022

186publishing.co.uk

Welcome to Marmot

Population 32

Chris Mason

Part One

* * *

Mayor Material

Bad Directions

Monday, August 16

There was a wide shoulder ahead. Kevin Calenda pulled his Subaru wagon over onto it and switched off the engine. He rubbed his eyes; he could feel a massive headache coming on.

Stepping out of the car was like walking into an oven. Despite the shade of the Douglas Firs that crowded the narrow road, it was hot and so dry he could feel his skin threatening to crack. It was early afternoon in mid-August, but this was ridiculous. When he'd left Portland this morning the projected high had been 72; this felt like 90.

Kevin did a few stretches before reaching back into the car to grab his notebook. It hadn't sounded that hard when the young woman at the Inn of the White Salmon—more of a girl, really—had given him the directions. He had tried not to let the religious tattoos, nose and eyebrow piercings, and spiky violet-and-black hair sway him, but on reflection he believed he had made a mistake to trust someone who looked like a devout myna bird.

His notes were clear; his handwriting had always been excellent, and his speedwriting was just as legible, to him at least. He was accustomed to transcribing quotes perfectly, word for word. He read, "You've gone the wrong way if you see Bethel Congregational on the left, New Beginnings on the right, and Our Savior on the left. Turn right from our parking lot. You'll see the Mormons on the right, then Grace Baptist on the left. The road will merge with 141A, then after a while you'll pass Husum Church of God on the left, and Mt. Adams Baptist on the right. Bear left in Trout Lake, then pass the

3

Presbyterian Church on the right. After that it's easy, just look for Forest Road 88 then 8810 and it will lead you right to it."

He'd just wanted to do one last hike before leaving the Northwest, and a friend had recommended Sleeping Beauty. All of his hiking books had gone to friends or the Goodwill, so he had to rely on vague—or precise but wrong—directions from strangers. As a result he had made several bad turns and found himself on the outskirts of nowhere three times. He checked his watch: 12:45. He'd hoped to be on the trail almost an hour ago.

There was no traffic at all on this road. He was pretty sure he was back on 141, but he hadn't seen a sign for a while. He did a few more stretches and got back in his car, deciding to give it fifteen more minutes before giving up.

But it didn't take that long. The view suddenly opened up, revealing Mt. Adams in all its glory, the snow pack completely melted but a few glaciers still clinging to the slopes. A few minutes later he entered the town of Trout Lake, which was more like a crossroads than any real town he'd ever seen. The road curved to the left, then he passed the Presbyterian Church, just as the myna bird had said he would.

"Thank you, Jesus," he shouted at the top of his lungs. He felt safe doing that only because his windows were rolled up and the AC was on max. Otherwise, given the rundown rustic look of things around here, he might have been in danger from a random blasphemy-avenging shotgun blast.

Because he was so late, and the myna had turned out to be right in the end, he didn't even consider pulling in to the Forest Service ranger station and asking for real directions. He was just looking for road 88, that should be simple enough.

An hour later Kevin pulled off the road again. The threatening headache had receded with the echoes of his blasphemy, but it was coming back full force now. There was no Road 88. There had probably never *been* a Road 88. He'd be willing to bet that they'd stopped at Road 66. After realizing that he was lost again, he'd turned back and driven more slowly. He hadn't reached the ranger station yet—if it was even still there—but he'd seen plenty of Forest Service road signs, just not an 8810, an 88, or even a lowly 8.

He closed his eyes and rested his forehead on the steering wheel. It was getting too late to safely start a hike. He was going to have to give up.

That's when he heard a car pass him, going away from Trout Lake, in the direction he'd been searching before he turned around. He opened his eyes and looked in the rearview mirror. It was a mail truck. *If anyone could find a way out of this maze,* he thought, *it would be a mail carrier.* So he did a quick U-turn and followed the truck.

He'd thought perhaps the carrier would stop at a roadside mailbox, and he could pull up beside him and ask for directions, but there *were* no roadside mailboxes on this stretch. So he kept following. After a short while they turned onto what looked like a two-lane gravel driveway, but it had a sign proclaiming it to be Trout Lake Creek Road. He hadn't noticed this before, he'd been so intent on finding fictitious numbered roads. But then a new sign said they were *on* Road 88. The myna had neglected to mention that the road had a name as well as a number.

Then—it took his breath away—they passed Road 8810, which was the route to Sleeping Beauty, but after a slight hesitation Kevin kept following the mail truck. He wasn't sure why, except that he knew it was too late to start out. And he was hungry. They crossed the Pacific Crest Trail, which he thought was cool; he'd never hiked that one but he'd often thought he would like to. The truck turned left onto 8871, so Kevin followed it.

This road looked like a *one*-lane gravel driveway. He stayed far enough back so that he wouldn't be blinded by the dust. After another mile or so the truck turned left again. When Kevin reached that spot, he saw a handmade but handsome sign proclaiming Jack Rd. He was feeling a tingling in his fingers, as though he were in a horror movie and had just walked down—alone—into an unlighted basement looking for a weapon to fight the zombies. But he took the turn.

Then he suddenly realized that, unlike the Forest Service roads, Jack Road, while narrow, was paved.

Another left, another handmade sign, this one saying Fish Lk. St., which was also paved. He drove past a small lake on his left, evidently Fish Lake, and glanced back to the right just in time to see a roadside welcome sign, but all he had time to read was "Population 32." After a few more curves he found himself in another town, even smaller than Trout Lake.

"What is a town doing out here in the middle of the woods?" he said aloud.

There were a dozen or so decrepit houses, most of them collapsed in on themselves, but another dozen that were in good repair, with small gardens, freshly-painted siding, and lawn decorations. At the first intersection in town he saw a small cafe and some kind of shop on catty-corners, then he passed another that was surrounded by tidy little cottages, and then the mail truck stopped in front of a modern stone civic building, with Town Hall carved into the marble above the portico and clearly-marked straight-in parking spaces in front. There were some beautiful, tall firs across the street from the hall that looked like overgrown Christmas trees.

Kevin parked his car and got out—and felt his mouth flop open. On a tall stone plinth in front of the handsome Town Hall building was a six-foot high bronze statue of an animal. Maybe a beaver. Kevin walked up and read the plaque on the base. It said simply, "The Marmot."

Little Fish Cafe

By the time he recovered, the driver of the mail truck had vanished, presumably into the hall. Kevin looked around: tall Douglas Firs, squat vine maples, a Ponderosa Pine here and there—and little yards carved into the gentle slope, surrounding modest houses. Off to the left beyond the Town Hall was a cemetery surrounded by a ramshackle fence, but inside the fence the grounds seemed to be tended regularly; there were trees but no overgrown shrubs.

He didn't see the point anymore in tracking down the mail carrier, and it was long past his lunchtime, so he walked downhill, following the narrow, curving asphalt to the second crossroads, where the cafe was.

The Little Fish Cafe stood at the intersection of Little Fish Street and Marmot Lane. It had a handsome painted wooden sign hanging from a post out front. The two-story building was sided with clapboards painted buttery yellow, with a dark green metal roof and wide, tall windows on either side of the central door. A small lawn separated the building from the street, with flagstones leading up to the door and low ornamental shrubs of some kind hugging the building. Directly across Marmot Lane from the cafe hulked the grey ruins of a cottage, collapsed in on itself like a jack-o-lantern in late November and surrounded by scrubby trees.

The outer door was open. Kevin pushed open the screen door and walked inside. The cafe was small but cheerful, the walls a lighter shade of yellow than the outside. Despite the lack of air conditioning the room was significantly cooler than it was outside.

Half a dozen tables were scattered around the room, and a bar with tall stools separated the main space from the kitchen. A bookshelf stood in one corner, with one shelf full of well-used cookbooks, one of homemade jams for sale in jars capped with gingham cloth and ribbons, and the other two crammed with rustic stuffed animals that looked handmade. The rest of that wall was filled with deep shelves with a variety of dry and canned goods for sale; so this was a sort of mini-market as well as a cafe.

A large and very old German shepherd lay asleep on a big fuzzy bed in front of the bookshelf. It didn't bother to look up as he walked in.

As his eyes adjusted Kevin realized that a woman was standing behind the bar looking at him. She was in her mid-thirties, petite, a bit below average height, with delicate features, very dark hair in a pixie cut, and pointed ears like a Vulcan.

Kevin did a double-take and looked again. No, her ears were normal. He decided he must be hungrier than he'd thought.

"Are you open?" he said.

She glanced at her watch; Kevin involuntarily did the same. It was 2:01.

"Just," she said, and he felt a shiver run up his spine. Somehow that single word was crammed full of something... a promise, a hint of magic? He felt as if his feet had been nailed to the floor.

"Uh. Kind of late to just be opening, isn't it?"

She gestured at the bar and he discovered that he was still actually capable of walking. He took a seat right in front of her.

"Reopening, actually," she said, and her voice was even better than he'd thought from the first word. Melodious, with a touch of mezzo. He must have looked confused. "We close at the normal lunchtime to discourage the hikers, then reopen at 2:00." He didn't

feel any less confused. "You're not a hiker, are you?"

"Not today."

"Good. What can I get you to drink?"

"Lemonade?"

"Of course."

There was a wire holder for laminated menus. Kevin grabbed one and studied it. The breakfast options looked good: waffles, French toast, pancakes, cinnamon rolls, scones, eggs. Lunch was mostly soup, sandwiches, and wraps. There were no dinner options; he noticed a line at the bottom, "Open for breakfast and lunch, six days a week." It took a moment to realize there was no meat anywhere on the menu.

When the woman came back with his lemonade, he said, "This is a vegetarian cafe?"

"Yes," she said guardedly, as if she were preparing to defend the choice.

"Wow. That's great, because I'm a vegetarian too. But it's called the Little Fish Cafe."

She studied his face for a moment. "The fish are diners," she said slyly, "not dinners."

He laughed and set the menu back in its holder. "Can I have the Jamaican tofu wrap, please?"

"Surely." She went into the kitchen, but he could still see her through a pass-through behind the bar. She started working on his food.

He tried to think of something to say that would draw her out so he could hear her voice again, but— uncharacteristically—nothing came to him for a while.

"I don't think I would have found this town if it hadn't been for the mail truck," he said at last.

"That would be Jeremy," she said without looking up. "Were you actually looking for us?"

"No, I was trying to find Sleeping Beauty. Someone recommended it and I got really bad directions."

She did look up at that. "So you were *almost* a hiker."

"Yes. I've been a hiker before, but not today. Today I'm just a little lost, medium confused, and very hungry."

She smiled. "Why are you confused?"

"This town. What's it called, by the way?"

She hesitated, as if she needed to think about it. "Marmot."

"Yeah, okay, that makes sense. I saw the statue."

"Why does the town confuse you?"

He took a long sip of the lemonade. It was tart but sweet and very cold. "Well, it's stuck out on the edge of nothing. Half of it is fallen down, and the other half is very nice. The town's roads are all paved, but the access roads aren't. The Town Hall would look right at home in a city with a population of thirty thousand, but you only have thirty-two. And it can support a vegetarian cafe. I find that confusing. Wouldn't you agree?"

"I've lived here all my life. I don't think it's possible to find your home town confusing."

"Hah! You haven't been to Portland."

"Yes, I have. Once."

"Only once?"

She came out with a plate that had the biggest green wrap on it that he had ever seen. It was enormous. He hadn't known they made tortillas that big. There was also a pile of potato chips and a multicolored slaw. He looked up from the plate at her.

She smiled sweetly. "You said you were very hungry."

11

It was cut in three pieces. He took a huge bite out of one of the ends and thought about staying here forever. It had to be one of the most delicious things he'd ever crammed into his mouth. The tofu was jerked, spicy and savory, surrounded by julienned vegetables, all of it permeated with a tangy mayonnaise-based sauce that cooled the heat while somehow enhancing the flavor.

"Thank you," she said, and went back into the kitchen. He hadn't said a word.

The screen door squeaked a little as someone opened it. Kevin didn't turn around—it would take a volcanic eruption to get his attention off his food—but he heard two people arguing indistinctly, a man and a woman. Her voice seemed normal and friendly, but the man was obviously older and grumpy.

"Oh, shit," the man's voice said. That made Kevin turn around. A grey-haired guy in his seventies, with a slight stoop and a scowl on his stubbled face, was glowering at Kevin. "I thought you were going to keep these freaks out of here, Elizabeth."

"Relax, Ernie," the cafe owner said. "He's okay."

The man peered at Kevin's face. "You could have fooled me, but if you say so, I guess I'll just have to put up with it. Coffee, okay?" He sat down at a table right in front of one of the big windows, and his companion settled across from him. She was mid-forties, with thick brown hair tied back off her face, not pretty but with a pleasant expression.

"You'll have to forgive Ernie," the newcomer said to Kevin. "He's a congenital jerk. DNA. Can't help it."

"Shut up, Jodie," Ernie said. "Are we going to have lunch or what?"

"No, not if you keep talking to me that way." Ernie mumbled an apology and picked up a menu. "Why do you always look at the menu? You always order the same thing."

"Because someday Elizabeth will change the line-up and I don't want to miss out on anything."

"How the hell has Bev stayed married to you for forty-five years?"

"Inertia," Ernie said.

"More lemonade?"

Kevin looked up and found himself staring at her eyes. They were sort of blue; no, maybe they were grey. He thought they flashed silver for a moment.

"Uh. Your name's Elizabeth?"

"Yes."

"Kevin."

She smiled. "Lemonade?"

"Uh, please."

The door creaked again and this time Kevin turned to look. Five people came in together, but it immediately became clear that they weren't a group. A woman in her early thirties took a seat at the bar two spaces down from him. An old couple, both grey and somewhat bent, took the other table by the windows. And a pair of men in their late twenties, dressed absurdly well for the venue in dress slacks and expensive shirts and shoes—no ties—took one of the three tables in the center of the room.

Elizabeth was busy getting drinks and taking orders from people who already knew what they wanted, which seemed to be just about everyone. Kevin was finishing his lunch but trying to keep track of everything that was going on in the suddenly-busy room. The old couple were talking very softly, Ernie was grumbling about something, the young men were discussing some kind of leveraged investment, and the woman at the bar was reading a hardcover novel.

"Pie?" Elizabeth said, showing up suddenly at his elbow.

"Uh, sure. What—"

"Cherry, huckleberry, and pecan."

"Huckleberry. Thanks."

She just smiled and moved off.

He felt completely disoriented. The bustle around him seemed so normal, and so out of place in this remote location. If he were still in Portland he'd feel right at home. But he had the weird feeling that if he dug his compass out of his pack in the back of the car that the needle would point somewhere other than North, or maybe it wouldn't point to anywhere, but just keep swinging around from side to side.

"Hey, Elizabeth," one of the businessmen called out. She stuck her head out the door to the kitchen. "Who's the stranger?"

The room fell completely silent. Everyone was looking back and forth between Kevin and Elizabeth.

"He's okay," she said in her beautiful, fluid voice. "His name is Kevin, until very recently he lived in Portland, and he's the one I've been waiting for."

Introductions

What? he thought. We just met. What does she mean?

There was another long moment of silence, then the man who had spoken stood up and walked over to Kevin. He slapped him on the back, grabbed his hand to shake it, and pulled him off his chair.

"Congratulations, you lucky S.O.B. Come sit with us. Melissa, come on over."

The woman at the bar closed her book and carried her plate over to the table. As soon as Kevin sat down Elizabeth put a huge slice of pie in front of him. All he could think was that it looked delicious, and he had no idea what anyone was talking about.

"I'm Upton," the man said. "This is my partner Travis." The other man gave a little wave and a smile. Upton indicated the reader: "Melissa." She smiled shyly. Upton pointed a fork at the two tables up front. "Jodie and Ernie— not a couple, obviously. Ha! What an idea. Paul and Martha," that was the elderly pair, "definitely a couple for what, fifty years, Martha?"

"Fifty-two," she said proudly in a deep, scratchy voice.

"Town record, I think," Upton said with a propriety air, as if it were his doing that they had been married almost twice as long as he'd been alive.

"I'm confused," Kevin said.

"I don't wonder," Upton said. "Elizabeth can have that effect on a person. If she hadn't vouched for you you'd probably be picking yourself up off the ground right now and dusting off your ass."

"But we just met. What did she mean by—"

Elizabeth appeared suddenly at his elbow. "You haven't tried the pie yet."

Everyone was staring at him. He picked up a fork and put a piece of the huckleberry pie in his mouth. He thought his head would explode.

"Oh my god," he gasped, "that is the best pie I've ever had." And he meant it, too. Elizabeth beamed at him and walked back into the kitchen.

Upton slapped him on the shoulder. "You're going to fit right in here," he said.

"What?" His first thought was, *Hotel California.* But his second thought was that he had no idea what was happening.

"Can someone explain what's going on?" Kevin said. "I mean, I got lost, I followed the mailman to this town, I was hungry so I came in here for lunch—which was terrific, by the way. And now it feels like I'm being adopted."

"Yeah," Upton said, "or kidnapped, right? It's like Hotel California meets Brigadoon."

Melissa the reader piped up for the first time. "When I first got here," she said in a thin but friendly voice, "somebody told me that Marmot *is* like Brigadoon. You can't find it unless you know where it is."

"That's not the real name," Ernie the grouch said.

"Ernie," Jodie warned him.

"Well, it's not." He looked around. "What? You all *know* it's not."

"The town isn't called Marmot?" Kevin asked.

"Not technically," Jodie said. "We're trying to unincorporate so we can change the name."

"Some of us," Upton said. "Not all of us. Not even a majority."

"Sixteen percent," she retorted.

16

"Fifteen point fifteen." To Kevin he explained, "That's five people out of thirty-two."

"Anyway," Ernie said, "the town has already been unincorporated. In 1953. Which was before you were even born."

"Not me," both of the old people chimed in together.

"So what *is* it called?" Kevin asked.

No one spoke for a moment. Then Ernie said, almost grudgingly, "Kill Marmot."

"*What?*"

"Yeah," Upton said. "Horrible name, isn't it?"

"But there's a marmot statue by the—"

"Of course there is," Elizabeth said. She was standing by his elbow again. "Haven't you finished that pie yet?" He took another bite and his head went into orbit just like the first time. "The marmot was the hero of the story, so *he* gets the statue."

Kevin looked helplessly at Upton, who laughed and said, "Okay, here it is. I got this straight from my grandfather, who got it from his grandfather, who was there. It was right around 1900. There wasn't a town here then (not that there's much of one now), it was just a logging camp. Bunch of canvas tents, a trench latrine, and piles of old-growth logs. One day the loggers were sitting around eating their lunches when a marmot stumbled into the center of camp."

"It was rabid," Melissa said confidentially.

"*No it wasn't!*" Upton and three other people said at once. Upton continued, "They *thought* it was rabid, but my guess is that it was drunk."

"Fermented huckleberries," Ernie grumbled. "Happens to the bears all the time."

"Right. So this innocent little rodent—"

"They weigh ten to fourteen pounds," Jodie objected.

"—*relatively* small rodent," he continued, "wandered into town and the loggers decided to kill it."

"And they spent all day trying," Ernie said.

"Right, but they couldn't."

"Because they were probably drunk too."

"It was a *wily* marmot," Upton said forcefully to shut him up. "They chased him all over, in and out of the log piles and the tents until dark, then they gave it up—"

"And got *seriously* drunk," Ernie said.

"Who's telling this story?"

"*We are!*" everyone else chimed in. Kevin laughed and so did some of the locals.

"The next morning they shook off their hangovers and looked around. They had trashed the entire camp looking for a rodent they never found. The tents were all collapsed, the equipment was strewn everywhere, the logs were scattered like pick-up sticks. Which my great-great-grandfather thought was some kind of metaphor, not to mention so funny that he passed a kidney stone. So when a town grew up around the old logging camp, they called it Kill Marmot, in honor of that crazy day. I think they were being ironic."

Kevin asked, "So they built a statue to the marmot?"

"No," Elizabeth said. She was standing at his elbow again. "We did that. Eight years ago, when we refurbished the Town Hall. Would you like some coffee?"

"No thanks."

"Everyone, let this poor man finish his pie."

They obeyed her and were quiet for the few minutes it took him to wolf it down. When he pushed the plate away, there was a noticeable change in the mood of the room.

Jodie said, "Kevin, tell us about yourself. What's your last name?"

"Candela. Uh," he chuckled nervously, "to tell the truth I'm more accustomed to asking questions than answering them. Let's see. I'm a journalist. I've worked for a small weekly paper in Portland for the last six years, but with the Internet now… you know. The paper folded last month. So now I'm on my way to the other Portland, in Maine; a similar paper has offered me the same kind of job."

"What kind of writing do you do?" Upton said.

"I had a column, humorous anecdotes about the local scene, you know, and I also did serious pieces pretty regularly. Investigative stories. Nothing worth a Pulitzer, but I think I did my part to help out."

"How did you end up in Marmot?" Melissa asked.

"Kill Marmot," Ernie mumbled, but everyone ignored him.

"I got lost. Then I saw a mail truck and thought maybe the carrier could help me out, and it led me here."

"Married?" Jodie said.

He laughed nervously. "No."

"Never?"

"No."

Jodie looked over his head. Kevin turned and saw Elizabeth just swiveling to go back into the kitchen.

"How old are you?" Melissa said.

"Uh. Forty-three."

"So what do you think?" Upton asked his partner Travis, who hadn't said a word so far.

"His beard is scruffy," Travis said in a surprising baritone. Kevin involuntarily felt his beard; it was a little full but not mountain-man long. The same as it had been for ten years. "Otherwise I think he'll do fine."

"He's right, you know," Upton confided to Kevin. "You should get Mary to trim that up for you."

Kevin felt her presence again and looked up. Elizabeth was standing beside him, rubbing her finger on her lips thoughtfully. She nodded slightly, which hit him with the force of a booming voice from the mountaintop.

Lay of the Land

"The first house on the right after Cemetery Lane," they'd said, which was so clear and simple compared to the directions that Kevin had got this morning that he didn't trust it. But when he walked up the paver path to the front door of the cedar-shingled one-story house, knocked on the door, and said, "I understand you're the town's barber," the woman had stepped aside to let him in without comment.

Mary Wyan was in her mid-thirties, a little plump, with shoulder-length hair framing a pointy face. Her eyes were sparkling as if she had just finished laughing at something really, really funny.

"I'm the barber if you need a barber," she said in a soft voice. "Or a stylist if you need that. Offhand I'd say that you need a barber right now. That beard..."

He followed her into the back of the house, which was larger than it looked from the outside. The front room seemed very lived in, with worn, comfortable-looking armchairs and sofa and a jigsaw puzzle of a European castle half-done on the oversized coffee table. The room she took him to was very different: small, painted a dark plum, with several modest tables and cabinets around the walls. A stylist's chair stood waiting in the center of a grey rubber mat that touched the cabinets on either side. This room had probably been designated "Den" on the construction blueprints.

"Have a seat," Mary said. She put a barber's cape around his neck.

"You know, no one has ever criticized my beard before today," he said.

"You must have very polite friends." She touched his hair lightly here and there. "I can do something with your haircut if you want," she said, "but I think you're fine for another two weeks."

"Just the beard, then," he said. "But don't cut it off."

"Just a trim," she agreed.

When she started in with scissors and comb, he said—being very careful not to move his jaw more than necessary— "Do you mind if I ask: what's the objection to hikers around here?"

Mary laughed. "It's not universal. Some locals have a problem with people wandering in from the woods, lost as a Girl Scout on the Moon, wearing their Gore-Tex shorts, flannel shirts, fleece vests, and $300 boots, and complaining about the lack of a decent latte. I never minded myself, not that any of them ever spent any money in here. But they boost the economy some. I suppose you've met Ernie?"

"Yes, at the cafe."

"Town grouch. He and a few others asked Elizabeth to change her lunch hours to discourage strays from crowding out the locals. She asked people what they thought, and no one really minded, so she did. It's funny: it shifted most peoples' dinnertime from around 6:00 to 7:30."

"Didn't that hurt her business?"

"Nope. Locals who'd been staying away made up the difference. A lot of us eat there almost every day. You might have noticed that her prices are reasonable."

He looked at her in the tall mirror hanging in front of him. She paused in her work.

"Reasonable? They're ridiculous. The wrap I had for lunch was one of the most delicious things I've ever eaten and it would have cost three times that much in Portland."

"Ah. Portland. Nice city, but we don't go there often. Supply runs, mostly."

Someone knocked on the front door. "Excuse me a moment," Mary said, and left the room. Kevin looked around while he waited. There were no posters for hair products or styles on the walls; he didn't think he'd ever been in a salon without them. Of course, this wasn't a real salon; it was a small room off the kitchen in a cottage. There were several framed pictures of three average-looking children ranging from middle school to high school age.

"Sorry," Mary said when she returned. "I had to sign for a package."

"UPS comes back in here?"

"No, it was Jeremy." When she realized he had no idea who she was talking about, she said, "The local mailman. Adie's nephew."

"I followed him in here," Kevin said. "That's how I found this place."

"It must be your lucky day." She worked in silence for a moment. "Software engineer?" she said at last.

"Journalist. What you said before—*does* UPS deliver to Marmot?"

"Not that I'm aware of."

"FedEx?"

"Nope."

"How do you get packages, then?"

"Post Office, usually. Or Mike's shop."

"I haven't seen that one yet."

"You should check it out. It's catty-corners from the cafe."

"OK, I will. Um… about the cafe. What's the story with Elizabeth?"

She chuckled. "It would take fifteen haircuts for me to even get started on that story. And you're done."

She gave him a hand-held mirror. He had to admit that they'd been right: the beard looked much better short.

"It looks great," he said.

"I think it's a better fit to your face and your haircut."

"What do I owe you?"

"Ten."

"You're joking."

"Too much?"

He gave her fifteen dollars, which is what he would have paid back home *without* the tip, and refused to take any change.

"Thanks," he said.

"No, thank you. Do you think you'll be staying in town long?"

"I was planning to head out tonight. I've got a long trip ahead of me."

She tipped her head and studied his face. But she didn't say anything, just smiled and led him back to the front door.

"Come back sometime," she said. "If you're still here."

He thanked her again and shook his head as he walked down the path to the road. Far off to his left he saw a youngish man in a blue uniform, with a substantial canvas bag slung across his body, just starting up the driveway to another house.

He stood in the street for a moment. To his right was the Town Hall and his car. He really had no reason to stay here; the hike he'd been planning was a bust and he didn't want to delay getting to Maine. But his plan had been to go back to White Salmon tonight and stay at the Inn before heading out in the morning. It wouldn't hurt to explore a little, since he had the time. It was just after 4:00.

24

He checked his phone and wasn't really surprised that there was no signal. He hadn't seen a cell tower in a while, and the wide wooded hill behind the Town Hall rose steeply for hundreds of feet above the town. It was nearly a cliff. The sun was going to set behind it in another hour or so. It occurred to him that afternoons must be very short here in the winter.

He strolled back down Little Fish Street, away from the Town Hall. The town was nestled right up against the foot of that sprawling hill, between the escarpment and the lake. In that habitable strip there were many small hills. The Town Hall stood atop one of them, and nearly all the rest had houses perched on them. The rest of the houses occupied the gentle slopes of the hills, while the paved roads followed the swales between them.

There were no ruins between Mary's place and the cross street where the cafe stood— Marmot Lane, he recalled when he saw the sign. Three houses on the left, three spaced alternately on the right—and what was that? He walked a few feet off the road into weeds and discovered the foundation for a fairly large building, but it didn't look like one that had fallen down. There was no sign that anything had ever been built on that foundation. There were small trees and shrubs growing out of the cracks in the concrete, but no debris at all.

At the intersection of Little Fish Street and Marmot Lane, Elizabeth's cafe was at the far-left corner, the crumbled house he'd seen before was at the near left corner, and a building larger than the cafe was on the near right. A hanging sign out front, done in the same style as the cafe's, said "Mike's Shop." There was nothing at the far-right corner; nothing would fit, because the streets came together at too small an angle on that side. Kevin debated for a moment going back to the cafe, but he didn't know what he would say if she asked him what he wanted; then he thought about taking Mary's advice and checking out Mike's, but he wasn't really interested. So he turned right and walked down Marmot Lane.

Beyond Mike's this street was nothing but fallen-down houses. He counted six in various states of decay, from a merely sagging roof with intact windows to a pile of lumber with vine maples growing out of it. Fifty-year old firs grew close to the twisting road. When he came around a final right-hand bend the road widened into a cul-de-sac, at the end of which was an intact building with another hanging sign: "Marmot Bar." The woods crowded in close behind the building, which had grey cedar siding and a blue metal roof.

How could a town of thirty-two people support a cafe, a shop, and a bar? And the Town Hall was still a mystery. Kevin turned to go back into town and saw Elizabeth walking around that last curve, head down as if deep in thought. She looked up and saw him and burst into a smile that he was sure was giving him sunburn.

She gestured at the bar. "It's a good place to eat," she said, "if you're still here at dinnertime."

"It's competition, isn't it?"

"No. I'm only open for breakfast and lunch. Jodie's only open for dinner."

"This is Jodie's bar?" She nodded. "So you two have a cartel."

"It's a very small cartel. Price-fixing is rampant, though."

"Maybe I'll try it tonight."

"Will be you leaving after that?"

"Probably. I have to be on the road tomorrow morning."

She nodded. "Have you seen the rest of the town?"

"Not really. Uh... would you like to show me?"

She smiled and turned around. He fell in beside her and they started back toward the cafe.

"I can't get over the contrast," he said, pointing at the fallen-down houses, "between the ruins and the intact houses. Half of these look like they've been abandoned for a century. But the ones that people live in are really very nice."

"Well, the people who live here love it. Except for a few of the teens, of course. The people who hated it walked away, and these are the monuments to their choice."

"Were most of the locals born here?"

"About half." She glanced at him and smiled. "Including me, in case you were going to ask. The rest of them just found us somehow."

"Maybe by following the mail truck."

"No, I think that's just you."

They had reached Little Fish Street. By unspoken consent they kept walking straight on Marmot Lane. This had only two ruins, the one across from the cafe and one just past it. Beyond the cafe were two more nice, small houses, then just as the road ended they came to what was clearly a school, a wide, one-story brick building with a fenced play area out front. The playground was part grass, part rubber mulch, with a swing set, slide, jungle gym, several rocking animals on giant springs, and a very large rocket ship.

"You have a school," Kevin said incredulously. "With a rocket ship."

"It's Montessori," Elizabeth said. "Helen runs it. And the rocket ship landed here in the seventies; the little green men said they didn't need it anymore, so we kept it." He stopped and looked at her. She looked back straight-faced, then she laughed. "Come look."

She opened a gate in the fence and they walked over to the ship. It was painted in bright colors, red, blue, and silver;

27

about twenty feet tall and six feet wide. On the building side was an opening about four feet high, and inside was a nest of ropes going all the way up.

"It's just another jungle gym," she said.

"I've never seen anything like it. Where did it come from?"

"Someone built it when I was little. I can't remember who, but Adie would know."

Kevin rapped on the side. It was apparently made of steel plates that had been welded together, with sturdy eye rings for the rope attachments. Elizabeth put her palm flat against the outside hull. "Rocket girl," she said almost too quietly for him to hear.

* * *

There was another ruined house past the school and another cul-de-sac at the end of the road. Elizabeth led him on a well-worn footpath behind the school building. They passed what was clearly the wreckage of an old church. Tumbled stones larger than his head were strewn around the foundation, but three of the walls were almost intact, though there was no sign of a roof at all, and the window openings were empty. The path led them to a cluster of three mobile homes, one single and two double-wide, clustered around yet another cul-de-sac, with another shell of a house at the very end. It wasn't clear why all the tiny roads in this town ended in circles big enough to allow a panel truck to turn around without having to do a three-pointer. Just another mystery.

This was Cemetery Lane, Elizabeth told him. They turned left and were at the cemetery. Elizabeth walked ahead of him into the grounds.

He had noticed the falling-down fence when he parked his car. And he'd been right: someone was tending the graves. The grass was almost ready for mowing, but there was no scrub between the stones, some of which were leaning far over, while others were broken stubs. They just stood and looked for a moment in silence, then turned away and headed up the gentle slope. It didn't occur to Kevin until they left it behind that she might have family buried in that little graveyard.

Four intact houses were on the lower part of the lane, two on each side. He could see the Town Hall between the houses to their right. A moment later they reached Little Fish Street. Mary's house was on their right.

"And that's it," she said. "Other than a few more ruins on the approach into town. What do you think?"

He turned and looked around him. A handful of commercial buildings that by rights should not be prospering, though clearly they were, an oversized Town Hall, a dozen homes, three mobiles, and a cemetery. If it was Brigadoon, it was the compact, economy size.

"I think it's charming," he said.

First Night

Elizabeth said she had work to do and left him in the street with a parting smile that lingered in his memory. Kevin debated once again whether he should just go, but he still had plenty of time and he thought it might be interesting to have dinner at Jodie's bar. Maybe Elizabeth would be there. It was too early for dinner, though, so he walked back up the hill to his car, grabbed a notebook and a pen, and then retraced his steps on Little Fish Street, past the cafe, to where it curved around Little Fish Lake.

He plunked down on the reedy shore of the lake, which was in fact rather small (living up to its name) and almost perfectly round. He guessed it was about five hundred feet across, maybe four acres in area. He wondered idly if there were actually any fish in it, then he saw one splash the surface off to his right.

Kevin opened his notebook and started jotting down thoughts on what he'd seen and heard that day. He thought it might be worth staying for another day or two if he could get a story out of the experience. He wasn't quite sure what form the story would take: quirky travelogue, wistful almost-romance, or something else. He always gathered the facts first and let the story tell him where it wanted to go. If he was going to do this, he would need more information than he'd gathered so far.

He kept at it for an hour or so, jotting down people, events, and impressions in speedwriting, until he noticed that it was getting dark and suddenly chilly. After the heat of the day the cool was welcome, but he was shivering. He closed his notebook and walked up the hill back to his car, rummaged a light jacket out of the back, and put his notebook in its pocket.

It was after 6:00. The bar should be open for dinner by now. Once again he walked down the hill and turned right on Marmot Lane. At the end of the street, the bar was lit up with strings of lights, old-fashioned looking bulbs that when he got closer revealed themselves to be LEDs. Kevin walked up and opened the door.

He'd had no idea what to expect inside, but it wasn't this. Maybe a rough mountain-shack theme, or old logging implements hanging from the rafters, stuffed animal heads on the walls, country music blaring from a jukebox. What it actually was—was nice. High ceilings, honey-colored wooden paneling on the walls, adequate but gentle light from wrought iron chandeliers, three thick-cut pine trestle tables and a long high bar. There was no mirror behind the bar, and nothing on the walls but some large, nicely-framed prints of exceptionally good wildlife photos: black bear in a stream, bald eagle against a pure blue sky, elk on a ridge-top against the setting sun. A black wood stove squatted in one corner beside a big wooden box of logs. There was music, but it was quiet, some kind of soft melodic jazz.

Everyone turned to look at him as he stepped inside and closed the door.

He counted 6 customers—all men—two at one table and the rest at the bar. Jodie stood behind the bar, looking at him expectantly. He realized that the two at the table were Upton and Travis from lunch, and one of the guys at the bar was the grouch Ernie. He didn't recognize the others.

"Hey, Kevin," Upton called out. "Come on in."

One of the strangers sitting at the bar, a heavily-muscled redhead with tattoos on both forearms, used his foot to pull out the stool to his left. "Have a seat," he growled. Kevin hopped up on the stool. The man thrust out a huge hand. "Peter Johnson."

Kevin gave it his best manly shake. "Kevin Candela."

"I hear you made an impression on our girl today."

"Hey, Pete," Upton said, "give him a chance to order a drink before you start freaking him out."

"What can I get you?" Jodie asked.

"You have any dark local beers on draft?"

"Hmm. It's local if you call Eugene local. Oakshire Espresso Stout."

Pete guffawed. "That'll put hair on your ass."

"Sure, I'll try that."

"You'll have to excuse Pete," Upton said, getting up and coming over to them. "He's a truck driver, so he thinks he has to be the toughest guy in the room. It's all an act. Ask him about the Renaissance in sixteenth century France and you won't have to talk again for an hour."

"It's fascinating stuff," Pete growled.

"You've met Ernie, Jodie, and Travis," Upton said. "Down there at the end is Mike, he's our Amazon. On your left is Darren, who can do anything but mostly works as a handyman and property manager." A teenaged boy came out of the back room carrying a sealed box labelled Frito-Lay. "And that's Jodie's son, Matt. Hey, Matt."

"Upton," the boy said in a friendly tone, "how's business? You bankrupt anybody today?"

"Agh! You know we don't do that."

"So *you* say."

Jodie put his beer on the bar. It looked like a Guinness but when he tasted it there were chocolate notes in addition to the coffee, and it wasn't as sweet. "Good," he said, and Jodie nodded and moved down the bar.

"Upton and Travis run an investment brokerage from their home," Pete explained. "We have a lot of little home businesses here."

"Like Mary's hair salon," Kevin said.

"It's a barbershop," Pete said threateningly.

"Yeah, that's what I meant." He took another sip and glanced at Upton, who was still standing behind him. "How do you run a brokerage from here? Can you get a T1 line out in the woods?"

Upton just laughed. Travis said, "We have a satellite link, and we don't do day trading or any of that high-frequency trading stuff. No crap, just solid advice and reliable wealth management."

"Which is why almost all their clients are in Seattle and Portland and places like that," Pete said. "No wealth to manage around here."

Upton got a strange expression on his face and went back to his table. Kevin took another look around. The bar was really very classy in a rustic way. When Jodie walked back his way he said, "I like your place. No clutter."

"Thanks," she said. "There used to be a barn on this spot. We tore it down, remilled the lumber, and used it to build this place."

"That explains the wide planks. How old was the barn?"

"Late nineteenth century, as far as we can tell. You hungry?"

"I shouldn't be after lunch, but yeah, I am."

She handed him a paper menu. There was a lot of meat, but they did have a black bean burger. He ordered that with a side of garlic fries.

"How long you in town?" Mike said from two stools to his left. It was the first time he'd spoken. Kevin leaned forward to look at him.

"I was planning to head back to White Salmon tonight," he said.

"Too bad."

"I heard they have a killer breakfast at the Inn where I was going to stay."

"Yeah, literally. It will kill you."

"That bad?"

"That good. Way too many calories. Better to eat at the cafe here. It'll kill you slower."

Jodie rushed down to the end of the bar and slapped Mike on the arm. "Don't you talk about Elizabeth's food that way."

"Hey," Kevin said to change the subject, "what did Upton mean that you're the Amazon?"

Ernie, on the other side of Pete from Kevin, snorted and muttered under his breath. "Jodie, get me another," he said, and she brought him something on the rocks.

"Kind of hard to explain," Mike said. "If you're still here tomorrow, stop by my shop and I'll show you."

Pete nudged Kevin's arm. "Why you going down to White Salmon anyway?"

"I'm supposed to be in Maine next week. I was going to head out tomorrow."

"Hey, Pete," Upton said, "didn't you hear Jodie say he lost his job at the newspaper and was on his way to a new one?" *So it was* that *kind of town.*

"Oh, yeah. Newspaper guy, huh? That's like being the last buggy whip salesman in Dodge City, isn't it?"

"I'll hang on as long as I can," Kevin said. "I like it."

"Hey," Mike said, "you should stay here tonight."

"Why, is there a B&B in town?"

"No, but there's an apartment in Town Hall."

"What?"

34

"For the Mayor. But he's dead, so it's empty. What do you think, Upton?"

Kevin turned on his stool. Upton was staring at him critically. Finally he said, "He looks like mayor material to me." *What?* Kevin thought. "What do *you* think, Jodie?"

"I'll call Elizabeth," she said. She took a cordless phone from under the bar, which startled Kevin.

"What," Pete said, grinning. "You thought we didn't have phones?"

"I can't get a cell signal."

"That's Steamboat Mountain," Mike said. "It blocks everything but satellite. That's the basis of my business."

"And I didn't see any phone lines." Or power lines, he realized, now that he thought about it.

"Buried," Upton said. "But you're almost right. The town uses a PBX system internally with no trunk line going out to the real world."

"Translate it into English for the man, Upton," Mike said.

"Geez. Okay, we have a private telephone exchange for the town. The phone company wouldn't let us tie into their system."

"Which means," Mike said, "that anyone can call anyone *within* the town, all at the same time if necessary, but no one can call in or out of the town."

"You're joking!"

"No, I'm not."

"I thought PBX systems were just for businesses."

"Well, this is sort of a business," Mike said.

"Kind of," Pete agreed.

"Ask Adie. She'll explain it."

Jodie butted in. "Elizabeth says to come to the cafe when you're done eating and she'll take you over to Adie."

"Adie?"

35

"Let Elizabeth explain it," Jodie said sharply, cutting off Upton, who seemed to have been on the verge of a lecture.

Matt brought his food out on a glass plate. Kevin asked Jodie for another stout. He took a bite of the burger, which was great, and gave Matt a thumb's up. Then he tried one of the garlic fries and seriously considered moving to this town.

"Pete," he said, "you called Elizabeth 'our girl.' What did you mean?"

There was a long moment of silence, broken by Ernie muttering, "God damned busybody strangers."

"Oh, shut up, Ernie," Jodie said.

"Well," Pete rumbled, "there are conflicting stories about where exactly Elizabeth comes from."

Mike said, "I heard somebody found her on a hillside and just kept her."

"I heard that one too," Upton said. "I don't believe it. I think she was adopted."

"Uh uh," Pete said. "She was switched in the cradle."

"Oh, give me a break," Travis said.

"Well that's what I heard, and I believe it."

Kevin had no idea what to make of all this. "Can't you just ask her parents?"

"Dead," Mike said. "Long time ago. Never got a chance to ask them."

"You knew them?"

"Yeah, when I was a kid, but I wasn't living here when they died. I came back years later."

"I knew them," Pete said. "And I was in school with Elizabeth. We're the same age. If anybody would know if she was a fairy child, it would be me, and I say she is."

"I knew them too," Ernie said. "Knew 'em well. Good people. But no damned idea where that girl came from."

"She came from the same place we all come from," Jodie said firmly, "her mother's womb."

That shut down the conversation.

"Ask Adie," Pete suggested confidentially to Kevin after Jodie had moved out of earshot. "She knows for sure."

Adie

Kevin left the bar without hearing a single word out of Darren, the handyman. Ernie had mostly muttered, Travis seemed to be the quiet type, but everyone else had been happy to talk—as long as the subject wasn't Elizabeth or Adie.

It was pitch black and he had to step carefully so he didn't fall off the road. His light jacket wasn't enough to keep out the chill. He stopped at the second turn on Marmot Lane, with the lights of the bar invisible behind him, and looked up. The Milky Way stretched across the clear sky with forty thousand diamond glints of light twinkling around it.

After the last curve in the road he could see a light at the cafe beckoning him onward. This stretch was fairly straight, so he quickened his pace. When he got to the cafe door and knocked, Elizabeth came around the side of the building instead of answering the door. She had a shawl or something wrapped around her shoulders.

"Hi," she said, and suddenly he felt like he'd had more than two beers.

"Hello. Thanks for helping me out."

"It's no trouble. Come on."

She led the way up Fish Lake Street toward Town Hall. It was about three times the length of the walk from the bar to the cafe, all uphill, and there were no lights except those inside the few houses they passed. Elizabeth seemed to have no difficulty, though, as though she could see as well in night as in day.

"You need some street lights," he said just to say something.

"No, that's the first step on a downhill slope. Next thing you know there'd be traffic lights at the corners, and then we'd have traffic jams."

The idea of traffic jams in this little hamlet was so funny he barked out a laugh.

"You sound like a coyote," she said. "Um. Sorry—that didn't come out right."

"It's okay. Do you mind if I ask you a question?"

"Go ahead."

He wanted to ask her what she meant by "he's the one I've been waiting for" but it seemed like a bad idea. "Who is this Adie? I've heard her name a dozen times today, but no one will explain who she is."

"Huh. It's not a secret: she's the Town Manager."

"This town has a manager?" He meant, this town *needs* a manager?

"Of course. She keeps it running smoothly. You wouldn't believe what this place looked like twenty years ago."

"What changed?"

"Adie found a new source of funds."

He wanted to ask, but didn't. Drugs? Illegal logging? Robbing lost hikers? They walked on in silence for a moment.

"She's also my best friend," Elizabeth said.

Now he *really* wanted to meet her.

They passed Cemetery Lane and Kevin was still nearly blind. But when they came around the sharp turn towards Town Hall he could see that the building was well-lit, with lamps under the portico and floodlights shining up onto the building's façade. He was surprised he hadn't been able to see the lights earlier; the woods weren't that thick.

The marmot statue was illuminated, too. Lit from below, it looked more sinister than it had in the daylight; when he'd first seen it high up on its plinth, it had merely been bizarre.

Elizabeth walked up the five steps to the top of the landing that ran all along the front of the building. She didn't knock, she just opened one of the big bronze-clad doors and walked in. Kevin followed.

It looked like most of the government buildings he'd been in while reporting in Portland, Salem, Corvallis, and Eugene—except it was cleaner. He'd been a journalism major at the University of Oregon and started investigative reporting while still an undergraduate, so he'd spent a fair amount of time waiting around in marble foyers just like this. But in Corvallis, the smallest of those four cities, City Hall serviced a population of over fifty thousand; this building was comparable and was used by just thirty-two people.

Their footsteps echoed as they passed closed doors marked Clerk and Community Room. Elizabeth stopped at a partially-open door labelled Town Manager. She knocked.

"Come on in, Elizabeth," a shaky contralto voice called out.

Elizabeth pushed open the door. Inside the large room was a modest desk piled with papers and magazines, and In and Out baskets that were both empty; a table with an impressive flat-screen computer monitor, keyboard and mouse; several black filing cabinets; and two tall bookshelves crammed with books. Facing the desk was a grouping of four wooden chairs that somehow looked comfortable despite the lack of padding. And behind the desk sat a grey-haired woman in her seventies.

She stood to greet them and Kevin was surprised at how tall she was, possibly a bit taller than him. Her silvery hair was coiled around her head in a tidy style he had seen once before; he racked his brain and recalled that it was a Dutch braid. She was very thin, but looked strong. Her face was friendly and open.

"Adie this is Kevin Candela. Kevin, Adie Eagle."

It occurred to him that he had never told her his last name; in fact, he didn't know hers either. The only person he'd revealed it to was Pete, in the bar. An hour ago. News travelled at the speed of light in this little town.

Kevin extended his hand and Adie shook it gently. "It's nice to meet you at last, Kevin," she said.

At last? He'd only been in town for seven hours. "I've heard your name a dozen times since I got here," Kevin said.

She laughed. "I'll just bet."

"I need to get back," Elizabeth said.

He nearly panicked. "You're leaving?"

"I have to, I'm sorry. Don't worry, Adie will take care of you. Come by the cafe in the morning for breakfast."

"I will."

"Goodnight," she said, and she turned and left the room. He could hear her footsteps echoing down the hall, then the door opened and closed.

"She leaves a vacuum, doesn't she?" Adie said.

He turned back from the doorway and looked at her. She was smiling benevolently, but he could tell she was amused by him.

"I don't even know her last name," he blurted out. Why did he say that?

"Kelly."

"She's Irish?" She didn't look Irish.

"She's American." She came around the desk and he saw that she was wearing flats, very sensible black shoes. And she was definitely an inch or so taller than he was. "Let me show you where you'll be staying tonight."

"I didn't mean to impose—"

"Don't be silly. The apartment's been empty since Bob died last spring."

So it was probably musty and smelled like Old Guy. "It's unusual to have a living space in a Town Hall, isn't it?"

"I'd say it might be unique. Come on."

He followed her to the back of the building, where a wide stone staircase led both up and down.

"You have a basement."

"Yep. Lots of spooky stuff down there."

They went up. The stairs curved around to the right. A long hallway led the length of the building; the stairs were right in the middle. Following Adie, he saw a door marked Police, and right beside it Mayor's Chamber. Across the hall were Voting and Library. She opened the Mayor's door and led him inside.

It was neither musty nor smelly. It was rather nice, actually. There was a gas fire already lit in a real stone fireplace. Several floor lamps illuminated the living room, which was furnished with contemporary fabric-covered sofa and two big chairs, and a large glass coffee table. An oversized flat-panel TV hung on the wall above the fireplace. Between two windows whose thick curtains were drawn stood a seven-foot-tall giraffe sculpture, which looked like mahogany.

Adie said, "There's a kitchen and an office on your left, bed and bath to your right. Fresh linens on the bed and in the bathroom. Maybe you'd like to freshen up first. Then I thought we could have a chat."

"Sure. I'll just be a minute."

This apartment was bigger than the one he'd had all through college. The bedroom was generous, with a queen-sized bed, and a really large dresser over four feet wide and as tall as his chest, both made of oak. Lighted lamps on nightstands on either side of the bed. A walk-in closet, completely empty. The bathroom was not extravagant, but it was spacious. A large walk-in shower, claw-foot tub, enclosed water closet, and a wide vanity with an etched mirror hanging above it.

Kevin used the toilet and washed his hands. The towels were deep green cotton.

When he came back into the living room, Adie said, "Can I get you a drink? Bob wasn't much of a drinker, but we have a few choices."

"Thanks, no."

"There's a really first-rate Scotch here."

"I never drink hard liquor, just beer."

"If you're going to waste it, I think I'll have a small glass. How about some water? Check the fridge."

The kitchen was adequate but smaller in scale than the bathroom, obviously designed for someone who didn't cook often or elaborately. There was no table to eat at, just a high bar with two stools. The refrigerator had bottles of Talking Rain and not a lot else; he took a black cherry and found a glass in the cupboard beside the fridge.

Adie had settled in one chair, facing the fireplace. Kevin took the opposing one. There was enough room for a second person in the chair, if they were friendly. She sipped from a highball glass, looking him over.

"Journalist?" she said.

"You know that. Something tells me that every word I've spoken since I got here has been relayed to you already."

"I'm not the spider woman, if that's what you're thinking."

"I'm not thinking anything, really. I'm accustomed to just listening to people and making judgments later, if at all."

She didn't say anything for a long moment. He waited it out. He'd seen this ploy many times before.

Finally she said, "A lot of people noticed you sitting down by the lake this afternoon. I think that a man who can sit still for an hour without looking at his phone, with nothing but a notebook and a pen to keep him company, that's a man who might be worth knowing."

He was at a loss for a moment. He'd had no idea he was being watched. "Thank you," he said.

"I understand you're on your way to Portland, Maine. For a new job?"

"Yes. I got lost trying to find a hike I wanted to do, and ended up following the mailman here."

"Jeremy, my nephew. Most people who find us just stumble on in, but that's a new one. You'll have to tell him about it."

"Sure, if I meet him before I go."

Adie didn't say any of the things in reply that he thought she might. She just sipped her drink and looked at him over the rim of the glass. He drank some more of his water. It didn't taste anything like black cherry, but he was thirsty.

"Perhaps you'll consider staying for a few days. Get to know the town a little. I know you've already had the tour, but it has depths you might not have noticed at first."

"Actually, I was thinking I might do that," he said. "I've been to a lot of towns, but I've never seen anything like this." He gestured to the room, swept his arm to include the whole building. "Like *this*."

"Well, there's a story there. I'll bet you like a good story."

"I do."

She nodded and stood up, finishing her drink before she set the glass down on the coffee table. "Get some rest, then. Elizabeth opens the cafe at 8:00. After breakfast I'll show you around the Hall, if you like. Do you remember where my office is?"

"I don't think I could miss it."

She nodded again. "Good night, Kevin. Thanks for the drink."

He laughed. "It was yours to begin with. And... thanks for letting me stay here. I really didn't want to go back to White Salmon."

"No. Who would?"

First Morning

Tuesday, August 17

Kevin woke up without an alarm around 8:30. The water pressure in the shower was excellent, which was a good start to the day. When he was ready he left the apartment. There was a lock on the door but he couldn't find a key anywhere, so he left it unbolted. At the end of the hallway was an elevator, but he spurned that and walked back to the stairs in the center of the building, leaving the rest of the second floor unexplored until the tour Adie had promised him. He passed her office on his way out, but the door was closed.

It was sunny and already warm outside. He strolled down the hill, smiling to himself, looking forward to breakfast and to seeing Elizabeth again. Kelly, Adie had said. Elizabeth Kelly.

The screen door squeaked a little as he opened it. There were only two other people inside, sitting at adjacent tables: Jodie the bar owner, and a woman in her early thirties that he hadn't met yet, who was smiling as she turned to look at him. There was a brown retriever of some sort lying across her feet under the table; the dog raised its head and studied him as if he might be useful later.

The old German shepherd he'd seen yesterday was still lying up against the bookshelf at the end of the room. Once again it didn't bother rising up at all, but this time its eyes tracked him as he crossed the room.

"Good morning, Jodie," he said.

"Morning, Kevin. This is Wanda," pointing to the other woman, "our resident artist."

"Really?" he said. "What kind of work do you do?"

46

"Painting mostly," she said, "but a little mixed media. Fantasy art."

"Dragons and fairies, that sort of thing?"

"Exactly."

"I'd like to see your work sometime. I love that stuff."

"Stop by my house any time."

He nodded and she smiled again. Elizabeth came out of the kitchen and met him at the bar. He sat down and they looked at each other quietly. He thought he heard the other women chuckling behind him, but he wasn't going to break eye contact to find out.

Finally she said, "You look like an egg man. Over hard?"

"Yes," he said without the slightest surprise.

"What kind of toast?"

"Do you have any scones today?"

"Chocolate chip and cranberry."

"How am I supposed to choose between those? You pick one for me."

"Okay. Coffee coming right up."

"She makes great coffee," Jodie said.

It was well after 9:00, which might explain why so few people were here in the cafe. Or perhaps fewer people ate breakfast here than lunch. But even if everyone in town ate here twice a day, how was Elizabeth able to make a living with a potential customer base of only thirty-one people? Or Jodi either, for that matter? Something screwy was going on with the economics of this little hamlet.

When Elizabeth came back with a black mug of coffee, she said, "Did you sleep well last night?"

"Yes, thanks," he said as he added cream and sugar. "It's a comfortable apartment. Nicer than any place I stayed in college." He sipped; it *was* good coffee. As if it could be anything else.

47

"Where did you study?"

"UO, in Eugene."

"Ah. Ducks."

He laughed. "I can't believe you know that."

"We live in a tiny town," she said, "not on another planet." She went back into the kitchen and was evidently cooking his eggs, but he could still see her through the pass-through.

"Did you know," he said, "that the Fighting Duck is really Donald Duck? From Disney?"

"Oh, are you one of those people that prefer Donald Duck to Mickey Mouse?"

"One hundred percent. Mickey creeps me out."

"Because he's a mouse?"

"Because of the squeaky voice."

He was aware that Jodie and Wanda were listening, but he didn't care.

Elizabeth came out with a plate of eggs, half an orange carved into a sort of flower, and a chocolate chip scone.

"That looks good!"

"Eat your breakfast." She went back into the kitchen.

He did. The eggs were perfect, and the scone was incredible.

"So, Kevin," Jodie said from behind him. He half-turned and nodded to acknowledge her. "You're still here. And you slept in the Mayor's apartment last night."

Then he turned all the way on his stool. "Yes."

"I thought you were due in Maine."

"It can wait a few days."

"Hmm." She stood up. "See you at lunch, Elizabeth," she called.

Elizabeth came out with the coffee pot. "Bye, Jodie." She topped up Kevin's and Wanda's mugs.

Wanda did not follow Jodie out. She was pointedly not looking at either Kevin or Elizabeth.

"What are your plans for today?" Elizabeth asked him.

"Adie's going to show me around the Town Hall. After that, I thought I would check out Mike's shop, and maybe Wanda's studio."

"Sure," Wanda said. She was still smiling. Kevin got the impression that she did that a lot. "I'll be around all day."

"And then?" Elizabeth said.

"That's it. I've run out of ideas."

"Maybe we could have dinner," Elizabeth said.

Kevin got the impression that it was taking all of Wanda's strength not to lean towards them. He said, "Well, you've cooked for me twice. How about if I cook for you tonight?"

"That sounds wonderful. Your place or mine?"

"Uh." It wasn't really his, but… "Mine?"

"What time?"

"7:30?"

"I'll bring something to drink. Dark beer, right?"

He just nodded. Elizabeth smiled at him and he tried not to fall off his stool. When she went back into the kitchen, he had to calculate the tip three times to be sure he wasn't stiffing her, which would send a very bad message, or over-tipping, which might send one just as bad.

Town Hall

As Kevin passed the marmot statue it seemed that it was looking down at him. He could have sworn it was looking up yesterday. It was an odd statement for a town to make: most places might have an equestrian statue of a local boy who became a general and won a glorious battle, but this town had a statue of a rodent that won a battle simply by not being killed; and the town *lost* that battle. It was a little like New Rumley, Ohio putting up a statue to George Custer in which he was surrounded by the Lakota and Cheyenne who had killed him.

Kevin pulled open one of the tall doors and walked in with the odd feeling that he was trespassing somehow, despite the fact that it was public building. Adie's door was half-open as it had been when he'd first met her. Before he had a chance to knock, she said, "Come on in, Kevin."

He opened the door. She was working on a laptop—an expensive one—facing away from the door, but turned to look at him. There must have been some odd expression on his face, because she just laughed.

"There's no witchcraft in this town," she said. "It's not Brigadoon, no matter what anyone says. If you drove away, you could find it again easily if you remember the turns. Elizabeth can't read your mind, and I can't see around walls." He stepped into the room. "Marble hallway," she explained. "Echoes like a canyon. I could hear you open the outside door, I could hear every step you took, and also that pause that people make before they work up the courage to intrude on a semi-closed door. Which, by the way, amplifies the sound more than if I just left it open."

"How did you know it was me?"

50

"I could have simply deduced that it probably was you, but the truth is that I know the footsteps of every soul in this town, and yours were new. I'd have been told by now if there was another stranger in town, so if I hear a stranger's footsteps, I assume it's the stranger I know."

"Okay, I believe that. But there *is* magic here, you know."

She stood up and smiled broadly. Her wrinkles proved that she had spent a lifetime doing that. "I've never heard a truer word. Let's have a look around, shall we?"

He stepped back outside her office and she followed him, and surprised him by taking his arm. "Top to bottom suit you?"

"Sure."

As they walked up the wide staircase, she didn't let go of his arm, and he was having trouble keeping up with her brisk pace, instead of the reverse that he might have expected for someone her age. She steered him right at the top and released his arm.

"Tax assessor's office."

She opened the door; like all the others he'd seen so far it had a frosted glass panel on the top half with large, sharp black letters explaining the room's function. Kevin was surprised that the spacious room was empty—utterly empty. There was not even any dust in the corners.

"Hold that thought," Adie said. He bit back what he'd been about to say.

She led him directly across the corridor to the police office. When she opened that door, this one too was empty. At the far end of the room was another door, which she opened. There was a short corridor, off of which were two identical jail cells, both with barred doors ajar. Other than the built-in sink, toilet, and sleeping platform, both were also empty.

Back in the main corridor, the room next to the tax assessor was labelled "Courtroom." Adie opened the door and they were in the back of a small court, such as you might expect in a remote rural county—which this was, of course. There were a dozen benches that looked like church pews, a swinging gate between them and the lawyers' tables, and a high bench for the judge. Everything was spotless and looked as if it had never been used. Behind the bench was another door leading to a small judge's chamber—empty. It had a door out to the corridor as well. When they went out, there were two restrooms directly across.

It took some self-control; the reporter in Kevin wanted to ask what the hell was going on. But he said nothing.

Down the corridor they went. Across from the Mayor's apartment was a voting room; this did in fact have four voting booths along one wall and a table with two chairs behind it at the front. It wasn't empty but it was very clean.

The next door down, the last one, was the Library. Adie opened the door and Kevin stepped in, expecting to see another empty room, but this one lived up to its label. Unlike most modern libraries, this one had no computers except one on the checkout desk, but it did have row after row of shelves, all of them crammed with books—all of them fairly new, as far as he could tell. It was small, but he'd seen libraries no larger than this in a handful of tiny Oregon towns, except those had been dingier.

"That's the top floor," Adie said. "You want to take the elevator down?"

"I'm fine with stairs," he said.

They walked side by side back to the first floor. Adie turned left. The first door on their left was the Mailroom, and this looked like it got real use. There was a bank of sizable cubbyholes against one wall with hand-printed labels beneath them, roughly forty by a quick estimate, and one of them had a package wrapped in brown paper in it. On the other wall was a large, heavy table with an office chair pulled up to it, a big blue wheeled recycling bin, and a locking metal supply cabinet.

"This is Jeremy's domain," Adie said. "You haven't met him yet, have you?"

"Not yet."

The next room down the hall, under the library, was the fire marshal's office. This had been stocked but looked as if it had never been used. There were a few desks with nothing on them but corded phones, cabinets for supplies, a tall filing cabinet, but no people.

Back down the corridor, under the tax assessor's office, was a filing room. This wasn't empty either: large black lateral filing cabinets covered both walls.

"Mostly empty," Adie said. "I keep most of my notes in my office."

The next room was labelled "Mayor" but was nearly empty. It was substantially larger than Adie's office, possibly twice as large, but all it had in it was a huge desk facing the door, with a tall-backed office chair behind it and nothing but a phone to mar its surface, three cushioned armchairs with their backs to him, and a low piece of furniture that Kevin suspected was a liquor cabinet. Across the hall were more restrooms.

Back into the foyer they passed Adie's office and she opened the Clerk's door: utterly empty. Across the way was the community room. This was a surprise, because this room looked like it got frequent use. There was a raised stage at the far end with a lectern off on one side, comfortable chairs

53

facing it—not the folding chairs he'd seen in similar rooms elsewhere—and a projector system hanging from the ceiling. A closed door at the back of the room was labelled "Equipment."

"Ready to go downstairs?" she said.

* * *

The basement was less brightly lit than it could have been. It had that weird lighting he'd seen in hospitals: you could always see well enough no matter where you were, but it looked dark even a short distance away. The ceiling panels had some kind of baffles to prevent scattering of light. He had no idea why they did that.

The first door to the right was the Utility room, water and power. It was very large, with lots of panels and pumps and piping that he didn't find very interesting. As Adie was closing the door, he took a chance and said, "I've heard some strange stories about Elizabeth."

"I'll bet you have. Was Peter going on about his fairy child theory again?"

"Yes. Why does he think that?"

They were standing in the bright-dim light in the spacious foyer at the bottom of the stairs. There were no side corridors down here, all the rooms led directly off this open space. In the distance he could see the elevator doors. The floor and walls were concrete, which definitely did not add any ambience.

"Well I could say that his brain is addled, but it's not true. He and Elizabeth did grow up here together, went to school together. To tell the truth, I don't know where he got his nutty ideas from."

"Someone implied you knew the truth."

"They think I know everything, the poor dears. In this case they're right, though. I knew her parents, Will and Anne. They were good, good friends. Now, you seem like a rational person to me, so let me reassure you. Elizabeth was born in a hospital in the usual way; I saw her there myself the day she was born. She was not snatched up and exchanged for a fairy, she was not found on a hillside, she was not delivered by a stork or an alien spaceship. There's something special about my girl, and I love her like the daughter I never had, but she's as human as you and I."

She waited instead of rushing on to show him the rest. He tried to think of how to respond to all that. What came out was, "I promised to cook her dinner tonight."

"Good for you, my boy."

"But I don't think there's much in the way of supplies in the Mayor's apartment. Can you tell me where I can get some groceries?"

She patted him on the arm. "I don't think you need to worry about that," she said enigmatically, and he already knew her well enough not to push it.

The next room was storage for leftover construction supplies, apparently. Cinder blocks, bags of mortar, slabs of marble, bins of hardware, all organized and stowed neatly. And the next three rooms, all very large, were utterly empty. By the elevator was a supply room, with rows of cabinets holding, he presumed, office supplies that would last the town—based on the storage capacity of all these cabinets— a hundred and fifty years.

Across the hall was a generator room with a gigantic backup generator in it. And next to that was the IT room, which absolutely blew him away. There were racks of blinking rack-mounted computers and, he could tell from the labels on some of the equipment frameworks, the heart of their PBX switchboard. It looked like it could service Eugene. He reined in his curiosity once more. He figured the answers were coming momentarily.

* * *

They went back to Adie's office and he took one of the chairs facing her desk while she resumed her former place. He leaned forward and put his chin on his fist, trying to think of how to ask the questions that were bubbling up in his journalist brain. She was grinning at him.

"Let me just forestall that," she said, with nothing but kindness in her voice. "You want to know how a hamlet that is barely more than a crossroads could afford such a building, and *why* we would build it, and why two-thirds of the building is unused. And why what *is* here is so over-engineered and sophisticated. Then I suppose you've noticed some quirks of the local economy you'd like to ask about." He just nodded. "I appreciate your curiosity, I really do. But at this time, I'm afraid I will not be answering any of your questions."

"*What?*"

"I'm not going to tell you. Not yet."

"Why not?"

"Because you haven't decided to stay yet. And if you're not going to stay, it's none of your business."

He spluttered for a moment before he got himself under control. "Who said anything about staying? I have to be in Maine in a week."

"I know that was your plan. But you never planned on this, did you?"

She watched him keenly as he mastered himself—swallowing indignation, blocked curiosity, bluster, professional outrage, and something that it took a moment for him to recognize as hunger. Hunger for place, hunger for attachment. Hunger for love.

He stood up. She looked enormously pleased. At his frustration or his self-control, he could not have said.

Instead, he simply said, "Let's leave the questions as read, shall we?"

"Absolutely."

"Thanks for the tour."

"It was my pleasure. Enjoy the rest of your day."

The Shops of Marmot

He needed to calm down before he faced anyone else, so he walked down the hill from the Town Hall to the cemetery.

He would have thought that in a town this small, anywhere he went he'd have a nearly one hundred percent chance of being alone. But someone was in the cemetery, hunched over one of the gravestones. For a moment he reconsidered, but then his stubborn streak reared up and he continued walking. As he got closer he recognized Darren, the quiet handyman from the bar last night. When he was nearly to the low, broken-down fence a small dog started barking. He couldn't see it, but evidently it could smell him. Darren stood up and looked at him. He looked back, in a cross mood because of Adie's evasions and not inclined to back down an inch.

After a moment the dog shut up, and Darren said, "Kevin, is it?"

"Yes. You're Darren, right?"

The other man walked to meet him and stuck out his hand. Kevin shook it; it was like shaking a tree branch. A middle-sized terrier, not a breed Kevin recognized—probably a mutt—scurried around from behind a stone and looked up at him, ears high. It seemed willing to give him the benefit of the doubt, but was clearly ready to start barking again if necessary.

"This is Ivan," Darren said.

Kevin squatted down and held out his hand with his fingers curled under. The dog approached cautiously, took a sniff, and came a little closer so Kevin could pet it. He scratched behind its ears and patted its shoulder. Then he looked up at Darren.

"Wait— Ivan the Terrier?"

Darren looked embarrassed. "Yeah."

Kevin stood up. "That's a great name." He looked past Darren at the graveyard. "Is this still in use?"

"Well."

Kevin waited. It wasn't clear that he was going to say anything else. "It's complicated?"

Darren thought about it for a moment and seemed to come to a decision. "The town lost its license for the cemetery when it was unincorporated. The state wouldn't renew it when the town started growing again. So technically no one is allowed to be buried here anymore."

"But actually…" Kevin prompted.

"We ignore them and when someone wants to be buried here, we do it."

"Huh. Fair enough." Darren looked relieved, as if he'd been afraid Kevin was going to report them. "You're the caretaker here?"

"Yeah, I keep it tidied up." Darren looked behind him at the sorry state of the fence, and turned back looking embarrassed again. "I'd like to rebuild the fence but I haven't had the time. Or the money to buy the materials."

"You mind if I look around?"

"Go ahead."

Kevin stood just inside the busted fence line and looked around. The cemetery was a little less than an acre in size. There were fewer than a hundred headstones visible, but there might have been many more flush markers that had been partially or completely buried over the years.

Darren was still standing nearby. Kevin said, "If you don't mind my saying so, you're a lot more talkative today than you were last night."

"Yeah," Darren said. "Well, it's usually more trouble than it's worth trying to talk over those motor-mouths in Jodie's bar."

"I know what you mean."

Kevin wandered around aimlessly. Some of the headstones looked to be a hundred years old or more, but it was easy to pick out the relatively new ones. One said, "Ida Eagle Bennett, 1949 to 1999." He finally found the one he was looking for, a double arched stone marked, "William James Kelly, 1951 to 1995. Anne Harroway Kelly, 1954 to 1995." Dead fifteen years. Elizabeth must have been young when it happened. He stood for a moment looking at the marker.

Something moved at the corner of his vision. Ivan the dog was sitting off to one side, looking solemnly at the stone. As he turned to look at the dog, it cocked its head up to look back at him. Then it stood up and walked away.

"Thanks," he said in passing to Darren, who was using hand clippers to cut back blackberry runners trying to make some headway along the fence line. "You're welcome," Darren said without looking up.

* * *

Kevin took the cross-country shortcut Elizabeth had used yesterday to get from the cemetery to Marmot Lane. At the corner with Little Fish Street he stopped and examined Mike's Shop from the outside. Other than the sign out front, it just looked like a house. It was a little larger than average for the town, clapboards painted marine blue, with dark shingles on the roof. There were three cars parked in the wide driveway off Fish Lake Street.

A hand-carved wooden "Open" sign, raised black lettering on a white background, hung on the front door. Kevin opened it and walked in.

What had once been the living room was now more like a home theatre. Reclining seats— upholstered in plush red, each with its own cupholder—sat in two rows facing a truly gigantic flat-screen TV hanging on the wall. Mike was sitting at a small desk off to one side, working at a laptop. He looked up as Kevin came in, smiled, and gestured to a coffee service on a sofa table against the wall opposite the TV. It had two large, pump coffee thermoses, a variety of sweeteners, real and artificial creamers, and glossy black mugs. Kevin helped himself and ignored the Danish shortbread cookies set out on a tray.

The TV was flipping through webpages at an impressive speed. Kevin's home Internet connection in Portland hadn't been this fast. Meanwhile Mike and a woman that Kevin couldn't see were speaking softly and constantly. Apparently this was a hunt for the perfect waffle maker. Kevin took a seat at the end of the second row.

"Too expensive," the woman said. "No, I don't like square ones. Well, that flips but the handle's the wrong shape. Wait."

The display stopped at a round waffle maker that stood upright with a long protruding handle. There was a small gallery of other images at the left of the page. Mike went through them slowly.

"That's it," the woman said. She stood up. Kevin had never met her before. She was in her early sixties, plump, with long hair that had probably been blonde when she was young, but was now a washed-out brown. "Do I pay you now?"

"That depends," Mike said. "If you want it delivered to your home then yes, I'll take your payment now. But if you want to come back here to inspect it when it arrives, then we'll defer payment until you're sure it's the correct item."

"No, I'm sure that's the one I saw at my daughter's house. You can send it to my place. Is Visa okay?"

"Perfectly okay."

He gave her the total and she handed over her card. Mike used a tiny reader to scan the card, then turned back to the laptop and quickly went through the checkout process online, using PayPal to make the purchase. He was a good typist, Kevin noted, no hesitations and no mistakes.

"They say it should arrive within three days," Mike said. "Call me if it doesn't, and I'll let you know if I hear anything from them."

"Thanks, Mike," the woman said. She took a printed receipt and left.

"Sorry, I've forgotten who's next."

"I am," a man said. The chairs were so tall and close together that Kevin couldn't see the people sitting in the front row.

"Jonathan. How can I help you?"

"I need some new flannel shirts from L. L. Bean."

"The same kind as last year?"

"Yeah, but I'd like to see what colors they have."

The whole thing took less than ten minutes. This man also paid before he left, and again he was a stranger to Kevin.

"Now, Margaret, what do you need today?" Mike said.

"I have a couple of kitchen things, and I'm looking for a baby shower gift for my best friend's daughter."

This took a little longer since she wasn't sure what she wanted, but they ended up with a plush singing kangaroo, which Kevin thought was unbearably cute, but then he'd never had much interaction with babies. The new stainless-steel pots were quicker. The woman chose to wait to inspect the items when they arrived. When she was gone, Mike closed his laptop and the TV went dark. He stood up and Kevin followed suit. Mike offered his hand and they shook.

"Sorry," Mike said, "you caught me in a very rare rush hour. It's usually not like this except at Christmastime."

"I think I get it. You do Internet shopping for people with no Internet connection?"

"About a third of them do have Internet, or could if they wanted to. They just don't know how to use it, or don't want to do it themselves."

"You can make a living off this?"

"Yes, actually. I always get free shipping when they wouldn't, so after I add in my service charge they're paying just a little more than they would if they bought it themselves. And they don't have to navigate the web themselves, or drive to the city. People like doing it this way; it's like going to an infinite shop. And a lot of times I can make suggestions, or warn them off iffy products. I think I earn my commission."

"You must be drawing in people from all over. I didn't recognize any of those people."

Mike laughed. "You know, you look up at these wooded hills and think they're just forest, but there are little villages and lonely houses scattered all over the place. And some of my customers drive just as far to get here as they would to get to a real town."

"How do you connect? I thought the phone service was limited out here."

"Satellite. I use the same system Upton and Travis have. Very fast, fairly reliable."

Kevin sat down in the front row this time.

"This is a cool business idea," he said. "I'm impressed. And I like your setup; the home theatre is a good model."

"Thanks. People seem to like it. Sometimes they have… um, private things they want to look for. Then I turn off mirroring and we go in the back room. But that doesn't happen very often."

Kevin sat and thought for a few minutes. There was an economy at work here unlike anything he'd ever seen in his years of reporting in Oregon. That alone would be worth a series of articles. If he could figure out how to approach it— not to mention figure out how it worked. Adie knew, apparently.

"Well, thanks," he said at last.

"Come back if I can help you with anything."

"I will." But he probably wouldn't; he was pretty good at navigating the web himself.

They shook hands again and Kevin left the shop. There was a faded teak bench in the garden outside. He sat down and took out his notebook. It took him a little while to gather his thoughts, then he wrote a few paragraphs about Mike's business and this tiny town's economy. When he was done he just sat for a little while longer, enjoying the sun while he looked across the street at the cafe.

* * *

When he got up from the bench, he realized that he had no idea which house was Wanda's. But since most of the houses were on Fish Lake Street, and he figured he could probably tell an artist's house when he saw it, he walked up toward the Town Hall.

The first one he passed, on the right almost across the street from Mike's Shop, had two satellite dishes on poles in the yard, nearly hidden by shrubs; that must be Upton's place. The next one was on the left, and it had that indefinable air of old folks. The third one, on the right, had carved wooden birds atop the white posts of the fence, a stained-glass panel in the front door, and the house was painted three different pastel colors; he'd bet anything that was an artist's house. When Wanda answered the door, he won his bet with himself.

She smiled at him. "You came!" she said.

"Of course. I told you I would."

"Well come in."

Like all of the houses he'd seen in town, this one was modest in size. On the left of the foyer was a tiny sitting room, but the more spacious living room on the right had been converted into a studio. It contained cabinets of supplies, a stained drafting table, canvases stood up in rows against the walls, and an easel near the window with a half-finished oil painting resting on it. The painting depicted a dragon standing on its hind legs with its front paws in the air, like a dog begging for a treat. This creature was begging from a row of fairies sitting on a tree branch, one of whom was dangling something from

one hand that was still merely a sketch. Kevin could swear that the dragon was smiling.

"You have good light here," he observed.

"Yes, the window faces nearly due south. Can I get you something to drink?"

"No, thanks." He gestured at the easel. "This is kind of fun. What's the treat going to be?"

"A knight."

He laughed. "Of course."

"Would you like to see a few others?"

"Yes, please."

65

She brought out several canvases, all of them quite well done. The fourth one made him raise his eyebrows. Two dragons were intertwined, a white and a black, both breathing fire, but not menacingly—almost as if they were dancing.

"Wait... I've seen this picture before."

"It was commissioned for the dust jacket of a book that came out last year."

"I remember that book. It didn't live up to its cover."

She laughed lightly. "They seldom do, do they?"

"But I remember the image. It's really good."

"Thanks." He looked at a few more and then she invited him to visit for a bit in the other room. "I heard you talked to Darren this morning," she said when they were settled.

He chuckled. "You don't really need phones here, do you?"

"Oh, word gets around."

"Yes, I met him in the cemetery. Also Ivan."

"Ivan's a good dog. Darren relies on him a lot; I think he talks to Ivan more than he does any of us. Not that I blame him for not talking to me."

"What do you mean?" he said.

"He used to live here."

"What? You mean *here,* in this house?"

"Yes, we were married."

"But you both still live here. I'd think that would be awkward. I mean... it's a pretty small town."

She laughed out loud. "What are you talking about? It's a *tiny* town. But we both grew up here, and neither of us wanted to leave. It wasn't a bad split, as they go, so he moved into the old Wibberley trailer and I spread out a bit." She gestured at the studio.

"That's… unusually civilized. I've heard of people who had to move to different *states* when they broke up."

"We still collaborate sometimes. Did you see the birds on the fence posts?"

"Yes. They were nice. They looked realistic."

"They are. Darren made those. It's a passion, maybe his only passion. Occasionally I do wood sculptures and I try to incorporate his birds into them. He gets a cut of the sale price and we're both happy. Well—I'm happy, he's slightly less depressed."

"I noticed that he didn't seem very animated," Kevin said. "He was at the bar last night and he didn't say a word the whole time I was there."

"Yes, it was very unusual that he spoke to you in the cemetery today. Usually he just pretends that other people aren't there. That's why I had to divorce him."

"He pretended you weren't there?"

"Not exactly. But I'm basically a happy person, and he's basically not. After a few years my constant good moods irritated him, and his perpetual gloom wore me down. I just couldn't live with Eeyore anymore. He took it pretty well when I told him. I think he'd been expecting me to ditch him since we first started dating in high school."

"There's not a high school here in town, is there?"

"No, the kids go to the one in Trout Lake. It's not a great school, but it's good enough for us."

"How do they get there? Do the parents have to drive them?"

"No, Marmot has a school bus."

Of course they had a school bus. They probably had a helicopter. If the town were on the ocean they'd have an aircraft carrier. How the hell could a hamlet like this afford this stuff?

He realized that he'd been quiet too long. "Well," he said, "thanks for showing me your work. Um… Is that book cover painting for sale?"

"Yes, it is."

"How much are you asking for it?" She told him. It was incredibly reasonable for such a great piece. "I think I'd like to buy it. But I don't have that much cash."

"Oh, just ask Mike to ring it up. We have an arrangement."

"Okay. Can you hang onto it for me until I leave?"

"Of course."

He stood up and she showed him to the door, which was five feet away from the sitting room's open archway.

"I'm glad I stopped by," Kevin said. "I love your paintings."

She grinned a million-lumens smile at him. "Thanks."

* * *

He walked back to Mike's Shop. When Kevin told him that he'd bought one of Wanda's paintings, Mike asked which one, then wrote up an invoice on his computer and took Kevin's card. There was no one else in the shop, so the whole thing took two minutes.

Then he trudged back up the hill to the Town Hall. It occurred to him that in the last two days he'd done more hill walking than he would have if he'd managed to find that trail he'd been looking for.

He had offered to cook dinner for Elizabeth, but there was nothing to cook. He went up the stairs to the Mayor's apartment, intending to get his keys and drive to the nearest town with a grocery store—all the way back to White Salmon if he had to. He would take the chance of not finding his way back; Adie had said he'd be able to, and even if there *were* a spell that kept the town hidden, he knew where it was now, and he trusted that he'd be able to make it back again.

But there was a basket of food sitting on the floor outside the door, fresh home-baked bread, jars of capers and olives, olive oil, cans of tomatoes and artichokes, and several other things he couldn't immediately identify. There was a note on which someone had scrawled, "Her favorite is Italian." And when he carried the basket inside, the refrigerator, freezer, and cupboards were full.

He sat down at the bar in the little kitchen and tried to shake off the feeling that someone was watching him.

First Date

He found a few candles in an otherwise empty linen closet. There was no music—no CDs, LPs, cassettes, or even eight-track tapes—but there was a sound system below the TV that accepted a mini-jack plug, so he spent a few minutes making a mellow playlist on his phone and plugged that in.

There were no cookbooks, but Kevin had two decades of practice cooking for himself at odd hours with no advance warning or chance to shop, so this was easy. He used the ingredients from the basket and some spices he found in a cabinet to make a slow-simmered green olive, caper, and artichoke tomato sauce.

After studying the contents of the refrigerator and cupboards he whipped up a lemon and garlic salad dressing from scratch. There was lettuce and plenty of vegetables for the salad.

Dessert was an issue. There was vanilla ice cream in the freezer and fresh blackberries in the fridge. He dug a bar of dark chocolate out of his hiking supplies to shave over the berries.

When he was ready he had over an hour left in which to sit and fret.

* * *

Elizabeth was so punctual that Kevin suspected she'd been waiting outside his door until the second hand hit 12. She had a bottle of wine in one hand and a pair of dark amber beer bottles in the other.

"Welcome," he said. "It's not home, but it'll have to do." She stepped in and he closed the door.

"Hey, it smells good in here," she said.

"Thanks. I thought the candles would be too strong, but they're not."

"I meant the food smells."

"Oh, that. Let me find you a glass. Hmm. And a corkscrew. I thought I saw one..." He walked into the kitchen and opened a drawer. "Here. May I?" She handed him the bottle and he peeled the wrapper and pulled the cork easily.

"You're pretty good at that for a beer guy," she said as he poured her a glass.

"I like beer but I seem to be drawn to wine drinkers."

"Well, here's to diversity." She raised her glass and he touched it lightly with a beer bottle, then twisted that open and took a sip. It wasn't a brewery he'd heard of, but it was good. They sat on the stools at the bar in the kitchen. There was a pillar candle burning at each end. "You've been busy."

"It didn't take that long."

"I didn't mean just the dinner."

"Oh." He took another swig of beer. "Let me ask you something. Does everyone know everything that happens in this town?"

She laughed lightly. It sounded like a Bach cantata to him. "No. Some things stay private, and everyone has their little secrets."

"What are your secrets?"

"They're secret." She sipped her wine and set the glass down. "You have to understand, not a lot happens here. We get a new resident only every six or seven years, and visitors are pretty rare too—at least, ones that stay longer than it takes to discover
that both the cafe and the bar are closed."

"Hmm. I've never been a nine-day wonder before."

She laughed. "How do you know it will last nine days?"

71

"You're right," he said. "I'll probably get up tomorrow and find that everyone's forgotten all about me."

"Well. Maybe not tomorrow." She had a twinkle in her eye that made him wonder if she knew something he didn't. Then he mentally kicked himself. *Of course* she knew something he didn't; tons of it.

"Are you hungry?"

"Very."

"Okay. I just have to cook the pasta."

He got up and turned on the burner under the pasta pot, and dialed up the heat on the sauce a little. It was a small kitchen but he'd found everything he needed in terms of utensils and pans. He wasn't sure if that stuff had been here when he arrived, or if it had come with the food.

"You know," he said, "I thought I was going to have to drive down to the Gorge to get supplies for dinner. When I came back this afternoon, this place was fully stocked." He took a small chunk of Parmesan out of the fridge (domestic and vegetarian, not Reggiano—he'd checked).

"Nice. I wonder who could have done that?" Elizabeth said.

He laughed, then she did too. They both knew that she knew who it was. Some of it had probably come from *her*.

It was a small stove but had plenty of power. It wasn't long before the fettuccine was ready. While it was cooking he tossed the salad and cut some of the bread that his benefactors had left. It crackled when he sliced it: soft crumb and crunchy crust. There were herbs in it, too.

When he'd dished up their food he turned off the kitchen lights, leaving just one lamp in the living room and the two candles on the bar.

"This is really good," she said with her first bite. He smiled, and they didn't talk much while they ate, just enjoying the ambience and the food.

When they were both finished, Kevin said, "There's ice cream with berries and chocolate for dessert, if you're interested."

"Actually, how about just the berries and chocolate?"

"Coming up." He washed and drained the blackberries, portioned them out into bowls, and used a paring knife to shave small curls of chocolate onto them. "Want to eat them in the living room?"

She nodded and he carried the bowls in and set them down on the coffee table. It was August but the evenings were cool, so he started the gas fire, which he had had to figure out in order to turn it off last night. They sat in adjacent easy chairs; she curled her legs up under her, and he spread out with his feet on the edge of the table.

"It was really nice of whoever to bring me the groceries," he said.

"We're lucky," she said. "We have only good people in Marmot, no one nasty or mean. The closest we come is Ernie, who isn't really bad, just perpetually grumpy."

He wondered if it really was luck or something else; some kind of field that repelled people that wouldn't fit in, or who would ruin the town's character. At this point he would have found it difficult to refute any mystical hypothesis.

She asked about his family and he told about growing up near Portland. His father died in the last years of the US's involvement in Viet Nam, but his mother and younger sister still lived in Lake Oswego, and he owed them a phone call soon. He talked about going to college in Eugene, the years of working up the ladder as a journalist until he found a job he loved at a small local paper, and his mixed feelings of sadness and adventure when the paper folded and he found a new job on the other side of the country.

He suggested that it was her turn, and she told him what it had been like to be a child in a town so small that it was almost like living in the woods. Coming across bears and coyotes on solitary walks in the forest; the animals had never seemed dangerous to her, merely cautious. She'd been home schooled until high school, but switching to the school in Trout Lake had not been the shock she'd been warned about. She'd known a few people already, like Pete, and made friends quickly. He ventured to ask about her parents, hoping it wouldn't make her sad, and mentioned that he'd seen their graves that morning, but she was happy to talk about them: loving, caring, fiercely indifferent to the outside world. They'd died on vacation in Mexico when she was twenty, their very first time outside the country, and she didn't know or want to know how, preferring to remember them excited and intrepid on the day they left home.

Then it was late and she said she had to go; the cafe opened at 8:00 and she had to get up early to prepare.

"Thank you for a lovely evening," she said. "And considering you had to prepare dinner without cookbooks or Internet access, it was impressive."

"Well, I'm really glad you came," Kevin said. "I've never had a better date. Let alone a first date."

She smiled and didn't kiss him, just took his hand and squeezed. It was better than most kisses he'd ever experienced: her touch sent a jolt through his body like nothing he'd ever felt before. She said good night and he walked her to the door.

Then he wanted to go find Adie and tell her she could explain everything now. Because he didn't care about his plans, or the job that was waiting, or his old life, or anything. He was staying.

Election Week

Wednesday, August 18

It was a little cooler when Kevin left the Town Hall the next morning, which might have been because he woke up earlier than the day before. He was in a superb mood, and his resolution to stay in Marmot was, if anything, firmer than it had been the night before. So it was a bit of a shock when he was halfway to the cafe and glanced over at the house of Wanda the artist. There was a political sign in her front yard that said, "Kevin for Mayor."

He stopped in his tracks. *What the hell?* He looked closer. It was very professionally done, but it looked hand-painted, on a heavy white board with letters that were blue on the top and red on the bottom. He turned to go up the walkway to ask her what was going on; then stopped and took a step toward the cafe, because he was hungry and wanted to see Elizabeth. He vacillated again, then he froze and looked around. There was no one else visible. Was this a joke?

His brain was an utter blank. He didn't know what to do. Finally his stomach told him what the first priority should be, so he continued on to the cafe with one parting glance at the sign.

When he opened the screen door into the cafe Elizabeth was pouring coffee for Jodie, and Ernie waved her away. Kevin forgot all about the sign. Upton and Travis were at another table, Melissa was at the bar, the old couple whose names he had forgotten were at the window. There was a middle-aged couple he didn't know sitting at a table with two mixed-breed dogs at their feet. And the old dog was sleeping on its bed over by the bookshelf again.

If there had been conversation going on before he entered, it died the moment he opened the door. Elizabeth was standing beside Jodie, beaming at him with the coffee pot forgotten in her hand, and everyone else was studiously ignoring him. Except Ernie, who was scowling at him.

"Hey, dummy," Ernie said, "you coming in or what? You're blocking the breeze." Jodie slapped him on the arm and he grunted at her.

"Good morning, everyone," Kevin said. "Elizabeth."

"Kevin," she said, before turning to go back into the kitchen.

Kevin tried to ignore the fact that everyone in the place except Ernie was now smiling like idiots. He took his same seat at the end of the bar and Elizabeth brought him coffee. He reached for the menu and she said, "Don't bother," so he pulled back.

"Have a nice evening?" Upton said.

Kevin turned on his stool. Even Travis had something like a smile on his face; Upton looked like he'd just won the lottery.

"Very nice, thanks."

"We missed you in the bar last night," Jodie said.

"Oh shut up, Jodie," Upton chided her gently. "You knew he wouldn't be there."

"Doesn't mean we didn't miss him."

The man with the dogs stood up and came over to Kevin with his hand outstretched. Kevin stood and took it.

"Jack Durgan," he said. "My wife, Sharon," Kevin waved at her, where she still sat with one hand lightly on the scruff of each dog. She smiled back at him.

Upton chimed in. "Jack runs a really nice auto shop out of his garage, so if your car has a problem, he's the man to see. And Sharon is in real estate, based in White Salmon but she works from home a lot."

"Nice to meet you both," Kevin said. Jack went back to his table.

Elizabeth came out of the kitchen and set a plate of French toast on the counter in front of him, with a bowl of mixed berries and a pile of home fries. She handed him a small glass pitcher of syrup. He smiled and she smiled back as she turned away. He poured on the syrup, dumped some berries on the toast, and tried it. It was real maple syrup and the French toast was—of course—the best he'd ever had.

"Good, isn't it?" Melissa said.

"It's delicious."

"She's a pretty good cook."

Kevin choked. *"Pretty good?"* He looked around the room. "Pretty good? You folks really need to get out of town more often! Everything I've had here is *incredible*. If Elizabeth opened a restaurant in Portland she'd be making money faster than they could print it."

He turned back to see her looking at him. She wasn't smiling, which worried him for a moment. "Thank you very much," she said, absolutely seriously.

"You're welcome."

"I think you're a pretty good cook, too."

"It's hard to tell from one meal. That might be all I know how to make."

"I doubt it." She went back into the kitchen.

"That was a challenge, boy," Ernie said.

Kevin didn't respond, just turned his attention back to his breakfast.

When he was finished Elizabeth brought him more coffee. "You liked it, then?" she said.

"How did you know that was just what I wanted?"

She shrugged. "How does anyone know anything?"

Excellent question, but it wasn't an answer. He decided not to press the issue. "Can I see you again tonight?"

"Yes, you may. You've probably already figured out that I'm busy all day, but come to the back door around 6:00. That all right?"

"Very all right."

"Okay. What are you going to do today?"

"I thought I'd go to the library."

"Good idea. I'll see you later." She carried the coffee around and topped off people's mugs, then vanished back into her kitchen.

Kevin was aware of a sort of vacuum behind him. He turned and caught nearly everyone just looking away. Upton raised his eyebrows at him. Kevin took that as an invitation and joined him and Travis at their table.

"I noticed that dogs are welcome here," he said.

"Yup," Upton said.

"Whose is that one?" He pointed to the old dog sleeping by the bookshelf.

"Oh, that's Owl. She belongs to Adie. Owl can't handle stairs anymore, so Adie doesn't take her to work like she used to. She spends most of the day sleeping in here and dreaming that people are giving her food."

"Adie used to take her to work?"

"Yes. She still has the other two with her every day."

"Huh. I didn't see any dogs when I was there."

"Did you look under the desk?"

Adie's desk faced the doorway, so there could have been five dogs under there, and if they'd been quiet he never would have known. "No."

"You've got to pay attention, Kevin," Travis said, "or you'll miss the important stuff."

Kevin smiled. "Thanks for the advice. I did notice one thing, though." They looked at him expectantly. "I haven't seen any kids around."

"There are actually nine. School's out, so they spend all day in the woods with the other wild animals."

"Nine? Really?" He hadn't seen a single sign of any of them—no toys in the yard, no screaming tag games, no bicycles—except for the pictures in Mary's salon.

"Melissa has a daughter. How old is she now?"

Melissa spoke up from her place at the bar. "Twelve."

Kevin turned to face her. "What's her name?"

"Tika."

"That's a beautiful name."

"Thanks. We were afraid she'd hate it here, but she absolutely loves it."

"Where did you live before?"

"In the Bay Area. We used to live right next door to Mike, but after he moved here we followed him."

"Wow. He must have given it a glowing report."

She smiled and patted her lips with her napkin. "I have to get to work. Nice to talk to you again."

"You too."

When she had gone, he turned back to Upton and Travis. "What does she do?"

"She's a cleaner," Upton said. Kevin had a momentary vision of the ruthless guys who vanish people for mob bosses, but that couldn't be what he meant. "She had some kind of high-powered career in San Francisco, but she won't talk about it. Now she cleans houses and seems to love it. Adie hires her to clean the Town Hall, too. Her husband works at the hospital in White Salmon. He's a nurse."

The old man sitting with his wife at the window table spoke up for the first time. "You a church-going man, Kevin?"

"I'm afraid not."

"An atheist, then?"

"No, I'm agnostic. I don't have any specific beliefs, but I don't have anything against people who do. I've talked to a lot of people as a reporter, and I've seen what a comfort religion can be to people."

"But you don't believe in God yourself?"

"Leave him alone, Paul," his wife said. "It's not like you're going to invite him to service. You don't even have a church anymore."

"The *town* doesn't have a church anymore," Paul said.

"And it hasn't since 1942," Upton said.

"It was 1941," Ernie chimed in.

"My dad said 1942."

"I was there when it burned down," Ernie said. "In September, 1941."

Upton silently mouthed "1942" to Kevin. Aloud he said, "Candles."

"Lightning strike, you ignoramus," Ernie said.

"Too many candles," Upton whispered.

"Doesn't matter," Paul said. "Kevin, I used to be a Methodist minister in Connecticut and New York. If you need someone to talk to, I'm always available."

"When he's awake," Upton whispered.

"How did you end up here?" Kevin asked.

"We just kept driving until we found a place we liked."

"You're kidding. But how did you *find* it?"

"We got lost," his wife said. "I'm Martha."

"Nice to meet you again. So you got lost and ended up here? That happened to me, too."

"We know," she said, chuckling. "But we didn't have a mailman to follow in. Just a stubborn driver who refused to turn around."

"Lucky for you I'm so stubborn," Paul said. "We might have ended up in Seattle."

"This *is* better," she agreed, putting her hand over his.

Upton looked at his watch. "Time to get to work. Ready, Travis?" Travis nodded and tossed some money on the table. "See you later, Kevin."

"I guess I'm heading out, too," Kevin said.

The rest murmured farewells. He looked back to the kitchen. Elizabeth gave him a wave and a smile that made his fingers tingle.

He hadn't gone ten feet past the cafe's front-yard fence when he stopped dead. There was a "Kevin for Mayor" sign outside Mike's Shop, just like the other one he'd seen. It hadn't been there when he came in. He turned back to the cafe, but who would he ask? He looked down the street. Upton and Travis's was the next house, on the opposite side, and they had a sign too. Maybe he should ask them. But they'd made it plain they were going to work.

He gave up and strolled back toward Town Hall. The original sign was still outside Wanda's house. At the big curve, he stopped again. Mary the stylist also had a sign identical to the others. Wanda had been busy this morning.

How could they want him to be Mayor? They didn't know him. And how could it be *legal* for him to be Mayor? He didn't even live here!

* * *

Adie's door was half-open, so Kevin paused and she called out for him to come in. She had her back to him, working on her laptop, but she closed the lid, turned, and smiled at him.

Her hair was done up exactly the same as before, in the tidy Dutch braid, but today she was wearing black jeans and a yellow blouse instead of the dress she'd worn yesterday. It made her look younger, somehow, but didn't change the fact that she was probably nearing eighty.

"Nice breakfast?" she said.

"Yes. They mentioned that you always bring your dogs to work, and I was surprised that I hadn't seen them before."

"They spend a lot of the day sleeping under my desk. None of them are young anymore."

"Can I meet them?"

"Of course. Bunny, Wombat—post."

He heard scrabbling from under her desk and two dogs popped around the corner, standing at attention with their eyes locked on his. One was a golden retriever, the other a terrier mix a third the size of the golden. So he doubted he was in any danger. He dropped to one knee and they relaxed a little.

"I'm guessing the terrier is Wombat." It looked as if it had just come out of a clothes dryer where it picked up static from a load of towels.

"Good guess. Guys, say hello."

The dogs approached him slowly and he held out his hands to be inspected. Wombat licked one hand tentatively and then retreated, but Bunny wanted to cuddle. He scratched behind her ears, the scruff of her neck, and under her chin. She wagged her tail.

"On your beds," Adie said, and they vanished back under the desk. He could hear Bunny throw herself down on something soft.

"How old are they?"

"These two are both eight. Owl—you must have seen Owl, right?" He nodded. "Owl is almost eleven."

"I guess the Health Inspectors don't come out here."

She laughed. "If they did, they'd have to give Elizabeth a ninety-nine percent rating. And the one percent would be for the dogs. But no, they don't."

"Do you mind if I sit?"

She waved at a chair. "Please."

"There are some weird signs out there this morning," Kevin said.

"I assume you mean Wanda's signs and not some celestial portent. Yes, I've seen them. How many are there now?"

"I saw four."

"You missed the one at the bar."

"Yeah, I didn't walk down that way." She didn't seem to want to say anything else about them. "I don't understand."

She looked at him severely for a moment. It felt like having an X-ray.

"Well, you've decided to stay, haven't you?" she said.

"How the hell did you know that? Are there microphones in the walls of the apartment?"

"Why, have you been talking to yourself?" He just looked at her. "If you make it to my age, Kevin, you'll find that some people are open books. There are plenty of people that I don't understand at all—but you are not one of them. You have an expressive face and no guile whatsoever, which is remarkable for someone who's been a journalist for so long. I don't need to listen to you talk to yourself; everything you're feeling is all over your face. And I'll bet Elizabeth has seen it all, too." He felt himself blushing. "Elizabeth told me that you are the one she's been waiting for."

"She said something like that when we met. I don't know what it means."

"Oh, come on," Adie protested. "You know what it means. You just don't know how it's possible."

"I met her *five minutes* before she said that."

"It would only have taken her two minutes."

"Is she..."

"No, she can't read your mind, and no, I told you, she's not a fairy. She's just very observant and extremely wise about people. And you have that face."

"But what if I'm not..."

"Not for you or me to say. That's up to her. Your job is to decide what *you* want."

"So why do those people want me to be Mayor?"

"Because we need a Mayor, and Elizabeth likes you." She chuckled. "In this town, that's way more than enough."

"Why does the town need a Mayor? You seem to run the place."

"I do run the place. That's my job. The Mayor's job is to be the face of the town. I've never wanted that. You know how in—oh, France for example—they have a prime minister who runs the country and a president who shakes the hands of visiting dignitaries? That's our town. The Manager keeps things running and the Mayor is the figurehead."

"Why would I want to be the figurehead?"

She laughed. "Because it's fun. I wouldn't wish *my* job on you, and I don't want to be Mayor myself. But if you're the Mayor you are one step closer to being, in the eyes of the townspeople, worthy of Elizabeth. Because they may like you, but they'll never see what she sees. What I see."

He thought about it for a moment. But he wasn't going to figure this out sitting here in this old woman's presence. She was too unsettling; almost as if she were a super-intelligent alien wearing a human body as a disguise.

"Let me think about it."

"Of course."

"In the meantime, I'd like to look at the library. Is anyone working there?"

"No, we don't have a librarian."

"At all? Who ordered the books? Who keeps things in order?" She didn't respond immediately. "Oh, of course."

She said, "When people are finished, they put the books back where they got them from. Melissa cleans the room occasionally. That's all we need. No one here is a book thief."

"Okay. Is there a checkout procedure?"

"Yes. Write down what you've taken on the clipboard on the circulation desk. When you return it, scratch it off."

"I saw a computer on the desk. You don't use that?"

"It's there in case we ever decide to use the online system we bought. I doubt we ever will. I'm thinking about repurposing it soon."

He decided not to ask. He'd probably get another "none of your business."

"Okay, thanks for your time."

"Come by anytime, Kevin. I mean it."

He nodded and left, putting the door back just the way he'd found it.

* * *

He found a history of Klickitat County and a couple of novels by female authors that he liked. As Adie had promised, there was a clipboard on the counter inside the library door with several sign-out sheets. He spent a moment looking at who else had checked out books. H. and M. Murphy had nearly a dozen; he didn't know them. P. Johnson had several; that must be Pete the trucker. T. Keyes. G., I., and C. Wyan; they must be Mary's kids. P. and A. Chadha; really, Indians in Marmot? S. Durgan; he'd met her in the cafe this morning, with her husband and the dogs. It looked like the library got pretty good use.

Following the convention that seemed to have the force of law, he wrote down the date, the titles, and K. Calenda for the three books he was taking.

He made himself a cheese sandwich for lunch and had a peach for dessert. By mid-afternoon he had given up on reading the Klickitat history in full (the style was stilted and dry) and was just skimming it, stopping now and then to read paragraphs that looked interesting, especially anecdotes about the old-timers. He'd been hoping to find something that would at least give a hint about this town, but though he thought it was the most interesting small place he'd ever visited, there was no mention of it anywhere in the text, and it wasn't listed in the index.

Someone knocked on the door. He looked up from the sofa where he'd spread out. He could see the silhouette of someone standing outside the frosted glass. It didn't look like Elizabeth; it looked like a guy.

He hoisted himself off the sofa and opened the door. A well-groomed, dark-haired man in his early thirties stood outside, dressed in blue Post Office uniform: dark blue pants and a lighter blue short-sleeved shirt. But he noticed that there were no official patches.

"Mister Calenda?"

"Call me Kevin."

"Hi. I'm Jeremy."

"Ah. The mailman."

"I have a letter for you. Aunt Adie said you were staying here for now."

For now? "Yes. Uh… I'm a little surprised. No one knows I'm here. Is it from someone local?"

Jeremy handed over the envelope. It was from his mother in Lake Oswego, and it was addressed to Kevin at his old Portland address. She must have sent it at the last minute, hoping he would get it before he left, but mistimed it. Kevin looked up at Jeremy. He realized that his mouth was open.

"What the hell?" he said.

"Pardon?"

"How did this get here? It was sent to my old address. They're supposed to forward my mail to Maine!"

Jeremy scratched his head. "Huh. Yep, that's a puzzler. I picked it up with the rest of the mail in Trout Lake. Barb saw me come in and told me I had a general delivery letter."

"Uh. Would you like to come in?"

"Sure, I can visit for a minute."

"Can I get you something to drink?"

"Oh, thanks, I'd love a Coke or something."

"Okay, I saw some in the fridge. Ice?"

"Yes, thanks."

"Have a seat, Jeremy."

Kevin tried to clear his head as he went through the mundane steps of getting a glass from the cabinet, filling it with ice from the dispenser, and grabbing a Coke from the refrigerator door. He handed the glass and can to Jeremy and sat back down on the sofa. Jeremy had flopped down into the armchair nearby.

"What was that about Trout Lake?" That was the little town where the Forest Service ranger station had been. *Little.* It was a metropolis compared to Marmot.

"I guess I should explain," Jeremy said, "since you're new. The Post Office won't deliver mail to Marmot."

"Why not?"

"Because we're unincorporated. As far as they're concerned, we don't exist."

"Okay, I got that."

"They wanted us to put our mailboxes out on Highway 141, but that's almost fifteen miles' driving from here and, as you can imagine, not very convenient."

"No, I wouldn't think so." Kevin was trying to be patient. Sooner or later they'd get to the letter.

"And not safe, either. So most folks here have boxes in Trout Lake. That's even farther away, of course, so my job is to pick up the mail from everyone's boxes at the Post Office in Trout Lake, and packages too if there are any. I also collect outgoing mail here and take it there for them to send it on."

"Okay, that's weird but I understand it. You have keys for everyone's PO boxes?"

"Exactly. All the people in Marmot give me permission to pick up their mail, which I do six days a week. Most people don't want their junk mail, so I recycle that, sort the rest, and hand-deliver it house to house. People seem to like the service."

"I can see why. It's like the 1960s without the funny hairdos."

"Sorry?"

"Never mind. So how did my letter end up in Trout Lake?"

"Sorry, I have no idea. Like I said, I was picking up the mail and Barb saw me and gave me your letter. I asked Aunt Adie where you were staying, and she sent me here."

Kevin thought about it and couldn't come up with any plausible way that this letter could have arrived here. He looked at it: perfectly normal, the addresses written out in his mom's shaky hand, a flag stamp, and no forwarding stickers. No pixie dust, no sign of any magic spell.

"I should be getting on," Jeremy said. He stood up. "I still have other deliveries to do. Thanks for the Coke"

"Thank you for taking the time to talk to me," Kevin said, standing too. "Hey, I also wanted to thank you for leading me here."

"What?"

"I was really lost on Monday and saw you drive past. I followed you, thinking I could ask for directions, and you led me here."

"Huh. People have strange ways of finding us, but I think that's a new one. Anyway, I'm glad you did. Welcome to Marmot." He held out his hand and Kevin shook it. "I'll be seeing you around."

"No doubt," Kevin said. He let him out and closed the door behind him.

Alone again, he held the letter up to the light. There was nothing unusual about it. He didn't have a black light or he might have tried that. He wondered if he should try rubbing the envelope with lemon juice to look for hidden writing.

Fairyland

A narrow path led from the cafe's entrance around the side of the house. It was made of pavers, expertly laid and very level. Although it wasn't dark yet, low-voltage lights spaced every six feet were already on. Both sides of the path were bordered with high evergreen shrubs of some kind, blocking his view of both the road and the side of the building.

In the back Kevin walked by a large raised vegetable garden, with an edging of herbs growing against the timbers that formed the sides. Flowers of over a dozen species grew in clumps here and there between the widely-spaced fir trees. The path ended in a stairway that hugged the side of the building and led up to a spacious, unscreened porch. Kevin ascended and knocked on the door.

Elizabeth answered the door wearing a deep blue knee-length halter dress and sandals. This was the first time he'd seen her in anything other than jeans and a blouse.

"Would you like to come in?" she said, and he realized that he'd been staring. Possibly for a while.

"Sorry. Thanks."

The entry was to the kitchen, which was smaller than he would have expected for such a good cook, but it was open to the large living room to his left, separated only by a half-wall. There was no telling how this floor of the small house had been laid out before, but now half of the space was the living room and kitchen, and the wall that cut the space in two had only a single, closed door—to the bedroom he supposed. The rooms he could see were simply furnished, with a small bistro table in the kitchen and a sectional sofa, coffee table, and bookshelves in the living room. Notably, there was no TV. The ceiling was vaulted; the bisecting wall rose all the way to the peak of the roof.

Simply furnished, but not simply decorated. Kevin realized that he was staring again.

Everywhere he looked he saw fairy lights: running across the tops of the kitchen cabinets, along the fireplace mantel in the living room, above the bookshelves. The living room also had lit sconces that looked as if they'd been fashioned from twisted, handmade paper, and a reading lamp beside one end of the sofa. The walls were a deep color, difficult to identify in the gentle light: perhaps dark purple, perhaps nutty brown. It could have been oppressive, but it wasn't.

Also visible everywhere were sparkles: crystals hanging in all the windows; shimmery silvery things draped along the tops of the curtain rods and twined in among the mantel lights; a complex, graceful mass of glass and curled metal on the coffee table that threw glints all over the ceiling. There were a few paintings on the walls; he recognized Wanda's work, but they weren't fairies and dragons, they were all animals in motion: horses in one, a mixed herd of zebras, giraffes, and wildebeest in another.

The balance of simplicity and lushness, brilliance and shadow, was unlike anything Kevin had ever seen before, not even in the decorating magazines he'd glanced at while waiting for appointments throughout his career.

"It's absolutely enchanting," he said.

She flashed that overwhelming smile that made his fingers tingle. "Thank you. Would you like a beer?"

"Just some water for now, thanks."

"Have a seat. I'm still working on dinner."

Elizabeth brought him a glass of ice water and he hitched himself up onto a seat at the oversized bistro table.

He'd never been able to watch her work in her cafe kitchen because of the wall that separated it from the seating area. It was like watching ballet: graceful, powerful, no wasted motion. He wasn't quite sure what she was making. She was rolling out balls of dough with quick, sure movements and filling them with something buttery yellow, then folding the dough up into miniature pies, with a twist at the top. The finished pies went on a waiting jellyroll pan.

When she finished she popped the pan in the oven and washed her hands, then turned to him. She'd been working with flour and dough but there wasn't a smudge on her dress. If he'd been doing that he'd have had flour from hair to shoes.

"We have some time. Let's go get comfortable." She picked up a glass of red wine and he followed her into the living room. "What kind of music do you like?"

"Oh, lots of different things. Nothing too jangly, and no blues. Anything else would be fine."

One of the bookshelves had a miniature stereo on one shelf; she put in a CD and it started playing soft jazz. She sat on the short end of the L-shaped sofa and gestured for him to sit beside her. It seemed impertinent to sit too close, so he settled in the curve a few feet away.

"Where did you learn to decorate?" Kevin asked.

"Nowhere. I just experimented with styles until I found one I liked. What did your Portland home look like?"

"Ugh. I hate to admit it: single guy contemporary. I like comfortable furniture but I don't have any talent at decorating. It was Spartan compared to this."

"Did you live in a house or an apartment?"

"I had a house. It was small and pretty old, but the couple I bought it from spent a lot of time renovating it. So it had modern plumbing and wiring, and they opened up some of the smaller rooms."

She sipped her wine. "How long did you live there?"

"Seven years. That's the longest I've ever lived in one place. How long have you lived here?"

"All my life."

That startled him. He looked around. He couldn't figure out how a couple and a young girl could have lived in this house together. He must have had a silly expression on his face, because she laughed.

"This was my mother's house," Elizabeth said. "She inherited it from *her* mother. I was only twenty when my parents died, and there was some insurance money, so I used it to spruce up the cafe and redo the living space. I completely gutted the upstairs here, which used to have two bedrooms and a poky bathroom. And the kitchen was very old-fashioned."

"So your parents ran the cafe before you?"

"Just my mother. Dad grew up in Bingen, and that's where he worked."

Kevin tried to imagine this open space broken up into smaller rooms. Just like his house in Portland, this one had benefitted from being converted to fewer and larger spaces.

"You learned to cook from your mom, then?"

"Yes, I used to help her in the cafe when I got old enough. She started me out baking and then we moved on to more advanced things."

"That's how I learned to cook, too. My mom taught me to make cookies."

"What kind?"

"Chocolate chip. Ginger snaps. Peanut butter. Oatmeal raisin. Um... That's all I can remember, but I know there were more."

She nodded and set her wine down. "Excuse me for a moment."

He heard her open the oven, and shortly afterward a really amazing smell reached him, savory and buttery. She came back and resumed her corner of the couch.

"Another fifteen minutes," she said. She watched him over the rim of her wine glass as she took another sip. "Tell me more about your family."

"We were very close when I was growing up. My sister and I used to play together all the time. I guess that might be a little unusual, for young boys and girls to get along so well, but we did. I thought she was the cutest thing on Earth, and she looked up to me like a hero."

"What's her name?"

"Jo. Short for Josephine."

"Are you still close?"

"We're still friendly, but after I went to college and she got married and had her kids, we lost touch a little. I went over to their house pretty often, but it was never the same."

"It must have been nice to have a sibling. I envy you."

He wasn't sure what to say to that. "What about your mom?"

"She's gotten a little crotchety the last few years, but we're still on good terms."

"Crotchety?"

Kevin shrugged. "She's in perfect health but she's convinced herself that she's going to die soon. It's a little irritating; I don't like talking about funerals with a woman who can still lift a giant bag of dog food with one hand. And lately she's been nearly demanding that people do things for her that she's perfectly capable of doing herself, as if she were infirm."

"How old is she?"

"Sixty-six."

"And what's her name?"

"Annabella."

"That's pretty." She glanced back at the kitchen as if she'd heard something, but he hadn't. "I feel like I'm interrogating you, so it's your turn. Ask anything you want."

He hesitated. "Do you mind if I ask about your parents?"

Elizabeth looked down at her wine glass, then looked up at him. "You want to know why I never tried to find out how they died."

"Yes."

"It's simple, really. I've imagined a hundred scenarios, some of them utterly ridiculous."

"Like what?"

"There's a whole class of them that deal with aliens. Outer space aliens."

"Like they're not really dead, just beamed up to the mother ship?"

"That's one of the milder ones." She rubbed the rim of her glass, making a soft, clear tone. "Imagining is one thing. If I *knew*, then I'd visualize it; I'd see it in my head. And no matter what it was, I don't want to think of them that way."

"Okay. I have to admit, that's not the way I felt about my dad's death, but I understand it." She nodded in acknowledgement or thanks, he wasn't sure which. "Tell me what you remember about them."

"My mom was always laughing. She found comedy in everything, especially anything having to do with people. Sometimes I'd ask her to explain what she was thinking, and when she did I would burst out laughing too."

"Can you give me an example?"

"Hmm." She thought for a second. "Pants."

"Pants?"

96

"You know that expression, 'He has to put his pants on one leg at a time, just like everyone else'?"

"Yeah, I've heard it," he said dryly. As a journalist reporting on politics, he'd heard every cliché known to man at least a hundred times.

"What about Olympic gymnasts? Couldn't they grab their pants, leap into the air, and pull them on—both legs at the same time—before they landed?"

Kevin laughed out loud. The image was just too ridiculous.

"Right," Elizabeth said. "That was my reaction when I first heard that, too."

"I wish I could have met her," he said, and immediately wondered if that was presumptuous.

But she didn't seem offended. "I wish she could have met you, too. Excuse me, I have to do a few last things before we eat."

He followed her into the kitchen and offered to help. She took a thin wooden salad bowl out of the refrigerator and tossed the greens already sorted in it with dressing from a small white ceramic bowl, then handed him the salad and asked him to serve it onto the small plates on the table. While he was doing that she filled another glass with water and handed him that too. He turned down a beer once more. Then she opened the oven and the rich aroma he had smelled before filled the kitchen. She took out the pan and set it on the stovetop.

The little pies she'd made had opened up like flowers, revealing a browned, slightly crusty filling. She asked him to bring over the larger plates from the table, and put two of the little pies on one plate and one on the other.

"Let's eat," she said.

Of course it was delicious. Kevin was beginning to suspect that Elizabeth couldn't burn toast if she wanted to.

The conversation during dinner stayed light. Kevin said that he recognized Wanda's paintings on the walls, and they talked about Wanda's work. He mentioned that he'd bought a wonderful painting from her yesterday that he knew from the miserable book whose cover it had been. Elizabeth joked about her mother's delightfully terrible taste in art and jewelry.

When they were finished he asked if he could use the restroom, and she told him it was through the bedroom. He opened the door, stepped inside, and stopped dead in his tracks.

The bedroom was like the living room on performance-enhancing drugs. There was a four-poster bed with a short canopy, and the sheer fabric was somehow threaded with more fairy lights. In one corner stood a comfortable reading chair with an ottoman and an unlit floor lamp. The nightstand lamp was lit though, shining through a golden lampshade fringed with small hanging crystals. The bed was covered in a quilt of deep blues and gold.

The left and right walls as he entered both had doorways, but the one on the right was open and clearly the bathroom. The other must be a closet. He went in and turned on the light. This was definitely a woman's bathroom: orchids on the counter, unlit candles around the soaking tub, sheer curtains over the big window behind the tub, three bottles of shampoo or conditioner in the glass-enclosed shower, and plush towels.

When he came back out Elizabeth was sitting on the sofa with her legs tucked up under her. He sat down close to her, but not too close.

"What are you going to do about your job in Maine?" she said when he was settled.

Of *course* she knew that he had decided to stay. She probably knew everything he'd discussed with Adie too.

"I'm not worried about that," he said. "They'll find someone else if they want to."

"But you needed the job, right? You don't look like a millionaire. Do you have any idea what you'll do here?"

"I think Adie has something in mind."

Elizabeth laughed. "Adie *always* has something in mind. She's my best friend, but I can say without malice that there's no bottom to her plans."

"How did you two become friends?"

"She was my mother's best friend before me, even though Adie's old enough to be my grandmother. I'm not sure how they connected. But she and her sister Ida were always around when I was growing up. I'd find them in the cafe or our kitchen when I came home from school. I never knew any of my grandparents, but Adie was like a second mom. Until my parents died, and then she became more than just a neighbor; more than just a relative. She held me when I needed a cry, helped me get started with the cafe, gave me advice during the remodeling."

"I've never had a friend like that. Maybe my sister, when we were young. But not since."

Elizabeth rested her chin in one hand with the elbow propped up on the arm of the sofa. "I don't know what I would have done without her. I don't know what the *town* would have done."

"What do you mean?"

"When I was growing up the town was in the process of dying again. People were having a hard time staying afloat, and some were talking about moving out. Adie fixed that."

"How?" The answer to that one question alone would be worth an article, maybe a series. There were thousands of struggling towns across America, mostly much larger than Marmot, that could use some advice.

Elizabeth smiled impishly. "You need to ask Adie that."

He settled back against the sofa. "I've noticed that Adie is the answer to an awful lot of questions here."

She laughed. "Don't go paranoid on me, Kevin. There's no cabal. There's just a really smart, very talented lady who has lived here nearly all her life, and been the Town Manager for more than half of it."

"Okay. I'll trust you. I guess that means I have to trust her, too."

"Yes, you do. To both." She glanced at a wall clock near the bookshelves.

"I guess I need to be moving on," Kevin said. "You have an early morning again." He stood up.

"Thanks for not making me toss you out the door."

"I don't doubt that you could. Thanks very much for the delicious dinner. And it was wonderful spending another evening with you."

"You're welcome. I enjoyed the company."

She followed him to the kitchen door. As he turned around to say something—he hardly knew what it would be—she kissed him lightly on the mouth. They stood close together, looking into each other's eyes but not touching.

"You are the most astonishing woman I've ever met," he whispered.

She smiled, the wattage turned up so high that he felt it in his toes. She opened the door and he walked out. Later he couldn't remember going down the stairs, around the building, out to the street, and up the hill to his apartment in Town Hall. For all he knew, he floated all the way back.

Open Secrets

Thursday, August 19

Kevin rushed through his shower the next morning. He glanced in Adie's office on his way out of the Town Hall but didn't see any sign of her or the dogs. It was another hot, sunny day, and he was beginning to think that Adie was using some kind of weather control. He'd seen a few cumulus clouds since he arrived, but otherwise the sky had been the deep uniform blue that you only found in high country. Little Fish Lake was at 3,600 feet, and it was over a hundred feet gain between the lake and Town Hall.

Past the big curve in the road, just past Mary's salon, two more houses had "Kevin for Mayor" signs. He didn't even pause, just shook his head. Wanda needed to get back to her dragon painting. But when he got to the cafe, he did stop: there was a sign there too. And the next house down Marmot Lane had one as well.

He stopped again just inside the door in surprise. The regulars were all present, as well as Jack and Sharon and their dogs, who he'd met yesterday, Mike the Internet shop guy, Pete the truck driver from the bar, Darren the handyman, Wanda, and Mary. His usual seat at the bar was the only unoccupied spot in the cafe. He counted quickly: fourteen customers beside him, plus four dogs. Elizabeth was having a busy day.

"Good morning, Kevin," a bunch of them chorused together, like kindergarten kids greeting their principal.

"Good morning, everyone. Thanks for saving me a seat."

Darren was sitting next to Kevin's spot at the bar. "I'm going to install a plaque on it with your name later today," he said.

"You're kidding!"

"Yes, I am."

Elizabeth appeared suddenly in front of him with the coffee pot. She had a serious expression on her face but a gleam in her eye. Kevin could feel a gigantic grin breaking out on his face; he couldn't help it.

"Breakfast, sir?" Elizabeth said.

"Yes, ma'am. Please."

"Coming right up. Who else needs coffee?"

A few people waved their hands and Elizabeth refilled their cups. Kevin turned on his stool to face the room.

"I'm new here," he said, "but I've never seen the cafe this crowded before, so I'm guessing that you folks might have something you want to ask me."

They all looked at each other. No one said anything until Ernie piped up with, "Yeah —when are you leaving?" Jodie smacked him hard on the arm and he shrank down in his chair, sulking.

"I guess we'll just save it for tonight," Upton said.

"Tonight? What's happening tonight?"

"Ask Adie."

Of course.

"Kevin," Wanda said, "would you like me to bring you your painting later on?"

It looked like *everyone* knew he was staying. "Um. I guess I'll stop by on my way back after breakfast."

"That works too. Well, folks, I have to get back to work. Later."

As she opened the screen door Ernie grumbled something, but Kevin couldn't hear what it was. Jodie lifted her hand to smack him again, but the threat was enough; he shut up.

Darren nudged Kevin, who turned to find his breakfast waiting for him: two fried eggs, a bowl of fruit, and the biggest cinnamon roll he'd ever seen. It had white icing on top in a tidy crosshatch pattern, but unlike most cinnamon rolls he'd ever had, the icing wasn't overdone.

He looked up at Elizabeth, who was clearly suppressing a grin. "You must think I'm too skinny," he said.

"No one's making you eat it all. Save some for lunch if it makes you feel virtuous."

But he didn't. And the weird thing was, when he was done he didn't feel stuffed, just pleasantly full. While he was eating, the locals had drifted out in ones and twos, until only Jodie and Ernie were left, nursing their coffees at the window table. Jodie smiled at him but Ernie wouldn't look up from the table.

Elizabeth picked up his plate. "Want to come back?"

"Back there?"

"Sure."

"Bring your coffee."

As he walked behind the bar and through the door into the kitchen, he could clearly hear Ernie say, "What the hell?" and Jodie hissed at him.

The kitchen was spotless. There was a commercial stove and oven combination below the pass-through so she could look out while cooking, two large refrigerators, a commercial dishwasher next to a double-wide stainless-steel sink that was continuous with a long stainless counter top, a butcher block island in the center of the room, metal wire shelves with cans and boxes of food and supplies. There were two closed doors: one in the side wall that he'd bet was a washroom, and one in the back wall that probably led to a storage or mud room and then outside. Near the back door was a small, round dining table covered with a floral-print tablecloth, with two ladder-backed wooden chairs.

"Have a seat," Elizabeth said. "Let me get you some more coffee."

Kevin took the chair nearest the door. Elizabeth filled his cup, and sat in the other chair, then pushed the cream and sugar towards him.

"What was Ernie going on about?" he said.

"No one comes back here except for bathroom emergencies," she said. "My mother had a strict rule, and I've maintained it, and everyone knows it."

"Wow. I feel honored."

She smiled. He sipped his coffee, but he couldn't take his eyes off her. Her elfin face seemed always just on the verge of breaking into a smile—if it wasn't already smiling. It was contagious.

"I guess there's something going on tonight?" he said.

"Stop by and see Adie after breakfast," she said.

"Adie is the answer to all questions," he joked.

"Not *all* questions." She looked at him with a very serious expression that somehow made him burst out laughing. Then she trotted out one of her magical smiles. Kevin knew right then that he was *never* leaving this place.

They heard the door close behind Jodie and Ernie.

"Can I help you clean up?" he said. But when he looked around there didn't seem to be much to do.

"I like to do it myself, but thanks for asking. What's on your list today?"

"Pick up my painting from Wanda. Gaze into Adie's crystal ball. Then I thought I'd have another walk around town. I'm starting to build up a mental map, but there are still gaps."

"Map gaps?"

"Yep."

She chuckled. "You'd better get to it, then. Will you be back for lunch?"

"Probably not. I don't know how long Adie will keep me, so I'll just grab something from the apartment."

"Okay. See you tonight then."

"Really?" He'd been hoping she would say that.

"You should plan on having an early dinner at the bar. I'll see you after."

"Great! Uh… where? When?"

"You'll know after you talk to Adie."

He should have known she would say that.

* * *

When Kevin stopped at Wanda's house, she looked busy (probably making more signs) and he had things to do too, so he didn't come inside. She handed him the painting, wrapped in heavy brown paper, and smiled knowingly, thanking him again.

Just for fun, when he got back to the Town Hall he opened the door as quietly as he could, then walked, as far as he could tell, utterly silently to the door of Adie's office, where he paused. After almost a minute, he heard her sigh.

"Are you coming in or not?" Adie said.

He shoved open the door. "You can't expect me to believe that you heard me. I was totally quiet!"

She'd been working with her back to the door again, but now turned to face him. "It was a good try." She pointed at the paper-wrapped painting. "But I could hear that paper rustling slightly as you breathed. Also." She grabbed her laptop from the return and turned it to face him. He looked at the screen: a spreadsheet was peeking out from behind a word processing window, but there was also a small window at the top right with a black and white video feed from the hallway outside. She laughed at his expression. "You told me yourself there was magic in this town. There are all different kinds of magic."

He sat down heavily in one of the guest chairs and had to laugh. "Okay, you got me."

"Now you think maybe the stuff I told you the other day about hearing you come in was a tall tale. Not true. I did hear you, but I *also* saw you on the security cameras."

"How many cameras do you have?"

"Eighteen. There are none in the Mayor's apartment, if that was your next question. We're not voyeurs. Mostly in the hallways and public spaces like the courtroom and library. A few around the outside of the building."

Kevin shook his head. "Why would you need security cameras in a town like this?"

"It was necessary to make it convincing." She held up a hand and he clamped his mouth shut. "Everything will make sense eventually. We'll go through it all later. Go ahead and ask me what you came to ask me."

He bit back his frustration—again. It took a moment to calm himself enough so that his voice wouldn't shake. "Apparently you have me scheduled for something tonight."

"There's a town meeting at 8:00. You're the guest of honor."

"Were you going to tell me about it?"

"Yes, as soon as you finished breakfast and came back to harangue me."

"I'm not..." He took a deep breath. "Sorry."

She chuckled and put the laptop back on the other desk. "Kevin, I know this is confusing. I can see that it might look like entrapment, or something even worse."

"Like a con."

"Yes. I don't expect you to trust me, but can you trust Elizabeth?"

"How do I know she's not part of..." He ran down. The idea was ludicrous, and he could see Adie watching him realize it. He had spent almost twenty years working the political beat in Oregon's major cities. He'd seen plenty of honest politicians and some that were seriously bent. He didn't deny that it was possible to fool him, but he didn't think Elizabeth was capable of that. He'd never known a woman who was so simultaneously open, honest, and mysterious. If she was involved in some con, it was time for him to retire to a monastery in Romania.

"You're right," he said, "it is confusing. Three days ago I thought I knew where I was going. Now I'm not even sure where I am."

"Life is like that sometimes."

"Not my life."

"Until now, you mean."

"Right." He took another deep breath. "Can I assume that this meeting tonight has something to do with me being elected Mayor?"

"That's correct."

"Can you tell me what the job entails?"

"Speeches, mostly. We have a movie night in the community room once a month. Free popcorn, you'll like it. The Mayor usually gives a short speech beforehand. Fourth of July, Christmas parade—"

"You have a Christmas parade?"

"A very small one." She settled back in her chair. "As I mentioned before, my job, the Town Manager's job, is to keep this place from going back to the ghost town it was in the 1950s. The Mayor's job is to help with that task by making these people feel like they're part of a community."

"Actually," Kevin said, "I would have guessed that was Elizabeth's job."

"Good point. Jodie and Jeremy do their part too. But the Mayor plays a vital role. Purely symbolic, but vital. Everyone that provides services to their neighbors, that keeps people from needing to go to Trout Lake, BZ Corner, Bingen, White Salmon, Hood River, or God forbid Portland—all of these things bind the community together and keep people living here."

"I like the town, but why is that so important?"

"It's not important to the world. Just to us. You've had three days of this little miracle. Don't you think it's worth preserving?"

He didn't even have to think about it. "Yes, I do."

"Good. I'm very happy to hear it. Will you come to the meeting?"

He was starting to understand her a little. "You mean, will I accept the nomination to be Mayor of Marmot?"

"That's exactly what I mean."

"Yes, Adie, I will."

* * *

After stashing the painting in his apartment—it was already starting to feel like his apartment—Kevin headed back outside. It was a tiny place, but he wanted to get to know it better. Especially if he was going to be Mayor; the very idea made his head swim.

If his phone had a cellular connection he would have used the map app to look at a satellite image of the town. But then he remembered the room full of computer equipment in the basement of Town Hall. He went back to his apartment and found his phone on the dresser; he hadn't used it since he arrived since there was no signal. There were no bars on the cell, but the WiFi for the "MarmotTH" network was at max. He typed "Little Fish Lake WA" into Google Maps and in a moment, to his utter astonishment, without needing to enter a WiFi password, it showed him the area around the town. But there were no streets on the street map other than National Forest Road 8871. When he switched to the satellite view, he could clearly see the Town Hall and the streets of the village, and make out a few of the other buildings including the cafe. Google's hordes of drivers hadn't found this town, which after a moment's reflection he realized was inevitable.

The land on which the town was built sloped up relentlessly toward Town Hall, behind which Steamboat Mountain loomed, looking like an enormous humpback whale just rising above the waves of green forest. The grade from Little Fish Lake to Town Hall was gentle enough for walking, but just past the Hall was an escarpment that would be a technical climb if Kevin were into that sort of thing.

The satellite image on his phone showed the many twists and turns that the little streets took to follow the grade. Coupled with the abundant trees growing between the houses, this meant that the pedestrian's view was never a far one, and little surprises— like Wanda's bird-capped newel posts or the marmot statue—appeared around every bend.

Paying more attention to the houses this time, Kevin suddenly realized that the two directly across from Town Hall were clearly empty. He wasn't sure at first how he knew this, because the tiny yards were mowed and the houses were in good repair, unlike the many collapsed buildings scattered around. He stood with his back to the statue for a moment and worked it out. Unlike all the other houses that he happened to know were occupied, the curtains were drawn, the front porches had no plants or chairs, and the yards were completely empty of ornaments, toys, or tools.

Kevin took the path that led from the Town Hall to the cemetery. He didn't enter it this time, instead walking across Cemetery Lane to the church ruins. He walked in through the narrower, fallen wall and looked around. Although there were big blocks of stone lying between the saplings and shrubs that grew out of chinks in the stone floor, there was no evidence of roof debris; someone must have cleared it away. He walked closer to one of the walls and could clearly see signs that there had been a fire here: soot marks were still visible on the walls sixty years after the lightning strike. Or overturned candles, whichever it had been.

He walked through weeds and trees toward the schoolhouse. It was a small, single-story brick building with a red metal roof. It might have been built as a house originally, but it was hard to tell. When he got to the school he walked right up to it and peered in the windows. Most of the space inside was a single room, with three thick, square columns holding up the roof. On the far side from where he stood were two separate rooms whose doors were open, one clearly a restroom and the other, he surmised, the teacher's office.

"Hello," a woman said from behind him. He straightened up and turned. A short, pretty black woman in her early thirties was looking up at him, one hand shading her eyes from the sun. "You're Kevin, I suppose."

"Yes. Kevin Calenda."

She lowered her hand to shake his. "I'm Helen, the schoolteacher. I saw you looking around and thought I'd introduce myself since we haven't met yet."

"Nice to meet you," Kevin said. "I guess you live nearby?"

She turned and pointed at the nearest mobile home, the single-wide. "Right there. You weren't planning to break in to my school, were you?"

"Ah… no." Then he realized she was kidding. "Sorry. I'm just trying to learn my way around town."

"That should take about five minutes. Do you want to see inside?"

"No, thanks. I was just curious what the layout was. I saw your playground the other day. I love the rocket ship."

"That's our claim to fame, I think," Helen said. "The one and only Montessori school in the world with a rocket ship in the yard."

"How many students do you have?"

"I'll have five this fall. It was six last year, but one is shifting to the high school in Trout Lake."

"You do all grades, then?"

"The kids range from six to thirteen. I could go older, but by the time they reach their teens they're usually ready to get involved with other kids their own age."

He looked into the building again and then back at her. "If you don't mind me asking, how did you end up in Marmot?"

"The same way you did. I followed Jeremy."

"Ah, nuts. They told me I was unique."

She laughed gently. "Well, it wasn't *exactly* the same. I was in Trout Lake interviewing for a teaching job, and I stopped in at the Post Office. Jeremy was there collecting the

112

mail and he introduced himself. We got to talking and he mentioned that his little town had an opening for a teacher. I was skeptical, but Mechelle loved it the moment she saw it, so we moved here."

"Mechelle—is that your daughter?"

"Yes, she's nine."

"You know," Kevin said, "I've heard that there are kids in this town, but other than Jodie's son I haven't seen one yet."

She smiled. "They're like a pack of wolves. Run around in the woods all day long and only settle down at night. If you hang around outside at dusk you'll probably see them popping out of the trees one by one, trudging on home for dinner."

"That sounds spooky."

"It is. Wraiths of the forest, or something like that." She shaded her eyes again and looked up at him. "Well, Kevin, it was nice to meet you. Don't get lost wandering around town, now."

"I'll try not to. Thanks for the chat."

She nodded and walked back toward her trailer. Kevin watched her go for moment, and then realized that he could just make out campaign signs outside the other two mobile homes.

* * *

From the school Kevin walked down Marmot Lane, past the cafe, and turned left toward the lake. He passed the welcome sign— "Welcome to Marmot, Population 32"— and decided to walk all the way around the lake. If he stayed far enough away from the water the walk was dry and not too

113

shrubby. It was less than half a mile; it took him about fifteen minutes.

He sank back down in the same spot where he'd sat three days ago, but this time he didn't make any notes. He just stared out at the water and the reeds, listening to a few frogs beeping like cell phones and the birds chirping in the trees, and thinking.

Town Meeting

Jodie's bar menu included a few vegetarian options, but none of them looked as appealing as the veggie burger he'd had last time, so he ordered it again. Jodie recommended a different beer, brewed in the Northwest but in a bottle instead of draught, and he liked it fine.

Upton and Travis invited him to sit at their table; actually, Upton did, but Travis nodded congenially when he sat down. Pete, Ernie, and Darren were at the bar again, like last time, but Mike wasn't.

"How did you find the town today?" Upton said when Kevin was settled.

He was confused for a moment, thinking that Upton meant "how did you locate the town," but then he realized he was referring to his second walking tour.

"It was fine. I discovered that the WiFi signal is good enough to show the satellite image on Google Maps. But there are no roads shown in the map."

"Ah," Upton said. "That was rather intentional, I think."

"Google didn't want you on its map?"

"Adie didn't want us on Google's map."

That took him aback. "How did she manage that?"

"She got Jeremy hired as the local street view driver. Thirteen dollars an hour for two months, and he conveniently forgot to turn off onto Jack Road."

"It's forgivable," Travis said. "It looks like a driveway."

Pete boomed out, "It *drives* like a god damned driveway!"

"Intentional," Upton said. "You want more hikers in here at night?"

"No," Pete said. "One new guy a year is plenty."

"He means you," Travis said to Kevin.

"Yeah, I got that."

Matthew brought him his burger and Parmesan fries; he'd skipped the garlic since he was supposed to be talking to the town tonight.

"So you met the schoolteacher," Upton said. It wasn't a question.

"How the hell did you know that?" Kevin said. "Does Adie have security cameras on every Doug fir?"

Upton and Travis laughed, and Kevin caught Darren chuckling too.

"If she does," Upton said, "she doesn't tell us about it, and the webcam URL is secret. No, you could figure it out yourself with one little byte of data that you're missing."

"Which is what?"

"Helen and Jeremy are a couple."

It took him a moment. Then he got it. "Helen told Jeremy. Jeremy told you when he delivered your mail this afternoon."

"Hole in one!" Pete shouted.

Kevin thought that maybe Pete had had one too many beers. Upton glanced at his watch. It was an Omega, Kevin noticed.

"Better eat up, Kevin," he said, "you're on in twenty minutes."

* * *

The whole gang from the bar, including Jodie and Matthew, walked him to the Town Hall.

"Want some Dentyne?" Pete asked him quietly. Maybe he wasn't drunk after all.

"Yes, thanks." He chewed quickly, because he didn't want to be chomping like a cow when he was standing in front of the whole town.

There was still plenty of light to see by when they arrived at the steps up to the portico. Kevin wrapped his gum in the paper it had come in and put it in his pocket.

It was just a few steps in to the community room, whose doors were already open. Upton held out his arm to invite Kevin to go in first, but he only made it two steps before he stopped.

It did look like the whole town. And everyone had brought their kids.

Adie was sitting on a chair on the stage at the far end of the room. She caught his eye and motioned him up, and he walked what seemed like a mile between the two rows of nice chairs up to the stage. No one was talking as they watched him go by. He didn't bother going up the shallow steps on either side, but stepped up directly onto the stage from the aisle.

"Welcome," Adie said quietly. "Have a seat and don't be nervous. The fire-breathing dragons were kicked out of town long ago."

People started to settle into chairs, beginning in the second row, leaving the front row empty. Then most of the crowd from the bar filled that in, leaving one spot free on the aisle. Now that they weren't milling around, Kevin was able to count them. Thirty-one, including Adie: twenty-two adults and nine children of various ages, but he didn't see Elizabeth. That meant that everyone in town except her had come out for the meeting. Or grilling, or interrogation, or interview, or whatever this was.

"She'll be here in a moment," Adie whispered to him, and she was right. Elizabeth strolled into the room calmly,

117

walked up the aisle, and took the center seat in the first row, right in front of him. She raised one eyebrow at him, and then smiled at his expression.

Other than the people he had already met, he saw a teenaged girl sitting with Mike the Internet shop guy, an Indian couple in their twenties with two young kids, a tough-looking guy sitting with Melissa the house cleaner and a pre-teen girl, a chubby-faced man sitting beside Mary the hairdresser and the three children whose pictures he'd seen in her salon, a young girl sitting with Helen the schoolteacher and Jeremy, a sunny-faced old woman sitting next to Ernie the grouch, and no dogs. That was strange. He thought these people took their dogs everywhere.

And he also saw Darren the handyman sitting beside his ex-wife Wanda the artist, with their heads together, whispering. What was that about?

Adie stood up and smiled. "Good evening," she said. "Thank you all for coming out tonight. We have a different kind of entertainment planned for this evening; no popcorn, but I think you'll find it enjoyable anyway. As you all know, there's been a grass-roots movement to elect our new friend Kevin Calenda as Mayor. He has agreed to stand up here and let you throw tomatoes at him."

What? Kevin thought in panic, then he realized she must be joking.

"So Kevin, would you tell us a little about yourself?" She sat down.

Kevin considered standing, as she had, but he decided it would be better if no one saw how he was shaking. He was used to confrontational interviews, but not to speaking in public.

"Hello, everyone," he said, and was relieved that his voice was steady. "I've only been here a few days, but I can already tell you that I think this place is very special. I've done a bit of traveling, in the Northwest a lot and around the world a little, and I've never found anywhere quite like this. Um." He cleared his throat and Adie handed him a bottle of water. After he took a sip, he went on. "Thanks. I grew up just outside Portland, went to the University of Oregon, and since I graduated I've worked as a newspaper reporter for several different papers in Portland. My dad died in Viet Nam, but my mom and little sister still live in Lake Oswego." He glanced at Adie and she nodded. "So if you have any questions, I'll try to answer them."

"I have one," Mike's daughter said.

"Dear," Adie said, "could you stand up so everyone can see you?"

"Sure." She stood up with more nerve than Kevin had. "How can we trust you?" Kevin laughed nervously. *Tough crowd,* he thought. "I mean, if you're a politician, you're basically a professional liar, right?"

Her father tugged on her arm and whispered something, but she stood her ground.

"Can I ask your name?" Kevin said.

"Viola."

"Ah, like Twelfth Night. Viola, I'm not a politician. Usually I'm the one lobbing hard questions *at* the politicians, and you're right, a lot of them are professional liars. Not all of them, though. As for how you can trust me, I can't answer that. I'm a pretty straightforward guy, but you'll just have to get to know me."

Adie spoke up. "I did a background check on Kevin."

"What?" he said, along with a handful of other people in the room.

"It was a reasonable thing to do," she said, staring him down.

"Of course. Sorry."

"He's easy to find on Google. All of his articles are available on the Internet, and he has social media pages too. His investigative stories are pretty darned good, and his lifestyle columns are rather funny, I thought. There's an index on the town website on the Mayor page, password *mayorkevin*. Look at it for yourself. Nothing he's told us so far has been less than the utter truth. Except that he forgot to mention that he was planning to write an article about us at first, but I think perhaps he's given up on that idea. Am I right?"

Kevin just nodded. He was past wondering how she'd figured that out.

"Anything else, Viola?" Adie said. The girl shook her head and sat down, and Mike immediately started whispering to her again.

Matthew, Jodie's son, stood up. "How old are you?"

"Forty-one," Kevin said.

"And Elizabeth likes you, right?"

He sputtered, unsure how to answer. Elizabeth turned and looked at Matthew. Kevin couldn't see her expression, but Matthew nodded.

"Good enough for me," the boy said, and he sat down.

Ernie stood up. "I've got one, dopey. What's your position on unincorporation?"

Kevin thought for a moment. "I'm not sure I understand the issue, Ernie. Could you explain it to me?"

"What?" the old man said. "What kind of god damned politician are you, admitting that you don't know something?" His wife smacked his arm with the back of her hand, but he ignored her.

"I'm not a politician. I thought I said that, but I'm pretty nervous, so maybe I didn't."

"Well, maybe you're not such a goober. I'll tell you. In 1954—"

"1953," Upton said.

"Shut up," Ernie retorted, "it was 1954."

"Ernie," Adie said, "it was 1953. It was my family, I should know."

"Okay, okay," he groused, "1950-whatever. The town of Kill Marmot had just two living residents, Adie's mother and her sister Ida. The state of Washington decided to unincorporate the town and they didn't bother asking the residents or any of us expats. They just up and did it. I guess they thought it was completely depopulated. A few years later Adie started convincing people to move back, and we discovered that as far as the state and the county were concerned, we didn't exist anymore. So we decided to ignore their stupid law and carry on anyway."

"Okay, I understand so far. So what's the issue? Do you want them to repeal the act?"

"Damned right I do. So this time we can *vote* on it and unincorporate *ourselves*!"

He coughed to hide a burst of laughter and took another sip of water. "You want them to reinstate the town so you can unincorporate the right way?"

"That's right."

Kevin looked around the room. He decided not to try to find a consensus. "I think people have the right to vote on issues that affect them. That's the basis of our republic."

"God damned goober's got my vote," Ernie said, and he sat down.

It got easier after that.

* * *

121

People were standing and stretching, talking in small groups. Elizabeth jumped gracefully up onto the stage, which seemed to grab everyone's attention. Kevin had been talking to Adie, but he turned just in time for Elizabeth to put one arm around him and kiss him firmly on the mouth.

"Good job," she said. "See you for breakfast."

She hopped down off the stage and walked out of the room. Kevin didn't take his eyes off her until she had vanished, and only then noticed that everyone else had been tracking her just as intently.

"Welcome to the family," Adie said.

* * *

Back in the Mayor's apartment, which looked like it might actually become his, Kevin dug out his laptop from his luggage. He hadn't used it since his arrival. It wasn't hard to find the town's website, which appeared to have been professionally designed. But every page other than the uninformative home page and "Contact Us" required a password to access. He clicked on the *mayor* link and typed in the ridiculous password that Adie had assigned.

There were links to everything, including the entire archive of all his articles for the Portland Rocket, the last paper he'd worked for. Also stories from his previous two jobs, at the Oregonian and Willamette Week, but he couldn't be sure that all of them were there; it had been too long. He was astonished to see that many of the articles he'd written for the UO newspaper, the Emerald, were also listed. And of course there was a link to his Facebook page.

Adie had found stuff that he didn't even know was online. Kevin closed the laptop and sat in the half-dark of the apartment. He could still feel Elizabeth's lips on his.

The New Mayor

Tuesday, August 24

Adie's efficiency put the British election system to shame. Apparently there was a private email exchange within the town, which was one of the ways that information had been passing so efficiently behind Kevin's back. She gave him an account the morning after the town meeting—kevin@kmarmot.org—and the first time he logged on there was a message already in his inbox, from Adie and apparently blind copied to everyone else, informing him that the voting office would be open for the mayoral election between 7:00 am and 7:00 pm the next Tuesday.

Adie informed him privately that he was not yet eligible to vote—not that it would make any difference to the outcome. There was a residence requirement of thirty days, which she said was intended solely to give them time to boot out undesirables before they could have an effect.

In the intervening four days he saw Elizabeth every morning for breakfast, most days for lunch, and every evening for dinner. Sunday was Elizabeth's day off, so they went walking on some easy hiking trails leading out of town away from Steamboat Mountain. They passed half a dozen lakes even smaller than Little Fish Lake. Kevin amused them both by coming up with ever-smaller names for them: Tiny Fish Lake, Minuscule, Wee, Itsy-Bitsy, Eensy-Weensy, and Nano.

Monday, the day before the election, they went to Jodie's bar together for dinner for the first time and put up with good-natured ribbing from Mike and Pete about their matching vegetarian meals.

When Kevin walked into the cafe the morning of the election it was full again. "Good morning, Kevin," everyone sang out in perfect unison, as if they'd been practicing it.

"Morning, everyone," he said.

Elizabeth came out of the kitchen with the coffee pot. "Good morning, Mr. Mayor," she said with a smile.

"Not yet."

She leaned in to whisper. "Almost everyone's voted already. I think you'll discover that you're already the Mayor."

"Well, not officially then."

"Hey, Kevin," Upton called from his table. "What will be your first act as Mayor?"

"Declare a town holiday, of course," he said, and everyone gave a mock cheer.

"Anything in mind for breakfast this morning?" Elizabeth said.

"Nope. You know me better than I do." She nodded and went back to her kitchen.

He turned to face the room, knowing there was a reason they were all here. Melissa the cleaner said, "I thought the meeting went well last night."

"I did too," Kevin said. "The teens were the toughest on me, I think."

"I don't know," Jodie said. "I thought Ernie gave you a pretty hard time."

"I did not!" Ernie shouted.

"He wasn't that bad. It was a reasonable question, and at least he didn't smack me between the eyes with, 'How can we trust you?'"

"What *do* you think you'll do first?" Jack asked.

"I think I have a lot to learn. So I'll probably spend a lot of time with Adie the first few days."

"Good luck with that," Ernie said under his breath, loud enough for everyone to hear. There was a deep silence in the room. "What? She's not God, she's not a dictator, and she's not a witch. She's just the Town Manager, and I don't care if she has been doing it for forty years, we could still vote her out if we wanted to."

"Why the hell would we want to?" Jack said.

"She gives me the creeps," Ernie said sullenly.

"Why," Upton said immediately, "because she knows more about this town than you do and isn't afraid to correct you?"

"She does not! Anyway, it's because of the way she hangs out in that mausoleum all day and half the night."

"You'd better be careful, Ernie," Jodie said. "She's got a voodoo doll that looks just like you, and a basket of knitting needles too."

"Oh sh—" His voice cut off suddenly.

Kevin realized that Ernie was looking in his direction, but off to the side. He turned to see Elizabeth standing beside him with an expression on her face that he hoped to God would never be directed at him. The room was utterly still.

"Ernest Katzenberg," Elizabeth said. "I've been listening to your griping since I was a toddler, and I've had enough. You are no longer welcome in my cafe. Please leave— now." Ernie got up slowly and reached for his wallet. "I don't want your money," she said.

He shuffled to the door and glanced back into the room before leaving. "I'm sorry," he said, quietly but clearly. The screen door slapped shut.

No one said anything for a long moment. Then Jodie turned to look at Elizabeth. "I don't blame you, honey," she said. "But Bev is going to be upset."

"She married him, not me," Elizabeth said.

"I know. You had the right to ban him, and I think all of us would agree that he went too far this time."

There were murmurs of assent from around the room.

"Thank you," Elizabeth said. "Everyone has a right to an informed opinion, and I have no problem with polite debate. But Ernie should know better than anyone how much Adie has done for this town, and I draw the line at people abusing my friends in *my* restaurant."

"That's right," a few people said, and everyone turned back to their food and their coffee.

Including Kevin. There was a plate waiting for him with waffles topped with huckleberries and whipped cream, and a side of home-fried potatoes. He looked up at her.

"Didn't scare you, did I?" she whispered.

"Not me. But it *was* scary."

"Come on back when you're done."

"Okay."

Kevin was pretty sure that more people would have liked to pester him with silly questions, but after what had just happened they seemed to feel it was more prudent to finish their breakfasts and get on with their day. By the time he was done only a handful of people were left, including Jodie and Melissa. He waved at them and walked back into the kitchen.

Elizabeth was sitting at the little table, looking dejected, and gestured for him to join her.

"That was pretty intense," Kevin said.

"It makes me feel ill," Elizabeth said. "I've never had to throw anyone out before, except that one hiker who wouldn't leave Melissa alone, and I think he was drunk."

"Ernie was being pretty spiteful."

"He's been getting worse every year. Especially since he retired um... eleven years ago. Bev can hardly stand having him in the house any more. I'm going to have to do an intervention eventually."

"What do you mean?"

She waved her hand. "It's not important. How are you this morning?"

"I'm feeling a little odd. Eight days ago I was on my way to a new life on the other side of the country. Now I've found a new life, but it's here. And I have a new job, apparently. And I met you."

She gave him a brilliant smile. "The results are being announced at the Town Hall at

8:00 tonight. Want to come over to my place for dinner after?" "Absolutely." "Okay. Come here." He stood up and leaned down and she grabbed the back of his head and kissed him.

He had to steady himself on the table edge; it felt like he might faint.

"You'd better go enjoy your last day of freedom," she said. He wasn't sure there wasn't a double meaning to that, but he didn't ask. "I have to clean up and get ready for lunch."

"You don't think people will stop coming because of ..." He wasn't sure how to finish that sentence.

"No, I don't. I think people will be relieved, actually. He was getting on everyone's nerves."

"Good. I'll see you later then."

"Git," she said, and slapped him on the leg.

* * *

Kevin walked back to the Town Hall. Adie's office was empty, so he jogged up the stairs and walked down the hall

128

past his apartment, to the voting room, which was right next to the library.

Jeremy and Adie sat behind the table near the entrance. He was working on a tablet computer, she was reading a book. They both looked up as he came in.

"Hi," Kevin said. "I know that I can't vote, but I just wanted to see where the action is."

"Not much action," Jeremy said. "The big rush was about an hour ago."

"How was breakfast?" Adie said.

"It was fine until the drama."

"There was drama in the cafe?" Adie said. "That's nearly unprecedented. Usually Elizabeth doesn't allow it." "She didn't like it today, either," Kevin said. "She threw Ernie out." The other two looked at each other and then back at him. "Why?" they said in unison.

He wasn't sure how to put it. Now he was sorry he'd even mentioned it, but he couldn't take it back. "Um. She said she wouldn't have people insulting her friends in her cafe."

Jeremy seemed about to ask something more, but Adie put a hand on his arm.

"I'll talk to her later," Adie said.

"It might be best to get it straight from her," Kevin agreed.

Someone appeared in the doorway. It was Mary the hairdresser. "Hi," she said. "I finally got the kids out the door and the kitchen washed up."

"Kevin," Adie said, "we can't allow candidates to be here while people are voting."

"Of course. I understand. I'll just..." He nodded at Mary, who smiled and moved aside to let him out. Jeremy checked

129

Mary's name off a list on a clipboard and they gave her a ballot. From his place by the door, Kevin couldn't see what was written on it.

"Enjoy your last day of freedom," Adie told him. He felt a chill run up his spine. It was word for word what Elizabeth had said.

* * *

He spent some time in the cemetery. At first he was just walking up and down the rows of headstones, looking at the dates and reading the inscriptions. But then Darren showed up with a rotary push mower and gardening tools.

"Can I help?" Kevin said.

"Sure. The mowing's a bit tough, why don't you work on the blackberries. Here." He handed Kevin some heavy gloves and a pruner.

Kevin had some experience with Himalayan blackberry from working in his mother's yard, and he recognized it immediately. While Darren mowed the grass, Kevin worked around the fence line, trying to pull it out by the roots when he could, cutting it off at the ground when he couldn't. Ivan the dog lay nearby, watching him intently, probably hoping for a treat. Kevin was sweating heavily by the time Darren finished the mowing.

"That's enough for one day," Darren said. "Nice work pulling them out. I can't do that, hurts my back."

"I hate these things," Kevin said.

"Yeah, nasty plants. They give good fruit if you're willing to sacrifice everything else to them."

"Not worth it."

"No. Well, see you later. Thanks for the help." He took his tools and rolled the mower toward one of the mobile homes.

Kevin went back to his apartment and took a quick shower. It was past lunchtime, so he heated up a bowl of soup and read while he ate. Then he had five hours to kill until he could find out whether his life had changed again. He wondered what Elizabeth did in the afternoons after lunch. She always deflected his attempts to get together before dinner. He'd have to ask her sometime.

* * *

Just before 8:00 Kevin walked downstairs to the community room. As before the door was open and most everyone had got there before him, including Elizabeth this time. He sat down beside her in the front row and she took his hand in hers. Adie and Jeremy were sitting up on the stage. A few minutes later Adie stood up.

"The last person voted at 5:00," she said, "so there was plenty of time to tabulate the results. Jeremy?"

She sat, and he stood up and cleared his throat nervously. "As usual, one hundred percent of the eligible voters participated. The voting committee, consisting of Adie Eagle and Jeremy Cooper, has triple-counted the ballots and we have official and final results, which are as follows. For the position of Mayor of Marmot. Kevin Calenda: twenty-six votes. Mickey Mouse: one vote. We hereby declare that Kevin Calenda is the new Mayor of Marmot. Congratulations, Mr. Calenda."

"That's twenty-seven votes," Kevin whispered to Elizabeth while the crowd applauded politely. "I thought there were only twenty-three adults in town."

"I'll explain later," she said.

"Mr. Mayor-elect," Adie said, "would you like to say a few words?"

Kevin jumped up onto the stage and faced the townspeople. A few people applauded again. He scanned the faces and found mostly wry amusement. He noticed that Ernie was present, which surprised him, but looking typically sour, which didn't.

"Thank you for your confidence, and for that ringing applause," he said, and the crowd laughed. "As I think I made clear last Thursday, I have no idea what I'm doing." They laughed again. "But I promise to work hard and to do my absolute best to represent this wonderful town as Mayor. Thanks again."

He hopped down off the stage, and a few people came up to shake his hand. Darren, Mike, and Upton were at the head of the line. When the crowd had thinned out, Adie walked down the stairs at the edge of the stage and stood face to face.

"Congratulations," she said.

"Thanks."

"Scared?"

"I'm too ignorant to be scared."

"That's something we can fix. Come by my office at 9:00 tomorrow morning. I'll get you up to speed and answer those questions that have been burning a hole in your throat all week."

"Will do."

She and Jeremy walked out of the room.

"Hungry?" Elizabeth asked.

"Starving."

"That's something we can fix. Come on."

She paused at the door to turn off the lights and they walked back to her apartment, holding hands.

* * *

Elizabeth had put a casserole in the oven before she left, so she had little to do to finish dinner, just pan-roasting some root vegetables and preparing a glaze for them. The table was already set, so Kevin sat on one of the bistro chairs and watched her work.

"Can you explain the vote count?" he said when she could spare him some attention.

"Sure. The Town Manager sets the voting rules, so Adie decreed that anyone thirteen and older could vote in town elections. We have four kids above that line, and five below, so with twenty-three adults that makes twenty-seven voters."

"That's unusual. Most places set eighteen as the lower limit."

"That still applies for elections outside this town, but it's clearly an arbitrary age. Some people aren't competent to vote at seventy and some are ready at ten."

"No kidding. Look at all the people who voted for George W."

She laughed. "I think he won by courting the puppy dog vote."

"What do you mean? Puppies can't vote."

"No, *he* was the puppy dog. A lot of people thought he was cute and bumbling, always tripping over his ears. Better than the robots who ran against him. Not cute at all."

"Jeremy said it was usual for everyone to vote," Kevin said. "Usually you only see full voter participation in countries where it's a crime *not* to vote, and maybe not even there."

"Are you getting conspiratorial on me again? Do you think this is a Stepford town?"

"No. It's just that unanimous anything makes me suspicious."

"Well, I unanimously think you're being silly."

"Okay, then."

She stopped stirring the sauce and looked at him. "This town almost died twice. The people who are still here care about it. Everyone who just wanted to hitch a ride on the easy train left long ago. So we make an effort."

"That makes sense. It's inspirational when it's not unsettling."

"You'll get used to it. Bring over the plates, please."

Over dinner he told her about working in the cemetery with Darren and she told him about Adie's dog Owl waking up unexpectedly at lunchtime and going table to table begging for food, which she hadn't done in over a year.

"It must have been the prospect of having a new Mayor," Kevin joked.

"Yes," she said, looking at him thoughtfully. "That will probably change everything."

Connecting

Wednesday, August 25

On his way to the cafe the next morning, Kevin noticed immediately that all the "Kevin for Mayor" signs were gone. He thought about walking down Cemetery Lane to check for sure, but decided he already knew the answer. Considering how this town was run, if people had been slow to do it, Adie would probably have gone out at 5:00 in the morning to collect them. But on second thought he decided it could have been Wanda, reclaiming her art materials.

The cafe was back to normal. *Thank goodness,* he thought. Melissa sat at her usual spot at the bar, Upton and Travis at their table, Paul and Martha together at one window table, and Jodie alone in the other. But when he walked in, everyone shouted out a hearty "Good morning, Mr. Mayor" in unison.

"Thank you," he said, saluting them with a beneficent wave, "my loyal subjects and serfs."

There were some chuckles, and everyone went back to their breakfasts and coffee as if he'd been there for a decade.

Elizabeth came out to greet him, grinning one of her radiant smiles. "You look like you need some eggs," she said.

"I do. I'm going to spend all morning with Adie."

"Eggs and potatoes and a scone, then."

"And a lot of coffee."

She poured him a cup and went back into the kitchen.

"Don't worry about Adie," Upton said. Kevin turned to face him. "Now that you're actually part of the town, she'll be more open with you."

"I hope so. Every time I tried to ask her anything interesting she turned into the Sphinx."

"That's just Adie. I think she has confidence in you."

"Good, because someone thought Mickey Mouse would be a better Mayor than me."

Travis piped up. "Don't discount the possibility that it was *Adie* who voted for Mickey."

Upton laughed, and so did Jodie and Melissa. He didn't think Paul and Martha had heard; they had their heads together, whispering.

Elizabeth brought him a big plate of food, including a cherry-and-chocolate-chunk scone which he was tempted to gobble up first. But he acted like an adult instead and ate normally.

He was nearly done when Paul came up to stand by his elbow. "Congratulations," he said.

"Thanks. I don't know how much of a triumphant victory it was, running unopposed. Except for Mickey."

"You'd been in town for eight days and we elected you Mayor. I'd call that a triumph."

"Well, thanks."

"Kevin, I just wanted to let you know that, despite being retired, I am a licensed minister in the state of Washington. In case you need one."

"Um... thanks. I'll remember that." He couldn't think what might have brought that on. But Paul had said something about counselling last week, too, so maybe that was what he was referring to.

"Okay. Enjoy your first day on the job."

"I'll try." Martha waved to him from the door, and the old couple left.

Elizabeth came back and refilled his coffee. "You have about five minutes before you have to leave."

Kevin glanced at his watch. "You're right. I'd better get going." He reached for his wallet, but Elizabeth put her hand on his arm.

"Kevin, your money is no good in here anymore."

"But I—" He had paid for every meal he'd eaten here so far. But the look she gave him made him slide his wallet back into his pocket.

"Go be the Mayor," she said, and kissed him lightly on the lips.

He tried not to notice the smirk on Upton's face as he walked out the door.

* * *

Kevin ended up outside Adie's office one minute early. She let him knock this time, and he had the eerie feeling it was out of courtesy, not because she didn't know he was there.

Bunny and Wombat came out from beneath her desk as he opened the door wide. He held out his hands and let them sniff him. They seemed most interested in his right hand; he'd held the scone in that one while he ate it.

Adie stood up and came around the desk. "Let's walk down the hall," she said, and told the dogs to lie down.

She led him around the corner to the end of the hall and the Mayor's office. He hadn't been there since his first tour with Adie, over a week ago. She opened the door and gestured him inside.

Someone had been very busy. Although the liquor cabinet was gone, the desk and three chairs remained, but it looked like a different room. An Oriental carpet now covered the bare floor, several potted plants softened the room, and two large matted and framed photographs hung on the walls, one of Portland's skyline at night with a lightning bolt splitting the sky, the other of Mount Hood on a cloudless winter day. *How had they found those so quickly?* The large desk now had a blotter, a pen and pencil set, and a computer monitor on it. It looked like a place you might actually want to spend some time in, and maybe get some work done.

"Wow," Kevin said.

"Let's sit down," Adie said, and they took adjoining seats in front of the desk. "You've heard how this town got its name." He nodded. Of course she would know that he'd heard that story. "It started as a lumbering camp in the late nineteenth century, became a very small but prosperous village, but then shrank slowly over decades until in 1953 there were just two residents, my mother and my little sister Ida, Jeremy's mom. I was quite a bit older than Ida, and the year before I'd gone off to Portland to work. All the other previous residents had done the same thing. Ida was only four that year, but she remembered until her dying day what it was like to live in a ghost town."

"So how did you turn it around?"

"It wasn't easy. I started by convincing a few people to move back."

"How?"

"To start with, I moved back myself. I renovated our house, and I cleaned up the yard that had gone to weeds and brambles."

"But how did you survive? You must have been fairly young."

"I came back in 1955, when I was twenty, because my mother died—to raise Ida. Mother's insurance wasn't much, but it was enough for me to make the house livable. The next year I got married, and convinced my husband to live here too. He was hardly ever at home anyway, so it didn't matter much where he called home."

"What did he do?"

"He was a logger. Worked all over the Northwest and down into California. He made a pretty good living from it, and though I hated his job and what it did to him, it was good work."

"What happened to him?"

"Heart attack at forty-six, in 1978."

"I'm sorry," Kevin said.

"Thank you. As you will discover, I'm a very good money manager, and Ryan was a good man, a good provider, not a drinker or a gambler, and as far as I know he was faithful, so we were able to save some money, and he had life insurance too. I would have asked him to buy some, but he did it on his own, to provide for me and Ida in case his job killed him. But in the end it wasn't that, just a congenital heart defect."

"Did you have any kids?"

Adie looked wistful, possibly the first time he'd seen her with an expression that wasn't either stern or amused. "No. We tried, but it never happened." She was silent for a moment and Kevin let her take her time.

"Anyway," she went on, "with Ryan and me and Ida living here, I was able to convince Bev and Ernie to come back. Then Mike's parents, then Elizabeth's parents, and so on."

"But how did you talk them into it?" She just smiled at him. After a moment he gave up. "Okay, you can be very persuasive. Can you tell me how *they* made a living?"

"The same way anyone makes a living. They already had jobs or they got them. There was work to be found. The point was to make this a living town again. All I asked was that they live here, fix up their homes, and form a community. I convinced the county that this area was prime timberland, so the property taxes were incredibly low. The houses had all been abandoned but about half were still structurally sound. We pitched in on weekends and fixed up the ones we could, cannibalizing the lost causes for materials. The availability of cheap, livable houses brought back more ex-residents."

Kevin thought about it. It might have been possible. It didn't explain the thriving local economy though. Or the great hulking building they were sitting in.

"Now you're thinking about the economics," Adie said. It wasn't a question. He nodded. She got up, went around the desk, and sat down in his desk chair. *Hey, that's my chair,* he thought, and smiled at himself. She gestured for him to join her and he went to stand behind her shoulder.

She logged in to the local network as "adie" and started an app. It brought up a window that looked like a very complex spreadsheet.

"This is not a spreadsheet," she said. "It's an economic model of the town. This is just the tabular view. Watch this."

She typed a keystroke and another window opened that showed two dozen circles connected by pulsing lines of various color and thickness. The size of the circles slowly changed, expanding or shrinking as the lines seemed to deposit glowing drops of honey into them, or carry them away. The web of lines between the circles was complex and shifting. Then he noticed that there were also lines coming in from the edges, bringing their throbbing drops of whatever into the network, and also lines going out. It was utterly mesmerizing: it would make the best screensaver he'd ever seen.

"What the heck is this?" he said.

She hit a key and the image froze. "It's Marmot. Well, to be precise, it's a visualization of the economic model of the town. The run you just watched was roughly one year."

"What app is this? I've never seen anything like it."

"No, you wouldn't have. I wrote it." He stared down at her, gaping like a fish. "What? You think because I'm seventy-five years old I can't program a computer?"

"No. No. I just..."

She laughed gently. "Never mind, Kevin. Everyone is deeper than they seem to be, even you. Let's sit down again."

They returned to the comfortable chairs on the other side of the desk. Now that he'd got over the initial shock, his reporter's mind was kicking into gear.

"Okay, I get that the circles represented—what, households?"

"Economic units. Household is a good approximation."

"And the lines are the flow of capital between them. The... pulsing? That was money changing hands?"

"Not just money. Unlike most economic models mine also tracks barter and other non-monetary exchanges."

"Okay, first big question. Where do you get the data?"

"Voluntary reporting."

"That can't be complete."

"You'd be surprised. Even if one party to a transaction doesn't want to report it, or remember to, the other usually does. I estimate that I've got 99.5% of our economy here."

"Why do they bother?"

"Because I asked them to, Kevin."

That set him back for a moment. "Okay. But why do you want all that data?"

She considered him for a moment. "After I got people to start coming back to Marmot, things looked up for a while. But the seventies were hard, and things never quite turned around for us completely. Starting around, oh, the late eighties, I could see that what I'd done so far was temporary. The national economy was good, but not good enough for people to continue to live in this lonely little hamlet so far away from the jobs that could have made them really comfortable. My models were really crude back then, but I could see that it was a long, slow slide back to oblivion."

"But that didn't happen."

"Obviously not."

"Why not?"

"9/11."

"*What?*"

"DHS."

"Huh?"

"Department of Homeland Security? You're an educated man, you've spent some time in government buildings, are you telling me you don't know what I'm talking about?"

"But what has that got to do with Marmot?"

"Did you notice the pipeline in the model?"

Kevin felt as if someone had opened a trap door beneath him. He had no idea what she was talking about. Adie reached out and turned the computer monitor around. She pointed.

At the very top left a line came in to the model from outside, a line he hadn't noticed before. It was much thicker and the pulse traveling down it was huge. He didn't understand how he had missed it; perhaps because it looked more like a structural feature or a glitch than like part of the web.

Adie went on. "When DHS was first created, they had a fund that communities could tap into for Homeland Security issues. Some big cities used it to turn their police forces into quasi-military units—better guns, armored vehicles, helicopters, surveillance networks. Do you know what I'm talking about?"

"Sure. Portland got its share, and squandered most of it."

"Marmot got its share too." He was gaping again. "More than our share, actually. You're a good writer, Kevin, but I'm a pretty good writer too. I spent months honing our proposal. I'm afraid that the DHS people may have been a little muddled about our situation here, although there were no outright lies in my submission. I can't be responsible for mistakes some bureaucrat makes if he thinks he sees what he wants to see. It's possible they may have got the wrong impression about what a marmot is; Kill Marmot might have been mistaken for an intent to take out an Al-Qaida terrorist named Marmot."

She paused and he tried to close his mouth, but it wasn't working.

"So they paid for this building, our IT infrastructure and the PBX system, the mail truck and school bus, renovations to every inhabited home and business, and we had enough left over to provide living wages for me, Jeremy, and—I should mention—you. Plus a sizable rainy-day fund. Travis manages the town investments, and the income from those is what I call the pipeline, that thick line on the model."

He floundered for a moment, then got his metaphorical feet under himself again. "I'm going to get a salary?"

"Of course. You're the Mayor." She mentioned a sum. "It's not lavish, but the apartment is rent-free, and the cost of living here is pretty low. I think you'll find it sufficient to support you. And of course you'll be spending a lot of it here in town, which pumps up the economy even more. That's

143

one reason we need a Mayor. Things have slowed slightly but noticeably since Bob died last spring."

With the free rent the salary she had named would be more take-home pay than he'd made in Portland. More than his new job in Maine would have paid him.

"I can see," Adie said, "that this was not what you expected. It's not magic, it's just cleverness. I'd forgive you for calling it devious." She stood up, and he did the same by reflex. "I'll leave you to settle in. Oh, I should mention that you have an account on our system now, it's 'kevin' of course. There are lots of useful documents on the public server, including the town history that I've been working on, though it isn't quite finished yet. You might want to poke around."

She walked toward the door of the office and he followed. She turned in the doorway and patted his arm. "Come see me when you get over the shock. Oh... I almost forgot. There's a movie night tonight, 8:30. Your first official duty. See you there?" He nodded and closed the door behind her.

* * *

The tall window on the long wall of his office looked due west, over the rolling, wooded foothills of the Cascades. The short wall also had a window, this one facing south, which let him look up the steep slope to Steamboat Mountain which lay to the southwest. Kevin spent a while looking out first one window, then the other, and back again, thinking.

He had expected something exotic, perhaps even mystical, to explain the prosperity of the town. He'd been prepared for a surprise. But not this. The whole town was built and maintained on a scam, a ruse—a lie.

144

No, not a lie. And not really a scam either. Adie had not made the rules, nor had she bent them, precisely. She'd just found a way to use the chaos, stupidity, and flailing that followed 9/11 to save her town. Compared to the way that other cities had grabbed and then wasted the funding that DHS had provided, Adie's ploy seemed virtuous. There didn't seem to be any misspent funds. It had all been used for worthwhile projects, except perhaps that the Town Hall was a few orders of magnitude grander than it had to be. Then Kevin remembered what she had said about the security cameras: they were "necessary to make it convincing."

Perhaps in order to get any funding at all, she had had to blow up the proposal, including the plans for a new Town Hall, so it looked as if the funding was going to a much larger community. Why would DHS care if terrorists took out a town of 32 people? But a larger, more prosperous city would be a better target, and therefore need more protection.

And she had actually put some of the money into investments to preserve the future of the town. He'd bet his next year's salary as Mayor that no other recipient of DHS funds had done that.

Kevin sat down at his new computer—probably the one that had been unused in the library, which Adie had said she was repurposing soon—and logged out of her account. He logged in as "kevin" and the system asked him to create a password. He typed in FairyChild816, for the woman he still thought of as fey, despite the lack of pointed ears, and the day they'd met.

He searched through the town documents, found Adie's history but didn't open it, and kept looking. He was hoping to read the proposal she had written for DHS, but couldn't locate it. Finally he gave up and logged out.

He needed some air. He walked downstairs, and when he realized that he was tiptoeing past Adie's office he forced himself to walk normally. He went out of the building into the hot, dry late-August day. The sun was shining as it had ever since he'd arrived, and not a cloud was visible.

He strolled down Little Fish Street, past the cafe to the lake. He stood looking out at the water and the trees beyond it—ruler-straight, magnificently tall Douglas firs and Ponderosa pines. Birds were chirping, but he didn't hear any frogs today.

When he turned to go back he noticed the welcome sign. It now said, "Welcome to Marmot, Population 33." He was official.

* * *

He didn't feel like being alone, and he didn't know what to do as Mayor—other than giving the occasional speech, he didn't know if he had any duties at all—so he walked back to the cafe for lunch.

"Hi, Kevin," they said when he came in. It was the usuals: Upton and Travis, Melissa, Jodie (without Ernie of course), and Paul and Martha. Pete was here today, too.

"Hello," he said and sat on his stool.

"You look befuddled," Elizabeth said when she came out. "You had your talk with Adie."

"I did."

"You look like she smacked you in the head with a trout."

"Pretty close. I think I'm still in shock."

"You need to eat something. It'll be right up."

He put his head in his hands. It was beginning to sink in that he'd hitched his wagon to a team of horses that might be insane and planning to drive him off a cliff.

"Cheer up," Upton said. "There was nothing illegal about it. They aren't going to ask for it back."

Kevin turned on his stool. "What if they do?"

"Well, first they'd have to find us. And if they manage that somehow, I've seen Adie's records, and I've read the proposal—and so has a lawyer friend of mine. He was so impressed that he waived his fee in exchange for a copy of the document. Adie kept a scrupulous account of every dollar we spent. It's all above-board. And she followed the RFP precisely. If someone misinterpreted what she wrote, she can't be blamed."

"RFP?"

"Request for proposals."

He thought that over. "Just how much is left over from the building and equipment purchases, anyway?"

Upton looked at Travis, who said, "Just over twenty-six million as of this morning."

"What?"

"It's diversified, all in very safe investments. Even if the US economy tanked we'd still have enough to run the town and deal with emergencies."

"As long as there was still an Internet," Upton said.

"Well, yeah," Travis retorted with a smile, "but if it got that bad we could just go back to shooting moose for our food."

"No moose around here for a hundred years," Upton said. "Elk, maybe."

"Just as good."

"Some of us," Kevin said, "are vegetarians."

147

"Well, you can grow carrots and starve if you want to," Upton said cheerfully. "But not today." He gestured and Kevin turned to see Elizabeth putting his plate down. With her other hand she set down a smaller plate with a really big brownie on it.

"You looked like you could use this," she said with a twinkle in her eye.

* * *

Kevin went back to the Town Hall after lunch and saw Jeremy just going in with a bag of mail. He followed him to the mail room.

"Hi," Kevin said.

"Hey," Jeremy replied.

"Do you want some help, or do you like doing this by yourself?"

"I love delivering it, but the sorting isn't that much fun. I'd appreciate the help."

"I feel like I need to do something to earn my keep."

Jeremy smiled almost sadly. "I'm sure you will. But you're welcome to come down and do this too if you want to."

"Okay. Tell me what to do."

Jeremy showed him a printed list above the sorting table. "These are the people who would prefer not to get junk mail. So for those folks, anything that isn't personal goes in the blue recycling bin. All the rest is sorted into piles for the recipients, then I organize it into my bag and go out on my rounds."

"Sounds straightforward. How do you organize the piles?"

"Oh, I didn't think of that. That's the part that might be confusing to you. I put them in the order I deliver them. Hmm. Wait a second." He went to the supply cabinet in the corner and got a roll of masking tape and a Sharpie pen. It took only a few moments for him to make a small label for each house or business and put them in rows and columns on the table. "I've been doing this so long I don't need the placeholders, but this will help you until you get used to it."

"Good enough. Hand me a stack."

The work went quickly, and they didn't speak during the process. Kevin was concentrating, but he suspected that Jeremy was simply taciturn. When they were done, Jeremy straightened the piles and tucked them into his bag. Kevin wasn't sure, even watching him do it, how he kept them separate from each other. Maybe he didn't.

"Thanks for the help. You don't have to do this every day if you don't want to, but if you feel like a break, I'd appreciate it. I usually get back from Trout Lake between 2:30 and 3:00."

"Okay. I'll see you tomorrow. Maybe I could ride in to the Post Office with you sometime?"

"Sure. Glad to have you. Well, I've got to get going."

"Of course."

Jeremy walked out toward the building entrance with his bag. Kevin followed him as far as Adie's office.

"Come on in," she said before he could knock.

"Hi," he said.

"Recovered yet?"

"No, not yet. I'd like to read over your DHS proposal but I couldn't find it. Is it confidential?"

"No, I just filed the early-days stuff in a different place. I'll email you the link."

"Thanks."

"You're welcome."

It was in his email In basket by the time he got back to his office fifteen seconds later. He spent the rest of the afternoon studying it and taking notes. It was a masterpiece of buzzwords, obfuscation, innuendo, paranoia, and misdirection. The farther he got into it, the more he felt a sense of bewildered awe at the sheer bravado of it—not to mention, of course, that it had worked.

* * *

Elizabeth had invited him over for dinner before the movie. They'd been taking turns cooking for each other, which had exhausted Kevin's repertoire of off-the-cuff recipes in just a few days. So he'd spent part of his dinner days looking for recipes on the Internet, using one of Mike's laptops. Elizabeth didn't need to do that, and although she had cookbooks both at home and in the cafe, he never saw her open one. When he had the opportunity to watch her cook, she simply worked with an impressive efficiency, without a moment's hesitation, as if she knew every recipe ever invented by heart. But he also got the distinct impression sometimes that she was improvising—but her improvisations were as good as anything he'd ever eaten in a restaurant, and there was no discernible difference in her proficiency. He wasn't even sure how he could tell she was making it up, he just could.

He was quiet during dinner and she didn't try to force conversation. Kevin complimented the food, and it was utterly delicious, but afterwards he couldn't remember what it had been.

Then it was time to go to the Town Hall. There was a small crowd gathered already. They sat together in the front row while Jeremy puttered around, pulling down a projection screen at the back of the stage, moving the lectern a little farther to the side, gathering up the chairs from last night—was it only last night they'd announced the results of the election? —and tinkering with something in the equipment room that he'd opened up. Adie was busy with a small movie-theatre style popcorn machine and a cooler with iced sodas. Soon the smell of fresh popcorn filled the room, and people began lining up to get themselves a bag.

When it seemed that everyone who was coming had arrived, Jeremy closed the doors and came up to Kevin, handing him a DVD case. "This is what we're watching."

"Mr. Mayor," Adie said.

Kevin jumped up on the stage. The audience was about twenty people, including all the kids, as far as he could tell. He glanced down at the DVD case.

"Good evening," he said. "Welcome to my first movie night. Today has been my very first day as Mayor, and I'd just like to say that I've enjoyed it thoroughly, especially the part where, as Elizabeth put it, Adie smacked me upside the head with a trout." He got a laugh at that, so he decided to go for it. "Jeremy tells me that tonight we're watching *Alice in Wonderland.* I don't know *anything* about this movie." A few chuckles. "I knew an Alice once. She wasn't that wonderful, but maybe this one is better." A few more. "I suppose some of you have read the book, as I have, in which case I'm a little surprised that you're here. Unless you're trying, as I did when I was in college, to decode the mathematics of Lewis Carroll's books. The best I could do was to disprove the idea that Alice was really Albert Einstein and that Wonderland was based on quantum mechanics." Pete was the only one who laughed at that. "Anyway, here comes a movie that has a vanishing cat and a lot of people with really big heads."

Adie was chuckling but the rest of the audience seemed perplexed. Jeremy turned off the lights and started the movie.

Elizabeth leaned in to whisper in his ear, "You are deeply disturbed."

"You've got that right," he said.

Kevin didn't really like the movie much, but he'd seen far worse. When it was over and most everyone had left, they were left alone in the front of the room. Jeremy was putting things back to rights and Adie was nowhere to be seen.

"Let's go upstairs," Elizabeth said. They walked slowly up the steps, hand in hand, to his apartment. Kevin got her a glass of water and after a sip she curled up in his lap and stayed there for a long while.

She didn't leave until morning.

Power

After that first night with Elizabeth, Kevin never slept in the Mayor's apartment again. She had to start her breakfast prep pretty early, so it was easier if she didn't have to walk down the hill to the cafe in the pre-dawn light. Kevin didn't mind in the slightest; he liked spending his evenings and nights in her beautiful home, he liked that it was easier for her, plus her bed was more comfortable than his, and when she got up in the morning he just rolled over and went back to sleep.

It didn't feel like they'd only known each other for seventeen days. It felt like ten years, or maybe ten lifetimes. Kevin had breakfast in the cafe every day, and lunch a few times a week. They still alternated cooking for each other, but he spent more time looking through her cookbooks. Every time he saw her after a few hours' separation it felt like his heart was overflowing with sunshine, and her smile of greeting made him think, *Who needed the sun anyway?*

He was learning more about her, and vice versa. When he wrote a letter to his mother just after they got involved (since he couldn't reach her on the phone), Elizabeth asked him to read it to her and then wrote a page of her own to be included with his. She told him about her own mother: watching her effortless mastery at everyday baking, Christmas decorating, and Scrabble. That launched a Scrabble marathon that cooled down into a daily game, but they never kept score.

Kevin shared his childhood memories of Christmas, just his mother and sister and him taking their time unwrapping gifts, then spending the whole day together reading, or playing in the snow on the rare occasions that they had a white Christmas.

At the end of that first week Kevin realized suddenly that he was happy, and furthermore that it had been a really long time since he could honestly say that. He didn't have to ask Elizabeth if she was happy. She glowed, and sometimes out of the corner of his eye he thought he saw sparkles drifting around her dark hair like specks in a snow globe, but they always vanished when he turned to look right at her. And he did that a lot.

One morning he sat in the cafe finishing his breakfast coffee and he realized that the regulars were staring at him quietly. He turned on his stool and looked from one to the other. Upton was grinning, which seemed to be his default expression. Jodie looked wistful, Melissa hopeful, and Paul and Martha thoughtful.

"What?" he said. One by one, they shook their heads and turned away. Elizabeth came out of the kitchen and kissed him before shooing him out to go to work.

* * *

He and Adie were sitting in her office for one of their morning talks. They did this every few days, to discuss happenings in the town or to continue Kevin's education. Adie never commented on the fact that Kevin spent so little time in the Mayor's apartment, and he didn't volunteer anything either. He figured she knew—that everyone knew—what was going on.

Wombat the terrier was sitting in Kevin's lap. He had apparently adopted Kevin, who was clearly homeless and needed protection. Sometimes the dog sat there alert, ready to protect his new friend, but other times, as now, he just curled up and fell asleep.

"Let's talk about utilities," Kevin said "Upton explained the phone system to me: the PBX works within the town but you can't call in or out. What about electricity?"

"You've noticed that there are no power poles," Adie said.

"Yeah, I saw that right away."

"During the renovation I had them all buried. They go underground at the Forest Service road, so we do lose power occasionally, but not very often the last few years since they replaced all the power poles on 141."

"Okay, but how is it that you have any connection at all?" He had a sudden thought. "You're not pirating the power, are you?"

She laughed. "Kevin, you have such a melodramatic view of the world! No, the agreement with the power company goes way back to the forties, and they decided to keep us connected even when the government abandoned us. They're really happy that they did, too, because now this place sucks a ton of juice."

"And you have backup generators here?"

"Just for the Town Hall. The outages are infrequent enough, and usually short enough, that everyone else just suffers through them. Except Upton and Travis. They have a generator too."

"I suppose in the worst case, everyone could just come and hang out here if it happened in the winter."

"True, but no one's ever done that. People have fireplaces and wood stoves."

"Okay," he said, "what about water?"

155

"The town is a private local water district. You probably didn't notice the pumps and filtering system in the equipment room in the basement."

"I'll check it out some time. So it's a well?"

"Yes. We're right at the base of Steamboat Mountain, so the aquifer is bountiful. We'll never deplete it."

"Who checks the water quality? The state? The county?"

"Jeremy. The state and the county refuse to acknowledge our existence."

"But you'd think they'd want to regulate... Oh, never mind. We're on our own, right?"

"Yep, pretty much."

"The water pressure is really good," he said.

"The pumps are up here. It's all downhill to the rest of the town."

Kevin thought for a moment. "What about trash pickup?"

"Darren."

"What?"

She settled back in her chair. "Everyone composts and recycles what they can. And I'd say that the average amount of trash per household in Marmot is half what the rest of the county produces. There are benefits to living so far away from towns and shops. So people separate for recycling, collect what trash they can't compost, and every other week Darren loads it into his pickup and takes it to the county landfill. People pay their share of the dump fee and his transportation costs and time, which amounts to less than $5 a month per household."

He thought some more. "Groceries?"

She laughed aloud. "That was a major coup, if I have to say it myself. We have them delivered."

"Huh? From where?"

"White Salmon. There was a grocer there who was a friend of my late husband. I made a deal with him back in the seventies, and his son still honors it. Mike emails him what we need and once a week he sends a driver up here with boxes for every house. The driver is a nice young lady, my old friend's granddaughter. She stays for tea, she gets a very hefty tip, and we all save gas money."

"What if someone runs out of something? Do they run into Trout Lake for it?"

"They borrow from the neighbors. This is a small town, Kevin. You have to get with the program."

"I'm trying. I'm going with Jeremy on the mail run today."

"Yes," Adie said, "he told me you've been helping with the sorting every day. That was nice of you."

"It's not hard work, and I like him, even though he doesn't talk much. Anyway, it makes me feel like I'm earning my salary. Which, by the way, I haven't seen any of yet."

"Payday's every other Friday, which is tomorrow."

"Who's on the payroll, anyway?"

"You, Jeremy, and I have salaries. Darren gets a small fee for maintaining the cemetery. That, and the property management fees, and his odd jobs around town are enough to keep him afloat."

"Property management?" Kevin said.

"You've noticed the empty houses?"

"The ones right across the street from here?"

"Yes. All owned by families that once lived here, who want the homes maintained. I know that two are planning on moving back someday, and I'm working on the third one."

Kevin stroked Wombat's head. The dog shifted so his legs stuck up stiffly like fence posts. Kevin rubbed his belly.

"It's a nice system."

She looked smug. "Thanks."

* * *

The ride with Jeremy to Trout Lake was the first time Kevin had left Marmot since stumbling onto it. He was trying not to be superstitious about it, trusting that Jeremy could get him back, especially since Jeremy was the reason he'd found it in the first place. But he couldn't help feeling a little nervous.

The mail truck was surprisingly comfortable. It looked just like a real mail truck, right down to the paint job, but without the Postal Service logos. There was one other odd thing.

"This is a left-side drive vehicle," Kevin said when they were heading down a Forest Service road about ten minutes out of Marmot.

"Yeah," Jeremy said, "it's not a real mail truck."

"It looks a lot like one."

"We had it custom built on a pickup frame."

"Wasn't that expensive? Wouldn't it have been cheaper to buy a used mail truck at auction?"

"Maybe. It didn't cost as much as I thought it would. Adie knew somebody in Hood River who gave us a good deal."

"Is there anyone within fifty miles that she doesn't know?"

Jeremy looked over at him and grinned. "I doubt it."

A while later Kevin found another topic of conversation, since it was clear that Jeremy wasn't going to offer one.

"Helen told me that you found her at the Post Office, and that's how she ended up in Marmot."

"She did, huh?"

"So she and I have something in common. We both found paradise because of you."

Jeremy laughed and scratched his head. "I like the place, but I wouldn't call it paradise. You haven't lived through a winter yet."

"Why, are they bad?"

"We're smack in the middle of the Cascades, Kevin. I hope you like snow."

He didn't have a lot of experience with snow. Portland had the occasional snowfall, but it never lasted long. He'd never got interested in winter sports, skiing or snowboarding, so he stayed away from the mountains and the passes in the winter.

"Have you met Mechelle yet?" Jeremy asked him.

"I've seen her with Helen a few times but I've never spoken to her."

"She's real nice. Helen's done a great job with that girl."

"Where are they from originally?"

"Near L.A. I can never remember the name, something Spanish."

"L.A.? Really? How did she end up looking for a job in Trout Lake?"

"I think she got lost."

A few minutes later they passed the ranger station. This part of the route looked familiar, probably because Kevin had driven it two or three times while he was flailing around that first day, trying to find the trailhead. Jeremy pulled the truck into the small parking lot outside the Post Office and they went in.

It was a tiny place, probably the smallest post office Kevin had ever seen. There was a small bank of post office boxes in the outer room, and enough space for perhaps four people to line up for the counter inside. Jeremy took a big key ring out of his pocket and started opening boxes with the keys. Kevin held his delivery bag while Jeremy extracted the mail and stuffed it in the bag. There were two package slips, so when he was done they went into the inner office. There were no other customers there.

A woman in late middle age, plump and stern-looking, with streaks of grey in her brown hair, was standing behind the counter. Her face improbably cracked into a smile when she saw Jeremy.

"Jeremy!" she bawled. "Happy Thursday."

"Same to you, Barb. How are you today?"

"Great! I got to chew someone's head off this morning, so I'm feeling terrific." She didn't seem to have a volume knob; it must have broken off at max.

"Who was it?" Jeremy said.

"Some local numbnuts, I don't think you know him. Gave me grief for a mangled letter and I ate him for second breakfast. How are things up in the ghost town?"

"Pretty spooky."

"So who's this guy?" She turned a glare on Kevin and he realized how idiotic anyone would have to be to antagonize the broom-riding postmistress in a place this small. Your mail would never be safe again.

"This is our new Mayor, Kevin Candela."

"The Mayor, huh? Where's your top hat, Mr. Mayor?" she asked Kevin.

"It fell off when a grizzly was chasing me down Main Street. Last I saw it the bear was wearing it, and I wasn't going to ask for it back."

"Haw! You can bring this guy back anytime. Okay, what you got?"

He handed over the package slips and she quickly found the parcels, one just too big for the box and the other too big for Jeremy's bag. Kevin took that one for him.

"Thanks, Barb," Jeremy said. "See you again soon."

"Yeah, but I might not be in such a good mood next time, so watch out."

When they were safely inside, Kevin said, "Holy shit!"

"She's not so bad," Jeremy said. "You get used to her after a while. You just have to be polite, then she's fine."

"I would not want to get on her bad side."

"Not if you ever wanted your mail again, no."

"Has she been here a long time?"

"As long as I can remember. Adie would know for sure."

Kevin looked around, then climbed up into the truck. "I guess there'd be no point in looking for a jewelry store around here?"

Jeremy looked at him for a moment thoughtfully, then put the truck in reverse. "Talk to Mike."

* * *

"When do you need it by?" Mike said.

"Soon. Uh… probably very soon."

"Well, I have a few things that have accumulated over the years. Problems with returns and so on. Let me look." He disappeared into the back of the shop for several minutes. He came back empty-handed and Kevin knew what he was going to say next. "Sorry, I don't have anything on hand that you'll be happy with. Why don't you talk to Adie?"

* * *

161

"Really?" Adie said. "Hmm. I guess I should have seen that coming." Kevin didn't know whether to believe that she was surprised. It seemed unlikely. She thought for a moment. "I have an idea. Come with me."

She led him out of the building and down Fish Lake Street to the first house on the right, after the big bend.

"This is your house?" he said. Kevin hadn't learned where everyone lived yet, but he should have known. It was by no means the largest house in town, but it was flawlessly maintained, with a beautiful, fenced front yard bordered with flowering shrubs. There was a flagstone path leading from the street to the front door.

"Jeremy and I live here," she said.

She invited him in, and they went past a spacious, elegant living room to a small den off the kitchen. It seemed to be the same floor plan as Mary's house, almost directly across the street. Adie rummaged around in a tall antique dresser that seemed to be serving as a storage cabinet. She pulled out a small box and opened it for him.

"This was mine."

He looked at her. She was smiling at him sadly. He looked back down at the box.

"Are you sure? I mean..."

"Absolutely. I can't think of a better use for it."

He reached out and she snapped the box shut and put it in his hand.

Sleeping Beauty

Sunday, September 5

On her next day off, Elizabeth proposed that they go for a hike while the weather was still nice.

"Why, is it going to turn bad?" Kevin said. He'd got out of the habit of checking the weather since he arrived, since it was the same every day: eighties, sunny, and dry. It was like Los Angeles without all the people, tall buildings, or freeways.

"The rains will start around the middle of the month," Elizabeth said, "and after that the weather can be unpredictable."

He readily agreed to go. After a simple breakfast of eggs, toast, and berries they loaded their hiking gear into the back of Kevin's car and headed back out to the world.

Elizabeth didn't own a car. He hadn't got around to asking her if she knew how to drive because he couldn't quite figure out how to phrase it without sounding insulting or patronizing. He assumed she could, because she'd gone to a normal high school, but since she had no vehicle and didn't seem inclined to go anywhere, perhaps she'd never bothered to learn.

"Where are we going?" he said when they reached the Forest Service road.

"A little place I know. Turn right here."

She guided him through several turns until he saw the sign for Sleeping Beauty. This was the trail he'd been searching for when he found her instead. He looked at her and she just grinned.

"Better late than never," she said.

He parked in a gravel-strewn lot in a wide spot at the end of the road. There were no other cars there. After putting on their day packs she led the way up a steep path leading from the parking lot through thick woods.

The trail eased up after the first hundred feet. It was well-maintained and clearly heavily travelled in season, because it was worn down well below the forest floor grade. The trees were huge pines and firs, with thick underbrush between them. When they'd been hiking for a while they came to a place where the trail curved around the edges of a ravine. It reminded Kevin of a cathedral somehow: there was a canopy above them but the ravine left a vast open space on their right. Even the birds that had been chittering since they entered the woods seemed hushed.

They were over a mile in when they came out of the woods onto a slope of bare rock. Loose scree was everywhere on either side of the trail, but the path itself was clear. A little farther on the trail started to switchback, and here someone had piled the loose rocks into a dry-stacked wall. It was too low to prevent anyone from falling back down the hill, but it served as a reminder to watch your step.

The switchbacks ended on a rounded, bare granite knob. The trees were all below them, only naked rock here. Kevin walked to the edge of the cliff and was able to look straight down the face of an escarpment, six hundred feet or more. He stepped back a little nervously.

The view was incomparable. Mount Adams hulked in the near distance like a sullen giant, its snow cover gone, leaving only the cracked, dirty white tongues of glaciers. On his left Mount Rainier sat on the horizon like Adams's older brother. Way off to the right, past the long grade down to the Columbia River, he could see the steep slopes of Mount Hood. It was recognizable but looked strange, and it took him a moment to figure out why: he was looking at its north face, but he was used to seeing the west face from Portland. The air was a little hazy, but not enough to obscure anything. A stiff, cool breeze blew up at them. It was probably twenty degrees cooler than it had been when they set out.

Elizabeth took off her pack, took a drink from her metal water bottle, and sat down on the rock facing Adams. A hawk flew by overhead, screaming at something—maybe at them. Somewhere far off was a machine sound, a chainsaw or a badly tuned tractor, but it was so faint that each gust of wind made it inaudible. Kevin shucked off his pack and sat beside her. They just looked at the view for a while in silence.

He tried to gauge whether enough time had passed. He didn't want to ruin the moment, but maybe this would make it better. So he pulled his pack toward him and dug around in the small pocket on the front until he found it.

She looked at him calmly. Somehow he knew that she knew.

"Elizabeth," he said. "I've only known you a little while—less than a month, actually. But it feels like we were born to be together. I've been wandering around my whole life not knowing what I was supposed to be doing, or where I was supposed to be. But now I think I know." He held out the small box to her hesitantly. His mouth was suddenly very dry. In what he hoped was not a croak, he said, "Will you marry me?"

She took the box from him and opened it. The thin, carved ring and its modest diamond sparkled in the sunlight. She looked up into his face and smiled so brilliantly that he thought the sun had gone out.

"Of course I'll marry you," she said, and fell into his arms for the best kiss in the history of mountain kisses. A long time later she looked at the ring on her finger. "I think I know this ring."

"It was Adie's wedding ring. She said she wanted you to have it."

"Oh, Kevin, I would have been happy with something out of a Cracker Jacks box, but this just makes it perfect."

The next kiss turned into something more, and for a long timeless stretch there was nothing in the world but the sunshine warming their skin, the breeze cooling it, the haunting screech of the hawk, and each other.

* * *

On the drive back, with the sun already down below the trees but the sky still a brilliant blue, Kevin looked over at her. They were both grinning like dopes.

"I don't want to wait," he said.

"I don't either. How about next Sunday?"

"A week from today? Great!"

"If it's okay with you," she said, "I'd like to have the service in the ruins of the old Catholic church."

He laughed. "Somehow I find that utterly appropriate. Were your parents married there?"

She laughed back. "How old do you think I am? It burned down the year before my mother was born."

"Oh. Um. How old are you?"

"Thirty-five." They drove for a few minutes without speaking. "How do you feel about kids?" she said.

He looked at her. "With you? I am completely in favor of kids. I think you would be the best mom in the history of the world."

She laughed and tousled his hair, which was already pretty mussed.

When they got to Marmot he parked his car at the Town Hall, where it had been for the last three weeks. "Do you think she'll be in her office?" he said.

She shook her head. "Probably at home. Let's go."

They walked to Adie's house and knocked on the door. She answered it, immediately looked at Elizabeth's left hand, and pulled her into a hug. Then she dragged them into the house and they sat in her living room.

"When?" Adie said.

"A week from today."

"Good. Waiting would just be a waste of time. You'll need to get a license right away, though. There's a three-day waiting period."

"Where do we need to go?" Kevin said.

"Goldendale. It's at the other end of the county, unfortunately, about an hour and a half away."

"We can go tomorrow after lunch," Elizabeth suggested.

"Okay," Kevin said.

"I'm happy for you both," Adie said earnestly, and despite Kevin's misgivings about Adie, he believed her. "Paul will want to officiate."

Kevin said "Oh" just as Elizabeth said "Great."

"What?" both women asked Kevin together.

"Paul told me that he was licensed as a minister in Washington. I had no idea why he

said that. Do you think he knew somehow?"

Elizabeth put her arm around him and pulled him close. "Everyone knew, silly. Except you."

* * *

Kevin borrowed Mike's Internet connection to look up the licensing requirements, which were ridiculously lenient, and told Elizabeth she just needed to bring a photo ID. She held up her driver's license, so now he knew that she knew how to drive.

He had lunch in the cafe on Monday and then helped her clean up. Everyone wished them luck as they left. They drove out of town together for the second time, and she directed him to and then past Trout Lake, down winding country roads past farms and patches of forest. It took almost exactly an hour and a half, as Adie had promised.

Elizabeth had never been to the County Auditor's Office in Goldendale, but Kevin's phone was working again, so his GPS told them where to go. Inside the boring office building there were two couples ahead of them. The male clerk, a gaunt man with thinning hair and a bushy black moustache, took their IDs, had them fill out a single-page form, and then said that the fee was $32. Kevin paid in cash.

Their license was valid starting on September 9, for sixty days.

Neither of them felt like lingering in the odd, ugly town of Goldendale. It felt like a metropolis to him after the weeks spent in the tiny village in the woods, which was weird considering how much of his life had been spent in Portland, a city that was two hundred times bigger. Kevin stopped for gas and they headed back the way they'd come.

After a while of driving in silence, Elizabeth said, "Do you want to go on a honeymoon?"

Kevin thought about it. "To be honest, I feel like I've been on a honeymoon since the day I arrived in Marmot. Do you?"

She squeezed his hand and said, "No. We'll have opportunities for travel later." She looked out the window and he decided not to ask what she meant.

* * *

There was no music but the sound of the birds. Kevin stood within the ruined walls of the church in his best suit (one of two) with Paul and Upton at his side, waiting. Someone had cleaned up the interior, chopping back the shrubs and saplings growing from cracks between the floor pavers and sweeping out the debris. Even the fallen wall stones had been hauled away, leaving a bare, level, open space that should have been depressing but wasn't. Just minutes before, the sun had risen high enough to shine over the remaining walls and brighten up the space.

As far as Kevin could tell, everyone in town had come. He was too nervous and preoccupied to count them, but he couldn't think of anyone he knew who wasn't there. There was nowhere to sit, so everyone stood, facing away from him. He realized that they had naturally separated into two roughly equal groups, left and right, leaving an aisle down the middle.

Without any warning Adie and Elizabeth appeared at the opening in the collapsed wall. Elizabeth was wearing a white knee-length dress, with sleeves that ended just above her elbows, a sculpted bodice, and a billowing skirt that seemed to flow as she moved. There was no veil. She was holding Adie's arm, but she looked as steady as the stones on which Kevin stood. Silently and slowly, they walked up the aisle the townspeople had made, until they reached the front. Adie stood beside her and Upton turned with Kevin to face Paul, who had taken two steps back. The guests had been silent since Elizabeth appeared, but now a deeper hush fell over the old church. Kevin thought that the birds had stopped singing too.

"We've come here to join Kevin Isaac Calenda and Elizabeth Faye Kelly in marriage," Paul said. *Her middle name is Faye?* Kevin didn't really hear the rest. He turned to face Elizabeth and took her hands. The words he had heard so many times, in so many variations, and always for other people—the words he had never thought to hear for himself— flowed over him like the calming sound of waves on a beach. What he needed to do and say he simply did, at the right times, without knowing why. He couldn't see anything but her face, and he couldn't take his eyes off hers.

Below the unruly, dark brown pixie bangs that just reached her eyebrows, blue-grey eyes looked back at him steadily. Her nose and chin were small, her cheekbones sharp, her lips were full, and he could tell that she was having to restrain herself from smiling. Then she stopped trying, and the roofless church got immeasurably brighter.

The world came back to him as Paul said, "You may kiss the bride."

Kevin took her limber but slight form in his arms and touched his lips to hers. He felt a distinct but painless spark pass between them, like static electricity, but he didn't pull back.

Part Two

* * *

Fairy Child

Wedding Party

"We've come here to join Kevin Isaac Calenda and Elizabeth Faye Kelly in marriage," Paul said. Of course Elizabeth knew that Kevin's middle name was Isaac, but she didn't remember how she'd learned that. From the brief flash of surprise on his face it was clear that he *hadn't* known that her middle name was Faye, and he'd probably invent some overblown significance for it when he had time to think about it.

She heard everything that Paul said, and everything that Kevin said in response; the words were etched on her brain forever. She felt like her senses had all been enhanced, turned up to a maximum she'd never experienced before. She could hear every rustle of the people watching them, every bird calling from the woods, Owl moaning from the cafe because she was left all alone; she thought she could hear a cloud floating by overhead when it dimmed the sunlight.

Elizabeth had never seen Kevin wear anything but casual clothing; he looked sharp in his grey double-breasted suit. Someone had given him a white rose for a boutonnière; probably Upton, who grew roses behind his pair of satellite dishes. With her heightened senses she noticed again the slight, pleasing asymmetry of Kevin's face: the left cheekbone slightly more prominent, the right eye slightly higher.

Then it was done, and Paul said, "You may kiss the bride." *That's me!* Elizabeth thought joyfully. When Kevin's lips touched hers she felt a distinct electric spark that thrilled her more than the kiss. She knew exactly what it was.

* * *

She had not seen her neighbors looking so cheerful since the day that Adie called a town meeting to explain that her long efforts to secure DHS funding had worked and their future was secured. It made her even happier to know that she and Kevin were the cause of their good mood.

A few people threw rice, a few threw flower petals, but most people didn't make it out of the church ruins in time, and the stragglers probably hadn't planned to throw stuff anyway. She held on tightly to Kevin's arm as they walked up the hill to Cemetery Lane and then to the Town Hall. As they passed the cemetery she whispered "Look, mom!" at her parents' graves. Kevin heard her, but no one else did; he turned to smile at her and patted her hand.

She had been gently excluded from the planning for the reception, so it was a surprise when they walked in to the community room and she saw how beautiful everything looked. Seven round banquet tables had been brought out from storage, the rows of chairs rearranged around them. Every table had a lovely centerpiece of white flowers—roses, baby's breath, and carnations—and a pair of white tapers. White banners and streamers hung from the walls and the light fixtures. Heavy cobalt curtains, hardly ever used, had been drawn across the stage, hiding the only part of the room that could not be beautified.

Long tables across the far wall held chafing dishes and platters of food, and a modest three-tiered white cake decorated with white fondant flowers. The lights were off, the only illumination coming from the windows that ran the length of the wall above the food. She and Kevin stopped inside the door and made a little receiving line, but most people didn't do more than smile and pause. They all knew each other and saw each other every day, and Elizabeth thought cheerfully that they were probably eager to get to the food.

Jeremy was fussing in the equipment room, and suddenly there was music coming from the wall speakers—but not appropriate music; she thought it was AC/DC, which she recognized from her high school years and did not like. She met Jeremy coming out of the equipment room with a smile on his face and asked him if he had any classical playlists. He got a sheepish look and apologized, and a moment later Debussy had replaced the twanging guitars.

When everyone had arrived, Elizabeth and Kevin started the food line. Since she hadn't been available to cook, as she usually did for this kind of celebration, Adie had catered the food. It wasn't bad, but Elizabeth couldn't help thinking what she could have done with the opportunity. More spices, for one thing.

The cake, however, was exquisite and just what she would have ordered: white cake with lemon curd between the layers, and a white icing that wasn't too sweet. Without discussing it first, she and Kevin dispensed with the vulgar modern habit of smashing cake into each other's faces; they dispensed with feeding each other altogether. The guests murmured, perhaps disappointed, but she didn't think so.

Then people insisted on getting up and making toasts. Adie said, "I couldn't love this darling girl more if she were my own child. She's been waiting all her life for the right person to come along, and though I trust her judgment, I just want to remind everyone—I don't necessarily mean you, Kevin—that anyone who hurts her will wake up with their heart cut out and served up to them deep fried with hush puppies. So please raise your glasses to our wild child and her new partner in life."

Pete had had too much champagne, evidently, because he gave a long, rambling, incoherent speech that Elizabeth suspected was intended to be a lament that he had not tried harder to win her for himself—but which no one seemed able to follow. During this baffling soliloquy, she noticed Mike looking wistful; she knew that for many years he'd stifled his feelings for her, and also knew that he thought he was too old for her, which was true. Finally Upton stood up, clapped his hand over Pete's mouth, and said, "I think what Pete is trying to say is, 'Good luck to the happy couple.'" And everyone cheered and emptied their glasses.

Jeremy also stood up and everyone got quiet. It was unprecedented for him to make a speech, but here he was. Without hesitation or stuttering, he said, "Adie has always been like a second mother to me, which is an experience that Elizabeth and I shared growing up. That makes Elizabeth the sister I never had, and I just want to say that I will always love her, and I'm very happy for her to have finally found someone to share her astonishing life with. To Elizabeth and Kevin!"

No one had anything to add to that, which was a relief. Kevin leaned over and whispered, "Do you think anyone would mind if I had some more cake?"

She laughed and shoved him up off his chair. Several people followed him to the cake table for seconds.

Adie whispered something to Jeremy, who walked back to the equipment room and stopped the music. Then Adie went to the seldom-used upright piano to one side of the stage and waited for everyone to quiet down. Elizabeth recognized her cue: she took Kevin's hand and led him to the open space at the head of the room.

It was a waltz, one she didn't recognize, slow and sweet. She had never danced with Kevin before, but he was surprisingly good, a confident and steady leader.

"Where did you learn to dance?" she said quietly.

"My mother taught us. I used to dance with my sister while she watched."

"The benefits of being raised by women," Elizabeth said, and he laughed gently.

When the song was over, several other couples came out on the floor. "I think

perhaps," Kevin said, "we could make our exit?" She smiled and nodded, caught Adie's eye, and gave her a little wave. Adie nodded back and played something a little more energetic, which was enough of a distraction for them to walk out with only a few goodbyes. They were nearly to the outside door when Elizabeth heard the rock music start up again, and people cheering.

* * *

Elizabeth woke up from a nap and found Kevin lying on his side next to her, watching her. She smiled and he grinned back. "I liked your dress," he said. It was hanging in the closet again; she had taken a

moment before they tumbled into her bed to preserve it. "Where did you get it?"

"I've had it all my life. It was my mother's wedding dress."

"It looks brand new."

"Well," she said, "it's only been worn twice."

176

"So you wore your mother's dress and Adie's ring. That takes care of *old* and *borrowed* I guess. What was *new* and *blue*?"

"New underwear." He chortled and she nudged him playfully. "Nothing blue."

"Nothing blue?"

"I'm too happy to be blue!"

"Ha!" He looked thoughtful for a second. "Actually, it's pretty hard to imagine you melancholy. But I guess when—"

She knew what he'd been about to say. "Yes, I was sad for a long time after that. But though I'll always miss them, I was able to recover my balance and get on with life."

"So you're basically a happy person?"

"Yes. Is that so unusual?"

"In my experience it is." He propped himself up on an elbow. "I think most people get knocked around by life until they realize that the best they can hope for is contentment. And that's enough, really. Being happy all the time must be exhausting."

"Not if you practice hard."

"How do you practice that?"

"I have a new technique. Want to see it?"

"Sure."

She knocked his arm down and climbed on top of him.

"I'd like to move in here with you," he said later.

"Oh, would you really?" she said tauntingly.

"Yes. I think it would set a bad example for the Mayor and his wife to have separate houses. Especially when the Mayor's house is so extremely grand, and includes a police department, a courtroom, and a dungeon."

"A dungeon? Is that what's down there?"

"It is now. Adie just released the funds for it on Friday."

"So, it's torture for the miscreants, is it?"

"Yep. It's the rack for missing movie night, branding irons for littering, and the iron maiden for failing to decorate your house at Christmas."

She tried to look serious. "I shudder to think what the punishment will be for not mowing your lawn."

"I haven't worked that out yet, but I'm sure that horses will be involved."

He kissed her. It still startled her how much she liked it when he did that. He wasn't the first man she'd ever kissed, although to be accurate his predecessors were really just boys. She liked his beard; it was soft on her face, not scratchy, and it made him look serious, somehow. The boys she had kissed in high school had not been able to grow beards yet.

"Move your things in tomorrow," she said while his lips were still touching hers.

"I can't believe I understood that. You said to salute my pigs in a burrow."

"Yes, and that's just what I meant, too."

"I thought so. Are you hungry?"

"No. Are you?"

"No, I had two pieces of cake. I won't need to eat again until Wednesday."

"What kind of example would you be setting if you didn't eat breakfast in your wife's little restaurant?"

"You're right. I'll have two breakfasts just to show people how it's done."

"Let's get up and make room in the closet." She made a move to roll off the bed and he caught her arm.

"I've seen your closet," Kevin said. "It's nearly empty. I've never met a woman who had fewer shoes than you do."

178

"Ha!" Elizabeth said triumphantly. "Then you missed my shoe vault in the Town Hall basement when you were planning your dungeon."

"Nuts. I must have. That will put a dent in my plans."

"So you don't want to get up and rearrange my stuff?"

"Oh, I want to rearrange your stuff, all right. Come back here."

Married Life

Monday, September 13

Elizabeth left Kevin sleeping the next morning, took a quick shower, and walked outside and down the stairs to the cafe's back entrance. This door was never locked.

It was a baking day: scones were quick and easy, but there was just enough time to make cinnamon rolls before her first customers arrived. Upton would want one, possibly Jodie, and definitely Kevin. She started the yeast dough rising first. After mixing up the scone dough she added in some dried cranberries and just for fun some crystallized ginger. Into the oven they went.

It was Monday so Darren would want pancakes. French toast for Melissa and Travis. Jack and Sharon would probably order eggs and scones. She made the pancake batter and covered it, checked out the fresh fruit situation—pretty good, she had plenty of oranges, strawberries, and the last of the fresh huckleberries—and carved some oranges into flowers.

Then it was almost time to form the cinnamon rolls. She mixed cinnamon with sugar, made up the glaze for the top, melted some butter, and got the raisins down off the shelf. By the time she had them rolled out and cut the scones were done. She turned down the oven temperature and opened the door for a moment to let out the excess heat before popping the rolls in.

Time to start the coffee. Then she used the press to juice a dozen oranges; Upton and Travis would only drink freshly-squeezed juice, so she didn't bother with any other kind.

Her iPad pinged. It stood on a stand in a corner of the countertop so she could monitor Adie's messages throughout the day. The first one for today was, "How's the beautiful bride this morning? All ready for breakfast?" She told Siri to respond, "Ready. When are you going to let me make *you* breakfast?" Adie responded almost immediately, "As soon as I lose those five pounds," which made Elizabeth laugh, because if Adie lost five pounds she would be invisible when she turned sideways.

At 8:00 she unlocked the front door—which was locked not for security but to keep people from piling in before she was ready—and Upton and Travis were already waiting, as usual.

"You're one minute late," Upton said with mock-seriousness. "I'll chalk it up to getting married yesterday, but don't make a habit of it."

She stood aside to let them in. "Your fancy Swiss watch is one minute fast, but I won't hold it against you. You should get it checked."

Travis went ahead to their usual table but Upton stopped and scanned her up and down. "You're looking remarkably... rested this morning."

She swatted him on the arm. "Go sit down."

Elizabeth brought them coffee and juice. "French toast?" she asked Travis. He nodded. "Strawberries or huckleberries?"

"Straw."

She looked at Upton. "Cinnamon roll?"

"Of course. Some eggs too, please."

"Coming up."

By the time she got the bread soaking in the egg mixture the rolls were done. She put them on a cooling rack and laughed when Upton said theatrically, "*Oh my God*, what just happened in the kitchen?"

The other regulars started straggling in and she took their orders. She glanced at the wall clock. Kevin would be waking up in a few minutes.

Elizabeth didn't mind lunch, but she loved serving breakfast. She adored breakfast foods, and liked seeing people first thing in the morning before their days got hectic or disappointing. While she worked she listened to her neighbors bantering back and forth— mostly Upton, of course—kept an eye on the iPad, and made sure everyone had what they needed, whether they knew it or not. Even if she didn't have to do this for a living, she would still want to do it.

She could hear Kevin close the door to the house as he left to come down. She started his eggs and filled a coffee mug, so by the time he walked in and everyone said, "Good morning, Mr. Mayor," she was nearly ready with his breakfast. She came out with his mug and everyone chimed up again with, "Good morning, *Mrs.* Mayor," which nearly made her drop the coffee laughing. Kevin took his usual place at the bar and she handed him the mug.

"Good morning, indeed," he said quietly. "Sorry I was asleep when you left."

"No reason for you to wake up too."

"I would have liked to kiss you before you went off to work."

"Well, I think I would have liked that, too," she said, grinning.

"You only think? Oh my, that's a steep drop-off. Yesterday you seemed pretty sure."

She smiled again. "Your breakfast will be ready in a minute."

It was less than that. The eggs went on the plate where the cinnamon roll and a bowl of mixed berries were already waiting, and she took it out to him. He looked down at it, then looked back up into her eyes.

"How do you always know exactly what I want for breakfast?"

She raised her eyebrows. "Have you considered the possibility that you decide in a split second that whatever I've given you is what you really want?"

He took a bite of his cinnamon roll while he thought about it. "Nope, I don't believe it. You can rationalize it if you want, but I know it's some kind of magic."

Elizabeth chuckled and stroked his head and went back to her kitchen.

Now that everyone had what they needed, she sat down for a moment and ate her own breakfast, some fruit and the small scone she'd cut and set aside for herself. Kevin had already fallen into the trap that almost everyone else in town, with the possible exception of Adie, had wallowed in for her whole life. She knew what they thought of her, and she didn't mind; it was often useful. Fey; magical; unusual. Well, maybe she *was* unusual, because she *paid attention*. But she didn't believe that magic existed, not the kind of magic they meant.

There was magic in the purr of a sleeping kitten and the lifelong devotion of a dog; in the splendor of a sunrise or the majesty of mountains and deep woods; in the stars and the galaxy flung wildly across the night sky; in a bird flying so far overhead that you couldn't identify it, even though it knew what color your hair was; in love that could bind two people together until they could barely sense the boundary between them; in the goodness that made some people devote their lives and bend their whole minds to helping other people.

183

But there was no magic within *her*; she would have felt it. She had a spark, she had a clear mind and a keen eye, she had a gift for listening to what people wanted—the spoken and the unspoken. But no magic wand. She also had a deep gratitude that she lived in a time and place that did not punish her for performing what frightened, superstitious people would once have called witchcraft.

Elizabeth could hear Kevin finishing up so she got the coffee pot and went back out. He held up his mug and she filled it.

"I guess you have to work today," he said with a sadness that was only partially pretense.

"I guess you do, too."

"I'll be back for lunch."

"And then we'll have the evening."

"Let me take you out tonight."

"Hmm," she said. "How about... the only dinner restaurant in town?"

"Or we could go out of town. Someplace nicer. Quieter."

She leaned in. "That would be a waste of at least an hour round trip. If you can't think of something better to do with an hour, that's a steep drop-off indeed."

He leaned forward to kiss her lightly on the lips. "I apologize. I wasn't thinking clearly due to lack of sleep and consumption of a gigantic cinnamon roll. That's a date, then."

"The old cinnamon roll defense, huh? Scoot."

He waved goodbye to Melissa and Jodie, the only ones left in the cafe, and went out.

"So how's married life treating you?" Jodie said, and cackled.

"Jodie, you sound like a cockeyed hen with sunstroke. No more coffee for you."

"You look happy," Melissa said. "Happier than usual, I mean."

"I feel happy. Like I'm on the first day of a vacation I've always wanted to take."

Melissa smiled and put some money on the counter. "Gotta go. Big clean-up today."

"Oh," Elizabeth said, "I didn't think about that. I'm sorry."

"Don't be. It was a great party. It's more than worth it to see you so happy."

Elizabeth beamed at her. "Thanks."

When she was gone, Jodie tossed a bill on her table and came up to the bar. "You two lovebirds left too early. The party was just getting started."

"We had a prior engagement."

"Was that a pun? Never mind. You should have seen it. Darren and Wanda dancing all night like they were newlyweds themselves. You don't think there's something in the wind there, do you?"

Elizabeth gave it some serious thought. She knew Wanda had been feeling lonely lately, despite her perpetually cheerful exterior. And Darren had never wanted to split up in the first place. Wanda thought her good spirits had chafed on Darren, but Elizabeth knew that wasn't true. Darren had been heartbroken when she told him they needed to split up, and he only left because he wanted what was best for her. In fact, Wanda had always kept him from sinking further into gloom, which his behavior in the last few months had proven. He talked less than he ever had, kept to himself more and more. But Wanda never got a corresponding equalizer from Darren; she didn't need to be subdued the way he needed to be lifted. He corrupted her every happiness, and though she still had warm feelings for

185

him, Elizabeth knew Wanda couldn't bear to go back to trying to smile in the face of misery. Darren probably needed some medication; the last thing Wanda needed was Darren. "No," she answered less than two seconds later. "I don't think there's any chance of that."

* * *

Adie sent a text message as Elizabeth was finishing the breakfast clean-up and about to start lunch prep. "Kevin volunteered to help with the community room clean-up." Adie never used abbreviations when sending texts, or failed to use perfect punctuation.

"Who else?" Elizabeth replied.

"Jeremy, Darren, Melissa."

"Melissa's not a volunteer. You pay her."

"I'm going to come over there and swat your behind."

"I'll start a fresh pot of coffee."

Just as she was ready to reopen for lunch, Adie sent another. "He's coming with his first load of stuff."

Elizabeth went to the cafe window and looked up Little Fish Street. Sure enough, Kevin's dark blue Subaru wagon was rolling slowly down from Town Hall. The cafe, with her home above it, had no garage and therefore no driveway. There had once been a pair of ruts from long, long ago leading up beside the house, but she'd had the landscaper grade them over when she refurbished the cafe. She watched to see what Kevin would do. He ended up turning up Marmot Lane and parking just past the cafe on Marmot. She laughed softly. He wouldn't know about her parking arrangement with Mike, and she didn't see any reason to tell him: it wouldn't make his job any easier.

186

She was waiting when Kevin walked in a moment later. Without any hesitation he moved in for a hug and a great big kiss, and she gave as good as she got.

"You wouldn't believe it," he said when they could breathe again.

"No, I believe it. You've kissed me better than that."

"Ho ho, funny girl. I mean the community room. They completely, utterly trashed it. I think we may have missed the party of the century."

"No, we didn't."

He smiled. "No, you're right. We didn't." He took his seat at the bar. "I can't believe it after that cinnamon roll, but I'm hungry again."

"Would you be wanting lunch then?"

"Tease. Yes, thanks."

She got him some ice water and started on his favorite tofu wrap. "Adie told me you helped with the clean-up," she said through the pass-through.

"I heard a noise in there when I walked by and popped my head in. Darren was standing in the middle of the chaos like a tornado survivor. I couldn't just leave him like that."

"That was very thoughtful." He shrugged. She waited a moment before saying, "I think Darren could use a friend right now."

"Really? Why?"

The screen door slammed open; Upton and Travis walked in. Elizabeth looked Kevin in the eye and he nodded his understanding: *Later.*

"Married one day," Upton said, "and you're already separated."

"Hey, Upton," Kevin replied, "you know that song: 'No matter the distance, you're holding my hand?'"

"Nope."

"Vienna Teng," Travis said.

"Right," Kevin said.

"So what you're saying is, not even light years could separate you."

"Ever heard of quantum entanglement?"

"Nope."

"Spooky action at a distance," Travis said. "Einstein."

Kevin turned to look at Travis straight on. "You are good. You should be on Jeopardy."

"I live in jeopardy every damned day," Travis said, and everyone laughed, including Elizabeth.

Sharon came in with her big dogs and took her usual table. "No Jack?" Upton said.

"He's working on the mail truck," she said. "Jeremy says it's been stalling out, so he's trying to figure out what's wrong. The mail's going to be late today."

Elizabeth took a moment to send a text to let Adie know that. She listened to her neighbors chatter, took their orders, made their food. She could hear them perfectly well back in her kitchen, but the physical separation allowed them to forget she was there, which made the observation all the easier. You could learn so much just from tone of voice and phrasing.

On one trip back to the kitchen she touched Kevin's arm and told him that Owl was watching him. Kevin went over, sat on the floor beside the old dog, and patted her neck. She saw him sneak something into the dog's mouth, probably a piece of his wrap. She had known before that moment, of course, but now she was absolutely certain she had done the right thing.

When the lunch rush was over, she washed her hands and came out of the kitchen. "Do you want some help carrying stuff upstairs?"

"Sure," he said, "if you're not busy."

"I have some time."

"It would help if you had a driveway out back. Or an elevator."

She grinned. "Getting lazy?"

"Nah. Just griping."

The car wasn't packed with any discipline. She knew that when he had first arrived in Marmot, everything he owned was in this car, but since he was just moving it a few hundred yards from one building to another, he hadn't bothered to do it efficiently.

"It looks like you just threw this stuff in here," she said.

"I was hungry."

She took a laptop shoulder bag and a small suitcase. He grabbed a sturdy wooden box that looked like an orange crate, and they walked around the building and up the stairs. They dumped their loads in the living room. It took only one more trip to get it all.

"I'll sort this all out tonight," he said. "I just have one more load. Should I bring it right away or wait until tonight?"

"Leave it for tonight," she said.

"Okay." She could see that he wanted to ask her why, but she knew he wouldn't. One of the things that she loved about Kevin was that he was willing to let mysteries be until the time was right to reveal them. And she *would* do that, eventually, but she was thirty-five years old, and he was forty-one. They had both been living alone, with sharp boundaries around their lives, for a long time, and she didn't think it would be good for them to give up all their privacy and secrets at once.

"So, fancy dinner at Jodie's place tonight," Kevin said cheerfully. "I'll be back around six."

"I'll be waiting," Elizabeth said, and smiled provocatively. "We should have enough time for an appetizer before dinner."

"Then I'll be back at 5:45."

"Go on, get back to work, or Adie will fire you."

"Can she fire me? I was elected."

"She can *unelect* you, my dear. You'd be out on the street before you could pull up your socks, and I'd be the sad, humiliated wife of the ex-Mayor."

"Well, I wouldn't do that to you." He reached down and tugged up his socks, one and then the other. "Well, little missy, I'll just be moseying on."

She laughed and followed him down the stairs.

Counsel

Elizabeth had plenty of time before her 4:00 appointment arrived to clean up from lunch. Mike sent her an email when the woman pulled into his small parking lot. Their arrangement was that Mike let her clients use his driveway, since she had none. More often than not, they would wander into his shop after they were done, or beforehand if they arrived early, and he would get a new customer.

The client was nearly fifteen minutes late, but Elizabeth expected that with new people. Even with clear directions they underestimated the time it would take them to get to Marmot—or just plain got lost—and most people weren't that punctual to begin with.

Someone knocked lightly on the cafe door. Elizabeth didn't like to shout that the door was open—it made people even more nervous, which was not helpful—so she went to the screen door and opened it. The woman was around fifty, average height and slightly overweight, with undyed brown hair that was going grey. She wore old blue jeans that were on the verge of fraying, and a faded yellow shirt. They had never met before, which was typical for new clients. The arrangements had been made by letter, since Elizabeth had no phone and, like most people in Marmot, no Internet connection.

"You must be Darla," Elizabeth said.

"Elizabeth?"

"Yes. Please come in." She stood aside to let Darla in, then led her to the table in the kitchen. "Would you like anything to drink? Coffee, tea, water?"

"Some ice water would be nice. Thanks."

191

Darla sat and looked around while Elizabeth got them each a glass of water. "It smells good in here," she said.

"Thanks. I baked this morning. Here you go."

Darla sipped her water and looked at Elizabeth, who studied her in turn. She didn't seem nervous at all; actually, she was clearly one of the calm ones. Elizabeth had made a provisional judgment about education and intelligence from the writing in her letter, but she revised both upward. And there was something confident about the way she'd chosen to dress. Elizabeth didn't believe these were her best clothes, or even second best. It was as if she'd been gardening and suddenly realized it was time to go, but more likely she was making a statement, something like, "I'm not intimidated and I'm not in an inferior social position, so I don't need to dress up."

Elizabeth waited her out. It was not her style to draw people out, and it was usually helpful to let the client make the first move.

"How does this work?" Darla said finally. "Tarot cards, palm reading, or what?"

"Nothing like that. You wrote that Tanya recommended me."

"Yes."

"She didn't explain what I do?"

"She was... enigmatic."

Elizabeth smiled. "It's not a mystery. We talk, and I make some suggestions."

"And that's worth what you're asking per hour?"

"If it's not, you don't pay."

"Fair enough." Darla took another sip of water. "Where should I start?"

"Why did you ask Tanya about me?"

"She's been different lately. Calmer. Happier. It was hard to put my finger on it, but when I asked her she told me about the Witch of the Woods."

Elizabeth frowned. "She called me that?"

"Oh shit, I'm sorry." She didn't look sorry. "No, she didn't, but that's how I thought of you when she was done."

Elizabeth studied Darla's face again and came to a conclusion. She had been about to scratch Tanya off her mental client list, but now she realized that it wasn't Tanya's fault: the next thing Tanya needed was some different friends. She would find a way to tell her the next time she came back, if she did come back. Meanwhile she had to deal with this obnoxious woman, who was clearly one of the Bounds Testers. She considered just ending the interview immediately, but decided to give it a shot first.

"All right. How can I help you?"

"I don't know if you can. There's something wrong with my husband."

Elizabeth studied her expression and posture. Darla was struggling to hold back a smirk; she thought Elizabeth was a fraud. She didn't seem distraught, so it wasn't her husband's health she was worried about. And there was no trace of the despair, greed, or hope Elizabeth might have expected to see if what Darla *really* wanted was for her husband to die. She glanced at Darla's left hand: she wore a double band, and the wedding ring had a fairly large emerald-cut stone. It looked like it would not come off easily, so it was unlikely there was infidelity on Darla's side.

Job troubles? Money? Probably not with a ring like that, although it was possible that they'd been prosperous but fallen on hard times. Yet if that were so, Elizabeth would have expected Darla to dress *up* out of compensation, not down.

193

Was he having an affair? Darla didn't seem at all anxious. It was clear that she didn't expect Elizabeth to help her, and that wouldn't be a disaster; they'd just muddle on through. So: it wasn't her husband that was the problem.

"He's been acting more distant lately," Elizabeth said. Darla jerked in surprise. Elizabeth studied her face: traces of guilt. "You thought he might be having an affair, but you checked his bills and... his phone and his computer. There was nothing incriminating. It's not his work... no, that's going fine. But he doesn't talk about it anymore. He hardly talks at all anymore."

"You got this from Tanya," Darla said accusingly.

"No, I didn't."

"You checked my Facebook page."

"No."

"You *are* the Witch of the Woods, aren't you?"

"No," Elizabeth said, suddenly weary of this conversation. "I just pay attention. You don't have any kids, do you?"

"No, neither of us wanted kids."

"How do you spend your days?"

"What do you mean? I have friends, I have my dogs, I have a garden..."

Elizabeth studied her face for a moment. "Where did you go to school?"

"University of Chicago. Why?"

"What did you study?"

"Business and economics."

"Master's degree?"

"How the hell did you know that?"

Darla wouldn't have believed her even if Elizabeth could have explained. PhDs had a look and a feel to them; people with merely undergraduate degrees had another, and high school graduates were also different. And then there were the people with master's degrees.

"I can explain what's wrong with your husband. Are you sure you want to hear it?"

Darla stood up so suddenly that she knocked her chair over. She took two quick steps toward the door, then stopped. She turned around, contemplated Elizabeth, then righted her chair and sat down again.

"Nothing you say can hurt me," Darla said.

"I don't want to hurt you. I'm not a witch, Darla, I don't cast spells."

"Go ahead then." She crossed her arms over her chest.

"Your husband," Elizabeth said, "is confused and hurt because you've been getting increasingly bitter. The reason for your bitterness is that you feel useless. You have a good education, and you had great plans for using it, but once you got married and moved out here there was no opportunity to do that. You need to find an outlet, Darla. Start an online business. Or open a shop, something to do with gardening. Or form a charity, perhaps to rescue and find homes for dogs. A good way to start would be to work someplace that interests you first, so you could learn how they manage their business and, I'm sure, find ways they could be doing it better. If you can improve an existing organization, so much the better, but if not then start your own so you can do it your way." She took a sip of her water. "Then you'll be more fulfilled, your attitude will improve, and your husband will stop feeling like he's walking barefoot in a cactus field. And life will be good again."

Darla stared at her for over a minute. Then she reached into her pocket, pulled out some money, and carefully counted a stack of twenties onto the table. She left without a word.

Elizabeth put the money in the cash register and locked the front door. She leaned against it and sighed.

A moment later her iPad pinged with a message from Adie: "Bad one?"

She wrote back, "Yes. But another $100 in the pipeline." Go, Marmot.

Fall Rains

"Why did you say that Darren needs a friend?" Kevin asked when they were getting dressed for dinner after finally rolling out of bed.

Elizabeth explained that Darren and Wanda had been seen dancing quite a lot after they'd left the reception, but that she didn't think there was any chance they would get back together.

"I saw him a couple times today. He seemed in a pretty good mood."

"That was probably hope. Hope that will be dashed."

"Well, I'll try to get to know him better. Hey, your shirt is buttoned wrong."

She smiled and let him fix it for her. Then he seemed to change his mind and started unbuttoning it again, but she slapped him away playfully, saying, "Hey, I'm hungry."

"I would think so. You must have burned up a thousand calories just now."

They came out of the bedroom. Kevin surveyed his pile of boxes and bags in the living room. "I guess I'll sort that out after dinner."

"Take a jacket," she said, "It'll be cool out there."

It was getting dark, and she was right, it was already cool. They walked down Marmot Lane holding hands.

"Our hands fit together perfectly," Kevin said. "Have you noticed?"

"I noticed it the first time you took my hand."

"It's weird, because mine are about twice as big as yours."

She laughed. "Your hand is one octave above mine. That's why they fit."

"What are you saying, our hands are in harmony?"

They came around the last bend. The bar's lights illuminated the wide circle of road that was the cul-de-sac. Jodie's bar was the only surviving house on this stretch of Marmot Lane. Behind the building the trees loomed, standing out against the darkening sky like halted giants lost in thought.

Kevin held the door open for her and the smells of bar food and yeast washed over them.

"Hey, it's the Mayors," Pete called out. *He's trying to keep it light,* Elizabeth thought. *But he's hurting.*

"Actually it's the Mayor and the Cook," she replied. "I didn't change my name."

"Elizabeth Cook," Upton said from his table. "It has a nice rhythm to it."

"That's because it's iambic." *Well, almost.*

"No, it's cherubic," Pete said.

"Do I really look like a cherub to you?" Elizabeth demanded. Being called a fairy child was one thing, and sometimes useful, but she would not stand for being treated like an angel. She wanted to be fully human and nothing more or less, especially to Kevin.

There was a moment of silence. Finally Upton said, "I detect a distinct lack of wings," and everyone started breathing again.

Kevin led her to a four-top table in the corner. He held out a chair for her that would have put her back to the room, but she took the one next to it so she could watch the action, if you could call it that. Upton and Travis were at another table, Mike, Pete, and Darren were at the bar, and that was it.

Jodie came out of the back room with plates for Upton and Travis, then came to their table, smiling as if it had been her own wedding yesterday.

"Welcome!" she said. "I didn't expect to see you in here tonight. What can I get you to drink?"

"Dark and draught," Kevin said.

"Cabernet," Elizabeth said.

"Got it. Listen, I know you must be getting sick of the veggie burger thing. I can do something a little bit special for you, if you're interested."

Kevin looked at Elizabeth and nodded. "That would be lovely," she said, "thanks."

"So," Kevin said when Jodie was gone, "how was work today?"

"You were there for half of it. Gobbling, if I recall."

"I don't gobble. I occasionally guzzle."

"Oh, I'm sorry. I'll try to be more precise in the future. How was your day?"

"Tiring. It took us all morning to put the community room back to rights. When I got back from lunch Jeremy was sorting the mail, so I helped with that. And Darren mentioned he was planning to work on the cemetery this afternoon, so I pitched in there too. I didn't know that being Mayor would be so strenuous."

"The bigger the town, I think, the less work you have to do."

"Ha! If that's true, the Mayor of New York City must just lie around on a couch all day with gangs of beautiful women feeding him little morsels."

"Actually, I think I just read something about that in *Time* magazine." He rested his chin on his fist and looked at her intently. She was amused and tried not to show it, but she let it go on for several minutes before saying, "What?"

"I love you," he said.

"I think we've established that. But I don't mind if you say it every now and then, say every five minutes or so. By the way, I love you too."

"I know. That's the weird bit."

"What, you think you're unlovable?"

"No, I'm pretty sure I'm a lovable kind of guy. Can't you see this twinkle in my eye? But stumbling on this place, finding you, and getting married to you—it still seems like a dream that I'm going to wake up from."

"Maybe it's a dream that you woke up *to.*"

"Yes, I think so."

Jodie came with their food. It was fettuccine with roasted vegetables in a pesto sauce, with small salads and garlic bread on the side, and it all smelled incredible. They thanked her and dug in. When they were finished, Jodie came back to take their plates.

"I think you should put that on the menu," Elizabeth said. "It was very good."

"I agree," Kevin said. "I'd order that again in a minute." Jodie looked at him with her head cocked. "Not this minute, you understand."

They paid their tab and said goodnight to everyone. It was full night now, but the setting Moon, half full, hadn't quite vanished behind the hills yet, so they could pick their way back home. She could have done it with her eyes closed, but Kevin always seemed rather tentative walking at night, as if he needed to see where he was going. The small sounds of the trees and the night insects would have been enough for Elizabeth to stay in the center of the road, but she let him lead her anyway.

When they got back Kevin looked at the pile of his stuff, then looked at her.

"It can wait," she said, and took his hand to lead him to bed.

* * *

Kevin didn't manage to organize his stuff the next day, either. But on Wednesday the fall rains started and he came home from work determined to get his bags and boxes out of the living room. Elizabeth let him work it out, while she sat on the sofa and made a shopping list. Mike was doing a Costco run to Portland tomorrow, for himself and some client articles, and he always broadcast a notice so people could add on to his list.

Friday after breakfast Elizabeth walked over to Mike's shop with some cloth grocery bags to pick up her items and pay him.

"How's it going?" he said. "You've been married nearly a week. If you keep getting more happy and beautiful like this, the sun will refuse to come up in the morning."

She slapped him lightly on the arm. "It's going great. Kevin finally unpacked on Wednesday."

"I'm surprised you didn't move in with him to the Mayor's apartment. It's bigger than your place."

"You're right," she said. "But then I'd have to redecorate it, and it's a long walk to get to the cafe in the morning."

He grinned and took her money.

* * *

On Sunday, their one-week anniversary, the rain had stopped, so Elizabeth took Kevin back to Sleeping Beauty. She didn't tell him where they were going, since they had a little tradition to uphold, but he figured it out as soon as they saw the first sign to the trailhead, and grinned to himself for the rest of the drive.

The trail was a little muddy in places, but no trees had fallen yet. By spring the trail would be impassable and a Forest Service crew would have to come out with chainsaws, pickaxes, and shovels to repair the annual winter damage. It was twenty degrees cooler than the last time they'd come up here, exactly two weeks ago, when Kevin had proposed to her. When she thought of that, she had to stifle a smile so he wouldn't tease her about it all the way to the top.

They came out of the woods into the scree-lined open section. When they passed the stunted ruins of the old fire lookout, Kevin looked up and gasped.

Only two weeks ago the peak of Mt. Adams had been mostly bluish-grey, with tendrils of glacier running down the slopes. Today, after only four days of rain in the lower elevations—snow up there—the whole immense peak, from the craggy summit to way down below the tree line, was pristine white and dazzling in the patchy sunlight. It looked like the world's biggest Dairy Queen cone.

"How?" Kevin said.

"Nature is a goddess," Elizabeth replied.

He put his arm around her and they stood for a long while, entranced by majestic beauty.

Intervention

Tuesday, September 21

Elizabeth had another client Monday afternoon, but Tuesday was open, and it was long past the time she would ordinarily have gone to see Ernie. She thought she might be forgiven for delaying it until after her wedding, and if not then to hell with everyone.

No, she didn't mean that. It had been a tough morning. Everyone was cranky because of the shift in the seasons; it took a little while to get used to the idea that the beautiful, dry summer was over, and poor Kevin hadn't known what to make of his new neighbors turning into snarling wolverines in front of his eyes. In a week or so people would settle down and be back to their usual selves.

She took an umbrella, but she barely needed it; the rain was just a drizzle. Bev and Ernie lived in the first house on the left past Mike's shop, so it took less than two minutes to walk there from the cafe. It was a nice little grey cedar-shingled cottage. They had once had the nicest gardens in town, but over the last few years they'd found it increasingly difficult to keep up with the maintenance, so they hired Darren to manage it for them. Darren was a talented wood carver and a hard worker, but gardening was not his gift, so the beds were neat but had somehow lost their exceptional beauty and were now merely nice. There were still a few late blooms on some of the coreopsis, but clearly it was nearly time for the fall clean-up and deadheading.

Elizabeth walked up the paved path to the deep red front door and knocked briskly. She knew Ernie would never answer it, and Bev was getting a little deaf.

Bev came to the door looking a bit testy, but when she saw Elizabeth she relaxed and said, "Oh, thank God." She was in her mid-seventies, thin and still straight but her hair, pulled back into a messy bun, was completely white and her face was heavily lined.

"Bad day?"

"The worst I can remember. You're just in time. I think he was about to implode."

"Where is he?"

"Where is he usually?"

Elizabeth nodded and walked into the back of the house. What had once been a first-floor child's bedroom had been turned into a TV room for Ernie, where some days he spent all of the time he wasn't in the cafe or the bar. She paused outside and listened: there were people talking on the TV, but their voices were too indistinct for her to follow the conversation. Unlike Bev, Ernie's hearing was still excellent, and he liked the TV turned low so he could talk over it. Which he was doing now.

"Oh, bullshit! What do you know about anything, you merciless hag? You too, you bombastic flitterhead. Get out into the world and learn something, why don't you?"

There was no point knocking; he would just ignore her. Elizabeth opened the door and stepped inside.

The room was dim and sparsely furnished, just a flat screen TV on the wall, a battered old sofa, a sagging matching easy chair, and an end table between them. Ernie looked up from the sofa and muttered quietly, "Oh shit." She was fairly certain he thought she hadn't heard him. He pointed the remote at the TV and turned it off, then continued staring at it as if it were still on.

He wouldn't look at her again. That was okay. Elizabeth sat down in the chair and watched the blank screen for a moment. She could feel the springs in the seat but she stayed perfectly still, not shifting or fidgeting. She closed her eyes and breathed calmly. The room was a little musty; it probably hadn't been aired out all summer. Her nose was trying to identify the other scents in the room and she steered her thoughts away, imagining herself sitting on a high, windy ledge looking out at Mt. Adams.

The sofa creaked slightly. Elizabeth brought her attention back to the room, but kept her eyes closed, listening. Several more minutes passed. Then Ernie said, "I haven't heard from Thomas in two years."

Elizabeth opened her eyes and looked at him. "Your eldest?" He nodded. "He's in upstate New York somewhere, isn't he?"

"Central. Ithaca."

"Cornell?"

"Yep. Teaches geology. Can you believe that? He spent his whole childhood pitching rocks at his sisters and he ends up teaching rocks to rich peoples' kids."

"As I recall, he never actually hit anyone."

Ernie chuckled. "Yeah. I could never figure out if he was a good kid with a good arm, or a bad kid with a bad arm."

"I think he was a good kid," Elizabeth said.

"Maybe. Hard to remember now."

She knew better. He didn't say anything else and she waited him out.

"I think," he said finally, "that Bev is tired of me."

She thought for a long moment before saying, "Do you think that people are what they do?"

"What do you mean?"

"Well. Say you were an architect. Would an architect be *all* that you were?"

He gave it some thought. "Not unless I did it every waking hour. Probably I'd have a wife and kids, so I'd be a husband and a father too."

"You might go bowling now and then."

He snorted. "Architects don't go bowling. Golf."

"Okay, so you're also a golfer. Probably pretty good at it. Maybe you're a religious man."

"Not a Catholic. No offense."

"Methodist."

"Sure, maybe."

She waited for a minute to let all of this sink in. "Then one day you decide that golf is taking too much time away from your family. It's good for networking, but you're successful now and you've got all the business you can handle. And your kids are going to college soon; golf is expensive. So you give it up."

"Okay."

"And the minister has started preaching fire and brimstone on Sundays."

"Like one of those Trout Lake Baptists, huh?"

"So you try out the Unitarian church and discover that you really like it."

"That's a long shot, but okay."

"And ten years later your kids are out of college, you've maxed out your IRA, and your wife wants to travel. So you sell your share in the partnership and go on a cruise. In the line at the chocolate bar someone asks what you do." She turned to look at him. "You were a working architect, a Methodist family man who played golf. Now you're a retired Unitarian empty nester on a cruise."

"Yeah, so?"

"Ernie, are you still the same person?"

He did her the courtesy of thinking about it. "Yeah, I guess so."

"Bev isn't tired of you. She's tired of what you're doing."

"I'm not doing anything." She didn't speak, she just kept looking at him. "Oh," he finally said. She still kept silent. It was several minutes before he said, "I'm a retired businessman. I don't know how to do anything."

Elizabeth shifted in her seat. The springs really were a kind of torture device. She said, "You know that Adie is writing a history of the town, right?"

He started to get agitated, then remembered who he was talking to.

"Perhaps," she said, "it would be a good thing to have more than one point of view."

"What, you mean write my own history?"

"Why not?"

"I don't know how to write."

"You could learn by writing letters."

He scoffed. "To who?" She didn't say anything. She could see him mulling it over.

"I'd bet all four of them would be delighted to get a letter from you. No one seems to write letters anymore. It would be a novelty."

"They probably wouldn't know what it was. Think it was junk mail and recycle it."

"Not if you put a return address on it, silly."

The wheels were turning now. She saw his hands twitch.

"Not very good with a pen anymore. Arthritis."

"Computers are cheap. You wouldn't need a fancy rig. Mike could get you one."

"I haven't typed anything in twenty years."

"When was the last time you rode a bicycle?" she said.

"Longer than that. But I get your point."

She stood up. "You know who else might like to get a letter from you?"

He looked up at her suspiciously. "Who?"

"Bev," she whispered. She walked to the door and turned back to look at him. "See you in the cafe tomorrow morning."

He tried not to look surprised, but it was a moment before he could make himself speak. "I'll want a cinnamon roll."

"Of course."

Elizabeth walked out of the room and paused in the hallway. Bev stood by the front door, clasping her hands, watching her. Elizabeth waited for several minutes just outside the TV room. The TV didn't go back on. She walked up to Bev and touched her arm. Bev pulled her into a hug and whispered a thank you.

It was almost time for Kevin to get home from work.

Extended Family

Ernie showed up at the cafe the next morning just as he had for twenty years. Surprise was evident on everyone's faces, including Jodie's, but no one said anything. Elizabeth couldn't remember the last time something of this import had happened in town and it wasn't immediately broadcast all over the network. Neither Bev nor Ernie had said anything to *anyone*, apparently, which she could understand in Ernie's case, but it was unusual for Bev.

She had made a fresh batch of cinnamon rolls especially for the occasion, and everyone was ordering them. She set one aside for Kevin, who came in a bit later than usual at 8:45. He took his customary seat and smiled at her as if it had been six months instead of three hours since he'd seen her. Of course his eyes had been only half-open three hours ago. Elizabeth brought him coffee and shortly afterwards his roll, potatoes, and fruit.

Elizabeth could tell when she set the plate down that he'd noticed Ernie sitting with Jodie at their usual table by the window. Kevin raised an eyebrow and she tilted her head and smiled. He shrugged and dug into his food.

Ernie was trying not to show it, but he was clearly in a better mood than he'd enjoyed for a long time. Every now and then, as he and Jodie talked and griped over their breakfasts, Ernie would take a small notebook out of his pocket and jot something down.

When Kevin was done, after coming into the back to kiss her goodbye, he made a point of saying good morning to Ernie. Ernie grumbled something surly in reply, most likely just out of habit, but that didn't lessen the glow she felt at Kevin's gesture.

During the morning clean-up Adie sent her a text message: "Dinner tomorrow night?" Elizabeth sent back, "Yes, thanks." She was certain that Kevin would have reservations about socializing with Adie, but he wouldn't refuse.

Kevin was busy with Adie all day—he might even have been in her office when she sent the message about dinner, which would be just like her—so he didn't come to the cafe for lunch. She had no clients that day, but she didn't see him again until he came home from work.

Elizabeth heard him stomping up the back stairs to their home around 5:30. He liked to make more noise than necessary on the stairs; she knew for a fact that he was perfectly capable of walking up them without making any sound at all, but he'd given as various excuses that he didn't want to startle her, that he wanted to give her time to make herself presentable, and to give her time to hop into bed if she was so inclined.

He opened the door into the kitchen. She said, "Hail the galumphing Mayor!"

"Hail yourself," he said, and came over to where she was sitting at the bistro table, reading a magazine, to give her a kiss. He hoisted himself up on the opposite chair.

"How's the government?" she said.

"Crumbling, just as it should be. Adie kept me busy all day with plans for the Christmas parade. It's three months away!"

"Not quite. It's always on the Sunday closest to St. Nicholas day, December 6. That's the fifth this year."

"Okay. Two and a half months."

She smiled. He liked to gripe about it, but she had determined early on that he liked his new job and didn't mind working with Adie. Although she thought that perhaps Adie still scared him a little, or maybe just intimidated him. She *was* pretty smart.

"I guess you've forgiven Ernie," Kevin said. "He looked happier than I've ever seen him this morning. Still full of vinegar, but happier."

"I think he's worked out some issues that were bothering him."

"Like what?"

She just smiled again. He knew by now that she wouldn't gossip, but he kept trying— just for the sport of it, as far as she could tell. Kevin contemplated her for a moment with a hint of a grin on his face. Then he stood up and said, "Any requests for dinner?"

* * *

They were finished eating and not really excited about getting up to deal with the mess Kevin had made in the kitchen. Elizabeth said, "Adie's invited us to dinner tomorrow night."

"Really? Both of us?"

"Very funny. I used to go at least once a month, but it's been a while. I think she was giving us time to settle in before she put that burden on you."

"I don't really think she's that bad, you know."

"No, but you *are* still uncomfortable around her." He looked hesitant; he was almost certainly remembering what had happened when Ernie bad-mouthed Adie in the cafe. "Go ahead and say it."

"I can't escape the feeling... I'm not sure how to put it in words. She's... manipulative." He looked at her as if waiting for a blow.

"You're right, she can be." He looked a little surprised, and much relieved. "She had to be to do what was necessary, and once you develop those habits they're very hard to break. But she's not a bad person, and I think she likes you."

"Really?" he said. "I have to admit, she's never actually said anything harsh. She's been very patient teaching me how to be Mayor. Even if the job could really be done by a store mannequin with a microphone inside."

"You should suggest that at dinner tomorrow. Maybe you can run against one in the next election."

* * *

Kevin had only been in Adie's house once before—to get her wedding ring—but by now he knew all the houses in the town. They arrived just after 7:30 and before she could warn him Kevin knocked on the door. Elizabeth hid a smile; she knew what was coming.

After a moment Adie yanked open the door and glowered at him. "What's wrong with you, you blockhead? You're family now. You don't knock on the door, you just walk in. And you," she glared at Elizabeth, "I thought you'd have him better trained by now."

"We've been married eleven days, Adie," she said, laughing, as they walked in. "You can't train a *dog* in eleven days, let alone a husband."

"Ork ork," Kevin said, imitating a seal.

Adie examined him as if he were a bug on a leaf. "I have some anchovies if you need a snack."

She led them straight back to the kitchen. It was a lot like Elizabeth's mother's kitchen had been, the one she grew up in. The cupboards and counter space were completely inadequate; a third of the counter was taken up by an ancient microwave oven. The floor and the countertops were both worn linoleum. The refrigerator and range were old and chipped. But it had a battered, round, wooden table in it big enough to seat eight people, with matching spindle-back chairs that must have been repaired dozens of times. Shabby without the chic, it was like a second home to Elizabeth, and its mere existence had given her the courage to turn her own kitchen into something more suitable to her needs—trading a gathering space for ease of cooking and preparation.

Jeremy and Helen were already sitting at the table, with Mechelle, who was nine, in the chair back in the corner of the room, writing in a notebook. The adults said their hellos, then Elizabeth sat down next to her god-niece. She wasn't related to Mechelle even in law; Jeremy and Helen weren't married, Mechelle wasn't Jeremy's daughter, and Jeremy— Adie's nephew—wasn't related to Elizabeth either. But it felt a like a family anyway.

"What are you working on?"

"English homework," Mechelle said without looking up. "I have to write a story about an animal."

"What animal did you pick to write about?"

"Jungle cats. They're the great-great-grandfathers of house cats."

"How are you coming along?" her mother asked.

"Almost done."

"Good," Elizabeth said, "because I want you to meet my new husband."

Mechelle's hair was not straightened, it stood up in a fairly thick fuzzy halo around her head. So she was able to look up *through* it at Kevin. Then she moved her eyes but not her head to glance at Elizabeth.

"I think I met him. At the wedding."

"Well," her mother said, "it might be more correct to say that you've *seen* him. Were you introduced?"

"No," she said hesitantly.

"Did you introduce yourself?"

"No."

Kevin interjected lightly, "I can wait. She has important work to do."

This time Mechelle did tilt her head to look at him. "Thank you." She turned back to her notebook.

Helen smiled at Kevin and gestured at the empty chair next to her. "How's the new job working out?"

"No one's circulating a petition to have me removed," he said as he sat down, "and I haven't noticed any mobs with torches and pitchforks, so I think it's going okay. How's the new school year starting out?"

"Easy as pie. All five kids were with me last year, so everyone knows what to expect. I wish I had more students, but given the size of this little hamlet I can't complain."

"Sure you could," Adie said from where she was working at the stove. "What we like about you is that you *don't.*"

"Kevin," Helen said, "I've been meaning to ask if you would mind coming in to talk to my students about your career in journalism."

"I'd be happy to. Should I wear my Mayor's hat, or come like a normal person?"

"From what I've seen," Jeremy said with mock seriousness, "neither one of those is possible." Elizabeth laughed and leaned back in her chair. She had been pretty sure the evening would go well, but now she was positive.

* * *

Dinner was a complicated Mexican casserole, a little spicy and very flavorful, with salsa-infused rice and a small salad on the side. Adie had made it for her before, of course; she was long past being interested in new recipes. Elizabeth could think of three ways to improve the casserole, two to fix the rice, and thought that the salad dressing recipe should simply be thrown out. But she kept it to herself. It was good enough, and everyone enjoyed it, including her.

Kevin and Jeremy discovered that they both liked the Seattle Seahawks, and they agreed to watch some games together in Jodie's bar. Kevin was a little surprised to find that several people in town got TV by satellite—including Mike and Upton of course— then admitted to feeling foolish about being surprised. Later it turned out that he knew Helen's favorite neighborhood Italian restaurant in L.A. from a business trip he'd taken years ago. When he and Mechelle were finally formally introduced, he asked if he could read her jungle cat story, and praised it sincerely but not too lavishly—just right.

Adie didn't say much throughout the evening, she just sat back and watched the flow of conversation. Elizabeth knew that mood: Adie was feeling alienated, lonely, superior, sad, and tender all at the same time. She didn't try to jostle her out of it. It was a funk that she fell into periodically, and she'd come out of it on her own.

Helen and Mechelle left first; tomorrow was a school day. Kevin shook the girl's hand and said it was a pleasure to meet her, and Mechelle replied gravely that she would like to show him some of her other stories if he wouldn't mind, to which he gladly assented.

"You have a knack with kids," Jeremy said when they'd settled in the small living room.

"Peter Pan Syndrome," Kevin said.

"I doubt that," Adie remarked dryly, the first time she'd spoken in a while.

"Do you have a lot of experience with children?" Jeremy asked.

"No, just a sister one year younger. But it's easy for me to remember what it was like to be young. I think a lot of people forget. If you can remember what it's like to be that age, it's easier to identify with the kid's point of view."

"Empathy," Adie said.

Kevin nodded. Elizabeth had an inkling of where the conversation was about to go, and she didn't really want to talk about children right now. So she stood up and grabbed Kevin's hand.

"Time to go home," she said.

"Adie, thanks for dinner," Kevin said. "It was delicious. Jeremy, I'll see you for the next Seahawks game at Jodie's."

Both of the other two nodded and stood up to follow them out. Elizabeth hugged Adie at the front door.

"Good night," Elizabeth whispered.

"Yes, in both senses. See you soon."

It was chilly but not raining as they walked the short block back home. "You did well," she told Kevin. "It was easier than I thought it would be. Adie was quiet, though." "She gets like that sometimes." "Helen and Mechelle are nice. Is it serious between Jeremy and her?" "Not yet, but I think it's about to get that way." "I'd like to get serious with you." "Oh you would, would you? I thought we were pretty serious already." "Nah," Kevin said. "Just getting started."

Conjugal Sprite

Tuesday, October 5

Early in October Wanda lingered after lunch to ask for an appointment. Elizabeth was booked that afternoon, but they settled on the next day.

Wanda came to the back door of the cafe kitchen, as the locals usually did, and let herself in. Elizabeth had been passing the time neatening up her supply shelves, but she got Wanda some coffee and they sat at the little table in the kitchen.

"Twenty questions?" Wanda said.

"Darren?"

"Ha! You got it in one, as usual. I suppose you noticed what was going on at your wedding reception."

"I'm not sure I saw it all, but—"

"What!" Wanda said in mock outrage. "You were distracted from your true calling by a little thing like cutting your wedding cake?"

They laughed together. "I suppose he took all that as a sign that you wanted to be close again?" Elizabeth remembered the way they had been whispering together throughout the day, and shared more dances than some people might think appropriate for a divorced couple.

"I was feeling lonely. I shouldn't have done it, I guess. It was... maybe cruel, in the end."

"Are you asking *how* to redirect his interest, or whether you *should*?"

Wanda was quiet for a moment. Then she said, "I don't know."

Elizabeth waited for the obvious answer to occur to her, but Wanda didn't say anything else. "This is the easiest problem you've ever given me, Wanda. I'm not sure I would even call it a problem. When you and Darren were married, he was slightly less miserable—by transferring it to you in triplicate. No one should have to carry that burden. You just aren't suited for each other."

"I know. But I like him."

"Everybody likes him."

"Except Ernie."

"Sorry," Elizabeth said, laughing, "that goes without saying."

"Okay, I know you're right, but that doesn't solve my problem or Darren's."

"True. To be honest, I'm not sure there is a solution to Darren's problem that doesn't involve medication. If the most cheerful person I ever met can't budge him out of his self-imposed gloom, I don't think anyone can. But his problem is not your problem anymore. And it's not the solution to your problem, either. Do you *want* to divorce him twice?"

Wanda laughed. "No, once was plenty. So what should I do? Maybe it's time for me to move someplace where the dating pool is a little deeper."

"I don't think that's necessary."

That stopped her. Elizabeth gave her credit for taking the time to think about it, but she could see that Wanda hadn't made the connection.

"On the way here you passed someone nice who is also lonely, and who might be a good fit."

Wanda laughed and said, "I know you aren't talking about Ernie. Upton and Travis are spoken for. You can't mean Mike?"

218

"Why not?"

"Because he's in love with *you*. Everyone knows that."

"Everyone is mistaken. Mike is not in love with me, he's just infatuated. He's not the one for me, and if he didn't know that before, he does since my wedding."

Wanda chewed on that for a while. "Okay, but he has a daughter."

"So?"

"So, is there a wife?"

"No, he's never been married."

"Then how does he have a daughter?" Wanda said. Elizabeth didn't respond. "You know, right?"

"Yes, I do know, but it's not my story to tell. You should ask him… eventually."

Wanda thought about it. Elizabeth watched her transition from surprised skepticism to serious consideration to provisional acceptance.

"Maybe," Wanda said at last. "He does seem like a nice guy."

"He is a nice guy."

"I've always thought he was good-looking." Elizabeth didn't take the bait. "He's older than me, though. How old is he?"

"Forty-five."

"Jeepers. Thirteen years. You don't think that will be a problem?"

"Not for another thirty years or so, no."

Wanda laughed. "Any suggestions for how?"

Elizabeth was ready for that. "Paint him a picture."

"What kind of picture?"

"You're the artist. Think about what he might like." She could see the wheels turning in Wanda's head. It was a challenge, the kind that she enjoyed, and the process of creating the painting would cause her to explore her own feelings. She'd known Mike ever since he came to town over a decade ago. Elizabeth was confident that she knew him well enough to make something that would please him.

"Doesn't solve the Darren problem," Wanda said at last.

"The Darren problem isn't really *your* problem, except to tell him gently that the two of you are *not* getting back together."

"Yeah, I can do that. It should be a lot easier than telling him we're not going to be married anymore." She lapsed into thought again, and Elizabeth gave her time. "Okay. Good session. Thanks." She laid a bill on the table and they both stood up for a hug.

"I'll be interested to see what you do for Mike," Elizabeth said.

"Yeah, it'll probably be all over town before you know it."

"It's a small town."

"It promises to be a juicy story. Thanks, Elizabeth."

"You're welcome. See you soon."

* * *

A few days later Elizabeth was in the cafe kitchen figuring out her Costco order for Mike's next trip to Portland when she heard a quiet knock at the back door. If it had been a windy day the sound would have been inaudible. She got up from the table, walked to the door, and opened it. Adhira, the eldest of the Chadha's two children, was standing outside looking embarrassed.

"Adhira," Elizabeth said, "come in. Is school out already?"

220

"Just now," the girl said. She had a sweet round face, eyes so dark they were nearly black, and beautiful caffè latte skin.

Elizabeth got her a glass of milk and an oatmeal chocolate chip cookie and Adhira thanked her. They sat down at the little table together.

"How's school going this year?"

"It's pretty easy," Adhira said. "I thought third grade would be harder, but it's not. It's interesting."

"That's good." Elizabeth waited while Adhira ate her cookie, meticulously nibbling at it without dropping any crumbs. When the girl had finished it and pushed her half-empty glass of milk away, she still waited. Adhira didn't seem inclined to start the conversation, so Elizabeth said, "Your mother told me your name means *Moon*. It's pretty."

"Thanks. My brother's name is Anant, which means *Infinite*, and that's funny."

"Why is that funny?"

"Because he's infinitely stupid."

"Oh. Is Anant what you want to talk about?"

"Not really."

"He's not bothering you?"

"No, he's just a little kid." Elizabeth suppressed a smile. Adhira was eight, her brother was only two years younger. "He's okay, I guess. Just dumb."

"Sometimes people get smarter as they get older."

"I sure hope so."

Another silence fell over them. Adhira fidgeted in her chair as if trying to settle in, then was still again. Elizabeth didn't try to interrupt the quiet this time.

Eventually Adhira sighed. "There's a boy," she said. Elizabeth could think of several ways this could go, and she didn't want to derail it by suggesting the wrong thing, so she said nothing. After a moment Adhira continued, "He comes into my parents' store a lot." Her parents owned the hardware store in Trout Lake. After moving from Seattle they'd bought it from the former owner, who had been sentenced to fifteen years in federal prison. No one seemed to know why. "He hardly ever buys anything, he just wanders up and down the aisles. I just figured out that he's coming there to see me."

"What's his name?"

"Bobby something. He lives in Trout Lake."

"Why do you think he's coming to see you? Do you know him?"

"No, I've never seen him except in the store, and I never even talked to him. But I think he has a crush on me."

"Oh." She waited to see if Adhira had anything else to say. "Do you want him to go away or do you want him to talk to you?"

"I don't know. Both. Neither."

"Well, if he's nice, wouldn't it be good to talk to him? Maybe you'd like him. You could be friends."

"I don't know."

"Do your parents know about this?"

"I don't think so. They're usually busy with real customers, or restocking, or ordering. I saw my mom watching him once, but I think she was just trying to figure out if he was a shoplifter. When she decided he wasn't, she went back to work."

"Do you think you should talk to them about him?"

"No." That was pretty definite.

"You know, boys can be real shy when it comes to talking to girls. Can I make a suggestion?"

"Sure."

"When are you going to the shop again?"

"My mom's picking me up at 4:30."

"Okay," Elizabeth said. "The next time you see Bobby in the store, pretend he's a customer and you're the shop owner."

"Okay…"

"Ask him if you can help him find something. You know what will probably happen?"

"What?"

"His tongue will get tied up in a knot and he won't be able to answer you."

Adhira laughed. "That will be funny."

"Yes, it will. But then you can be nice to him, because he's probably shy and confused. You can ask him what his name is. You can mention that you've seen him in the store sometimes. You can ask him if he likes hardware stores—a lot of boys do. You can give him a tour. You can ask him what it's like to go to school in Trout Lake."

"Okay, I guess."

"That way, you can find out if he's nice. And if he is, you will have a new friend. If he's not nice, you can tell your parents and they'll make him stop bothering you. How does that sound?"

"That sounds okay. I guess I could do that."

"Someday you'll go to school in Trout Lake. It would be nice to know a few kids on your first day."

"Did you go to school there?"

"Yes, I did," Elizabeth said.

"Did you like it?"

"Yes. I learned a lot and I had a lot of fun. I made some friends there. I think you'll like it, but that's several years away. You have plenty of time to get ready for that."

"I think it's scary. It's a big school."

"It is big, but it's not scary. The teachers are nice, and if you have a friend or two when you start it will be easier."

"Okay. I'll think about it."

"Good."

Adhira fished around in her jeans pocket and pulled out a quarter. "My mom said you help people with problems and they pay you. Is this enough?"

"Yes, that's just right. Thank you." Elizabeth managed to keep a straight face but it was an effort.

"Thanks for your help," Adhira said.

"Stop by sometime and tell me how it went with Bobby. You don't have to pay to bring me news or just to talk."

"Okay. Thanks."

Adhira hopped off the chair. She looked calmer than when she'd come in. Elizabeth walked her to the door, waited until she was gone and the door was firmly closed behind her, then doubled up laughing.

* * *

The weather cleared for a few days in the middle of October. The sunny, cool days were sufficient to dry out the trails, so on her day off Elizabeth suggested that they go for one last hike this year. They dressed warmly but didn't plan to stay out all day. Elizabeth made some sandwiches to take with them, and Kevin made a thermos of hot chocolate.

They walked out of town. The locals knew all about the unnamed, unnumbered trails —ones not maintained by the Forest Service—where they would be unlikely to run into hikers from outside the area. And Elizabeth knew that the local kids, if they were out in the woods today, would be heading anywhere but *up.*

The path she chose was essentially a deer trail, narrow and hard to see in places, winding between the big trees and climbing gently up the slope of Steamboat Mountain. Side trails split off every few hundred yards, but she had spent her childhood exploring this area, usually on her own, and she wasn't fooled by the dead ends. She glanced back at Kevin every now and then; after about two miles she caught him with a worried expression on his face and laughed.

"We're not lost," she said.

"If you say so. Are you sure this is a trail?"

"Of course."

"It looks like a *hamster* trail."

"Do you want to take the lead?"

He laughed. "Absolutely not. I have no idea where we are, where we've been, or where we're going. Besides, the view is better from here."

She sashayed for the next few steps just to tease him.

About three miles in they came to a small clearing where a big tree had fallen a decade or so ago, and taken out a few of its neighbors when it went down. Saplings of Douglas Fir were growing among the grasses and scrub, vying with each other to fill the gap their elders had left. It was a temporary glade, which wouldn't last more than another twenty years, but in the meantime the view was superb.

They climbed up onto a nearly-horizontal stretch of old tree trunk and looked out. Mount Adams, completely shrouded in snow, dominated the northeast. To the southeast Kevin spotted a lake that was two or three times the size of Fish Lake, which Elizabeth told him was Steamboat Lake. Due east, glittering here and there through gaps in the forest—some of them clearcuts—they could see short stretches of the White Salmon River.

They spread out a poncho on the tree trunk and sat there to eat their lunch.

"How did you know I was the one?" Kevin asked.

"That day we first met?" He nodded. "It was your ears." The crestfallen look on his face made her laugh out loud. "I'm kidding. It wasn't any one thing. The way you held yourself, the tone of your voice, the expression on your face."

"Adie told me once that you'd have figured it out in two minutes."

"Yes."

"Well, what could you learn about someone in two minutes? Especially someone you just met, who spoke maybe three sentences?"

"You'd be surprised. I knew you were single and never married, that you were responsible, intelligent, modest, hard-working, funny. Faithful. And I knew you were ready to fall in love."

"It's hard to believe you could see all that so quickly."

"I know. But that's what I do. I see things other people don't see."

"I'm glad it wasn't my ears. But I have to tell you, the first time I laid eyes on you, for just a moment—I thought you had fairy ears."

"Really?"

"Well. I think I thought they were Vulcan ears. But pointy."

She laughed lightly. "Did you see wings, too?"

"Nope, just the ears."

Elizabeth took a blanket out of her pack and stood up. Kevin stood up too. She moved the poncho down onto a soft, level spot on the ground and put the blanket down on top.

She said, "Come here."

They lay down together and exposed themselves to the elements.

* * *

That night, watching Kevin cook dinner, Elizabeth felt a strange, very subtle sensation in her abdomen. It wasn't a pain, not even a twinge, more like something turning over gently within her. She focused on it closely and thought about it while he chattered about a long, funny sequence of events that had unfolded in the Town Hall that week. It took a moment, but she finally figured out what it was.

She thought about telling him, but decided to wait. She didn't want to frighten him; he already thought there was something weird about her. She wasn't afraid herself—it was what she had always wanted. She would wait to tell him until the time that any woman would know for sure.

Halloween

Sunday, October 31

At breakfast on Saturday, the day before Halloween, Wanda had suggested that Elizabeth and Kevin come over for lunch the next day. It was so unusual for anyone other than Kevin or Adie to cook for her that Elizabeth agreed immediately. She felt sure that Kevin would be agreeable, and when she told him he was happy to go.

"But why?" he said over dinner.

"I think she has a new painting she wants to show us."

That was all it took; he was instantly excited. The dancing dragon painting that Kevin had bought from her on his first day in town was now hanging in the living room with the two Wanda paintings that Elizabeth had already owned. She thought he would be inclined to buy another one if there had been room to hang it. Which there wasn't.

It was chilly and cloudy when they walked over just before 2:00 on Sunday.

"I hope it doesn't rain tonight," Kevin said. "You said there would be trick-or-treating, right?"

"Definitely."

"I remember trick-or-treating in the rain. It seemed like it did that every year when I was a kid. It was miserable."

"It's not supposed to rain tonight."

"Good."

Wanda opened the door when they knocked. "Come in," she said. "Let me take your coats."

The studio looked pretty much as it always did, except that there was a different painting on the easel—still in the pencil sketch stage, so it was hard to tell what it would be.

"Come on back," Wanda said.

The kitchen was small and about as messy as one would expect an artist's kitchen to be. There was a canning jar of turpentine on the counter with brushes soaking in it. No dirty dishes except for the ones that had been used to make lunch, but there was a lot of clutter and out-of-place items on the counters: a small sledge hammer, a pile of seashells (hopefully those two had nothing to do with each other), small coils of fine wire, a pile of pliers of various sorts.

Elizabeth and Kevin sat down at the table at a gesture from Wanda, while she went to the refrigerator and brought out composed salads of greens, olives, tomatoes, and cubes of cheese. There was a small wooden cutting board with some good-looking dark bread on it, and a wicked-looking bread knife.

"Kevin," Wanda said, "would you cut us some hunks of bread?"

He did the honors while Wanda opened a bottle of white wine. Kevin declined and asked for water instead, but Elizabeth had a glass.

The salad was tangy and herby, very nice. Elizabeth decided that the bread was a homemade pumpernickel, which Wanda confirmed. It was quite good, dense and slightly acidic, and the real butter Wanda offered with it made it perfect. While they ate they talked about the weather and the events coming up that night. Gordon and Mary and their three kids were hosting their annual party when the trick-or-treating was done.

"Well, that shouldn't take long," Kevin said, but neither of the women corrected him.

Wanda offered a fresh apple pie for dessert, and both Elizabeth and Kevin had a slice. Elizabeth could see where Wanda had gone wrong—she'd used an apple variety that gave up too much of its liquid when baked, so the top crust fell when the apples shrank, the water she'd used in the pastry hadn't been cold enough, and there wasn't enough cinnamon—but she didn't say anything other than how good it tasted, and that was true.

"Great lunch," Kevin said.

"Thanks. I thought you both might like to see a painting I just finished."

Kevin reacted enthusiastically as a fan of her work. Elizabeth said she would be delighted. She knew why Wanda was offering the showing, though she had no idea what the subject of the picture would be.

In the studio Wanda moved the sketched canvas off the easel and replaced it with another that had been standing covered on the floor. She removed the covering sheet and stood back.

Elizabeth nearly laughed out loud. She could tell that Kevin was appreciative but confused.

The picture showed a night scene. A gaggle of children were grouped around the front door of a house, whose door was open and porch light on. In the doorway a man stood, holding a black metal cauldron with one hand while he reached into it with the other. The children were all in Halloween costumes and holding out their bags, but none of them wore masks. Every one of their faces was easily identifiable as the nine kids of Marmot, and the man in the doorway was clearly Mike Winslow, the Internet shop owner.

Behind the children, supervising and almost out of the light, was a woman dressed in a tutu, holding a long magic wand and wearing large, butterfly-style fairy wings. And that woman was Wanda.

"It's absolutely perfect," Elizabeth said. "Inspired. I would never have thought of that."

"You think he'll like it?"

"He will love it. It will be his most prized possession."

"It's really very good," Kevin said with a puzzled note in his voice. He must have guessed who the "he" was but he didn't say anything about that. "I can recognize everyone in it. And I love the composition and the chiaroscuro. The lighting is really superb."

"Thanks," Wanda said. "I worked hard on that."

Kevin and Wanda talked some more about the painting—the colors, the menacing shadows the trick-or-treaters threw, the tall ghostly trees visible in the background. Elizabeth didn't say anything else, she just admired the work and the subtle suggestion it represented. The woman in the picture was open to an invitation to come into the light, to come inside, but she was standing far enough away that if that invitation never came she could just take one step back and be invisible. Elizabeth had no doubt at all that the invitation she was inviting would be extended.

They left shortly after the unveiling. Kevin waited until they were halfway back to say, "Wanda and Mike?"

"It makes sense to me."

"Yeah, I guess it does. Do you think he'll like the picture?"

"Wouldn't you?"

He smiled but didn't respond. She knew what he was thinking.

* * *

Kevin came out of the bedroom wearing a dark morning coat with matching waistcoat, striped dress slacks, a top hat, and dress shoes. Elizabeth gaped in astonishment.

"Where did you get that?" she said.

He looked smug. "You can find just about anything in the dungeons of Town Hall."

"No, really."

"It's a secret."

"Okay. So what are you, Prince William? You'll need to dye your hair. And maybe lose some of it."

"No, silly. I'm the Mayor."

She had to lean against the counter until she recovered from her laughing spell.

"Do you think I should wear this to work from now on?" he said with mock seriousness. "Really, I'll bet people would treat me differently."

"Of course they would. They'd lock you up in your dungeon."

He looked her up and down. "You look very naughty."

She was dressed in a tight-fitting black witch's outfit, including the pointy hat, and had applied a thin layer of green makeup all over her face.

"I'm a bad witch," she said.

"Who, you? You're not a witch at all."

"That's why I'm bad at it."

He looked at his watch. "What time does this get started?"

"As soon as it's dark. Another half hour or so."

"Want to be bad in the meantime?"

She laughed. "I've been told I need to make an appointment to meet with the Mayor. Pencil me in for later."

Kevin climbed up on the kitchen bistro chair. He looked down at the mixing bowl set on the table, which was filled with full-sized candy bars. "I think maybe you got too much candy. Who's going to eat what's left?"

"I'm going to make you eat every last piece that's left over before our appointment."

"Well, I've never vomited on anyone before, but it might be fun." He looked down at the bowl and back up again. "Really, I'm not crazy about milk chocolate. Why did you get so much?"

"Wait and see." She looked at the clock. "Let's go down. Could you carry the bowl, please? I need to hike my skirts to get down the stairs safely."

"Sure. I just hope no one spills any water on you."

"Don't worry, I'm only a *little bit* bad. It won't hurt me."

Elizabeth set the bowl just inside the cafe door and turned on the outside light. Five minutes later the first kids arrived, which were predictably Adhira and Anant—always the over-achievers. Adhira was wearing a cat suit with her long tail draped forward over her shoulder and a painted face. Anant looked a lot like a pirate, but he might have been William Shakespeare. It was hard to tell.

It took a little while before the next group, which was Viola and Matthew. They were dressed up as 1980s rock stars, tight leather and big hair. Elizabeth felt a little sad. This was almost certainly Viola's last year trick-or-treating, and possibly Matthew's too.

Then the kids started coming thick and fast, each group arriving before the departing one had reached the street, sometimes before they'd left the doorway. The parents waited on the street while the kids ran up the walk. Kevin looked dazed. She could tell that he was counting, and she could also tell the moment he lost count, when a group of seven grade-schoolers arrived all at once, half of them shoving to get to the front and the ones already in front demanding to know what Kevin was supposed to be.

Finally the kids thinned out. There was a single candy bar left in the bowl when Mechelle came up the walk dressed in a silver spacesuit with a helmet, although the helmet was hanging down her back. Fortunately it was a Butterfinger, which Elizabeth knew she liked. They closed the door and turned out the light.

"There are only nine kids in Marmot," Kevin said breathlessly. "That was at least seventy. I lost count."

"We're off the main roads, but the people who know our town know we only hand out the good stuff. So they go out of their way to come here. We like it—as long as they don't all come every day. Once a year is plenty, on both sides I think."

"I need to sit down."

"Don't get too comfortable. We're due at Gordon and Mary's party."

"Do we have to?"

"No, I don't have to. I often skip it. But you're the Mayor. You have to at least make an appearance."

"But I'm the Mayor. Who says I need to go?"

"Adie."

"Okay, let's go."

The party was nearly all the way up the hill to the Town Hall. They followed Jodie and Matthew through the front door. When the crowd inside caught sight of Kevin, they all yelled out in unison—at the very top of their voices—"Huzzah, Mr. Mayor!"

* * *

They didn't have to stay long. Kevin had a beer, Elizabeth managed a few sips of her wine. They watched the kids play the traditional games, including a few variations like dunking for apples in a big washbasin full of hollow rubber balls instead of water. Several people mentioned how much they liked Elizabeth's costume, which was amusing because she wore this exact same outfit every other year or so.

She tugged on Kevin's arm when she felt he had done his duty, and they walked back to their house to keep her appointment with the Mayor.

Thanksgiving

Thursday, November 25

Elizabeth spent all morning making her traditional vegetarian Thanksgiving casserole, Mrs. Gobblegoods. Kevin offered to help, but she assigned him to make a dessert instead, and he came up with a chocolate pecan pie that smelled just as heavenly as her dish did.

They found an hour and a half when they were both free of tasks, so they went outside for a walk in the first snowfall of the year. It was one of nature's oddities that Marmot's first snow often fell exactly on Thanksgiving day, as if the sky knew what day it was and wanted to make it pretty. Or difficult.

Elizabeth celebrated all the major holidays with Adie and Jeremy; they weren't just her honorary family, she thought of them as simply family, without qualification. All the indoor celebrations happened at Adie's house, because she was older, because both she and Jeremy lived there, and because the living space was on the ground floor. Adie was beginning to dislike stairways; even the handful of steps up to the Town Hall were starting to give her trouble this fall. She had always, as long as Elizabeth could remember, nearly run up and down stairs, but her hips were beginning to ache when she did that, and sometimes they'd lock up afterwards, so she had trouble standing up or sitting down.

"It's tedious," she had told Elizabeth recently, "but not serious."

Elizabeth wasn't so sure.

Adie didn't like to leave a lot of time for chit-chat before eating, so Elizabeth's casserole came out of the oven ten minutes before they were supposed to arrive. She slid the oblong pan into a warm/cool pack and zipped it up. Kevin put his pie into a pie saver and they shrugged on their coats.

The snow had only accumulated a few inches so far, but it was likely to be half a foot deep by nightfall. They trudged up the hill, past Mike's shop and the four other houses, two on each side of the street, that separated the cafe from Adie's house. Kevin had learned his lesson weeks ago, so he simply opened the front door without knocking and held it for Elizabeth.

It was warm and cozy inside. There were no holiday decorations, for this holiday or the next; Adie didn't do that. But the rooms were familiar and comfortable and Elizabeth didn't mind.

After shedding their coats and knocking the snow off their shoes, they went through to the kitchen. Jeremy, Helen, and Mechelle were there already, as well as Mike and Wanda, which was not really a surprise to her. Kevin made a big deal of it, exclaiming, shaking Mike's hand, and kissing Wanda lightly on the cheek. Wanda was grinning so hard her head would crack open if she went outside in the cold. Mike looked more cheerful than Elizabeth had ever seen him.

"What a great surprise," Kevin said. Elizabeth thought he probably welcomed any company that would dilute Adie. He was still a little uncomfortable around her, despite all the time they'd spent together at work. "You two look very well."

"Thanks," Mike said. "I think we are well." Wanda just smiled even more broadly, if that was possible.

"Kevin," Adie said from the stove, "get yourself and Elizabeth something to drink. Everybody sit down. Dinner's in five."

They sorted themselves out, Kevin taking the seat next to Mechelle and Elizabeth sitting beside him. The girl was just putting away a sketch pad and colored pencils.

"What is it today?" Kevin said. "Turkeys?"

"Koalas."

"Well, you don't need many colors to do them, do you?"

"I could draw them striped red and blue if I wanted to," Mechelle said seriously.

"Of course you could. It's your drawing."

"But I didn't. I want them to look real. The colors are for the background. Trees and birds."

"Will you show me later?"

"Sure. Wanda was helping me with... perspective." She said the last word slowly and carefully, as if she'd just learned it, which Elizabeth doubted.

"Wow. I was never any good at that. Did you know that European artists had to relearn perspective during the Renaissance? Before that everybody drew as badly as I do."

Mechelle laughed and Helen smiled at him.

Elizabeth saw that Adie was just about done, so she got up to put her casserole on the table and help carry the rest from the kitchen. Since Elizabeth had started making Mrs. Gobblegoods, Adie didn't bother with a turkey anymore. The first year she'd brought it everyone said they preferred it to the turkey, and Adie had abandoned with great relief her grim quest for the perfect turkey technique. She said she didn't miss the basting and the smelly, voluminous leftovers.

But there was a vegetarian dressing and gravy, mashed potatoes, roasted Brussel sprouts, and a broccoli salad that Elizabeth didn't recognize—which Wanda must therefore have made. When everything was on the table Adie tossed her apron onto the counter and sat down. Everyone dug in.

238

Mike and Wanda—not to mention Kevin—had never had Mrs. Gobblegoods before, and they all praised it enthusiastically. Wanda asked for the recipe, which Elizabeth promised to give her.

Adie was quiet all through dinner as everyone else chattered. Elizabeth could feel her watching intently, as if she were on an anthropological expedition to study a strange new tribe. Elizabeth had seen her in this mood many times. She had a theory that Adie's detachment had begun when she married Ryan, the local logger. She hadn't been forced to marry him; it wasn't arranged or due to an unplanned pregnancy. But it had made her life easier, and Elizabeth's theory was that she had despised herself for marrying a man she merely liked just to lessen her burden. Elizabeth didn't remember Ryan; he'd died when she was three. But she had seen pictures of Adie when she was young: pretty, willowy, brunette—and so, so serious. It was easy to understand how Ryan could have fallen truly in love with her, and loved coming back from his strenuous, dangerous jobs to the home she'd made.

When he'd died in his forties, that had only severed another connection to the world. And the final blow had been her sister Ida's death two decades later, when Elizabeth was in her mid-twenties and Adie was sixty-four. Elizabeth had noticed a steady withdrawal since then. She looked up from her food to see Adie watching her with a wry smile on her face.

"Don't read too much into it," Adie said.

Elizabeth smiled back. Adie could read her almost as well as she could read Adie. Kevin and one or two other people caught the exchange and looked puzzled, but the flow of conversation swamped that strange little moment, and they forgot about it.

* * *

Adie had made a traditional pumpkin pie; both that and Kevin's chocolate pecan were a big success. Everyone had a slice of each; the men rather large slices, the women small to tiny. Mechelle declared that Kevin's pie was her new favorite dessert. When dinner was over they unanimously decided to ignore the dishes and all went into the living room.

Kevin asked Jeremy if he ever watched football on Thanksgiving Day, and it turned out that neither of them had ever done that in their life. There was no chance of starting today, either, since Adie didn't own a TV.

Wanda had been helping out with art class at the school for several years. While Kevin and Jeremy nattered on about football, Wanda and Helen got into a parallel conversation about painting supplies and techniques; Elizabeth tuned both out as she watched Adie watching everyone else. Mechelle had her sketch book out again and was clearly waiting for an opening to show Kevin her koalas.

Elizabeth had no first-hand experience in how most people—any other people—spent this time on this day; only what she'd learned from movies and reading. Subtract TV for the men and mutual cleaning and gossip for the women, and what would be left in any other household? She didn't know. Since her parents had died, she had never spent a Thanksgiving anywhere other than this house. She could barely remember the Thanksgivings with her mom and dad. There had been turkeys until she became a vegetarian at twelve, she knew that. She didn't recall any TV or football. She had a fuzzy memory from when she was a girl of the Christmas decorations coming out and being sorted after the big feast, but she didn't know if that was a one-time thing or

240

every year. There had never been any relatives; she and both her parents had all been only children, and she had never met any of her grandparents.

So all she knew to look forward to was Adie's speech, although Adie would probably snort in derision if anyone actually called it a speech. Adie did not play games, either literally or metaphorically, so there would be no charades or Scrabble. Elizabeth watched as Adie monitored the flow of conversation, until Mechelle had had a chance to show off her work and Kevin to praise it, until Jeremy-and-Helen and Mike-and-Wanda had unconsciously nestled closer together.

Elizabeth judged the ingredient that was missing, and instead of standing by the wall as she had been doing sat on the floor at Kevin's feet. She wrapped an arm around one leg and he put a hand on her shoulder and stroked her hair a few times, still talking to Mechelle.

Eventually that last conversation paused and Adie stood up. Everyone turned to look at her. She paused dramatically for a long moment.

"Some of you know what comes next," she said, "but I'm going to disappoint you this year. Or maybe please you, depending on how you felt about my tradition. I'm not going to recite any poetry or quote Socrates, Thucydides, Marcus Aurelius, either Augustine, Erasmus Darwin or his wacky grandson Charles. There's a time for everything, and the time for my long-winded thanksgivings has come and gone.

"What I do want to say is that I'm grateful to all of you for helping me keep this little speck of a town alive from year to year. People come and go—I was born here, went away, and came back—but enough of us care about Marmot to make sure it endures. That's something we have to work at every year, and all of you have done that. Yes, even you Mechelle. Kevin has just begun to play his role, but we're grateful nonetheless. I think this place is something special, and it's not just the history but the people in it that make it so, that give it continuity and life.

"So—who wants more pie?"

* * *

There was a bustle as some of them gave in to their dessert addiction and others got coffee or tea. Adie caught Elizabeth's eye and made the subtlest possible nod toward the den. Elizabeth followed her in and Adie closed the door.

"You had something you wanted to tell me?" Adie said.

Elizabeth took a deep breath. "I'm pregnant."

There was no mistaking the elation on Adie's face. She studied Elizabeth's figure for a moment and looked directly in her eyes.

"Have you told Kevin yet?"

"Not yet. I'm only five and a half weeks. I want to wait until I miss one more period. And anyway, I wanted you to know first."

Adie pulled her into a fierce bear hug. Elizabeth could tell she was weeping. She felt a spark pass between them, all up and down her arms. Then she started crying herself.

Part Three

* * *

History Walking

Managing the Mayor

Thursday, November 25

Adie felt a shock run up her arms, like static electricity. It wasn't painful, but it couldn't have been more clear. She didn't have much time left.

She thrust that thought away and returned to the moment. Elizabeth's news was wonderful, and she was immensely happy for her, and she told her so. "Boy or girl?" she asked. It only occurred to her after she said it that most women wouldn't know for months yet—and not without an ultrasound. But she wasn't surprised when Elizabeth said confidently that it was a girl.

"We'd better get back," Elizabeth said, drying her eyes. She handed Adie a tissue so she could do her own. "I just thought you would want to know as soon as I was sure the baby was healthy."

Adie hugged her again. "Thank you. I'm so happy for you." She wanted to say, "I wish I could watch you raise this child," but she didn't want to frighten her. She knew it was time for Elizabeth to go, even if the dear girl didn't know it herself yet. But she probably did.

They rejoined the others in the living room, and the evening broke up shortly afterwards. Elizabeth and Kevin left first, followed almost immediately by Mike and Wanda. Those two as a couple had been genius on Elizabeth's part; Adie felt stupid for not having thought of it. It solved so many problems with one simple stroke. She made a mental note to stop by Mike's shop and see the painting that had sparked a love affair. Elizabeth had told her about it and it intrigued her.

Jeremy and Helen offered to clean up, and Mechelle said, "Me too." Ordinarily Adie would have done it herself, but she had other things to think about. She thanked them and accepted their offer. She left them sorting out the pans in the sink and clearing the table and went back to her bedroom to let the dogs out.

Owl, the shepherd, was the eldest and struggled for a moment to get up off her bed. When the dogs were younger it would have killed them to be locked away while visitors were in the house, but none of them were young anymore and they seemed to have lost interest in socializing. They just sniffed at her clean-up crew as they went past them on their way to the back door. It was dark out so Adie flicked on the lights before letting them out. She followed them and stood on the small porch while the three dogs scattered.

Bunny and Wombat were still young enough to want to take a few moments to play in the first snowfall of the year, but Owl squatted near a tree and immediately came back to stand at Adie's side. It had taken Adie a while to learn that Owl was afraid of the dark and wouldn't do her business at night if the light wasn't on. Adie looked up at the sky. The snow had let up for a while but it was coming down again, harder than before. The security lights she'd installed for Owl made cones of light through which the puffy snow drifted, momentarily visible before vanishing back into darkness. Adie felt a metaphor forming in her mind and squelched it. She had too much to do to get maudlin.

It took another five minutes for the other two dogs to work their way back to the house. Adie told them to shake and they all wiggled their coats to get the snow off. She had nothing but contempt for people who used that command to get dogs to shake hands with people; dogs did not have hands, but they did have an instinct to dry and fluff their fur.

The kids were still at it in the kitchen. It wasn't done by a long shot, but Adie could see that they had things organized and an assembly line of sorts in place. She left them to it and went down into the basement. Owl went back to the bedroom, but Bunny and Wombat followed her down.

She had a good basement. The ceilings were a little too low for her but it was dry. This house was older than she was, but it was still watertight and structurally sound, just like her. The concrete floor down here, she was sure, had been added long after the house was built, but whoever had done the drainage knew their business.

The open area at the foot of the stairs was the laundry room. There was also a set of metal shelves holding canned goods; she believed in redundancy and multiple backups, and not a tenth of it all would fit in the tiny kitchen. One shelf held jars of produce that had been put up by her or her neighbors, including some of Elizabeth's jams.

There were three other rooms. One was the utility room, where the furnace and the hot water tank were. Long ago there had been an incinerator in there, but Ryan had torn it out when they refurbished the house in the 70s. Adie didn't miss the nasty thing, but you could still smell the smoke oozing like ancient evil out of the cinder block walls.

The other two rooms were storage. Altogether the four spaces down here didn't run the full depth of the house; probably only half of it. The doors to the two storage rooms were right next to each other. Adie opened both and flicked the light switches. She stood back a bit so she could see into both rooms at once. They contained mismatched shelves, some made of wooden planks by Ryan, the rest metal shelves that she had bought from Costco or the hardware store over the years. The shelves were full of boxes, neatly labelled and fully organized. Adie recognized her sister Ida's writing on a few of the labels, but most of them were hers.

Christmas decorations, her own and Ida's, which she had stopped putting up after Ida died, but couldn't bring herself to discard. Easter decorations, for God's sake. Tax records, town history, personal files, several boxes of Ryan's things, airtight bins of spare bedding and clothing. One whole box of newspaper clippings and photographs—those were her mother's. Boxes of games; she couldn't remember where those had come from, probably Ida.

She made a mental inventory, then turned off the lights. The dogs were sitting at the foot of the stairs, tongues out, watching her.

"What?" she said. Wombat, the terrier mutt, woofed gently and went back to grinning. Bunny, the golden retriever, just sat contentedly without a thought in her head. "You guys want to help?" Their idea of helping was sitting on her feet while she was working.

She started for the stairs, which was the cue the dogs needed to race up. The kitchen was deserted, the lights out. There was a note from Jeremy on the table saying he'd gone to Helen's for the night. Good. She strongly approved of Helen, loved Mechelle, and thought Jeremy had found his soulmate, if he could only get up the gumption to do something about it. He needed something to get him in gear. Like a good kick in the ass. Adie laughed out loud at that and the dogs grinned at her.

She went into her den and pulled a pad of paper out of the side drawer. She started a new list. The first item was to sort out those history boxes. There were probably a few things she could use in there to finish her history of the town. She would make sure that some other things made their way anonymously to Ernie; she'd have to figure out how to do that, but not tonight.

That was another stroke of genius on Elizabeth's part, to give that old sourpuss a task, a goal for a life that had become meaningless. She didn't mind in the slightest that his history would compete with hers. It wasn't a contest, and she was utterly certain that whatever he came up with would be mostly fabrication and misremembered maundering, and the rest would be crap. That didn't matter. What mattered was to give him something to do other than gripe himself into the grave, making everyone else in town miserable while he did it.

She went on with her list, and had filled over a page when she decided she was too tired to think clearly anymore, and went to bed.

* * *

Kevin walked past Adie's office just after 9:00 the next morning. She called out his
name and he stuck his head in the door.

"Morning," he said.

"Could you do me a favor?"

"Sure."

"I have some file boxes at my house that I'd like here in my office, but I don't want to carry them in the snow." Even though Jeremy had ploughed all the town roads hours ago, she was afraid she'd slip and break her hip. But she wasn't going to tell Kevin that.

"Okay, I can get them for you. I might as well do it now while I've still got my coat on."

"Thank you. The front door is open, and the boxes are on the floor in the kitchen."

248

"Okay. Where do you want them?"

She pointed to the corner of her office and he nodded and went back out. It took him almost half an hour to bring the three boxes. They were too heavy to carry more than one at a time, and she didn't have a hand truck. Of course Mike had one, but she didn't think it would be any easier with the patches of slush still on the street. Although the yards were still white, on the asphalt that was all that was left of the three inches they got last night.

"Do you need anything else?" Kevin asked when he was done.

"No. I appreciate it."

He nodded again and left her alone.

It took her all day to go through the files, sorting them into four piles. The smallest was material she thought she could use for her own book, another quite a bit taller for Ernie's book, one pile for the filing cabinets, and the last for recycling. While she beavered away at it, she could hear Jeremy come and go. Kevin went to lunch, came back, and later helped sort the mail. Her hearing was still excellent and she also kept one eye on the surveillance cameras. But nothing unusual happened; it was just a normal Friday.

She was pleased that Kevin had assumed that today would be a work day. Of course, Elizabeth would have gotten up early to start breakfast, so he'd just followed her lead. But though he didn't always know what to do with himself in his official capacity, he wasn't afraid of work.

At lunchtime she let Bunny and Wombat out for a romp and a pee out the back of the Town Hall, waiting on the top step while they did their business. Then they lay down on their beds under her desk while she went back to her sorting.

When it was starting to get dark she carried her recycling pile into the mail room, where Jeremy kept a tall blue garbage can for used office paper. She shucked on her coat and didn't have to call the dogs; they knew what the coat meant. As she got close to home she decided to stop in now to see Wanda's painting—one less thing on her mental list. She let the dogs into her house, then continued down to Mike's shop.

When she told him why she was there he looked pleased. He ushered her into his personal living room, not the one he used for business, where the picture was hung above the fireplace.

Elizabeth had been right. The painting was masterful, and as clear a proposition as she'd ever seen without being explicit.

"It's wonderful," Adie said.

"I'll tell her you said so."

"Please do. She's studied Rembrandt, I see. I can't imagine that curly-headed scamp painting this, but it's something he would have admired."

Mike laughed and said, "I'll tell her that too."

She thanked him for letting her see it and went home to feed the dogs.

* * *

The next day, having finished her first purge, Adie was initially at a loss for what to do next. So she got out the list she had made on Thanksgiving evening, typed it up on the computer, and started adding new items and filling in steps for the old ones. When she was done with that she had a three-page document that looked like a college course syllabus. It would probably take her two years to do it all. She read it over a few times, then started prioritizing the tasks.

Finishing her history was at the top of the list, but she didn't feel like writing today. Finishing Kevin was close enough to the top, so she told the dogs to stay and ambled around the corner to the Mayor's office.

She knocked on the doorframe and Kevin called out, "Come in." He looked up and smiled lopsidedly. "Just the person I need to talk to. I can't figure out this clause in your proposal."

"Are you still working on that?"

"I pull it out every now and then and try to get a little further. I'm almost done, actually, but I keep getting bogged down in the language."

"Let me have a look." He slid his chair over and she pulled one of his guest chairs around the desk and dropped into it.

He pointed at his computer monitor. Adie took a moment to familiarize herself with the section.

"Right. I remember this. It has to do with how we can spend the grant money if we don't need it all for the stated purposes."

"It's a bird's nest."

"Yes, intentionally. The point was to tie any close reader up in knots so he'd just shrug it off and move on to the next section."

"To hide something?"

She gave him her best dry stare. "To give us flexibility. The last thing we want is to give any money back. Here, let me drive for a minute." She grabbed the mouse and selected a semantically meaningless phrase, highlighted it, and did it again until all the twisted fluff was marked. "Do you see that all this stuff I've highlighted doesn't really mean anything? It's just noise. What's left?"

She gave him time to analyze it. It took several minutes. Then he sat back and nodded his head.

"Once they give us the money we can do whatever we want with it."

"Exactly. Well done. It's not surprising you couldn't see through the obfuscation. That's the whole purpose of this section: confusion."

"Did you come up with this all by yourself?"

She smiled. "I did the outline and the meaningful content. The actual verbiage—I got some help from a lawyer friend in White Salmon. When it was all done he waived his fee in exchange for the right to reuse it, including my original outline. He said it was the Sistine Chapel of bullshit."

"I have to agree with him. Thanks for clearing it up." Kevin closed the document. "Did you want something?"

"Just an idle thought. Have you wondered what happened to the job that was waiting for you in Maine?"

He shrugged. "I'm more than a month overdue and they haven't been able to call me. I assume that they gave the job to someone else."

Adie thought that was likely but she wasn't going to agree out loud. "What do you think would happen if you just showed up someday?"

He chuckled. "You mean a decade from now when I lose my job here?" She shrugged back. He suddenly looked alarmed. "Hey, you're not firing me, are you?"

She laughed out loud. "Kevin, what do you imagine I would base *that* decision on? Is there some part of your *onerous* duties you think you can't perform?"

"Well, no one laughs at my jokes on movie night."

"You should have heard your predecessor. I never knew anyone who could slaughter a punchline like Bob. No, I'm not firing you. I was just curious if you'd given a thought to the path you didn't take."

"One or two. But nothing in Maine stacks up against Elizabeth. Or this town."

"I have to agree with you there." That was enough; she just wanted to plant the idea in his head and let it grow for a while. Now for the second seed. "You just have one sibling, right?"

He looked puzzled. "Yes, a younger sister."

"I had a sister too. Jeremy's mother."

"Her name was Ida, right?"

"Yes."

"What was she like?"

He meant, *Was she a tough old bitch like you,* but Adie wasn't offended. She was exactly as tough as she needed to be. "She was short and sweet. After high school I had to duck to go through doorways sometimes, and she always wore high heels. She wore high-heeled boots when working in the garden. I think her evening slippers had inserts. I loved her to pieces. Nicest person I ever knew, maybe tied with Elizabeth."

"I'm sorry I never got to meet her."

"Well. She came to live with me around the time she turned forty, when Jeremy was nine, after her husband died. She lived with me for eleven years until she went too. We were never closer, not even as kids."

"I'm sorry."

"Thank you. Sometimes I think it's odd that she had only one child and I had none. Like there was something wrong with our line."

"That can't be right. Jeremy turned out great."

"Yes, he did, didn't he?"

Kevin hesitated. "You couldn't have children?"

253

Thank you, she thought. "We tried. Ryan wanted to go to a doctor and find out why we couldn't, but I said no. Whatever it was, I doubt anything could have been done to fix it, and no matter whose problem it was, it would only bring strife. This was way before in vitro fertilization, not that I would have agreed to that. I believe that when your body is sending you a message, you should listen." She shifted in her chair. "Anyway, Jeremy and Elizabeth were so close to being my own children I'm not sure I could have told the difference. I saw them nearly every day, and after their parents died we got even closer. I'm happy with how things turned out."

She let a small silence fall over them. "So, you want kids, right?"

"Yes. I always have. I like kids."

"I've seen how well you and Mechelle get along. She likes you."

"Flattery is a very effective tool." He grinned broadly.

Adie laughed. "No, it's because you treat her like a real person, not the way most people condescend to children. You ask her questions and actually listen to her answers. Kids react to that."

"Well, I had some experience with my sister."

"She must have adored you."

"She did, until she got old enough to see I was just as full of it as anybody. We went through some stages, but it's better now. We like each other and treat each other as equals. I wish I'd got to see her more often before I left."

"She has kids?"

"Two."

"Well, maybe someday you can get the cousins together for a reunion."

He laughed softly, clearly full of doubt. "Maybe."

She stood up. "Okay, I need to get back to work. And I've made you slip your schedule, I think."

He looked at his watch. "Yep. Past time for my morning nap."

She smiled and slid the guest chair back to its spot. She went back to her office, patted both dogs and gave them a treat, and checked "Nudge Kevin" off her list. Only two hundred or so items left to go.

Managing the Heir

Monday, November 29

Adie spent most of the following Monday laboring on her history of the town. She didn't complete it, but for the first time she could see the finish line. Another week of writing and she would be ready to do a read-through from start to end.

While she was working she had a secondary train of thought running through her mind: Jeremy. She had no doubt that if she died, Jeremy would be elected Town Manager —he already drove the school bus and the snow plough; collected, sorted, and delivered the mail; and managed the town meetings including movie night. No one had a more obvious impact on the town. But she was worried that the manager's job might overwhelm him. When she had taken up the job half her life ago, it was a much simpler proposition, so she'd been able to learn on the job. There were no computers and essentially no money. She'd had decades of experience struggling to revive the town before they got the opportunity to actually fund the work that needed to be done. During that time she'd built up a network of contacts in the Gorge area that she still relied upon. Jeremy's main contact outside of town was the petulant fussbudget who ran the Trout Lake Post Office.

Helen wasn't joining them for dinner tonight, she was taking Mechelle down to the Gorge for some kind of social activity that Adie hadn't bothered to pay attention to. She and Jeremy would be having leftovers, so there was no need to rush home. When she was through writing for the day she dug out her Unix manuals and spent several hours refreshing her memory of the scripting languages and some of the more potentially-useful commands such as *cron* and *at.*

She had enough time before going home to sketch out a plan for a system that would solve the inheritor problem. When her eyes wouldn't focus anymore she put the manuals away and stuck her notes in a desk drawer.

* * *

Jeremy's only real problem was lack of direction. He was smart enough, and he had a good heart. It was utterly obvious, from Adie's point of view, what he should do, but she loved him too much to manipulate him directly. She just gave him little nudges now and then when she thought it might help.

That wasn't going to be enough if he succeeded her as Town Manager, and anyway she wouldn't be around to help. So over the next few days she spent part of each day trying to figure out how to get the system to tell him what he needed to know, when he needed it. She was inspired by a book she'd read once, a techno-thriller in which an extravagantly wealthy man wrote a series of scripts that kicked in after he died from his brain tumor, and step by step created a new worldwide social order. She wasn't that smart, but maybe she was smart enough.

There were other things she could do about his personal life. On Wednesday she and Kevin met to nail down the final details of the parade. When they were wrapping up, she said to him, "What do you think of Helen?"

"Helen?" He got that bemused look he often did when she changed gears on him without warning. She'd have thought he'd have learned to jink with her by now. "She's a nice lady. A little sarcastic for my taste sometimes, but maybe that comes from growing up in L.A.."

"She's pretty smart," Adie said.

"I guess so. I haven't had any deep discussions with her. To be honest, I've spent more time talking to Mechelle."

"She was smart enough to stay when we offered her the job as teacher."

Kevin laughed. "Yeah, like me."

"Like you," she agreed. "What do you think of Helen and Jeremy as a couple?"

"They seem to really like each other. They look comfortable together—um, like they understand each other." He looked up at her. "What are you thinking, Adie? You don't want to split them up, do you?"

She snorted. "Absolutely not. What do you think I am?"

"Sorry. I thought maybe…"

"I don't care what color her skin is. She's actually one of the prettier women I've ever met. Do you know how much of our genome we share with chimps?" After failing once again to follow her tight turn, he nodded. "Then can you think that anyone intelligent would believe there's any significant difference between the so-called races?"

"I agree with you."

"Good. I thought maybe you thought I was an idiot."

Kevin laughed explosively. "No, I don't think that."

"Good. You asked me what I was thinking about them as a couple. I'll tell you. I think Jeremy wants to marry her but he's waffling like he always does."

"Really?"

He left her office a few minutes later, looking thoughtful. Adie smiled after he was gone. Kevin and Jeremy saw each other nearly every day. Another seed planted.

* * *

Helen and Mechelle ate dinner with them the night before the parade, as they did about half the days of each week. Helen volunteered to do the cooking, with Jeremy and Mechelle helping out. Adie sat at the kitchen table, observing the dynamics between the three of them and nibbling on shiny seaweed-flavored rice crackers. The damned things crunched between her teeth as if they'd been varnished.

It was interesting watching the two adults move around each other in the kitchen. It was almost a dance. They clearly loved touching each other; he would lightly stroke her hand as he reached past her for a cutting board, she trailed her fingers across his shoulder as she stretched to get something out of the cupboard, he brushed something from her cheek. But they reined it in for her sake and Mechelle's, so the contact was never too explicit, never prolonged, always subtle and just in passing. Adie doubted that Mechelle even noticed it was happening. She wondered if the lovers did.

She had been aware of this *pas de deux* for months now, and subconsciously tracked its intensity, which was very slowly intensifying. At the beginning she'd had to make an effort not to start a spreadsheet. Too creepy, but now she had no record of a history that was self-evidently quantifiable.

"Helen," Adie said, "where did you learn to cook?"

"Not from my mom, that's for sure," Helen said with a smile. "She meant well, but she could burn water."

"So who did the cooking when you were growing up?"

"My older sister and I. In middle school Mom was regularly making us peanut butter and jelly sandwiches for dinner, so my sister got a cookbook out of the library and we taught each other."

"*Joy of Cooking?*"

"Betty Crocker. It was like having an auntie looking over our shoulder. She got us started and then we got hooked. We started competing to see who could make the most complicated meals. But I scaled it back when Mechelle came along."

She said it as if her daughter had wandered in from the street one day. Adie would have liked to ask her what the story was—who the father was—and she would have with anyone else. But she had a soft spot for Helen. Anyone who could envelop Jeremy as she had, pretty much the day they met, got special treatment from Adie.

"Well, I think if you went flat out you could probably compete with Elizabeth." That wasn't true, of course, but Helen *was* competent.

Helen stopped chopping something green (Adie couldn't make out what it was from here) and looked at her. "Thank you," she said sincerely. "That's a real compliment."

Adie nodded, but she was really watching Jeremy out of the corner of her eye. He was looking at Adie too, then turned to look at Helen as if he'd never seen her before.

Equating the two young women in his life. Good.

* * *

Jeremy and the others left after insisting on doing the clean-up. Adie didn't ask if he would be back; none of her business. She went out of her way not to track where he spent his nights. Despite the smallness of her house, their bedrooms were not right next to each other, and she couldn't sleep without a noise generator, so unless he threw a bowling ball against her bedroom door she wouldn't know if he came back or not.

When she was alone she went into the bathroom and studied her face in the mirror. She wondered if she were looking frail. Jeremy and Helen had been treating her a little differently for the last month or so, doing more of the cooking and cleaning, as if they were worried she couldn't handle it anymore. She didn't feel older or sick, just a little tired all the time. Which probably had more to do with Kevin's arrival than anything else. She had forgotten how much work it was to train a new Mayor.

Her eyes traced the wrinkles that had fashioned her face into a stranger's. She'd turned seventy-five this past summer. Who could have imagined she would live this long? Over thirty years since she'd buried her husband, eleven since she'd buried her younger sister. Yet she went on and on, even though everything seemed pointless sometimes. Everything except her two surrogate children.

She found no clues in the mirror. Maybe it had nothing to do with her; the closeness growing between Jeremy and Helen might be enough to explain the changes in their behavior. She switched off the glaring light and went into the living room. Sitting in her favorite recliner chair, she switched on the reading lamp and picked up the notebook where she was mapping out the scripts she would leave for Jeremy. She got in a good hour's work before she couldn't keep her eyes open anymore.

Christmas Parade

Sunday, December 5

Another snowfall Saturday night meant that Jeremy had to spend all morning ploughing. That left Adie alone for the day, which pleased her. She wanted to send a text to Elizabeth in order to gloat over the surprise Kevin was going to get tonight, but she doubted that Elizabeth would be anywhere near her iPad. Oh well, she knew Elizabeth wouldn't spoil the fun. Adie had had numerous opportunities to tell Kevin what to expect, but she'd been careful not to. It wasn't manipulative, she told herself; she just enjoyed surprising people pleasantly.

All the planning he'd helped with would not prepare him. She was looking forward to talking to him afterwards.

Usually on Sundays she stayed away from work—not out of religious observance, since she'd abandoned her Catholic heritage when she was in her early teens—but just to give her brain a rest, She'd discovered by trial and error that she was more efficient if she limited herself to six days of work per week. So she spent the day reading a one-volume biography of Winston Churchill she'd borrowed from the library. There were longer, more comprehensive biographies out there, but she firmly believed that *no one's* life merited more than one volume.

Jeremy came back from his special duties at dinnertime. She'd been simmering a homemade vegetable soup all day, which she served with a loaf of dark rye bread that Elizabeth had made and dropped off a few days ago.

"Cold out there?" she said.

"We've seen worse. At least the snow has stopped so I don't have to plough again."

"Everything ready?"

"As ready as I can make it."

"Good. You're a hard worker, Jeremy."

He looked up from buttering a slice of bread and smiled at her. "I don't like it when you shout at me, so I try to keep up."

She feigned outrage. "When have I ever shouted at you?"

"Never. Not once. And I want to keep it that way."

She got up from her chair and kissed him on the cheek on the way to the fridge to get him a beer.

Dusk fell early in the winter, so as soon as he was done eating Jeremy left to meet up with Kevin and start their preparations. Adie was starting to clean up when the phone rang.

"Hello?"

"Adie, it's Wanda. Mike has no candles."

"How many do you need?"

"Two, one for him and one for Viola."

"I'll be over in a minute. How is everyone else doing?"

"As far as I know, everyone's ready."

"Okay, see you soon."

It was nearly time for her to go out anyway. She grabbed a handful of the traditional, narrow white pillar candles—just in case someone else might need one—and a few barbecue lighters, and put on her warmest jacket, a scarf, and a knit cap that Elizabeth had made for her over a decade ago. On her way to Mike's house the small school bus and the mail truck passed her and she waved as they went by.

Wanda, Mike, and Viola were waiting at the street outside his shop. Adie handed over the candles.

"Do you have a lighter?" Adie said

"Yes," Mike said, looking sheepish.

"Two of them," Wanda added.

"You do realize the irony of this?"

"Would you like to rub it in a bit?" Mike said.

"Yes, I would. You can order anything in the world for anyone, but despite a full year's notice you don't have two measly candles."

"Oh, we have them," Viola piped up. "We just can't find them."

Adie looked at her. "If you can't find them how do you know you have them?"

"Because I remember seeing them last year. But they were in some obscure box and when we looked for it this morning we couldn't find it."

"The basement," Mike said. "It's a mess. I've been meaning to get down there and organize it, but..." He looked at Wanda and smiled. "I've been a little preoccupied lately."

"Forgivable," Adie said. She pulled back the sleeve of her jacket and checked her watch. "Time to take my place."

"Thanks, Adie," Wanda said.

Adie laughed. "Merry Christmas."

They echoed the greeting as she walked back up the street to her house, where she took up station at the street.

Despite the darkness she could see Gordon and Mary across the way standing in front of their place with their three children. Paul and Martha came out a few minutes later to stand outside their house, to her right. It was too dark to see if anyone else was out, but a few minutes later Paul rang a handbell and people lit their candles. Then Adie could see by the two wavering lights at Ernie and Bev's, and another pair at Upton and Travis's, that they were in place as well.

Then the visitors started arriving. In occasional pairs and singletons, but mostly larger groups of couples with their children, they walked up from the parking area that Jeremy had cleared down by the lake and took up station between the houses. As they got settled more and more candles lit up.

A few minutes later a middle-aged woman Adie vaguely recognized ran up to her. "I'm sorry to bother you, but someone said you might be able to help us. We couldn't find…"

Adie held out her spares. The woman took three, leaving her with one extra.

"Do you need a lighter?" Adie said.

"No, thanks, we have one. I meant to get into town this weekend but…"

"It's okay. Where's your family?"

"Down next to the cafe."

"You'd better hurry then."

"Thank you so much."

Adie nodded, but the woman was already half-running down the hill.

Over the next five minutes more visitors arrived, taking up positions between her house and Paul's, between Paul's and Ernie's, between Upton's and Wanda's even though Wanda was over at Mike's. Finally a set of stragglers with three kids took a position to Adie's left—the end of the line—and she gave them her last extra candle, because they only had two, and no lighter. The parents let the children hold the candles. Adie resolved to bring more spares next year.

Now the streets as far as she could see down the hill were lit by people standing on the verge of the street holding white flickering candles. Adie was pleased. In very warm years it could rain on parade day, and you had to use an umbrella to keep the candles going. About half the time it

265

was snowing, and most people used umbrellas then too. This year the sky was overcast but it wasn't precipitating, just cold, so the worst they had to deal with was an occasional gust snuffing out a candle and forcing the celebrant to light it again.

There was a lull. No new visitors arrived, and nothing happened for several minutes. Adie could hear the muttered questions and complaints of the children to either side of her, but she ignored them. She watched expectantly down the hill.

Then she saw a glimmer through the trees. It looked like a cloud of fireflies was headed their way. The lights slowly grew brighter, but no more distinct, until you could tell that they were different colors.

Adie's heart skipped a beat. She had invented this ritual personally, as one more way to turn this ghost town into a real, living place. Despite that, every year when it began she felt a little thrill. It was so beautiful.

The lights continued to grow brighter until, far down the street, almost to the lake, the school bus came around the last bend. Its warning lights were flashing red and yellow, but those were outdone by the multicolored Christmas lights draped all along the top and down the sides. It drove at a walking pace up the slope until it reached Marmot Lane, and turned right at the cafe. Then she could see that behind it was the mail truck, similarly festooned with lights and with its flashers blinking.

And behind that were pickups, campers, SUVs, panel vans, small U-Haul trucks, and even a sedan or two, all strung with brilliant colored lights. Altogether there were over two dozen vehicles, coming sedately and brightly into town.

The children were all exclaiming and clapping, and some of the adults too. As the last vehicle in the caravan passed the audience, people fell into line, walking behind the vehicles. The parade went down Marmot Lane to the end and turned around in the cul-de-sac, passing by the cafe again while heading to Jodie's bar at end of the other leg of Marmot Lane. The bus crossed Little Fish Street shortly after the last vehicle turned off.

Minutes later the parade, now swelled by more than forty pedestrians holding candles, turned left onto Little Fish Street again and headed toward Adie. When the first vehicles passed she could see Jeremy driving the bus and Darren in the mail truck. All the other drivers were from out of town, and after the first few she stopped trying to recognize them (because she didn't) and just enjoyed the spectacle of the lights. Cemetery Lane was directly across from her house, so the vehicles and then the people turned right there.

The last one was a pickup with a large throne in the bed; the throne, like the truck's cab, was hung with glittering lights. And on that throne sat Santa, waving at the children and tossing them candy canes. It was Kevin of course; this was one of the Mayor's most important duties. Adie had to admit that he made a pretty good Santa. He was a little too lean, but Elizabeth had found him some padding, and the fake beard and the city's classic red suit looked good on him. The beard made it hard to tell, but she was fairly certain he wore a stunned expression on his face, which made her smile. He'd probably been expecting five vehicles at best, and at her request no one had told him anything about the candles. She would have loved to see his face as all those other cars showed up at the marshalling yard on Jack Road.

Elizabeth was following close to Santa's truck. She waved and smiled at Adie as she walked past.

Adie waited for the tail of the procession and fell in behind, followed by Mary and her family and the last visitors

267

to her left. The procession went all the way up Cemetery Lane, picking up a few more people at Jack and Sharon's house, and at the mobile homes that Helen and Pete lived in. That was everyone, about a hundred pedestrians following over twenty vehicles.

The parade turned at the end of the road, which also had a cul-de-sac of course—this is why they were there—and went back down Cemetery Lane, turned onto Little Fish Street for the last time, and went around the big bend, ending up at the Town Hall. The vehicles lined up all the way past the Hall and almost down to the curve.

As they stopped, the drivers got out, leaving their colored lights on, and mixed with the audience to gather near the marmot statue. When the crowd was assembled, Santa strode up and faced the crowd.

"Merry Christmas," Kevin bellowed, and was answered by a chorus of the same.

He bent down to lift a weather-proof cover in the base of the statue's pedestal and flip the switch. The giant tree directly across the road lit up with thousands of white lights and everyone cheered. A woman, whose voice Adie didn't recognize, started singing Silent Night and the whole crowd joined in, including Adie.

Someone had once compared this part of their tradition to the Whos in Whoville holding hands and singing around the tree, in Dr. Seuss's Grinch story. Adie hated that idea; she hated that story. She didn't think this was anything like the story; it was better.

And when the song ended, it was over. Some people milled around, greeting others and looking up at the tree. A few of the drivers went to their cars or trucks, turned them around, and paused for their families to get in. That made it easier for the next set, and they for the next. Half an hour after lighting the tree, almost all the visitors were gone, leaving just the Marmot residents and a few stragglers, most with their candles still lit, standing around looking smug.

Santa came up to her and handed her a candy cane.

"Thanks," she said.

"You told me it would be a small procession," Kevin said.

"Well, it's not the Macy's Thanksgiving Day parade."

"Of course." He was taking it pretty well. "Well, that was just about the coolest thing I've ever seen. But—who were all those people?"

"Clients of Elizabeth, or Mike or Mary. Or people that we've hired in the past. Like Halloween, word gets around. This town has friends, Santa."

Before she could react, he stepped in close and gave her a hug. "Nice surprise, Adie Eagle."

"Thanks. Say hello to Comet and Vixen for me."

"Will do."

He turned away and Elizabeth came up and took his arm. She smiled at Adie as they walked past.

Adie looked up at the tree, then turned one hundred eighty degrees to look up at the marmot statue. "I love this damned place," she muttered, and headed on home—alone, for the first time ever on a parade night.

Gifts

Adie sat back from her computer and stared at the screen. The cursor winked at her with smug impertinence. She leaned forward again and saved the file, then chose the Print command.

She was finished with her history of Marmot. She still had to do a read-through, which would result in hundreds of edits, she was sure. But the project she'd been planning and thinking about for decades was done. She'd taken it right up to the Christmas Parade this year. That seemed like a good place to stop.

The dogs looked up at her from beneath her desk. She got up and grabbed her coat. Knowing what that meant, they jumped up and followed her out the back of the building for a pee and a romp in the new snow that had fallen overnight. It was melting already, as it tended to do. Almost every winter night the temperature fell below freezing, and until the hard freeze that came every February nearly every day would be above freezing, so snow had a tendency to settle into compact layers. It was good for making snowmen, but garbage for cross-country skiing. Not that she cared anymore; she'd given that up in her forties.

Wombat came racing back with snow all over his face; it was hard to make out the big grin behind it. Bunny ambled toward her with a more serious expression. In the five minutes they'd been out, Bunny had managed to get dozens of little snowballs embedded in her belly fur. They looked like white Christmas tree ornaments.

"Retrievers," Adie grumbled. She took a wide-toothed plastic comb from her jacket pocket and combed out the dangling snow. Bunny took it stoically, but Adie knew she hated this. Wombat's problem was solved more simply by scrubbing his face with her mittened hands. When she was done he looked even sillier, but he shook his habitual punk coiffure back into place.

When the dogs had been given a treat and settled back onto their beds, Adie was momentarily at a loss for what to do next. That didn't happen very often. Her daily tasks included entering data into the economic model that tracked the flow of money through the town, monitoring their investments (which was redundant because that was Travis's job, but she did it anyway), tweaking her short- and long-term strategies for the town, and passing information around the network.

But she'd done all of that. It was mid-afternoon and she'd finished her history. She had half-expected an earthquake or a thunderbolt at the very least, but not this— not nothing.

So she did what she always did when she was at a loss. She consulted one of her lists. She'd checked off half a dozen things already, but the big one at the top was still in progress: Jeremy's scripts. She took a deep breath, summoned up a well of motivation from somewhere, set aside her desire to just go home and read, and resumed work on the biggest programming project she'd ever undertaken.

* * *

Jeremy's birthday was December 24. Adie remembered when Ida had gone into the hospital early in the morning to deliver him. Her sister had said, "If this baby had waited until

271

Christmas I never would have forgiven it." But Christmas Eve was bad enough. There had been no traditional cinnamon rolls for Christmas breakfast that year. And every year afterward Ida had had to struggle with the temptation to fold the two celebrations into one. But she never did: every year Jeremy celebrated his birthday on one day and Christmas the following day. It was a one-two punch that might have derailed some children—what would they expect on December 26? —but not Jeremy.

Adie held a little dinner party for him that year. She varied the festivities, but he never wanted anything fancy. Some years it had just been the three of them, Adie, Jeremy, and Elizabeth. Lately Helen and Mechelle had always been involved. But this time Kevin was coming as well, of course, and she also invited Mike, Viola, and Wanda. Jeremy asked her to include Darren too. Adie wasn't sure that was a great idea, but she had sent a message to ask Elizabeth, who said it would almost certainly be fine.

Elizabeth brought a long, wide loaf of bread and a chocolate cake. Adie made a big pan of lasagna and a salad.

She kept an eye on Darren as the evening progressed, looking for anger or pain, but all she saw was occasional wistfulness when Wanda and Mike put their heads together. He never talked much at the best of times, so she couldn't use his silence as a gauge, but it seemed that he had accepted this new phase in his relationship with his ex-wife, and put away any hopes of reconciliation that might have sprung up at Elizabeth's wedding.

Jeremy and Kevin made sure Darren was included in their conversations, which were mostly about plans for more aggressive clean-ups around town when spring came. Darren knew a man who ran a waste disposal company and the three of them, being male, had a long, happy discussion about dumpsters.

When it was time for dessert, Adie turned off the kitchen lights and Elizabeth lit candles on the cake she'd made. They all sang the birthday song, which Adie secretly despised. In her middle years she had written several replacement songs, but could never convince anyone to use them. She'd finally given up, and—like most of her pet peeves— kept this one to herself.

Only Adie, Elizabeth, Helen, and Mechelle gave gifts; the others had been gently told not to. The women in his life knew that Jeremy preferred that they not make a fuss over him, but none of them could stop themselves from making him something.

Elizabeth gave him a knit cap like the one she'd made for Adie so many years ago. It was deep blue with a gold diamond pattern running around it, and Jeremy wore it for the rest of the evening. Helen and Mechelle gave him a book that the Montessori students had made, which had blank pages interspersed with drawings of Jeremy delivering the mail, driving the school bus, ploughing the roads, and playing with Adie's dogs. Many of the drawings were childish, of course, but several by Tika and Mechelle were exceptional.

Adie handed him a large, rectangular package that was only a few inches thick, wrapped in brown paper. He gasped a little when he opened it.

"What is it?" Kevin said.

Jeremy turned it around so everyone could see it. It was a sizable framed photograph of a woman holding a swaddled newborn. The woman looked blissful as she gazed down at her new baby; tired but ecstatic and fulfilled. The baby looked like every healthy newborn since the world began: scrunched-up face and pudgy cheeks. The original

273

photograph had clearly been in color that had long ago faded, perhaps a Polaroid, and rather small. Adie had enlarged it, and used Photoshop filters to turn it into a sepia-toned print, with a stipple effect that covered the lack of detail from the enlargement and made it look like a Madonna and child.

It was Ida and Jeremy of course.

"Thirty-one years ago today," Adie said. Jeremy handed the picture to Helen and came around the table to hug her. He didn't say anything. He didn't need to.

* * *

Adie gave up on Christmas the year her sister Ida died. She had never loved the holiday to begin with, not since she was very young, but that year she'd got out the boxes and bins of decorations and then sat in her living room looking at them for a long time, before putting them back in the basement. She just couldn't do it. She'd asked the few people who might be inclined to give her presents not to. She could tell it was hard for Elizabeth and Jeremy, but they complied.

She wasn't sure why she had soured on Christmas as a child. It might have had something to do with her alcoholic father and his predictable late-afternoon eruptions: storming around the house, bellowing and throwing things, and more often than not trampling the toys she and Ida had just unwrapped. Her mother's solution was always to dress them in their warmest coats and send them outside for an hour or two to play in the snow. When she called them back inside her father would be asleep in the bedroom.

But she'd quickly got used to the brutal, pathetic ritual, and soon learned to hide her favorite new presents and help Ida do the same. By the time she was eight the toys her father destroyed were always old ones that she had tired of anyway. He never seemed to notice.

It was Christmas evening now and she sat alone in her living room in the dark, alone except for her beloved dogs, and mentally catalogued everything she'd lost. Her parents, her husband, her sister. Her ability to have fun, to enjoy a sunrise for its own sake, to rejoice in the blossoms of spring.

Jeremy was with Helen and Mechelle in their sad little mobile home, as he had been for the last several years on Christmas night. The place was probably decorated beautifully, with a tree and garlands, construction paper chains, popcorn and cranberries strung on string, twinkle lights everywhere, the smell of cinnamon and ginger, the sound of laughter.

She thought briefly about going to her office to work.

The dogs looked up inquiringly as she bolted up from her chair. She went to the hall closet and put on her red wool coat and the hat Elizabeth had made her. She hurried outside before she could change her mind.

The Christmas tree across from the Town Hall was lit, as it had been every night since the parade. She could see it twinkling through the intervening trees as she strode up Cemetery Lane, past the empty houses that Darren looked after, past the Durgan's place where the couple were probably cuddled up on the sofa with their lovely mutts, watching *It's a Wonderful Life.* She passed the cemetery, nodding her head to Ida's grave, invisible in the dark; passed the school and its ridiculous rocket ship.

She walked up to the door of Helen's ramshackle trailer and paused for just a moment before knocking with her bare knuckles. It seemed a month before the door opened and she saw Helen's unabashed, unfiltered surprise and joy,

Mechelle's innocent grin, and on Jeremy's face a slowly growing smile that would split his head if he didn't watch out.

Behind them the trailer looked exactly as festive and welcoming as she had imagined, if not better.

"Merry Christmas," Adie said. "May I join you?"

Last Birthday

The day before Elizabeth's thirty-sixth birthday, Adie hit another milestone on her task list. The scripting engine she'd been working on for over a month was complete. All that was left was to actually write the messages that she wanted to leave for Jeremy. Her first impulse was to start composing facetious, jokey ones, but she stifled it and closed the script file. She wanted to sleep on what needed to be said. Instead she opened up the source code for her economic model. She had never been happy with the level of detail in the comments, and it was going to be hard for anyone else to modify the model without whatever help she could leave behind.

A few hours later, Kevin stopped by when he was done helping Jeremy with sorting the mail. "Got a minute?" he said.

"Yes, come in." Wombat and Bunny got up from their beds and came around the desk to say hello to Kevin, then went right back. He sat in one of the guest chairs, not quite looking at her. She let him take his time.

"What do you usually do for Elizabeth on her birthday?" he said at last.

Adie laughed. "Kevin, are you *worried* about this?"

He looked surprised she would ask. "Of course I am. I was worried about Christmas, too."

"Well, that went well, didn't it? I know she loved the necklace you got her." And she knew that Mike had found him a great bargain on *catbirdnyc.com*.

"Yes, but her birthday is something else, isn't it? It's just about her. This is the first one we've celebrated together, and I want to do it right."

"What did you have in mind?"

"Well... a small party. You and Jeremy and Helen, Mechelle, maybe one other couple. Any more and they wouldn't fit in our kitchen. I was thinking I'd make dinner and a cake."

"I wouldn't invite more than the four people you mentioned. Six is enough, and that's bigger than any party she's had since she was a little girl."

"Okay. Any suggestions on the cake?"

"Can you do seven-minute frosting."

"Sure. I've done that."

"Chocolate cake, seven-minute frosting. That's her favorite, and I know she hasn't had it for several years."

"Got it."

"You want me to tell the others?"

"No, I'll do that. Thanks." He got up and started to leave.

"Kevin."

He turned around again. "Yes?"

"*Very* chocolate."

He smiled and left.

* * *

The next morning Adie was working on the first of her scripted message trails when she got a text message from Elizabeth. "I told him."

She had to mean she'd told Kevin about the baby. She replied, "How did he react?"

"He said it was MY birthday, I shouldn't be giving HIM gifts."

278

"He's happy, then?"

"Ecstatic."

Well, that should help him get through his big day of cooking and baking.

* * *

Jeremy had said he'd meet her at Elizabeth's house, so after work Adie walked down the hill alone. She took her time, enjoying the cold dusk. The last light was fading beyond the western hills and the Moon wouldn't rise for hours, so the stars were popping out bright and clear. It had snowed again that morning, so everything was frosted with a fresh blanket except the dirty piles where Jeremy's plough had pushed the three inches of accumulation off the streets.

The cafe lights beckoned her once she passed Ernie and Bev's place. The walk up to the cafe was clear, and so was the path around back. Someone had even scraped the snow off the solar lights that lit the side path, so she had no trouble making her way back to the stairs that led up to the residence.

Adie paused at the foot of the stairs. Until just recently this little walk, all downhill from the Town Hall, would not have inconvenienced her at all. But she suddenly found she needed to catch her breath, and the prospect of climbing these stairs was unnerving.

It passed in a moment and she started up, thinking that for most of her life she had run up flights of stairs. She was nearly at the top when she felt a sharp, intense pain in her chest. She gasped, and leaned hard against the railing. But it passed almost immediately, leaving nothing but a sense of dread. Adie waited, expecting the pain to come back harder and fiercer, but it didn't. She felt fine. So she went up the last handful of steps and walked into the house.

Everyone else had already arrived, standing around in the kitchen as always. Adie decided not to mention the weird episode on the stairs. They would just make a fuss and distract themselves from what was important.

They were loud and boisterous, as young people tended to be, but that never bothered her. Kevin was standing at the stove, stirring one of several simmering pans, and apparently just finishing a story about—if she understood the snatches she heard as she came in—a pompous Eugene politician and a llama. Adie shucked off her coat, hung it on the coat tree, and joined them as they burst into laughter. Elizabeth turned and gave her a swift hug, then went to the fridge to get her some mineral water.

"I don't get it," Mechelle said.

"The donkey is the symbol of the Democratic party," Helen explained.

"So when the llama kicked the donkey…"

"Right."

"Okay. But *why* is the donkey the symbol for Democrats?"

"That would be a good research topic for you," Helen said. Adie reflected for the hundredth time that having a mother who was a teacher was a curse that in later life would reveal itself as a special blessing.

"Did you just get off work?" Jeremy asked Adie.

"Yes."

"Anything urgent?"

"Not really." She wandered to the stove to look over Kevin's shoulder. "Indian?" He nodded, still stirring. "No wonder I haven't seen you all day. How long have you been at it?"

He looked up at her and grinned. "Since 9:00."

She clucked and took her water to sit on one of the bistro chairs. Normally there were only two, but Elizabeth had brought out four more from somewhere, and they just barely fit around the table. She had a moment of difficulty hitching herself up onto the tall chair, but she made it.

"Hey, remember your birthday last year?" Jeremy asked Elizabeth.

"Oh, please," Helen said.

"Are you really going to bring this up again?" Elizabeth said.

"What?" Kevin said from his post at the stove.

"The cake," Jeremy replied. "The Cake that Tipped the Planet."

"It wasn't that big," Elizabeth protested.

"Tell me," Kevin said. "I'm her husband, I should hear all the good stories."

"Go ahead," Adie butted in. "Kevin's right."

"I liked that cake," Mechelle said, but no one else seemed to notice. Adie nodded at her.

"Are you going to tell him," Jeremy said, "or should I?"

"You brought it up. You tell it."

"No interruptions. No corrections."

"Fine. Tell it your way. I need some more wine."

Kevin half-turned away from his work, looking back and forth between Elizabeth and Jeremy.

"Okay, here it is," Jeremy said. "Elizabeth hadn't had a birthday party since she was a little girl. Last year she turned thirty-five and she decided that she wanted a little party. It was all of us except for you, Kevin, but none of us had the guts to bake her a cake like you did."

Adie wondered if they'd seen Kevin's cake yet. That would have surprised her.

"Since no one else was going to do it," Jeremy continued, "and none of us could have done it as well anyway, Elizabeth baked herself a cake. It was the Coon Killer Cake."

Mechelle said, "It was the Cake that Broke the Camel's Back."

"It was the Cake that Cracked the Juan de Fuca Plate."

"Oh, enough already," Helen said. "I've seen bigger cakes at parties in Hollywood."

Jeremy stopped short. "You've been to parties in Hollywood?"

"I was born in L.A., you know."

"Me too," Mechelle added.

"Whose parties?"

"Hey," Kevin said, "can we tell one crazy story at a time?"

Jeremy shook it off. "Okay, unless you've been to parties in Hollywood it was the biggest birthday cake you've ever seen. Three feet high—"

"Jeremy," Elizabeth said.

"—and at least three feet wide. Twenty layers, each one smaller than the one below it, with hand-made sugar roses on every step, and it sparkled like diamonds with all the sugar crystals."

Kevin turned to look at Adie. "Adie, as a rational observer, can you clear this up?"

"Sure," she said. "It was the most exquisite cake I've ever seen, and delicious too. It did have hand-made roses, but they were fondant mixed with gum paste, not sugar. And it was an eight-layer cake, not twenty, with only three steps."

Jeremy scowled at her. "Who's telling this story?"

"You mean who's making this story up?" Adie asked. She waved her hand. "Go on, get it over with."

"We all had a piece of the cake, and she gave us some to take home, too. But that was like chipping ice cubes off a glacier. It didn't even make a dent in the towering magnificence—"

"Oh, Jeremy," Helen said, laughing in spite of herself.

"Please skip the poetry and get to the point," Elizabeth said. "I'm hungry."

"Okay, here's the point. The leftovers wouldn't fit in the refrigerator. Or the freezer. Or both combined. Or the house refrigerator and the cafe refrigerator combined. So she did what any enterprising, deranged, brilliant cook living in the Cascades would do. She covered up the Leaning Tower of Fondant and put it on the porch overnight."

"That makes sense," Kevin said. "It was January, so it would freeze. What, did she serve it at the cafe the next day?"

"There was nothing to serve," Jeremy said. "The raccoons ate it."

"You couldn't salvage—"

"They ate *all* of it." Kevin's jaw dropped. "Yes," Jeremy said, "all of it. We found a dozen raccoons dead by the side of the road, round as puffer fish, with frosting all over their frozen paws and big smiles on their frozen bandit faces."

Elizabeth and Helen both had their heads in their hands. Mechelle was smiling. Adie shook her head. Kevin turned back to the stove and gave each pan one last stir. "Dinner's ready," he said.

* * *

It was an extravagant dinner, possibly the most complex homemade meal Adie had ever eaten. There was a cauliflower and pea stew, potatoes that were spicy and

283

sweet at the same time, glazed carrots, some kind of mushroom curry, and fragrant saffron rice that was also slightly sweet. Everything was heavily seasoned but not spicy hot. There was no room on the table for serving dishes, so everyone served themselves buffet style. And when they were all seated with their plates, there was no extra space whatsoever. The drinking glasses barely fit.

Everyone complimented the cook, including Adie, and Elizabeth looked very pleased. It occurred to Adie that her goddaughter had not had someone to cook for her regularly since she was a girl and her mother had reliably served up delicious and healthy but plain food. Not exotic stuff like this.

In those days the cafe had been a bit dingier but also a bit cozier, and the food had been very good but not exceptional. When Elizabeth took over and remodeled both the property and the menu, it no longer seemed the sort of cafe that belonged in an end-of-the-road hamlet like this. And that, of course, made it so much more special—magical even—than it had been before. Adie had loved Elizabeth's mother Anne, but the affection she felt for the daughter went beyond simple love and into the domain of ferocity. There wasn't anything she wouldn't do for Elizabeth, and it was occasionally maddening that for the last ten years there wasn't anything that Elizabeth *needed* her to do, except be a friend.

The conversation as they ate was sparse, as usual. This was sort of a tradition in Adie's family as well as in Elizabeth's: talking was for before and after. Mealtime was for appreciating the food. But Kevin whispered with Mechelle once or twice, brought up the Super Bowl with Jeremy—just a month away, apparently later than usual— and Helen also broke the code with both of those two.

When everyone was finished, Kevin looked at Elizabeth and she nodded.

"I thought you might like a little rest before dessert," he said.

"Rest?" Jeremy responded. "I need a nap and a three-mile run."

"So... Elizabeth and I have an announcement."

"You're kidding!" Helen said.

Kevin frowned. "No, I'm not. How did you— Never mind. We're going to have a baby."

Adie apparently was the only one who had known, though Helen had done well guessing from almost no clues. There was the usual furor and congratulations. Adie sat back and watched it, smiling but not speaking. She caught Elizabeth's eye at one point and they shared a moment of wry humor.

"When are you due?" Helen said.

"The second week in July," Elizabeth said.

"Ah, a summer baby, like Adie. Mechelle was born in winter, like you."

"Is this some kind of astrology thing?" Kevin asked.

"No, it's a 'getting to the hospital easily' kind of thing. Fortunately it almost never snows in L.A., so I didn't have that problem."

"Now I'm really in the mood for dessert," Jeremy said.

"Me too," Mechelle seconded. "Do you have any ice cream?"

Kevin got up and turned off the lights. He fussed around in the kitchen for several minutes and everyone was careful not to watch, even though he was in plain sight. But then he came back to the table carrying a tall, snow-white cake with six lit candles on top. Adie refrained as everyone else sang the song she hated most in the world. Kevin held the cake as

Elizabeth blew out the candles easily, and Jeremy jumped up to turn the lights back on as Helen moved dishes aside so Kevin could set the cake down.

Elizabeth served while Kevin got the ice cream. Adie was having trouble holding back tears. She knew she had every right to cry, but it would have been out of character and probably would have alarmed them all.

She felt so grateful that she'd had this last birthday with the woman she'd loved more than any other in the world since her sister died. She couldn't help remembering all those birthdays of past years, many of which Elizabeth had celebrated at Adie's house. The cloud of memories made it hard to concentrate on the cake and ice cream, the excited conversation and the modest gifts. Later she remembered kissing Elizabeth tenderly before she left, but not much else from the tail end of that raucous little party.

History

Monday, February 8

Adie resolved never again to come to work on the day after the Super Bowl. Kevin seemed intent on describing the game play-by-play, even though she'd told him she was not interested in football. The Saints beat the Colts, of course— because, she thought, *how could a mere horse from the Midwest defeat a supernatural being*? He was standing in her doorway, gesturing and nearly shouting in excitement. She finally got up, walked around her desk, and closed the door in his face.

That gave her a few hours of peace. But she didn't have anything critical to do with the time. Her scripting project had been finished for a week, and she was back to her normal routine of monitoring the town, with occasional afternoons spent on items from her list, mostly cleaning up and purging. The basement in her house was done. The files and storage rooms here at the Town Hall were still in pretty sorry shape, but she was making slow progress.

In the afternoon, after Kevin and Jeremy had finished sorting the mail, she thought it might be safe to try to talk to Kevin again. The two of them had probably rehashed the game again as they were working, and she was sure he'd have found someone in the cafe to discuss it with over lunch. So maybe it was out of his system by now.

When she got up she told the dogs to stay but they wanted to follow her, and—very unusually—she had to tell them twice more before they grudgingly lay down again.

She knocked on Kevin's half-open office door.

"Come in," he said. When she walked in he stood up. "I'm sorry about before. I got carried away. I didn't mean to—"

"Don't worry about it," she said. "I took as much as I could and then I stopped you. If you had opened the door and kept on talking I might have had to get violent, but you took the hint."

"Yeah, some hint. Sorry." He sat back down and gestured at the chairs facing him.

As she walked toward the nearest chair, she said, "I wanted to ask you about the—"

And then she stopped. There was the queerest feeling in her chest, a sort of tightness, but also lightness. She was dizzy. She felt herself swaying on her feet. Suddenly the sharp pain she'd felt on the stairs on Elizabeth's birthday came back, but this time it didn't stop. She thought she heard Kevin calling her name. But she didn't feel like answering.

* * *

She woke up in her own bed. Elizabeth was sitting on a chair on her right side, crying. When she saw that Adie was awake she wiped her eyes with a tissue and took Adie's hand.

"You had me so worried," Elizabeth said.

"What happened?"

"Kevin said you fainted and fell down. He carried you here."

Adie looked around. They were alone in the room. "He carried me? Where is he?"

"Out looking for Jeremy. They should be here any minute. Upton called for an ambulance on his satellite phone. It should be here in fifteen minutes or so."

"Ambulance? What for? I just fainted, dear. I don't need an ambulance."

"Adie!" she said indignantly. "You had a heart attack."

"That was a heart attack? No, I don't think so. Let me rest for a minute, then I'll get up."

"You're not going anywhere until that ambulance arrives."

Adie started to sit up but the dizziness came back. She gave it up and lay back. "Okay, fuss if you want to."

She could hear the front door open and loud, clomping steps came toward the room. Jeremy burst in, wearing his delivery uniform and still carrying the mail bag.

"How is she?" he asked Elizabeth.

"I'm awake, you know," Adie said.

"How are you?" Jeremy said.

"A little dizzy. I'm going to rest for a bit."

Jeremy looked at Elizabeth, who said, "Fifteen minutes. Maybe less." He nodded.

Kevin came into the room carrying another chair. Jeremy sat down on her left side and took her other hand.

"If I need to blow my nose one of you is going to have to hold the Kleenex," she said. "What are you looking so worried for? I'm fine."

"Of course you're fine," Elizabeth said.

Adie felt a spark pass from her to Jeremy where they were holding hands. It was the same thing she'd felt when she hugged Elizabeth at Thanksgiving, when Elizabeth had told her she was pregnant. But the spark was stronger this time; it really hurt. She wanted to look at her hand to see if it had burned her, but Jeremy was still holding it. He looked surprised and confused. She turned and looked at Elizabeth again. She looked confused too.

Everyone was confused and concerned—except Adie, who felt fine. Actually, she felt light. She hadn't felt so good in years. She remembered what it was like to run to school when she was a girl. Thinking back, she thought she must have looked like a deer: tawny, fleet, graceful, willowy. Why was she thinking about running when she was flat on her back?

The spark—that was what Jeremy had been waiting for. The thing that would give him direction, a focus in life. Good God, she should have found some way to pass it on years ago. She would gladly have traded these last few years of uselessness to give him a purpose for those same years. She should have… But then she realized that it hadn't been the proper time yet. He wasn't ready, and whatever it was she was passing on to her beloved nephew, she hadn't had it to give until recently. No, this was good enough. It was enough.

She looked at Elizabeth, who was crying again, and smiled; and then turned her head to look at Jeremy. He was crying too, the ninny. She hadn't seen him cry since he was a boy.

Adie looked up at the ceiling. She felt like she was holding her whole life in a bowl, intricately carved of maple with inset gold wires, like the ones she'd seen at the art show in Portland all those years ago when she was young. She had wanted to buy one, but she never had enough money. She would have liked to have had that sitting on her fireplace mantel all these years. She could have filled it with polished stones, or silk flowers, or something really special. And now there was one lying on her chest, holding her life like a warm, thick, sweet syrup. She could feel that bowl in her hands.

She closed her eyes and let go.

Part Four

* * *

Knight Ascendant

Orphan

Something like a shock of static electricity jumped from Adie's hand to Jeremy's, and he almost let go. But he managed to restrain the impulse and keep his eyes on her face, blurred through tears. So he saw the moment, mere seconds later, when she passed away. He was grateful that he didn't have to close her eyes; he knew he would have done it, but it would have disturbed him.

He'd never seen anyone die before. He'd been out of the room when his mother died in the hospital, also of a heart attack when she was only fifty. This was like losing his mother all over again, because for all his life Adie had been there like a second mom— but unlike his birth mother, Adie was strong, smart, and weird; just about the opposite of Ida.

Jeremy let go of Adie's hand and set it gently at her side. He looked across at Elizabeth, who was crying full on now, with deep wracking sobs, but his own tears had stopped. Behind her tears he could tell that something was confusing Elizabeth beyond the sudden, unexpected death. Maybe that spark had been meant for her. Jeremy didn't understand what it was. He didn't believe it was her life force or soul or anything like that; he'd given up those ideas when he was in grade school. He felt just as confused as Elizabeth looked.

Kevin had his hand on Elizabeth's shoulder, not speaking, just present for comfort. He looked upset, which made Jeremy feel better. He'd known that Kevin was somewhat intimidated by his aunt, and though he didn't blame him at all he was gratified that Kevin felt something beyond that. Jeremy wished Helen were here, but she was at school, working.

Now what? he thought.

Well, the ambulance was coming. They had no way to stop it, and he wouldn't have anyway. There were many things he had to do, but he didn't know what they were and he didn't know in what order to do them. When his mother died Adie had handled everything.

Someone knocked at the door. "I'll get it," he said, forestalling Kevin. He dried his face with his sleeve and walked to the front door. It was Upton.

"How is she?" he said.

"She died," Jeremy said. He could see that was the wrong thing to say. Upton's face crumbled in shock and he looked nearly ready to cry himself. "I'm sorry," Jeremy said.

Upton waved a hand and got himself under control. "No, *I'm* sorry. Do you need anything?"

"No, thanks. Um... do you want to come in?"

"No. I just— No. Uh, I'll get out of your way. I'm sorry, Jeremy. She was irreplaceable."

"Thanks."

He went back to Adie's bedroom. "Upton," he said. Elizabeth nodded; she looked calmer. She was drying her eyes with Kleenex from the box on the nightstand. When he came into the room she stood up and hugged him fiercely. "Is there something we need to do?" he said. He felt completely overwhelmed. "Don't people wash the body or something?"

"I think we should leave her until the ambulance arrives," Elizabeth said. "It will only be a few minutes."

Jeremy nodded and sat down again. Then he got back up and went into the kitchen to get a chair for Kevin, who thanked him and sat next to Elizabeth.

It was about five minutes later that they heard the siren approaching. Jeremy went outside and stood with his back to the front door. When the ambulance pulled up he walked down to meet the two EMS guys.

"We had a report of a heart attack," the lead one said. He had a trimmed black beard and shaggy, untrimmed eyebrows. The name tag on his left breast said "Matthews." His partner was a lot younger and blond; he looked like he was still in high school

"She died about ten minutes ago."

"Oh... I'm very sorry. Can you take us to her?" Jeremy led them into the bedroom. They checked Adie's pulse and breathing and confirmed that she was gone. "Did you notice the time that she passed?"

"It was 3:34," Elizabeth said. "She was talking to us, then she closed her eyes and exhaled deeply and didn't breathe in again."

The lead man made a note on a clipboard. "Was she under a doctor's care?"

"No," Jeremy said. "She was healthy."

"We need to take her with us," Matthews said. "In cases like this the law requires that we determine the precise cause of death. So... there will have to be an autopsy. Who is the next of kin?"

"I am. Jeremy Cooper. She was my aunt."

Matthews wrote that down. "Can you tell me her full name and date of birth?"

"Adie Constance Eagle. Born August 13, 1935."

"Okay, we already have the address. Did she have a doctor?"

Jeremy gave him the name of her doctor in White Salmon. "Yes, I know her. Okay, we'll contact her and let her know. Do you know if there's a funeral home she preferred?"

"Hang on, let me look." Adie had told him she kept a folder of important papers in the top right drawer of the dresser that she used as a filing cabinet in her study. He opened the drawer and saw a fat manila envelope with his name on it. Inside was a fact sheet giving her Social Security number and a lot of other stuff, including the name of a mortuary in White Salmon. Under that was a letter addressed to him, which he glanced at without reading—and a will. He took the top sheet back to show to Matthews.

"Thanks, you've been very helpful. If you folks will give us a little room, we'll take good care of your aunt now."

They went back out to the ambulance to get a gurney, and with swift but somehow reassuring efficiency they loaded Adie's body onto it, covered her with a sheet, and strapped her down. Matthews gave Jeremy a piece of paper with his name, the hospital contact number, and some other information on it. He had signed it and written in the date and time.

Jeremy followed them outside and then they left. There was a small crowd of people standing in the yard as the gurney went past, like an honor guard: Ernie and Bev, Upton and Travis, Jodie, Jack and Sharon, Melissa, Mike, Mary. Jeremy barely heard their condolences. It was all just a blur. Elizabeth and Kevin came out a moment later and talked to the other people, and then everyone went away but Elizabeth and Kevin.

Jeremy had a sudden thought. "I'll bet the dogs are still in her office."

"Bring them to the cafe," Elizabeth said. "They can stay there with Owl during the day."

"That's a good idea. I'll do that now."

It felt good to be doing something. He strode up to the Town Hall and went to Adie's office. The dogs came out from under her desk when he called and he put their leashes on. They didn't seem reluctant to go with him, but they did seem a little confused when he passed their house. They paused and sniffed for over a minute. He let them pull him into the yard so they could get the whole story, then they looked up at him.

"Bunny, Wombat," he said, "you're going to hang out with Owl from now on during the day. You'll like it there, people will give you food."

Jeremy walked them down to the cafe and let them inside. Owl looked up from her corner and thumped her tail. The other two had never been inside the cafe before. The three dogs snuggled up together in a pile and looked up at him. Elizabeth gave each of them a treat. Then she gave him another hug.

"I've got to finish delivering the mail," he said.

"You do that," she told him. "And take your time. Do it right."

He grinned at her and went back to the house to try to find his mailbag.

* * *

Kevin caught up with him when he returned to drop off his mailbag and change back into his regular clothes.

"Hey, Jeremy," Kevin said, "you doing all right?"

"I'm holding up."

"How do I call a town meeting?"

"Hmm. Adie always did that. Wait… There's an email alias for everyone in town, I think it's town@marmot.org. Just send an email to that. Whoever doesn't see it will hear about it the old-fashioned way."

"Okay, thanks. Anything I can do for you?"

"I'm okay, Kevin. Thanks."

He started tidying up the mailroom. Not because it needed it. Because he did.

* * *

Helen came over alone to make dinner that night.

"Where's Mechelle?" Jeremy asked.

"She's having a sleepover with Adhira tonight."

"Oh." He looked up from unpacking the bag of groceries she'd brought and found her staring at him with concern all over her face. "I'm okay," he said. "Sad, of course. Feeling a little lost. But I'm not… distraught."

She came over and gave him a long, long hug anyway. He didn't try to break away. He never did. If she wanted to hug him for twelve hours, that was okay with him.

Eventually she let him go. "News travels at the speed of light these days," she said. "I saw the message Upton sent when I took a break after art class. I called Wanda over and she couldn't believe it. She left right away. I wanted to, but I had the kids."

"I understand," he said. "I was probably out on my rounds, anyway." She looked about to say something—probably something sympathetic—but changed her mind.

"What's for dinner?" he said. "And can I help?"

After they ate he sat down in the living room with the envelope Adie had left for him. The contact list wasn't very interesting, except that it had the name of the White Salmon lawyer who was also on the letterhead of the will's cover sheet. The only other thing in the envelope was a computer-printed letter from Adie to him, which he hadn't even glanced at yet. He looked over at Helen; she was engrossed in a biography of Eleanor Roosevelt.

* * *

Dear Jeremy:

There's so much I wanted to tell you but never got the chance. No, not true. Let me be perfectly honest since if you're reading this there's nothing left between us anymore. I had an infinite number of chances to tell you everything, but never could work up the enthusiasm. It was so much easier to just live our comfortable life together.

You probably didn't know one of the most important things about your mother: that she was an alcoholic. You didn't know this because she got it under control when you were very small. But I know for a fact that there was not a day of her life after you were born that she didn't long for a drink. And more importantly, she never gave in to that craving after you were two. There was an accident at home when she was drunk, it was completely her fault, and she never forgave herself. That's where you got the long scar on your left leg. So the most important thing to know about this is that she was not just sweet, she was strong. She was as tough as granite.

I realize that some people in town think I am a control freak, a voyeur, and maybe a witch. Well, switch out some consonants and maybe they're right. I'm leaving you the keys to the system that let me play those parts, and it's completely up to you what to do with them. Don't use this unless you become the Town Manager, but I predict that will happen within the first week after my death.

login: jctm password: your middle name

I know you know this, but I want to say it anyway. I love you and Elizabeth as if you were my own children. It's always been hard for me to slough off the kevlar shell I live in and show my true feelings. But you can trust me when I say this: your mother and you, and your godsister Elizabeth, were the best things that ever came into my life. The only thing I loved nearly as much was this town. Take care of it.

Adie

* * *

He read it through again. The signature was utterly redundant. He would have known who wrote it by the end of the second sentence. He set the letter aside and skimmed the will. The last page listed assets, including bank account numbers and the balances as of a month ago. No surprises there: she wasn't rich, but she left a little money to Elizabeth and everything else to him.

Jeremy set the papers aside and watched Helen read for a while. She was so intent. He tried to clarify his thoughts about her, and found it surprisingly easy. They had always been so muddled before. He loved her, and he was pretty sure she loved him too. What else mattered? Why had he been so reluctant to take the next step?

Eventually she must have felt his gaze. She looked up and smiled, went back to her

book, but immediately looked back at him. "Bedtime?" she said. "Definitely."

Rites

Tuesday, February 9

After breakfast Jeremy dropped the dogs off at the cafe. They seemed happy to go there, especially together, and most especially since they were all confused about where Adie was. They had slept with her every single night since she adopted them, one by one over the years, from a shelter down in the Gorge somewhere. Last night they had slept in her room as usual, but without her.

He stopped at Upton's house and borrowed their satellite phone, then went to Adie's office and sat in her chair. It felt strange, like trespassing. There were two dog beds under the large, U-shaped desk, with hollows in their centers. It smelled faintly like dog, but more like his aunt. She'd been in the middle of something, obviously, when she went to see Kevin and collapsed in his office. There were papers and books on her desk, and she usually left it empty when she went home for the night.

Jeremy unfolded the contact sheet and called the lawyer. The secretary connected him immediately.

"Jeremy Cooper," the lawyer said in a voice that sounded as if he gargled with olive oil. "You're Adie Eagle's nephew, right?"

"Yes."

"How is she? I haven't seen her in months."

Jeremy hesitated; he didn't want to say it. "She left me your name and a copy of her will."

There was a long silence. "Did she pass away?"

"Yesterday afternoon."

"I am very, very sad to hear that."

"I don't have the slightest idea what to do next."

"Let me handle this for you. What you have is *just* a copy of the will. The original is filed with the court in Goldendale. I'll enter it into probate and take care of the other business that needs to be done. I assume you don't have a death certificate yet."

"No."

"I'll need a copy to enter the will. Who was her doctor?" Jeremy told him. "I know her. I'll take care of that too and have one couriered up to you as soon as it's available. Do you know what her funeral wishes were?"

"Yes, I have all that."

"Okay, I'll leave that part up to you and get back to you when there's been some progress. Let me just check... We have a mailing address but no phone number or email address."

"That's right."

He must have been used to that with Adie because he didn't miss a beat. "Okay, I'll be in touch via mail. Jeremy, I'm so sorry. She was a tough old girl, but I've never met anyone with a purer heart."

"Thanks."

He looked at his sheet again and called the mortuary. An unreasonably chipper young woman answered. He told her that Adie Eagle had died and that her remains would be coming to them when the coroner was through. The woman looked Adie up in their files.

"Yes, we have her. Everything is prepaid. It says here... You said your name was Jeremy Cooper?"

"Yes."

"Okay, it says the casket should be delivered to you for internment."

301

"Yes, there's a…" He wasn't sure how to say it. Unlicensed cemetery? Illegal? "Family mausoleum here. That's where she wanted to be buried."

"We can do that. But… no service?"

"No. She didn't want a formal service. We'll have a memorial here." That was a lie too.

"How can I reach you? The number you're calling from is unidentified."

"It's a satellite phone." He gave her his address.

"You don't have a phone?"

"It's a long story. Just give me a day's notice before you bring her up here."

"Very well. Our condolences, Mr. Cooper."

"Thanks."

* * *

When he went to pick up the mail in Trout Lake that afternoon, Barb the postmistress had her frowny face on. Nothing she did was ever subtle, refined, or restrained. She was like a giant puppy with a mean streak.

"Sorry to hear about Adie," she said.

"How did you…"

"Oh, word gets around. I am the Post Office, you know."

She thought she was. What she really was a tinfoil bureaucrat in the world's smallest mailroom. Of course, what did that make Jeremy, since he took a tiny bit of their mail and distributed it by hand?

"Well, thanks," he said. "See you tomorrow."

"Wait. What do you think will happen now?"

"What do you mean?"

"Will you abandon the town?"

He shook his head. "What?"

"Adie *was* the town, wasn't she? Will you all pack up and move out?"

He sighed and leaned on the counter. "It's a self-sustaining organism, a complex system in dynamic equilibrium. Adie helped set that up, but it didn't collapse when she died. That was the point of her life's work. There are enough redundancies and reinforcing dependencies that with a sufficient but small and steady input it demonstrates resilience in the face of minor chaos. Okay?"

Jeremy didn't smile at her shocked expression, but he wanted to. That was ten times longer than any speech he'd ever delivered to her before, and he'd just increased her estimate of his vocabulary by five thousand percent. He was quite sure she had no idea what it all meant, and that was just the way he wanted it. He waved, picked up his bag, and left.

He had never felt so strongly how much he was his aunt's nephew.

* * *

Jeremy noticed as he passed the town sign that Darren had updated it already: "Welcome to Marmot, Population 32."

* * *

Jeremy sat on the community room stage with Kevin. In the last several years there had always been at least three chairs for these meetings—Adie, the Mayor, and Jeremy. Now there were only two.

As far as he could tell without counting heads, everyone was here. The crowd was much quieter than usual at these

303

things. Typically town meetings were an excuse for a gossip festival and a party atmosphere—often there were refreshments afterwards. It was usually a lot like movie nights, without the movie. But none of that was true today.

At 8:00 sharp Kevin stood up and what little conversation there was faded away. He walked to the front of the stage and put his hands in his pockets.

"I'm not going to try to eulogize Adie," he said, "because I barely knew her. It's not my place, anyway. If Jeremy or Elizabeth, or any of you, want to say a few words when I'm done, I'll gladly relinquish the stage. I called this meeting because I thought, in keeping with Adie's terrifying efficiency—" Several people laughed at that. "—that we should talk about the vacant position of Town Manager. I've seen how you run elections here—" More laughter. "—but I'm not sure that's necessary in this case. So I thought I'd ask your opinion about just doing a voice vote.

"Adie made it very clear to me that she expected— maybe hoped would be more accurate—that Jeremy would take her place. That makes a lot of sense to me. Jeremy has lived here all his life, he knows the town inside and out, and he already does half of everything that ever gets done here. So if he's willing..." Kevin glanced back at Jeremy, and he nodded, resigned to his aunt's indomitable will.

"I propose a voice vote to hire Jeremy Cooper as the new Town Manager. Would anyone care to second the motion?"

"Seconded," half a dozen people said simultaneously, including Helen, Elizabeth, Jodie, and Upton.

"All those in favor?"

"AYE!" It sounded like everyone in the room had shouted it.

"All those against?"

No one said anything for a moment, then Ernie stood up. "I abstain," he said gruffly, and sat down again.

"Jeremy, congratulations," Kevin said, and invited him to the front of the stage before taking his seat.

Jeremy stood up and stepped forward. He was accustomed to being on display in these dog and pony shows, but not to speaking. He cleared his throat.

"Thanks for that. I know that some of you found Adie difficult, and I completely understand. I loved her, but sometimes I thought she was an alien, too." There were a few chuckles. "However, she was really good at this job, and though I can't compare myself to her, I will do the best I can." He paused for a moment. "When I was picking up the mail in Trout Lake today, the postmistress asked me if we were going to evacuate the town because Adie had died."

The outraged shouts that followed surprised him. Some people jumped up out of their seats. Kevin rushed up to the front and calmed everyone down.

When it was quiet again, Elizabeth called out, "What did you say?"

"Well." There was no way he was going to repeat his grandiloquent speech. "Adie was not the town of Marmot. She was *part* of this town, just as we all are. I'm not sure that we'd be here if it wasn't for her, but she set it up so it would run without her. And that's what I intend to do. If we even thought about abandoning her life's work, she'd come back from the dead just to kick our butts."

There were shouts of approval. He went back to his seat. He could see several people looking at him speculatively, as if they'd never really seen him before.

Kevin said, "Any questions? Anyone want to say anything at all?"

No one volunteered. Kevin gestured to Jeremy again. He realized that as Manager it was now his duty to open and close proceedings like this.

He stood up and said, "Thank you for your confidence in me. Meeting adjourned."

Kevin came over and shook his hand. "It will be a pleasure working with you outside the mailroom," he said.

"Don't think I'm letting you off the hook," Jeremy said. "Mailroom duties will be written into the Mayor's job description from now on."

"Okay, then. See you tomorrow."

Jeremy jumped down off the stage. Elizabeth came up to him.

"Well done," she said.

He hugged her and looked around for Helen. He took her hand in one of his, and Mechelle's in the other, and walked out to go home.

* * *

It snowed again that night, so on Wednesday he was busy with ploughing and didn't get a chance to use his new login, and didn't look at his mail until almost dinnertime. He had express letters from the doctor, the lawyer, and the funeral home.

Adie had died of cardiac arrest. The death certificate would be delivered soon, the will would be entered into probate on Friday, and the body had already been transferred to the funeral home. Adie's instructions forbade a public viewing, so her body wasn't going to be embalmed. The coffin would be brought up to Marmot on Thursday morning.

Jeremy sent a message to Elizabeth to summarize all this, then went looking for Darren. He found him in the cemetery, surprisingly, standing just inside the broken-down fence, looking at the ground.

"Darren," Jeremy said.

Darren shook off his reverie. "Oh, hi. What's up."

"They're sending Adie's coffin up tomorrow. Can we dig a grave?"

"Well, we haven't had our deep freeze yet, so it shouldn't be any problem. I'll go get the backhoe first thing in the morning. Are you going to have a ceremony?"

"She didn't want one."

"Memorial service?"

"She said no."

"Okay. It's her funeral."

He said this with a perfectly straight face. Jeremy looked up at him for a moment, then they both burst out laughing. He was ashamed of himself, but he couldn't help it.

"Probably just me and Elizabeth then. So let me know."

"Okay. Uh... I guess next to her husband, right?"

"No. Next to my mom." That's what the will said.

Darren looked at him speculatively for a moment, then nodded.

* * *

In the end there were five people standing around the coffin suspended over the empty grave: Jeremy and Helen, Kevin and Elizabeth, and Darren. The funeral home people had left the coffin at the edge of the pavement nearest the cemetery. Darren had attached nylon straps around it, then lifted and carried it with the backhoe bucket, which still held it suspended just above ground level. It was an undignified way to go to one's final rest, but Jeremy thought Adie would have found it hilarious.

No one said anything. Jeremy thought they might be waiting for him, but he had nothing to say. He'd loved his aunt, but speaking ritualistic or meaningless words at her corpse wasn't going to make him feel better, and she was past all that.

Darren glanced at him out of the corner of his eye and Jeremy nodded. Darren stepped up into the cab of the little backhoe, fired it up, and slowly lowered the coffin. When it was all the way down Darren jumped down into the hole, released the ratchet fasteners on the straps, and climbed back up. The straps were still connected to the bucket, so he pulled them out and looked at Jeremy once more. Then he started shoveling the dirt in on top of the coffin.

"I need to order a headstone," Jeremy said.

Kevin said, "I thought the cemetery was decommissioned."

"Yeah," Jeremy said. "They can arrest me if they want. But she's staying right here."

Elizabeth touched his arm, then she led Kevin away. Helen put her arm around him and they walked the short distance to the school, where Wanda was watching the kids while Helen took this odd funeral break.

He kissed her at the door and said, "Thanks for taking the time."

She didn't say anything, she just kissed him again and went inside. Jeremy turned and headed back to the cemetery. Darren was nearly done filling the hole. Jeremy watched him tamp the mound down with the back of the bucket, then he walked to the Town Hall to get the mail truck. It was time to go pick up the mail.

It was getting really cold. He turned up his collar. It was a good thing the mortuary people had brought Adie up today. It felt like the annual hard freeze was coming tonight.

Ghost

Friday, February 12

Although the temperature had dropped below ten degrees overnight it hadn't snowed, so Jeremy had very little to do in the morning other than spread sand over a few slippery spots on Little Fish Street. That was done by midmorning, so he decided to try to start learning how to be a Town Manager.

He went to Adie's office—his office now—and sat in her chair. His chair. He decided that the dog beds could stay, even though he doubted that he would bring Bunny and Wombat here with him, because he was never going to spend all day at this desk as Adie had. He'd probably be in and out all day, driving the bus to take the high school kids to Trout Lake in the morning and picking them up in the afternoon; picking up the mail, sorting and delivering it; ploughing the roads; or whatever else needed doing.

Now that he thought about it, "whatever needed doing" had been nearly a full-time job. Maybe he should think about delegating some of that. To whom, though?

He looked over the stuff Adie had been working on when she left her office for the last time. Four days ago. Only four days. There were spreadsheets for town finances, programming books, and pads with her small, tight writing all over them. He closed all the books and put them on the shelf in the corner. He knew a little bit of programming, but she'd been the expert, teaching herself three different primary languages and half a dozen scripting languages. He didn't expect to be doing much of that for a while, if ever.

At first glance the spreadsheets didn't make a lot of sense, but after a few minutes he worked out that she'd been tracking the progress of some of their investments. He decided right on the spot that he wasn't going to do that. That's why they paid Travis a retainer; he was an expert, he knew what their goals were, and he'd been managing their money successfully for almost a decade. Perhaps Adie had needed to reassure herself that their finances were secure, but Jeremy was willing to trust Travis.

The note pads, three of them, were full-sized sheets of lined paper. He spent almost half an hour puzzling out their meaning. They described the logic of some kind of scripting engine. Another one of her crazy projects, like the economic model she spent so much time on and that, as far as Jeremy could tell, had no practical purpose whatever. The model let her know what was happening in town, down to the last dollar, but it didn't *help* in any way that he could see. He'd have to think about whether to continue collecting that stuff from people. He knew that everyone was in the habit of giving Adie the details of their financial transactions, but he didn't think he needed that data to keep the town running smoothly.

He woke up her desktop computer. She was still logged in, and there were about fifty emails in her In basket, all reporting transactions from people in town. He decided not to delete them yet, until he figured out for sure if there was any reason to go on updating the model.

Her laptop was open and also asleep. When he woke it the video feeds from the security cameras showed empty hallways and no one outside the Town Hall. He closed the lid. He knew why they had security cameras—it had been part of the package that had convinced some government dope in D.C. that Marmot deserved a grant—but he saw no reason to monitor them. When the town was invaded by jihadists he was sure they would come in handy.

He turned back to the desktop monitor and logged out of her account. For the first time he used the new account she'd set up for him, *jctm*, and typed in his middle name, Spencer, for the password. His mom had been a fan of old movies, and Spencer Tracy had been her favorite actor. It was a good password; he doubted that even Elizabeth knew his middle name.

As soon as the login screen cleared and he saw the desktop, a window popped up in the lefthand corner of the screen. He saw a large, bold line that said, "Hello, Jeremy," followed by so much text that it wouldn't all fit in the window. He rocked back in his chair. It was a message from Adie.

Hello, Jeremy

I've been pretty sure since Thanksgiving that my time was running out. No one knew the dynamics of this town better than I did, so I figured there was a 99% chance you would be elected Town Manager before they could get the tag off my toe. I love and respect you, you're a hard worker, and your talents have been underrated your whole life, but this is a big pumpkin to drop in your lap without any training. Since I was the person who invented this job, I know whereof I speak.

So welcome to *Aunt Adie's Tips for the New Manager*. These little messages will pop up every now and then when you're trying something new, or when my script engine decides that it's time you knew something that you probably don't. Actually, that's a misstatement. The script engine isn't making any decisions; I've made all these decisions myself and programmed them into a series of scripts that are triggered by certain actions by you or other users of the town system. So don't go thinking there's a ghost in the machine. I'm gone, and all that's left of me is my works.

Speaking of which: the Marmot economic model. It was once an essential tool, but lately I've been thinking that it really doesn't serve a useful purpose any longer. It's hard to be

312

objective about something I've spent so much time on, but if you decide that it's not important to know how the money is flowing through the town, don't worry about how I would feel if you shut it down. You're the boss now. I'm nearly certain that you don't need the model anymore, and it's been several years since I made any decisions based on it, but I just couldn't stop. Keeping it up to date was an obsession, I know that, and watching the flow was hypnotic. No need for you to follow me in my addiction.

But I would appreciate it if you could find a way to get the code and the model data to someone in the outside world who could make use of it. Maybe Kevin could help with that.

You have a good crew. Travis knows what our financial goals are and you can trust him to manage them. Darren is perhaps even more hard-working than you are. Kevin is goofy but good-hearted, and I know he will help you when you need it. And you can always rely on Elizabeth. You don't need me.

She was such a Vulcan, Jeremy thought. *There's more to it than need.* He felt a pang of loneliness and realized that he missed her already. He called up the town calendar and another message window popped up. He wondered how long it would take for this to get really irritating.

First Calendar Access

Sunday is Valentine's Day and the following day is President's Day.

The next payday is Friday of this week. I used to handle the town payroll, but Travis has agreed to take over that task if you want him to, for a nominal fee.

Click <u>here</u> to hire Travis to manage the payroll.

Click <u>here</u> to turn off notifications of upcoming events on the calendar.

Jeremy clicked both links, dismissed the window, and sat back in his chair. He felt an urge to root out the script engine that generated these messages and delete the damned thing. But he had a feeling that would be like cutting

313

off a finger; not life-threatening, but messy, painful, inconvenient, and counterproductive. Years from now he might stumble across a dusty message from his aunt and feel tender nostalgia. Right now he felt like screaming.

He put the computer to sleep, shrugged on his coat, and went outside to find Darren.

* * *

The handyman was working in the freezing cold with his coat open, no hat, and no gloves. He was wrestling with part of the fence that surrounded the schoolyard. Darren looked up as Jeremy approached and went back to work. Jeremy didn't say anything, he just watched for a moment. The cap had popped off one of the chain link posts, so the top rail was sagging. Darren was having trouble getting it back on. When Jeremy felt that he understood the problem, he moved to the center of the rail about ten feet away and lifted; the damned thing resisted, so he put his back into it. This also raised the end of the rail where Darren was working, which allowed him to push the cap back on.

"Thanks," Darren said. Jeremy nodded. "How's the new job?"

"Confusing. I know what to do, but I don't. I watched her for years, but now that I have to do it myself, I feel like I don't have the first clue."

Darren nodded and started walking toward the cemetery. Jeremy followed. Darren said, "Some things are like that. Watching isn't enough, you have to get your hands on it, feel it in your bones and muscle, before you really understand it."

"There's something else. I guess she knew I was going to feel this way, because she programmed herself into the computer system."

Darren stopped and looked at him. "AI?"

"No, it's not that smart. Just messages when I do something for the first time. Some kind of scripting system. It's creepy, though. Like she's standing behind me telling me what to do."

Darren grunted and they continued walking. When they got to the cemetery they stood outside the failing fence and looked in. Snow had covered the mounded dirt but Jeremy could still see where the grave was.

"I've been thinking," he said.

"Oh?"

"The town has a boatload of money. I think we should spend a little of it."

"On what?"

Jeremy turned to face him. "I want to hire you full-time as maintenance man for the town. Call yourself a... hmm, a conservation engineer, if you want. You're already doing half the work anyway, you might as well get a living wage from it."

"What kind of living wage?" Jeremy mentioned a figure. Darren's eyebrows went up. "What would I be doing exactly?"

"Rebuild this fence." He kicked a broken slat on a section that leaned out from the graves as if a gale had blown it half down.

"Adie didn't want to spend the money to fix it."

"She's on *that* side of the fence now."

Darren looked at him silently for a moment. "Okay. That's maybe a month."

Jeremy gestured past the cemetery. Above the low fence, through the saplings, young pines, and shrubby vine maples, they could see the ruins of two houses poking up from the snow like bombed-out wreckage from a war.

"I want to clear out all these derelicts."

"*All* of them?" Jeremy nodded. "There's more than a dozen."

"I know. I'm sick of looking at them. They're relics of failures. They make the town look... I don't know..."

"Dilapidated?"

"Yes."

Darren thought about it for a moment. "Anything else?"

"Not that I can think of right now. But I want you available anytime for whatever needs to be done. Maybe some of the ploughing I've been doing, or driving the school bus sometimes. I might not have time for all the little stuff I used to do."

"I don't have a bus driver's license."

"We'll pay you to take a training course."

Darren stuck out his hand. "Deal." They shook and then looked back at Adie's grave. "She was a special lady," Darren said. Jeremy nodded agreement. "Scary as hell. But hey."

* * *

With his mind cleared, Jeremy went back to the office and, for the first time ever, opened up the code project for the town's economic model. A little window popped up with the title, "First Code Access." Jeremy groaned and stood up so abruptly that the chair slammed into the wall. He decided it was time to go get the mail.

Demolition

Wednesday, March 3

There was still snow on the ground, but this had not been one of the big snow years. In the worst winters Marmot would get eight feet altogether, and in March there would there would still be six feet of the stuff on the ground. Jeremy stood at the very end of Cemetery Lane, waiting for Darren, and scuffed down to the dirt with his work boots. Not even a foot of snow left.

He heard the dumpster coming long before he could see it. The truck hauling it in was belching smoke that rose up over the trees down on Jack Road, and the sound of the shifting gears was loud enough to be alarming if you didn't know what it was. Darren stomped up the road, with Ivan trailing behind, and joined him just off the pavement.

"Loud," Jeremy said.

"Bad driver," Darren replied. Darren thought everyone was a bad driver, but had an especially low opinion of the local short-haul truck drivers.

In a few minutes the trailer came into view, backing slowly up the road. It took a while to wend around the curves, then it stopped and the hydraulics raised the front end of the flatbed. The driver, a wiry old guy who looked too short to see over the steering wheel, jumped out of the cab, released the restraints, and hopped back up to unload the dumpster smoothly onto the cul-de-sac. It wasn't a small one such as a restaurant might use: this was almost six feet tall and at least sixteen feet long. When it was in place, the driver climbed back in, lowered the bed, and drove off without ever saying a word or even looking directly at them.

Jeremy looked at Darren, who shrugged and said, "Doesn't talk your head off, does he?" That was rich coming from the most laconic person Jeremy had ever met. Jeremy wasn't a big talker either, but apparently he was nowhere near the edge of the Neanderthal scale.

"Where do you want to start?" Jeremy said.

"Let's just look it over first."

They walked thirty feet or so off the pavement to the edge of the debris pile. This had once been a house much like Adie's—his, now. But years of neglect had let nature force its way in, and the roof had collapsed from water, rot, and termites. Vine maples and firs were growing through the shingles and the trusses.

"We need the Bobcat," Darren said.

"It's on order. Delivery in a week or so."

"Don't know why it takes so long."

"Me neither," Jeremy said. "You'd think they didn't want our money." They studied the situation. "I bet if you knocked out what's left of the walls, the rest would come tumbling down."

"Sledgehammers?"

"Yes."

"Dangerous."

"Not if you were careful and had a spotter."

They looked at each other. "Kevin," they said in unison.

* * *

"*Can you hear me now?*" Kevin's voice boomed.

"Yeah. It's working."

Jeremy had found a megaphone in his storage closet off the Town Hall's community room. He had no idea why it was there—no recollection of it ever having been used—but he

318

remembered seeing it the last time he'd organized the place. It took Kevin several tries to figure out how to use it.

Jeremy and Darren grabbed their sledgehammers and started toward the ruined house. But Jeremy caught a movement out of the corner of his eye and stopped. Helen was leading her students—all five of them, bundled up in parkas and plaid coats—up the trodden-down path from the school.

"What's this?" he asked her as they stopped in front of him.

Helen just smiled and turned to her kids. "Class, this is what happens when testosterone is allowed to override common sense. Who can tell me what testosterone is?"

Adhira raised her hand. "It's what makes boys stupid?" The other girls laughed, but her little brother punched her on the arm.

"Don't hit your sister, Anant. And that wasn't a very nice thing to say, Adhira, but in this case you may be correct. Anyone else?"

Iona said, "It's a hormone that affects the brain and the development of male fetuses. By making them stupid."

The girls all laughed again. Helen turned to Jeremy and cocked her head.

"Well done, kids," he said. "Well, I'm off to fulfil my biological destiny."

"By dying young?" Helen said.

"By impressing my mate," he countered, and walked away.

"Now class," he could hear her say, "who can suggest the proper procedure if one of our neighbors does something really stupid and needs urgent medical attention? Mechelle?"

"Ha ha," Darren said as he came up.

319

"You heard that?"

"Voices carry."

"You ready, Kevin?" Jeremy called.

"*Ready.*"

"I'll take the far corner," Jeremy offered.

Darren nodded. He looked around and found Ivan lying down at least thirty feet away. He widened his stance, turned a bit, and lifted the ten-pound sledge. Jeremy took up the same position, counted to three, and they both slammed their hammers into their respective corners, where the wall met the foundation.

"*Back off,*" Kevin screamed, and the two men jumped back from the building.

The wall shivered, then buckled inward. Everything that was left standing collapsed tidily into the center of the ruin.

Jeremy threw down his hammer, turned to the gawping children, and executed a deep bow.

"Time for a beer," Darren joked.

After they had each trundled several wheelbarrow-loads of debris to the dumpster, the kids evidently decided that no one was going to be maimed or killed and clamored to go back inside. Jeremy told Kevin he could go too, but instead he pulled out a pair of work gloves and started hauling long pieces of lumber by hand and flipping them into the container.

"When's the Bobcat coming?" Kevin said as he passed Jeremy on his fifth trip.

"Week or two."

"Well, that'll be fun too. Think I can drive it sometime?"

"Yeah. We have insurance."

"Very funny."

"Those things can tip over," Jeremy called over his shoulder.

"That's why they have cages," Kevin responded.

When Jeremy got back to the rubble pile with his wheelbarrow, Darren said, "Testosterone," and they both laughed.

* * *

That night Helen teased him about the risks that men took doing silly things, and he teased her back about the risks that women took living with crazy men. They ended up tumbling into bed laughing, and dared each other to do one outrageous thing after another, almost all of which they did.

A few days later Jeremy, Darren, and Kevin tackled a second house, which was easier because there were no standing walls, but harder because it was much farther away from the street. Cemetery Lane had once been a dirt road that went up to and then wrapped around the cemetery. They hadn't bothered to pave the whole thing when they rebuilt the town, so there were two ruined houses off the far corner of the graveyard, well beyond the one they'd already cleared, and they were much too far to take wheelbarrows in the snow. Instead they tackled the house off the end of Marmot Lane, near the schoolhouse.

Helen brought the kids to watch for a time, but there was no drama at all to this one, since there were no standing walls. The three men just broke up the chunks of debris into smaller chunks of debris and hauled them up the hill to the dumpster, so after a few minutes and some exclamations of boredom the spectators all went away.

When the Bobcat came in on a flatbed the following week, Darren filled it with diesel fuel from a fifty-gallon drum in the equipment barn behind the Town Hall, checked the oil and hydraulics, and fired it up. It started easily and idled with a throaty purr.

"Can I give it a try?" Kevin said. The three of them were standing together, admiring the white-and-orange machine with its black operator cage.

"After I've wrung it out a bit," Darren said.

"This is going to look great in the next Christmas parade," Kevin said, and the other two laughed.

The machine made short work of debris piles that would have taken them hours to move. It could hold as much as four wheelbarrows, and Darren drove it along faster than walking speed.

They let Kevin knock over the nearest of the two Cemetery Lane houses. The school kids came out to watch again.

"Don't scratch it," Jeremy said. "It's brand new."

He and Darren watched as Kevin drove hesitantly up to the house. The roof had caved in, but three walls were still standing. He fumbled a bit with the control levers at first, but he practiced for a few minutes until he understood how they worked. They were clearly labelled, so it wasn't a big mystery, and Jeremy was sure it was more the fear of looking foolish than the fear of what might actually happen that made him keep at it until he was comfortable. Darren was getting impatient, but when Kevin was finally ready to do the job, he raised the bucket to chest height and drove slowly forward.

The wood-framed wall buckled and went down like cardboard. Kevin drove right over it, wheeled slowly around the back of the building, and knocked down the second one. When he backed off the third one went down by itself. The kids cheered and Darren signaled for him to shut it down. They swapped places.

Jeremy stole a look at the Mayor. His face was flushed, and not with the cold.

"You did fine," he said.

"I've never driven one of those before," Kevin replied. "It was fun and scary both."

"Let's let Darren do it, then. You can drive it in the parade."

Kevin smiled and the two of them put on their gloves and started picking up scattered pieces of debris and tossing it into piles for Darren to collect.

* * *

Jeremy waited until everyone had arrived—he counted to be sure—and then stood up from his chair. It was the first town meeting since he'd been elected, and although he had often called them to order, he'd never presided before. He could feel Kevin's presence behind him, and he was acutely aware of Elizabeth and Helen in the audience, visibly worried; or maybe just trying to send him confidence telepathically. But he himself wasn't worried. He'd grown up with these people, and there was nothing they could do to unnerve him.

"Thanks for coming," he began. "This is one of the first town meetings in history that Adie wasn't in charge of, so if I fall off the stage you can blame her ghost." The younger kids looked around as if trying to spot the ghost, but most people just smiled.

"I'm not going to eulogize her again. You all know I loved her, but she did have her little quirks." Ernie and a few others grimaced at that. "Some of you may have heard that she left messages in the computer for me. This is true. Some of them are little tutorials, or hints for how something works, or just motivational notes. They were kind of irritating at first, like, 'Aunt Adie, I thought you were *dead!*'" That got a small nervous laugh. "But, as always, she knew what she was doing, and now I get excited when I see a new one. This is actually pertinent to our meeting tonight. You could say it's the reason for this meeting."

Jeremy glanced back and Kevin gave him an encouraging nod.

"If I had to sum up the point of all those messages it would be this: Adie did things her way, and I should do things my way. You elected me to be the Town Manager, not to be Adie Eagle reincarnated. So I've made some decisions, and we've started acting on them.

"First, you've probably noticed that Darren, Kevin, and I have been cleaning up the ruins. We bought a new Bobcat to help with this and also for other tasks around the town. It will be available for use by anyone over eighteen after some training by Darren. We're going to continue the clean-up until every one of the ruins is cleared away."

Ernie stood up. "How much did that thing cost?"

"A lot. But we can afford it, and it will be worth it in the long run. We'll recoup the cost of purchase over renting within the first year. I have all the documentation for anyone who wants to go into the details."

"Okay," Ernie said, and he sat down.

Mike stood up. "What about the foundations?"

Jeremy said, "Darren?"

Darren had been standing at the back of the room. He walked down the aisle until he was roughly in the center.

"About a third of the houses didn't have foundations. It looks like they were built on pilings or maybe just set on unmortared blocks. That's probably why they didn't make the cut for refurbishment when the town was modernized.

The rest of them do have concrete, but so far every one we've cleared is cracked." He retreated to his old position in the shadows at the back of the room.

Jeremy said, "It doesn't make sense to me to bring in a jackhammer or a backhoe to get rid of the concrete. It would more than double the haulage fees. The foundations should be overgrown with brush in a couple of years, and trees will crack them for us."

Mike said, "It took a lot longer than that for the Methodist church foundation, and it's still visible."

"That's a lot thicker than these house foundations. I think we're looking at years, not decades." Mike nodded and sat down. "Any other questions about the clean-up?" Jeremy said. No one stood up. "Anyone who wants to help, talk to one of us crazy guys who've been working on it and we'll induct you into the chain gang."

He grabbed a bottle of water from the floor by his chair and took a sip.

"Once the weather warms up, we'll start our second project. I'm releasing funds for Darren to rebuild the cemetery fence."

"About time," someone in the audience said. There was general agreement from the crowd.

"There are going to be a lot of tasks like this in the future, and I don't have time to do everything I used to do. So I've hired Darren as a full-time employee of the town to handle maintenance."

"About time," someone else echoed. He didn't hear any complaints.

Jeremy figured everyone probably knew all about that already, considering how news travelled in this town. He said, "Darren has been doing this informally for years for piecemeal pay. I think this will be better for the town and

325

more fair to Darren. Next month he's going to Vancouver to get a bus driver's license so he can be the primary driver. I'll be the backup driver. If anyone has other suggestions for things to keep him busy, let me know." There was louder laughter at that.

"Okay, last item. After thinking about this hard for a while, I've decided to shut down the transaction reporting system that's kept all of you on your toes since Adie installed it back in the seventies."

This time there was instant and loud cheering. Several people were on their feet shouting in support. Fists were pumping the air and almost everyone was smiling. Jeremy took a step back. He'd thought people would appreciate this, but he hadn't realized how much of a burden it had been. When they quieted down, he stepped back to the front of the stage.

"That system was very important for a lot of years, but I think we all know that it's outlived its usefulness. The town is doing well and we don't have to monitor the flow of small change to know that. So, on behalf of my aunt and the town itself, I want to thank you for the effort you've put in over the years. But as of right now, the system is retired."

There was more cheering. Jeremy gestured at Kevin and said, "Now for a word from our Mayor. Your honor?"

Kevin walked up beside him. "Meeting adjourned," he said. "Time for ice cream and cookies."

Everyone stood up and moved to the back of the room, where store-bought ice cream was waiting in the freezer and Elizabeth was uncovering the cookies she'd baked that day.

"I got a letter today," Kevin said.

"I know. I delivered it."

"It was from my old computer science professor."

"I thought you were a journalism major?"

326

"Journalists have to know how to use computers. I guess they thought it would help if we took a class about what's going on under the hood."

"Did it?" Jeremy asked.

"No. Anyway, he contacted an economy professor and showed him Adie's model. Apparently both of them had to be revived. The word they both used was 'ground-breaking.'"

"That's two words."

"Used to be, but now it's one. Like bedroom. Anyway, I thought you'd like to know that her work was appreciated and that someone's going to be using it."

"Thanks. Let's get back there before they eat all the chocolate chip cookies."

"Right. Can we get Darren to help us with a wedge formation?"

* * *

Mechelle was asleep and the dishes were cleaned. The lights in the cramped single-wide trailer were off. Jeremy and Helen sat on the lumpy couch that was also Helen's fold-out bed, snuggled up together and not talking.

So many times in his life, Jeremy had known what had to be done, but not how to do it. He thought of himself as an intelligent man; not well-educated but well-read and capable of thinking through a problem—as long as it wasn't in his personal life. Then he might as well be blind and deaf and have the brains of a cricket.

The Moon had set behind the mountains a few hours ago, and there were no street lights or security lights to disturb the darkness; no traffic to disturb the silence. Jeremy imagined it was like being in the womb, only without the wet and his mother's heartbeat. After a while he began to wonder if Helen had fallen asleep. But then she stirred.

"Pretty good for your first meeting," she said.

"I'm never going to get applause like *that* again."

"Not unless you liquidate the town's investments and hand it out in cash."

"Now there's an idea," he said. "That might be enough to buy you a new couch." She elbowed him in the ribs, but in a nice way. "I have a thought."

"Really? At this time of night?"

"Very funny. Let's toss this couch in the dumpster."

"I can't afford a new one."

"Well, my thought is that if you and Mechelle moved in with me, you wouldn't need a new one."

She went silent in that way she had. It meant that he'd crossed some line—like asking who Mechelle's dad was, which he had never done and never would. He was clumsy but not stupid.

"We talked about this," she said finally.

"I know. And I understand your position, I think. I just wanted to give you a chance to change your mind."

"I haven't changed my mind."

"Okay. So we'll keep the couch. How did it get so lumpy, anyway?"

"You know very well how."

"No, I think I forgot."

"You need a reminder?"

"My memory isn't what it used to be," he said.

"Geez. You're utterly hopeless." She pulled him even closer, and despite the bottomless darkness and the terrifying silence, she had no trouble finding his lips with hers.

Merging, Diverging

Wednesday, March 17

Kevin had suggested having a parade for St. Patrick's day, but no one could get enthused about it. When most of the snow had melted by the Ides of March, it had seemed that Mr. Winter was going to peter out early, but then he changed his mind and dumped another two feet on them over as many days. The demolition party was on hiatus and everyone was just hunkering down, burning down their woodpiles and griping to each other whenever they chanced to meet. Jeremy thought it would be a bad idea to add beer, green or otherwise, to the situation, and nobody wanted to tramp through the snow to celebrate the holiday, not even the few who were actually Irish—or Helen, who had an Irish family name but who clearly wasn't at all Irish.

That suited Jeremy just fine. He had his own plans for the day and they did not include straggling down a dark road in the cold with his neighbors.

He contrived to be outside the schoolhouse when it let out in mid-afternoon. As usual, Helen stayed behind for a while after the kids were released, to grade papers or clean up the art room or whatever.

The other kids walked past him as if he weren't there, but Mechelle stopped. "Hi, Jeremy," she said.

"Hey you. Is it too cold for a little walk?"

"No, you know I like the cold. Where do you want to go?"

"Up to the Marmot?"

"Long way, though, right?"

329

"Definitely." The shortcut past the cemetery was drifted to over three feet.

They walked in silence down Marmot Lane, passed the cafe, and turned uphill on Little Fish Street.

"Mom keeps the school too hot," Mechelle said.

"Do the other kids think so too?"

"Not Adhira and Anant. You'd think they were *born* in India, they like it so hot. Their *parents* have never even been there."

"But you were born in L.A. I'd have thought you'd like the warmth too."

"I don't remember it. But if we were there now I'd probably spend all summer playing ice hockey."

"Do they have ice hockey in L.A.?"

"Indoor rinks, dopey."

"Oh, right."

Presently they reached the statue. The bronze marmot was more than three times life size, taller than either of them, sitting up on its haunches as if waiting for a treat.

"It's kind of silly, isn't it?" she said.

"I think that's why Adie wanted it. The town has such a weird, twisted origin story, I think she was trying to tell everyone to lighten up. And anyway, the marmot won, so it deserves a statue. Like the statue of Rocky in Philadelphia."

"What?"

"Oh. Never mind. Hey, are you and your mom doing anything for dinner tonight?"

"I figured we were eating with you."

"Sure. I'd like to cook at my place, though. But I want to ask you something first. Don't get mad at me, okay?"

She frowned up at him. Her hair was getting puffy again. Helen usually kept it either fairly short or braided; maybe it was almost time to braid it again. Her face was perfectly symmetrical and sweet, dark chocolate brown, darker than Helen's. He felt the irrelevant curiosity about her father trying to bubble up and squelched it.

"Why should I get mad at you?" she said.

"I don't know. You're a girl. Sometimes I have a hard time figuring out what makes girls mad and what makes them happy."

"But you're a grownup."

"Mechelle," he said, "let me tell you the secret of life. And this might upset you, too. *No one* is a grownup. No matter how old you get, you'll still feel confused sometimes, still make mistakes, still misunderstand people and have them misunderstand you. That's just what it means to be human."

She thought about that for a moment. "I thought things would make more sense when I got older."

"For you, they might. Maybe you'll be the exception. But I... sometimes I feel like I'm still *your* age."

She thought some more. "Okay, I'll try not to get mad. What's your question?"

He took a deep breath. "Would it be okay with you if I asked your mom to marry me?"

She gaped at him. "Are you serious?"

"Yes, I am."

"You're asking *me* for permission to marry Mom?"

"I don't know, it seemed like the right thing to do."

She didn't answer, she just flung herself into his arms. He felt himself tearing up as he hugged her back.

"I guess that means *yes*?"

She pushed away from him and took two steps back. She wiped away some tears of her own.

"Two conditions," she said.

"Anything. Within reason, I mean. I can't afford to buy you a horse."

"I don't want a horse. I wouldn't mind a puppy, though."

"We'll discuss that. I'm inclined to say yes, after Owl is gone. I don't think she could handle a puppy. What are your two conditions?"

"I want to be the maid of honor."

"Unconventional. But as long as your mom agrees I don't see any problem. What else?"

"I want to call you Dad."

Then he did break down and openly weep. She had to hug him again to make it stop.

* * *

The dinner went well. Jeremy wasn't a great cook, but it was hard to ruin chicken and mashed potatoes. He caught Mechelle giving him sly little smiles and winks throughout the evening; she probably thought she was being subtle, but it wasn't possible that Helen missed them all. But she didn't say anything about it, which was typical. She usually let things unfold without pushing. She knew—and Jeremy knew it too—that sooner or later she would find out everything that was going on.

Jeremy took some of Elizabeth's pink cookies out of the freezer for dessert later. They went into the living room and Mechelle immediately commandeered her favorite reclining chair, a ratty old brown thing that Jeremy was fairly certain was older than he was. He and Helen sat together on the couch.

"What'll it be?" she said. "A healthy, stimulating game of Scrabble or a silly, mind-numbing movie?"

"Wait," Mechelle said, "why can't it be a mind-numbing game of Scrabble or a stimulating movie?"

"Okay, I admit that the possibility exists, but usually it goes the other way."

"I have a better idea," Jeremy said. "What about a silly, stimulating conversation?"

"Or," Mechelle said, "a healthy, mind-numbing conversation."

"Obviously you two clowns have a topic in mind."

"Yes we do," Mechelle said gleefully.

"We're not going to Alaska this summer, Mechelle. You know we can't afford it."

"I don't want to go to Alaska anymore."

"Really?" Mechelle had been hounding her mother for weeks to take her on a cruise up to the Arctic circle once school let out. Icebergs willing.

Helen looked back and forth between them. Jeremy had rehearsed this in his head a hundred times, but somehow he'd never imagined that Mechelle would be in the room with them. It seemed fitting, though, so he tossed out all his plans and just rode the wave.

"Mechelle and I had a little talk today. I wanted to ask her advice on something."

"*You* asked *Mechelle* for advice?"

"Yes. It was helpful."

"This I've got to hear."

Jeremy glanced at Mechelle. She nodded at him.

"She agreed with me that it would be a good idea if you and I got married. If you wanted to, I mean." Mechelle was holding her head in her hands. "That didn't come out quite the way I'd hoped it would."

"Jeremy, are you asking me to marry you?"

"Let me try again. Helen, will you marry me?"

She just stared at him for what seemed like a week. Then she looked at Mechelle and said, "And you're okay with this?"

Mechelle nodded. "I made some conditions."

"Did you now? What conditions?"

"I get to be your maid of honor."

"That's just weird. What else?"

"Jeremy lets me call him Dad from now on."

Something was going on behind her eyes, but for the life of him Jeremy could not figure out what it was. She didn't cry. But at least she didn't look angry. Finally she turned back to Jeremy and said, "And you're okay with that?"

"I would consider it an honor," he said. "And if the two of you want, I'll adopt the little lizard too."

Mechelle's mouth was open. Helen just laughed. Jeremy looked at her, and there must have been something on his face because she stopped laughing abruptly and got serious.

"I'm sorry, I never answered your question. *Yes.*"

Jeremy smiled and lunged for her. Mechelle covered her eyes, but couldn't hide the fact that she was laughing. The kiss went on for a very long time, but when it was done, Jeremy said, "You can look now."

"About time," she said. "Can we finally have some cookies?"

* * *

"I don't want to wait," Helen whispered in his ear when he might have been asleep. He wasn't; he might not sleep at all tonight. They were in his bed, and Mechelle was in the guest room.

"I don't either."

"Let's do what Elizabeth and Kevin did."

334

"Get married in the church ruins? There's no roof and four feet of snow on the ground."

She bit him lightly on the nose. "No, let's get married right away. This Sunday."

"I don't want a big wedding."

"No. Just Mechelle and Elizabeth and Kevin. And Paul and Martha."

"We can't get a wedding license that fast."

"Yes we can. We'll go tomorrow."

"The roads might be closed."

"Then we'll hold hands and levitate."

"Maybe we should practice," he said. She bit him again, not on the nose, and that led to something else.

* * *

On Thursday they found that the roads had been ploughed. Jeremy made a quick stop in the Town Hall to talk to Kevin, who told him what documentation they would need to bring to get their license, and promised not to tell Elizabeth until Helen had spoken to her. Which she did the moment they returned from Goldendale.

"How did she take it?" he asked Helen.

"She cried." Of course.

"Was she upset that I wasn't the one to tell her?"

"No."

That was all he really needed to know.

On Friday Jeremy took another day off work and spent the entire day laboring with Darren to get the house ready. The guest room needed to be cleaned out and repainted, the master bedroom closet still had a bunch of Adie's junk in it, and so on and on. They started right after breakfast and were still at it long after night had fallen.

Sunday at 3:00, Paul and Martha joined Elizabeth and Kevin in the living room of Adie's old house, where Darren had helped him push the furniture out of the way. Paul kept the service short, as requested, and by 3:30 the three of them were alone again. But Elizabeth had made them promise to come over for dinner that night.

They spent the afternoon moving Helen and Mechelle's things from the trailer to his house. Mechelle was delighted at the pale yellow that Jeremy had painted her new room, and smiled at them as she portentously closed her door to sort out and organize her stuff.

"You found a way to get me to move in with you," Helen said as she hung clothes in her half of the walk-in closet. Her belongings didn't come close to filling the space he'd cleared for her; she had never had the money, the room, or the inclination to build up her

wardrobe. She owned fewer pairs of shoes than Jeremy did.

"I should have thought of it earlier. I'm sorry I didn't."

"Better late than…" She stopped.

"What? Never?"

She didn't answer, she just shoved him so that he fell onto the bed, then she closed the bedroom door. "I think this mattress is starting to get lumpy," she said when she joined him. He was too busy to think of a smart retort.

* * *

Jeremy would have liked to skip the socializing on his wedding night, but he felt that this was better than a big reception, and he was grateful to Elizabeth for removing the burden of cooking from them.

When they stomped up the stairs to Elizabeth and Kevin's house above the cafe, Jeremy was surprised that he got fierce hugs from both of them. But so did Helen and Mechelle.

"How long have you been planning this?" Elizabeth asked him when they were all settled and she was back in the kitchen, stirring something on the stove.

"Planning?" he said innocently, and everyone laughed. "I think the idea had been growing on me slowly, but it accelerated after Adie died. Like I told Helen today, I should have done it sooner."

"Maybe you weren't ready yet," Kevin said.

"Maybe."

"Helen said you're going to adopt Mechelle."

"I am. It's the only way to keep her out of trouble."

"I never get in trouble, *Dad!*" Mechelle protested. Jeremy saw Kevin start a bit at that, then smile. He couldn't see Elizabeth's face from where he sat at the small table, but he could tell by her posture that she was amused too.

It was a fairly simple feast for Elizabeth: a complex tomato sauce, with mushrooms and little green things, over pasta with homemade garlic bread and a green salad. The conversation stayed on topic, mostly, dealing with the changes Jeremy had made to Adie's house to accommodate his new family, his plans for more work on it when summer came, speculation on what would happen to the mobile home that Helen and Mechelle had been renting. It wasn't in very good condition, and the owner—who lived in White Salmon—had made noises about having it towed away by a salvage company. Jeremy wanted to encourage that.

When the dishes were cleared away it became obvious why Elizabeth hadn't gone to great lengths over the main course. She went downstairs to the cafe briefly and came back up with a small wedding cake. It was the most beautiful cake Jeremy had ever seen, frosted pure white with candy flowers surrounding the base and covering the top, and sparkling crystals in swirls on its sides as if Tinker Bell had waved her wand at it in passing. It was smaller than the one at Elizabeth and Kevin's wedding, but he thought it was far more magnificent. Helen lamented that she didn't have her phone with her to take a picture, so Kevin went into the other room to get his camera, a fancy Nikon job with a zoom lens, and took a dozen pictures from every angle. He promised to drop the image files off the next day.

It tasted as good as it looked. There was a hint of almond in the cake, and the buttercream frosting was delicious and not too sweet. A quarter of the cake was left when they were done, and Elizabeth wrapped it up for them to take home.

They moved into the living room with coffee for the adults and a flavored water for Mechelle. Jeremy spent a few minutes examining the dragon painting that hung on the wall. It was clearly Wanda's work, and though he didn't care for the subject matter he told Kevin that he thought it was an impressive piece, and meant it. Jeremy preferred the paintings of real animals that Elizabeth had had for years, horses and African animals, which were also Wanda's work.

When they were all settled, Elizabeth leaned forward in her chair and looked at Jeremy and Helen sitting together on the couch.

"I'm so happy you two finally got married," she said. "I know Adie had hoped you would, and I've been thinking for a while now that if you didn't manage it on your own I would have to nudge you a bit."

"I'm glad to hear there was no nudging," Helen said. "I'd like to think it was all Jeremy's idea."

"It was," he said. "She never said a word to me about it."

"It's been clear to me for over a year that you two were perfect for each other," Elizabeth continued. "I can't imagine anyone else who could appreciate my godbrother the way you do, Helen. And Mechelle seems to like him too."

"Yeah," Mechelle said archly, "I think he's all right."

"Thanks very much," Jeremy said. "You're not a bucket of worms, either."

She made a face at him.

"So now I have a confession to make. With Adie gone and Jeremy settled, it's time for me to go."

"*What?*" he and Helen said together.

Jeremy looked at Kevin, who wasn't surprised. They must have discussed this already. "You can't leave," he said. "You're the glue that holds this place together."

"No," Elizabeth said. "I've never been that. That was Adie, and now it's you. If anything I was the fondant flower on top of the cake, but not the cake and definitely not the icing."

"You knew about this?" Jeremy asked Kevin.

"Since the day you told us you were getting married."

"But you just got here."

"It was seven months and three days ago."

"Not even a year."

"Elizabeth was the only reason I stayed," Kevin said. "I love it here, I love being Mayor, but frankly, I'll follow her anywhere she wants to go."

"Where *will* you go?" Helen said.

"Kevin interrupted a journey to stay with us. Adie and I talked him into it, and now it's time for him to complete the journey."

"So actually," Helen said, "you're following him."

"No. We're traveling together. Side by side."

"Where was it you were going?" Jeremy asked.

"Portland, Maine."

"Do you think your job is still waiting for you?"

"I have no idea. If not, I'll find something else."

Jeremy sat back and shook his head. Elizabeth had always been there, just as Adie had always been there, all his life. He looked up and saw her staring right into his eyes.

"It'll be all right," she said. "You needed to make a journey too, and now you've arrived. We may never live in the same place again, but I'll always be with you."

"It's a hell of a wedding gift," he said, and couldn't keep a touch of bitterness out of his voice.

"Speaking of which," Kevin said. He went into the bedroom and came back almost instantly with a sparkling package a bit smaller than a shoebox. It was clear that Elizabeth had wrapped it. No man Jeremy had ever known could have created the magical flurry of silver ribbons and bows that coiled around the box, not to mention the perfection of the paper wrapping itself.

"It's too pretty to open," Helen breathed.

"No, it's not," Elizabeth said.

Jeremy let Helen do the honors, and Mechelle came over to watch. Helen managed to uncoil the ribbons without cutting them, then borrowed a pair of scissors to gently remove the paper. It was a fairly fancy box, striated silver that matched the wrappings. Helen carefully lifted off the lid.

Nestled in tissue paper was a crystal rabbit with black eyes. It was sitting on all fours and looking up alertly as if greeting a friend.

"It's not a marmot, but it's as close as I could get."

"It's beautiful," Helen said.

"It's the prettiest thing I've ever seen," Mechelle said wonderingly.

"It belonged to my mother. I've had it packed away in the closet for years. It seemed ready to come out again and play."

"Thanks," Jeremy said. He knew he would never be able to look at it without thinking fondly of his godsister. Which, of course, was the point.

Mechelle smushed in between them on the couch and took the box from Helen so she could look at the rabbit more closely.

"What will happen to the cafe?" Helen said. "The town won't be the same without it."

"Ah," Elizabeth said. Jeremy felt one of her bombshells coming. "I was pretty sure, one way or another, that Kevin and I would be leaving this year. So for the past few months I've been training Melissa to take over the business."

"Melissa?" Jeremy said. "She's a cleaner."

"Oh Jeremy, no one is just one thing. Have you ever just been the mailman? When Melissa and Delmar lived in San Jose she was a restaurant manager. She's taken professional culinary courses. I've given her the recipes that I do have, and showed her how to make the things I never wrote down. She's been wanting a new challenge for a while now. I think she'll do fine."

"You didn't just *give* it to her, did you?"

"No, she bought it. But I gave her a very good deal."

"They live right next door," Helen said. "That'll be convenient. What about this place?" Meaning the apartment over the cafe.

"She's planning to rent it. The cafe and the rent will make a nice addition to their income."

"But what about the cleaning?" Jeremy said. "She cleans the Town Hall."

"Not to mention half the houses in town," Helen said.

"Tika's thirteen now. She and her mother will do it together for a while until Tika gets the hang of it. With the two of them working together, Melissa should have enough time after lunch is over to get it all done."

Jeremy looked at Helen and she gave a little nod.

"I think we ought to be going," he said. "Thanks for the dinner and the bunny."

"And the cake," Mechelle said enthusiastically.

"Thanks for everything," Helen said. The women all hugged everyone, but Kevin and Jeremy backed down to a brief, vigorous handshake. Mechelle was given the honor of carrying the rabbit home, Helen carried the wrapped cake leftovers, and Jeremy was left with the fancy pants wrappings.

When they were walking up Little Fish Street, Jeremy said, "This town will never be the same."

"Oh, sweetie," Helen said. "It never was."

Last Manager Standing

Wednesday, April 1

Kevin had called the town meeting this time, so Jeremy let him moderate it. He still wasn't comfortable being the center of attention, but he supposed he would get used to it in time. Adie had never liked it either, which might have had something to do with her chronic sour disposition at these things.

Elizabeth sat beside his family in the front; he still felt a little thrill every time he thought or said "family" referring to Helen and Mechelle. She smiled up at him and went back to discussing something with Helen.

Kevin stood up and everyone got quiet much more quickly than they usually did. He looked at Jeremy, then at Elizabeth, and took a deep breath.

"Even though I'm a newcomer," he said, "I know how things work in Marmot. By now you will all have heard that Elizabeth and I are moving to the Northeast in a week or so. I can see by the fact that none of you are carrying pitchforks or long knives that you know this is not my fault."

There was a small flurry of laughter.

"I think we can all agree that Jeremy has done a fine job so far as Town Manager. He's streamlined things that need it, he's working hard to improve the appearance of the town, with the clearings and the new fences that are coming. He's done a lot of the manual labor himself.

"That's why I'm calling for an election tomorrow. I know it's short notice, but I couldn't see a reason to wait. This is too important. There will be two items on the ballot. First, a proposal to fold the position of Town Manager into the

Mayor's office, so there's just one chief executive. Second, that Jeremy Cooper should fill that position."

Jeremy looked out at the faces of the audience. These were people he'd known since he was big enough to toddle off on his own. He didn't see any hostility, he barely saw any surprise. Once they knew that Kevin was leaving, they must have seen this coming. Everyone except him. He'd been surprised and perplexed when Kevin had told Jeremy he wanted to call this meeting.

"If anyone else would like to put their name forward to run in this election, you can shout out now or come talk to me by midnight tonight." He paused but no one said anything. "Anyone?"

Of course no one wanted the job. The only possible opponent Jeremy could have imagined was Upton, and Upton was too busy to want the job. Ernie might have run once upon a time, but only against Adie, not against Jeremy. He was obsessed with his town history now, which Jeremy had heard through the grapevine was already over three hundred pages.

Kevin adjourned the meeting and people started wandering out. Jeremy hopped down off the stage and put his arm around Helen.

"I'm gonna be the Mayor's daughter," Mechelle crowed.

"That just means you have to work harder than everyone else," Helen said, "and set a good example."

Mechelle looked disappointed. Jeremy had no idea what she'd thought the perks might be. Ice cream every day for lunch? Not having to go to school?

"Let's go home," he said.

* * *

Darren stood in as election monitor since Jeremy was on the ballot. Everyone had voted by 5:00, after which Kevin and Darren counted the ballots three times in full view of the voters. The whole town had wandered back in to hear the foregone conclusion. Kevin stood up on the stage with a small slip of paper.

"On the resolution to combine the offices of Town Manager and Mayor: thirty-one for, none against. On the election of the new Mayor, thirty votes for Jeremy Cooper, one vote for Bugs Bunny. As of tomorrow, Jeremy is the new Mayor."

There was scattered applause.

"On a personal note, I'd like to thank every one of you for letting me be part of this town for the last eight months. It's been one of the greatest experiences of my life, and I'll never forget any of you. Now, Jeremy: would you like to say a few words?"

"No," Jeremy said, and almost everyone laughed.

People wandered up to shake his hand or clap him on the shoulder. When the hall was nearly empty, Kevin came down from the stage, where he'd been hanging back, apparently in some noble attempt not to hog the limelight.

"Jeremy," he said, "I know you'll be great. I can't imagine anyone who could carry on Adie's legacy better." Jeremy had his doubts. But like most of his opinions, he kept it to himself.

* * *

Helen suggested a goodbye party for Elizabeth and Kevin. Jeremy would never have thought of that. If it were him, he would prefer a quick farewell with his closest friends and then slip away quietly. But the ex-Mayor and the goddaughter of the town's savior— who was also the best cook any of them had ever met, and the proprietor of the most popular daytime meeting place in town—definitely deserved a going-away party if they wanted one. Which, to Jeremy's befuddlement, they did.

To him it was like every other party they'd ever had in the community room at the Town Hall. There was music, food, a little dancing, loud talking, happy faces and sad ones. He was still trying to deal with the reality that Elizabeth was leaving the next day, and he might never see her again.

Jeremy and Elizabeth had not been raised as siblings, exactly, but he'd always felt that she was his true sister. In high school some clown had suggested trying to get to second base with her and he'd knocked the guy into the dirt of the baseball field.

Now, at the end of the evening, she came up to him and took his hands in hers. He looked her full in the face for the first time in years. She was getting little laugh lines around her eyes, but otherwise it was the same beautiful pixie face he'd known all his life. Small nose, piercing blue-grey eyes, short black hair, perfect skin. She looked a little sad and a little hopeful.

"It'll be all right," Elizabeth said. "I'll send you my address when we get settled and you can write to me now and then. Don't get that look on your face, I know you can write a coherent sentence, even if no one else does."

"First Adie, now you," he said.

"First your mom and Adie and me, and now Helen and Mechelle," she corrected him. "You have always had at least two loving women in your life, and you always will. You're strong enough for that to be enough."

"Don't you tell me I don't need you."

She tilted her head and looked up at him. "Adie said that, didn't she?" He nodded. "Well, I wouldn't presume to guess what you need or don't need." He snorted and she laughed lightly. "Okay, yes I would. But I wouldn't say it. Need me if you need to. But I'll always love you, and I'll always be ready to listen if you have something you want to say. Now give me a hug, I have to go finish packing."

He hugged her, and somehow he knew it was for the last time. But she was right. He could take it.

Kevin stepped up and wordlessly held out his hand. Jeremy gripped it strongly. He felt a shock pass between them, like a big charge of static electricity. He didn't jerk back, but let Kevin release the shake naturally. The two of them turned and walked out of the room, and out of his life. Helen came over and put her hand on his arm.

Even more so than at his wedding, Jeremy knew at last and for certain that a new phase of his life had begun.

Part Five

* * *

Push Play

Restart

Thursday, April 8

When the packing was all done, Kevin and Elizabeth lay entwined in bed with the lights off, talking occasionally but mostly just cuddling and waiting to fall asleep. It was hard for both of them. Kevin wanted to say something about the spark he'd felt pass from Jeremy to him, the same kind of spark he had once handed off to Elizabeth, at their wedding. But he couldn't think of a way to describe it that wouldn't sound silly.

The next morning they carried everything down from the house to Kevin's Subaru. He'd had to jettison half of his stuff to make room in the car for Elizabeth's things, but he'd found that to be easier than expected. Over the last few months he'd discovered what was really important to him, and it didn't include a lot of the memorabilia and books that he'd thought were indispensable. A lot of that was just junk that he'd thought he should care about, because in some way it traced his past, but when the crunch came he tossed it onto the discard pile without a second thought. The things that mattered did, however, include their three paintings by Wanda.

They closed the car but didn't bother to lock it. This was Marmot, not Portland. Or the other Portland, either.

The snow was almost completely gone and the little flagstone path was clear. They walked up it to the front door of the cafe. It was more crowded than usual, with all the regulars joined by Darren, Wanda and Mike, Delmar (who Kevin had never seen in the cafe before), Gordon and Mary.

Kevin hadn't expected to see Jeremy or Helen, and they weren't there, but almost all the rest of the adults were.

As they walked in, everyone chanted, "Good morning Mr. and Mrs. Mayor!" He supposed it was like being President: you could step down but you never gave up the title.

Kevin's usual spot at the end of the counter was open, and so was the one next to it. A hush fell over the room as Elizabeth took a seat on the wrong side of the counter for the very first time in her life. Melissa came out from the back with coffee for Kevin and a tea bag and a pot of hot water for Elizabeth. Kevin was about to order when Elizabeth touched his arm, and he stifled it. Melissa went back into the kitchen and started preparing their food.

"All packed up?" Upton said from his usual table.

"All ready to go," Kevin said.

"You can get gas in Trout Lake if you need it," Pete suggested. He was sitting two seats down from Elizabeth at the bar.

"Thanks," Kevin said, though he'd already known that.

"You can talk if you want to," Elizabeth said without facing the room. "We're not fragile."

Upton got up and stood behind her. She turned to look up at him.

"I just want to say," Upton said, "that you are the nicest person I've ever met, and the best damned cook on the planet. If Melissa picked up half of what you know, we'll still be the luckiest small town in the world."

"Who are you calling a small town?" Ernie demanded. He and Jodie were sitting in their usual table at the window. "Kill Marmot is not a small town. It's a *microscopic* town."

"It's a hamlet," Jodie suggested.

"It's a village," Wanda countered.

"It's not even a damned *crossroads*," Pete said vehemently.

No one had any other synonyms to offer. Elizabeth looked around. "Are you done?" There was a murmur from the townspeople. "Thank you, Upton, that was sweet. And the word the rest of you were searching for is *home*. No matter where I go, this will always be my home."

Kevin put his hand on her leg and squeezed. She put her hand over his and squeezed back.

Melissa brought out their food: a cinnamon roll, eggs, and fruit for Kevin, and fruit and a tiny scone for Elizabeth. Kevin cut off a piece of the cinnamon roll and tasted it. It was the second-best cinnamon roll he'd ever had; before he came to Marmot he might have thought it exquisite. If she worked hard for a decade or so Melissa might come close to matching Elizabeth as a cook. "Very good," he said diplomatically, and Elizabeth nudged him playfully.

People wandered out in ones and twos as Kevin and Elizabeth ate, some coming to say goodbye first, others just slipping away. When they were done eating, Elizabeth walked to each person who was left behind and gave them a hug. Upton was crying when he got his. Travis whispered loud enough for everyone to hear, "We'll miss you horribly." Darren didn't say a word, just accepted his hug from Elizabeth and nearly tore Kevin's arm off with a mighty shake before turning and walking out. Melissa came out and got the last hug.

"You'll do fine," Elizabeth whispered to her. "You're off to a great start."

They walked outside. When they got to the car Elizabeth turned and looked back at the cheerful cafe with the little apartment upstairs. She didn't cry, not that Kevin would have blamed her. She just smiled wistfully and got into the passenger seat. A few of the cafe patrons had come out to wave them farewell. Kevin started the car and did a three-point turn and then an immediate left onto Little Fish Street. They passed Little Fish Lake, and Kevin slowed to look back at the sign, which already read, "Welcome to Marmot, Population 30." Darren had been out early. He turned right onto Jack Road, and followed its twists and turns until they got to Forest Road 8871. Kevin stopped there, although there was no traffic visible in either direction.

"Are you okay?" he said.

"I'm great," she replied. "It's time for a new adventure, a new life. Are you ready?"

"I'm ready."

He turned right and they drove to Trout Lake, where he did fill the tank. He hadn't had to put gas in the car since September, when they got their wedding license in Goldendale; that was a lifetime record for him.

They drove down 141 and a few minutes later passed the school and then the hardware store. Sadeep and Priya were standing outside the store, and when they spotted the car they jumped up and down, waved and shouted. Kevin waved back and a moment later they were driving between thick trees with no sign of human habitation. The woods opened up again at BZ Corner, but then closed in once more.

Almost an hour after leaving Marmot they reached 141A and headed down the hill to White Salmon. The first glimpse of the Columbia River was breathtaking. It was a sunny day, with just a few fast-scudding clouds, so the water sparkled as if it had been strewn with diamonds. There were a few boats out, and even a few intrepid—or crazy—windsurfers, but for the most part the brown river rolled on down to the sea unpeopled.

It occurred to Kevin that he could probably get cell phone reception again. He reached into his coat pocket and pulled out the phone he hadn't used for almost eight months. He had charged it the night before; now he pushed the on button and waited.

They had to wait at a stop sign in White Salmon. Kevin glanced at his phone and gasped.

"What's wrong?" Elizabeth said.

He handed her the phone and continued through the intersection. "Push that round button at the bottom."

She read off, "Two thousand three hundred seventeen text messages. One hundred three voicemails." She looked up at him. "That sounds like a lot."

"It is."

He turned onto the approach to the Hood River bridge. Just before they reached the river, he had a sudden epiphany. Elizabeth was still holding his phone.

"Honey," he said, "would you do me a favor?"

"Of course."

"Throw that thing in the river."

"Really?"

"Really."

"Are you sure?"

"Absolutely sure."

"Okay," she said. She rolled down her window. He could feel her counting the beats as the trusses flicked by. Then she flicked her wrist and the phone went sailing through the air, flying though the gap between two trusses and disappearing below the bridge deck. There was no audible splash, of course, but Kevin imagined he could feel it hit the water, and a weight he hadn't known was there lifted from his shoulders.

"How will you contact the paper in Portland?" she asked.

"In person."

Elizabeth nodded.

They were back over land. The bridge road was bordered on both sides by fields of rounded river rocks. Someone had been building cairns from them, and the last one towered at least nine stones high.

Kevin turned onto the entrance ramp to I-84. When he'd merged into the light traffic, he reached over and took Elizabeth's hand. "The adventure begins," he said happily.

Elizabeth lifted his hand to her lips and kissed it. He felt a shock on the back of his hand, like a spark of static electricity.

Rebirth

Elizabeth felt a swift rush of joy when her lips were shocked. So the magic had come around again, from Kevin to her, from her to Adie to Jeremy, and Jeremy must have passed it back to Kevin some time very recently. She'd thought she'd lost it forever.

This spark didn't belong to any of them. She'd known that since the moment she'd first felt it, on her wedding day. Since then it had passed through more good people, accumulating power and purpose. She knew whose spark it truly was, and she would pass it on in turn when the time was right.

She rested a hand on her swelling belly. She felt so much happiness that she didn't know how she managed to hold it all in. She imagined she was like a butterfly about to hatch, although it was probably more accurate to say that her daughter, who she wouldn't meet for another three months, was actually the butterfly.

Elizabeth had left her past behind. The happiness and the sadness, the accomplishments and the frustrations, helping and being helped. For the first time in her life she felt truly free. Her beloved mother's legacy had been a burden that she finally found a way to set down, and now she could find her own path.

She turned a little to look at Kevin. She loved him so much, his good heart and his carefully-maintained façade of strength. He seemed to be focusing on the road, but she could tell that he was actually wondering what the spark was.

She knew he felt it was some kind of portent. Perhaps she would tell him some day.

Elizabeth didn't know precisely what it was that they were about to unleash on the world in the person of their daughter. But she knew that it would be something good.

Also by Chris Mason at 186 Publishing:

Mrs Bambi Knows

It's 1995. Braveheart, featuring Mel Gibson in a kilt, wins five Academy awards. People think it's cool to dance the Macarena, or at least, lots of them do it without getting too embarrassed. Maria Carey, Bon Jovi, TLC and Michael Jackson all chart, as do Annie Lennox, Van Halen, Shaggy, Bryan Adams and Coolio. Bill Clinton is President and DVDs are invented.

...And in a small town in Oregon, everyone wants to kill the local advice columnist, Mrs Bambi. If only they knew who she was.

Mrs Bambi's advice is so snarky that people have long since stopped asking for it, so instead she eavesdrops on conversations and writes the letters herself. The readers would lynch her, but no-one knows who she is.

In fact, Mrs. Bambi is not a woman. The column is written by Richard, a quiet widower with a young daughter.

The uneventful part of Richard's life is nearly over: he begins dating Pam, a well-known realtor and a sports addict. When people begin to learn the identity of Mrs. Bambi, Richard is threatened and humiliated in public.

Despite the pleas of his editor, his friends, and Pam, he refuses to stop writing the column.

The only thing that can prevent disaster is for the town to finally learn the whole truth about Richard, which is much larger than the simple mystery of Mrs. Bambi.

Available at www.186publishing.co.uk and from Amazon, in paperback and Kindle

Printed in Great Britain
by Amazon